Ben's hand c[...]

Despite his illness, it was [...] steel clamp. "[Why] are you doing this?" he asked.

Ryan's face creased in puzzlement. "Doing what?"

"Taking care of me like this?"

She regarded him sadly. "If you have to ask, Colonel, then I have no answer you can understand."

He let go suddenly, his hand feeling as if it had been burned. He had not expected the rush of heat that ran through his body when he touched her. His blood was like a river of fire, and when his eyes met hers again, he knew she shared the same warm sensation.

She stared at him, unable to understand the quickening of her blood, the desire that flooded her. Ryan remained still, unable to move, until she heard his low voice.

"You're right," he said roughly. "I don't understand it. I don't know if I ever will."

Dear Reader:

We're all delighted that you've been so enthusiastic about our Harlequin Historicals, but there are some questions we have. Are there any particular settings or types of stories you'd like to see more of? How do you feel about the levels of sensuality? Do you find the characters and their relationships appealing?

This month we're pleased to publish *Promises*, a romantic story of glamorous high society in Edwardian England, by Oscar award-winning screenwriter Pamela Wallace, and *Between the Thunder*, a second novel by Patricia Potter. Set in Colorado and Texas during the last years of the Civil War, it's the story of a woman torn between her loyalty to her Confederate brother and her love for a Yankee colonel.

I'd appreciate any comments, criticisms or suggestions. Please write to me at the address below.

Karen Solem

Editorial Director
Harlequin Historicals
P. O. Box 7372
Grand Central Station
New York, New York 10017

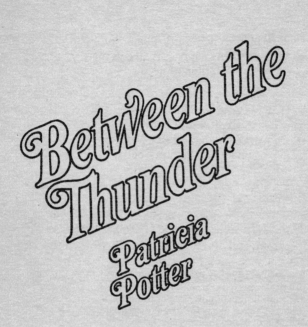

Between the Thunder

Patricia Potter

Harlequin Books

TORONTO • NEW YORK • LONDON
AMSTERDAM • PARIS • SYDNEY • HAMBURG
STOCKHOLM • ATHENS • TOKYO • MILAN

To my brother, Dr. William Potter,
whose strong support is always there
in time of need

And to Tracy Farrell,
editor and friend,
who understood Ben Morgan
and made his story better

Harlequin Historical first edition February 1989

ISBN 0-373-28615-5

Books by Patricia Potter

Harlequin Historical

Swampfire #6
Between the Thunder #15

PATRICIA POTTER

is a former award-winning journalist with a passion for history and books. As a reporter with the *Atlanta Journal*, she met and reported on three presidents and covered Southern news stories as varied as the space launches and the civil rights movement.

This resident of Atlanta, Georgia, has her own public relations and advertising agency. Her interests in animals and travel are not especially compatible, but she does manage to fit them both into her busy schedule. Her reading runs the gamut from biographies to espionage, and she is currently the president of the Georgia Romance Writers of America.

Prologue

The anguished scream shattered the early morning peace. It hovered there in that strange hesitant time between deep night and the first shards of an awakening dawn.

It was quickly followed by another, more childlike, more frightened. There was pain and terror and loss in the sound, and it haunted the soldiers, who lay strewn about the valley floor like pebbles flung from a giant hand.

They had heard the screams before. But each time it touched them deeper, because they had learned to care deeply about the person from whom the pain came.

Trained to react suddenly to any noise, they had awakened quickly. But only one among them could soothe the agony behind the sounds. The rest continued to lie there, listening to the screams, which would gradually dissolve into whimpers. Each would collapse just as quickly back into sleep once everything was quiet. It was instinct, sharply honed by four years of war, that allowed such immediate oblivion.

One man rose from the hundreds huddled in blankets. The days were still hot, but the late summer nights had a cold bite to them. It wouldn't be long before the winds came. And the snows. But the men planned to be gone long before then.

The tall wiry man hurried to the wagon, which stood alone in the clearing. Lifting the flap, he gracefully ascended in one effortless movement. With a practiced reach, he found the lantern hanging from a hook and lighted it, looking down at the twisting tossing figure who had cried out with such pain.

He knew she was lost in a nightmare. The capricious flame from the lantern captured the gold in her hair, which spread over the pillow, freed from its usual disciplined braid. Her face was tear-stained, and her body, under the discarded shirt she used as a nightdress, was bathed in sweat.

He gently put one hand to her face, trying to wake her without causing more terror. His other hand fingered a ringlet of the soft hair before brushing it behind her ear. He lifted her head to his chest, holding her in his arms. "Hush, Kitten, it's all right," he crooned softly. "You're safe. Everyone's safe."

He watched as her eyes opened, wide with fear. They still held tears, and their brown depths were dark pools of sorrow and confusion.

"It's all right, Kitten," he said again, wondering at the child/woman in front of him. His sister looked so young, so defenseless, so unlike the capable self-assured person who usually resided in her tall slender body. Protectiveness was new to him. He hadn't felt it in many, many years, and the ferocious nature of it surprised him. He wanted to protect her from everything, from all hurt, from the terror that continued to haunt her at night.

She leaned her head against his hard body and held his hand, saying nothing, sensing his concern.

"The dream again?" It was more a statement than a question. He had come to recognize it in the six months she had been with him. "The same as before?"

She nodded and then shook her head, trying to dismiss the remnants of fear that lingered there.

"I'm sorry," she said, shame in her voice. The dream was always the same, and its frequency did nothing to lessen its intensity. First the savage yells, then the scream and finally the heat. Always the heat. And the terrible fear and loneliness.

The man gathered her to him, holding her tight. "It's all right," he said. "I'm here."

"Everyone I love dies," she said in a small trembling voice. "Everyone."

He pulled back. "Only the good die early, Kitten. I should live for a very, very long time."

He was rewarded with a small smile that lighted the arresting face, which was usually touched by laughter. Only these dreams brought pain, and the man had come to detest them. Joy was a living thing in her, and it colored everything she did. Her unconscious warmth touched everyone, and her rare curiosity searched for beauty where one would least expect to find it. She had a zest for living he had never quite experienced before, and he didn't want anything, or anyone, to take even a part of it away.

"Sean," she said suddenly. "Please sing me a song."

He reached behind the bed, where he kept his guitar safe against the uncertain weather. He fingered one of her favorite tunes, a Spanish lullaby, and watched as the tension in her body slackened. His usually strong baritone voice was uncommonly soft as he mouthed the gentle Spanish words.

Ryan leaned back and watched him, one hand resting in his lap. When he finished, her eyes were almost closed, her body completely relaxed.

He leaned over and kissed her forehead. "Now sleep, Kitten. I'll stay here for a while."

She smiled softly at the brother she had come to love so well. "It will always be the two of us, won't it," she said sleepily. "Always and forever."

She was asleep before she saw the slight determined smile on his face and the silent vow in his eyes.

Chapter One

Colonel Bennett Avery Morgan took his eyes from the trail before him and allowed his thoughts to wander. It was an infraction he often warned his troops against and one he rarely committed.

But he relished the feel of the day that surrounded him. The Colorado territory was awash with jagged slashes of golden light darting through the overladen trees, and a small breeze took the sting from the heat. Morgan had been traveling hard for three weeks, one by train and the last two by horseback. He was tired and knew he was getting close to his destination. His usually sharp senses were lulled by the laziness of the afternoon and his own deep weariness. He had, as always, pushed himself and was now feeling the effects of the unrelenting journey.

He thought briefly, and unhappily, about the new assignment that had taken him from Washington, and couldn't shake a foreboding that had been with him for weeks. The feeling was uncommon, and he worried over it, seeking a reason that wouldn't surface.

He had been sent to find, capture and see to the execution of a band of Southern guerrillas operating in the territory. Their leader was to be brought back for public trial in Washington, but the sentence had already been privately decided. The operation was to be an object lesson, a deterrent to other guerrillas. Morgan had no compunctions about killing in battle, but the role of hangman did not set well with him.

But the war, now in its fourth year, had turned mean and ugly. The gallantry of the first months had disappeared in rising death tolls and Northern defeats. The North had stopped all prisoner exchanges, realizing it could withstand the loss of men at greater rates than the South. And it had taken a hard unyielding stand on guerrillas. They were to be treated as criminals and could be executed summarily. A number of Mosby's guerrillas in Maryland and Virginia had already been shot out of hand.

Those in Colorado, Morgan knew, were to be made an example. Their activities had become too effective to continue. The stream of gold trains traveling east had thinned to a trickle, and supplies were nearly impossible to get through. Finding different routes would mean considerably more time and manpower. The Union Command wanted the Southern guerrillas stopped, and in such a way that they would not be replaced.

Morgan's orders gave him access to as many troopers as he required from units already stationed in Colorado, orders that he knew would incense the local commanders. Not only could he override their decisions, it was a direct slap in the face at their inability to quiet the frontier.

He had argued against the assignment, asking instead to return to Virginia, where he felt the war would be won or lost. But the request had been denied, and Ben Morgan was, first and foremost, a soldier. He had spent the past thirteen years as a career officer, ten of them in the West and the past three in Maryland and Virginia in the midst of some of the worse fighting of the war, until a shoulder injury sent him back to Washington, where he had become an adviser on guerrilla activities. He had fought against and studied Wade Hampton, Jeb Stuart and John Mosby, all of whom had perfected the art of strike-and-run warfare.

As his strength returned, he had requested duty in the field. Instead, he had been saddled with a job no one else wanted. Not only was it a job he despised, it was one that would send him thousands of miles from his young son.

Morgan turned his thoughts from his assignment to twelve-year-old Bennett Avery Morgan III, better known in the family as Avery, after his grandfather.

He had visited the boy on and off during the early years in the army. The visits had been short and unsatisfactory, performed more out of guilt and duty than any fatherly affection. Morgan had carefully kept a distance between himself and the boy, unable to forgive or forget the betrayal by the boy's mother. The soldier, who had grown increasingly bitter through the years, found it difficult to separate Avery from his mother, and in the past five years had made no attempt at all to see his son. He had the excuse of distance and war.

But in this spring of 1864, at the death of his own father, Morgan had hesitantly brought the boy to Washington. But only after unmerciful badgering from his sister.

To his surprise the youngster opened doors he had thought closed forever. For the first time since his marriage had ended so disastrously, Ben Morgan allowed himself to feel something for another human being.

For years he had shied away from any kind of personal commitment. He had no friends, nor wanted any, wary that a friendship would again sour. His cynicism had grown as he quickly ascended from lieutenant to colonel. He was a difficult officer to serve under, intolerant of even the smallest error and completely tireless in the field. He seemed to take perverse satisfaction in hardship, a feeling not shared by his subordinates. His methods, however, were rarely criticized by superiors; he was uncommonly effective.

For himself, he had come to the conclusion that life was something to tolerate, a bad game designed by some master jokester who spread misery and destruction indiscriminately. He took no pleasure in being a part of it and didn't understand those who did. It was an attitude that made him fearless and, some of his men thought resentfully, invulnerable. Death seldom seemed to claim those who did not fear it, who even courted it.

Young Avery, however, had pierced that armor. The three months they had spent together were an unexpected pleasure and probably the happiest period in Ben's life. After a short period of reserve and strangeness, they had found an easy comfortable companionship together, the boy reveling in the rare attention from his father, and the older Morgan fascinated with the boy's curiosity and intelligence.

When he had received his orders, Ben had taken his son down a trail they both favored, one that led to a quiet riverbank hugged by willow trees.

Once there, they had crafted a pair of rough fishing poles and sat silently. They had learned to enjoy each other's company and had talked of small things: schools, an antic of one of young Ben's friends, the heat and dust of Washington city. It was late afternoon before Ben had told his son he was leaving and felt the boy's pain as his own.

"I'll be back for you," he had vowed. "And after the war, I won't leave you again. Where I go, you'll go. If that is what you want."

The boy had sat quietly for several minutes, then blurted out some words, wanting at last to confide in this man who had come to mean so much to him. "You know I've been helping Dr. Roberts at the hospital?"

Ben had nodded. He had been proud of his son who had gone to the army hospital daily after school, doing everything from mopping floors to writing letters for the wounded.

"I want to work at the hospital in Boston, too," the boy had continued softly. "Will you arrange it with Uncle Charles?" Then, as his father regarded him seriously, he had said in a rush of words, "Someday, I want to be a doctor."

Realizing how important his approval was to the boy, Ben had answered carefully. "If that's what you want, I'll do anything I can to help."

Avery had smiled suddenly, his face glowing. Ben felt a sudden pain. How much he had missed! The boy was something special. He carried a unique aura of gentleness about him.

"I was afraid you might be angry," his son had replied. "I thought you might want me to be a soldier. Like you."

Ben thought about the death he had seen in the past thirteen years. He winced at the images that never entirely went away: the young men torn apart, their eyes open and accusing; the horrible screams of dying horses; the stacks of bodies so thick you couldn't make your way through them. He had almost become inured to it. It had been the only way to survive.

But he had shuddered at the thought of the young boy next to him caught up in the twisted maelstrom of war. "No," he had said abruptly, reliving his own empty violent life. "I don't ever want you to be a soldier."

Ben had looked at Avery and touched him lightly. "I love you," he had said, realizing it was the first time he had ever expressed affection toward his son. The boy had looked at him and smiled shyly, his eyes shining.

Ben had lived with that farewell for the past four weeks. Carefully packed in his saddlebag was a copy of *A Tale of Two Cities* by Charles Dickens, which the boy had given him.

They had said goodbye sadly but with a shared knowledge and understanding that they had something special. In addition to being father and son, they were also friends....

Morgan was still thinking about that riverbank when his horse reared suddenly. His head hit the top of a branch and, unconscious, he fell from the animal and landed on his left leg, breaking it. As he lay there, the two rattlesnakes who had startled the horse, struck.

Chapter Two

Ryan Mallory, her dreams forgotten and her mood lightened by the success of her afternoon, laughed gaily as she rode along beside Lieutenant Tom Braden in the old farm wagon. She was imitating the frosty storekeeper in Center, the town they had just left. The man had been quite terrified that the urchin—Ryan—would steal him blind and had followed her the entire time she had browsed in the store. He had finally, angrily, shooed the disgusting lad from the premises.

Lieutenant Braden couldn't help steal a glance at his companion and take pleasure in the mischievous gleam in her eyes. It was quite impossible, he thought to himself, that a girl so pretty could look so disreputable. Ryan was clad in trousers and a dirty shirt from one of the younger troopers. Her golden hair was bound tightly under a floppy farmer's hat, and dirt was smudged over her nose and chin. She looked just as she had wanted to—like a squatter's boy who would attract little attention.

The two of them had driven to town, he to check the telegraph, she to listen at the store where soldiers from the nearby fort sometimes gathered. Braden was equally as squalid looking. He had let his black beard grow ragged, and his hair was long and dirty looking. There were few traces of the handsome young lieutenant Ryan had first met seven months ago in Richmond.

The telegraph message had been waiting. The man and boy had left town as quietly and as anonymously as they entered it.

As they turned at the fork, Braden pushed the horse into a canter, eager to get back to camp with the message.

A horse suddenly bolted out of the woods, startling their worn-looking mare. This was a lonely area, rarely traveled and frequently patrolled by their own men.

Ryan put her hand on Braden's arm. "Someone's in trouble," she said, the laughter gone from her voice and her brown eyes full of concern.

Braden turned the horse toward the break in the trees. He didn't recognize the other animal, nor the saddle, and he couldn't imagine who else might be on this deserted trail.

Ryan saw him first. A figure in a dark blue uniform lay, unmoving, at the base of a tree. She jumped off the buckboard before Braden could stop her and hurried over, only to stop suddenly at the sound of rattling. Several shots rang out while she stood absolutely still, afraid to move. She heard the rattling subside and watched the headless snakes writhe in their death throes, as though it were happening to someone else. Then she felt Braden shake her, and she quickly returned to the present. She looked at Braden gratefully, then stooped quickly over the unconscious figure.

She could see the blood on the man's trousers and quickly rolled the pant leg up, revealing two bites just inches apart.

"Tom," she said urgently, "give me a knife."

Braden took his knife from its ankle strap and handed it to her. He watched silently as she cut a piece of cloth from the man's trousers and tied it into a tourniquet, tightening it with a small stick. With two sure strokes she cut an arc just above the snake bites. Leaning down, she sucked blood from the cuts and spit it out. Over and over she repeated the process.

Finally, Ryan released the tourniquet, letting some blood circulate, then tightened it again. She turned to Braden. "You have to help me get him on the wagon," she said. "We can't leave him here."

Braden looked at her with amazement. "And take him where? You know your brother's orders. No prisoners. We can't take him into camp."

She looked at him impatiently. "There's no place else.... We obviously can't take him back to Center. How can we explain finding a Yankee officer in this area? We're supposed to be on the other side of town." She stared at Braden with determination. "And I'm certainly not going to leave him here to die."

"He's a Yankee!" Braden said. "Good Lord, we've been killing them for the past four years and now you want to save one."

Ryan's chin jutted upward in a familiar determined way. "If he doesn't go, I don't go."

Braden, much to his regret, had seen the gesture before. He knew she meant it. He also knew her brother—his captain—was equally adamant about bringing an enemy into their secret camp. It was not the first time he had been caught between brother and sister—and each time he vowed it wouldn't happen again. Either way he caught hell.

He stood there, undecided. It was a unique feeling for him. After four years of war, two of them with Captain Mallory, he was used to split-second decisions. But Ryan had a way of throwing him off balance.

Now impatient, Ryan tried to drag the Yankee by herself, but his size made it almost impossible. "Help me," she demanded. "He needs attention. And," she added in sudden inspiration, "they're expecting us. . . ."

"They're not expecting a damned Yank," Braden said stubbornly.

Ryan looked at him with an unspoken plea that melted his resolve, even as he knew he would pay dearly for it.

"I'll take the responsibility," she said. "If we're not quick, he'll be dead before we get there."

"That will suit me just fine," Braden answered, knowing that her assumption of responsibility would mean exactly nothing to Sean Mallory. He would be the one held to account. But he reached over and helped drag the Yank into the back of the buckboard.

"I'll stay back here with him," Ryan said. "Let's go."

He urged the horse on. Ryan sat in the back, cradling the Yank's head, bracing him as much as possible against the lurching of the wagon. She looked at him for the first time. His hair was nearly black, shorter than most, and thick. It curled slightly, creating an undisciplined look, an impression made stronger by the heavy dark eyebrows that framed his closed eyes. He looked about her brother's age, but his face had deeper lines. It looked, even now, hard and uncompromising. Dangerous.

She glanced up at Braden. "He's rather young for a full colonel, isn't he?"

Tom looked at her, his face bitter. "Yes," he said shortly. "He must be very adept at killing Southerners."

Ryan let the comment go without reply and returned her attention to the Yank. She felt the growing heat of his skin as the snake poison reached his brain, and she felt the spreading stream of blood from the cuts. She had loosened the tourniquet, afraid of cutting off his circulation. Tighten and loosen. Tighten and loosen. Over and over, her hands kept busy.

A mile down the trail, they saw the Yank's black horse. Tom Braden whistled and it cantered over obediently. Ryan stared at the horse, admiring its obviously fine bloodlines, then tied it to the back of the buckboard as it stamped nervously. The horse pranced behind the wagon, its fear slowly dissolving.

Braden directed the buckboard horse toward what seemed to be a wall of water tumbling down the side of a cliff. The horse, accustomed to the route and eager to get to the rich pasture beyond, offered no resistance as it was guided through the falls into a valley. As they entered the protected camp, they met several riders on the way out, each dragging long brooms. Ryan knew they would trace the tracks back a mile, then return, brushing away all signs of the wagon and horses.

Sean was not in sight, and Ryan said a brief prayer of thanks, then asked several of the startled Southern troopers to carry the Yank back to her makeshift hospital.

It was no more than a clear piece of ground sheltered by a canvas strung from trees. There was one young trooper there, recovering from a bullet wound. She had made several mattresses from branches, and covered them with tough hides, then blankets. At the very least, it kept the sick and injured from the cold and often damp ground.

Ignoring the disapproving stares of the Texans who composed the majority of Sean's command, she gently inspected her patient. He was wet, as she was, from the waterfall, but the heat of the day would soon correct that. She moved his leg lightly, only then observing it was slightly crooked. She had been too concerned earlier with the snake bites to notice the leg was also broken.

Ryan explored the rest of his body, noting its fit leanness and the muscles straining against the fine linen shirt he wore under the tailored uniform jacket. He had a bad head wound; blood seeped from an open cut, and the area was badly swollen. There were numerous other bruises and cuts. She wondered if there were any more injuries inside. Even without such complications, she thought, it would be a miracle if he lived.

She studied his face, already stained with sweat from the gathering fever. His cheekbones were high and his nose straight and narrow. His mouth was full and currently clinched in a firm tight line. It would be, she knew suddenly, devastating in a smile. A small but distinctive indentation in his prominent chin broke the severity of his thoroughly masculine features. His face was well tanned, and the taut leathery skin spoke of years in the open.

It was a fascinating face, strong and determined, even arrogant, yet made vulnerable by the long lashes and recess in his chin. She couldn't help wondering if the man himself was as contradictory as his face.

Chapter Three

The tall figure in gray stood up in the stirrups, stretching to see over the rocks without being seen.

The sun hit his ruffled bronze hair, causing it to glitter with specks of gold as he impatiently ran a hand through its thickness, pushing wayward strands from a forehead damp with sweat. His other hand held both his reins and a cavalryman's hat, the wide brim covering the front of his worn saddle.

He watched as the long slow line of blue uniforms and pack mules moved into range below him. There were only sixteen soldiers accompanying some forty heavily laden mules.

"They never seem to learn, do they," he whispered to a young private resting easily on the horse next to him. "Cocky bastards."

The young soldier just grinned at his commander. "Maybe they like supplying the Confederacy. Makes things a little more even."

Captain Sean Mallory motioned to a burly man in a tattered uniform with corporal stripes. The man moved up, holding his rifle so familiarly it seemed almost an extension of his arm. He fondled the rifle, much as some men would a woman. It was a repeating rifle, one of few owned by the thirty riders bunched behind the two men in front, and to Corporal Wilson it was the most important thing in his life. He was a master in its use.

Mallory quickly pointed out two men below, the blue-clad man in front and the back rider. The corporal raised the rifle and, almost effortlessly, sighted his targets. The shots rang out in quick succession, and the two marked riders fell from their horses.

The sound of the shots signaled the waiting gray figures. They spurred their horses, letting loose an ear-deafening cry almost in unison. The sound was designed to frighten, and frighten it did.

The startled soldiers at the foot of the hill were in complete disarray. Their lieutenant was down, clutching his shoulder, and gray riders were everywhere. The noise was overwhelming. One blue-clad figure after another threw his pistol down and grabbed at the air with empty hands. Only two tried to shoot, but they couldn't find a target. The gray was darting in and out among their own men, and there were no clean shots.

In just minutes the fourteen mounted Yankees had surrendered and were ordered down from their horses. They stood, hands behind their head, each still wondering exactly what had happened.

The bronze-haired officer, his hat now partially hiding his sun-brown face, dismounted and checked the two men who had been shot. One, a lieutenant, was sitting up, his hand covered with blood seeping through his uniform jacket at his left shoulder. The other was dead.

The officer looked at Corporal Wilson, a measure of censure in his eyes. He had issued standing orders that his men were to shoot to wound, not to kill unless absolutely necessary. The corporal merely shrugged and turned away. Sean Mallory swore to himself, wishing that Wilson was not his best marksman. Sean was tired of death. Wilson loved it.

Sean turned his attention to the overloaded mules. "Check them," he ordered his men, and permitted a rare smile of satisfaction when he learned they carried ammunition, fresh Union uniforms and blankets. They could use all of it. The household goods and dresses bound for some officer's wife were dumped. They already had a caveful of such odds and ends.

He gave orders to switch the bundles to the Union horses and to split the remainder among their own horses.

Sean knelt by the wounded officer, unbuttoning his coat and the shirt under it. He studied the wound for a moment, and then called to the young soldier who had waited with him at the top of the hill. "Jimmy, get some bandages and see what you can do for him."

Jimmy took his place next to the soldier, and Sean watched as the young Texan probed the wound. "The bullet's still there, Captain."

"Can you get it out quickly? While they're loading the supplies?"

"I think so." The young man looked at the Yankee officer. "It's going to hurt like hell."

The Yankee nodded, knowing that the sooner the bullet came out the better chance he had. He was slightly confused by the help he was receiving from the men who had just tried to kill him. He didn't wonder long as the young Reb poured alcohol on the wound; the intense burning pain was replaced by emptiness as he slipped from consciousness.

Several minutes later, Jimmy proudly extracted the bullet and quickly bandaged the wound.

The other Rebs had just finished repacking the supplies and turned their attention to the Union soldiers, who were now sitting, their hands still locked behind their heads.

"Take off your boots," Sean commanded, and watched carefully as each man slowly, resentfully, pulled off his boots and placed them in a sack held by one of their captors. "Now stand."

As they stood, one of the gray clad men went among them, cutting suspenders and buttons to their pants. Most of the pants fell immediately, and the men stood there looking both foolish and furious.

Sean's face showed little sympathy, although he cringed inwardly at inflicting the additional humiliation. It was not caprice but necessity that forced what was now routine. The partial disrobing would greatly hamper his enemy's efforts to recapture the mules and try to follow or obtain reinforcements. It would give him valuable time to cover his tracks and reach safety. But he didn't enjoy it, although he knew some of his men delighted in the discomfort the practice caused the Yanks.

"Who's the ranking soldier here?" Sean asked after the task was completed.

One man reached down to pull up his pants, and with as much dignity as he could muster, replied, "I am."

"I'm leaving you two mules, one for your lieutenant, another for him." He gestured to the dead man. "The rest of you can walk back. And soldier," he added, "be sure you use them for those purposes. We will be watching for some distance."

Without any additional words, he mounted and tightened his knees against his large bay stallion. The mules were too slow for them to take so they scattered them to hide their tracks. Once the animals were driven in forty different directions, Sean and his men disappeared with the Yankee horses and their newly acquired goods over the hard rocky ground.

It was dark before Sean and his men arrived back at camp. They had taken a long circling approach to the valley they had called home for eighteen months.

Once inside the entrance, Sean hunted for his sister. He didn't like her trips to Center, and only necessity had won his consent.

He was also growing more and more concerned about the length of their stay in the valley. They had been here too long. He knew it was past time to leave, but there was one essential shipment scheduled through the area. It would be carrying the new repeating Spencer rifles, and he had the strongest possible orders from Richmond to take it. The guns were crucial to a South struggling with outdated and woefully inadequate supplies.

Privately, Sean realized the war was lost and that it was only a matter of time. His superiors in Richmond knew it, too, and they were hoping only to make the last months so costly that a weary North would sue for a just peace. Sean doubted such an outcome. The war had become too bitter for any retreat, but he had made his choice four years earlier, and he was not one to give half measure. He was tired of war, tired of killing, but he would give the South the best he had until the end.

The numerous camp fires reminded him of the fireflies he used to catch as a boy. But one was larger and shone brighter than the others, and his eyes were drawn to the hospital area. He saw his sister bent over a still blue uniform.

"What the hell?" he swore, looking at Braden, who was approaching him on foot.

Braden, knowing what was coming, was grim and stiff. "We found him, sir," he said slowly. "He'd been snakebit. Your sister wouldn't leave him."

"And you let her?" The question was explosive and all the more intimidating since Mallory rarely disciplined his men. It was seldom necessary; they had all been handpicked and had been together a long time. "You know my orders, Braden. No prisoners inside the valley. Consider yourself busted to sergeant."

Mallory dismounted in one quick fluid movement and strode over to the Yank. His face, flushed with anger, suddenly went white.

Ryan looked up, prepared for his anger but not for the bleak strained look that replaced it. "Sean, what is it?"

"I know him," he whispered tonelessly. "It's Ben . . . Ben Morgan. We roomed together at West Point." He stood and stared for a few moments in disbelief, then turned away wordlessly.

Sean walked slowly to the camp's one large tent. He rarely used it except in meetings with his officers or for a personal matter. He preferred to sleep in the open with his men. There were several caves the troopers used when it rained, but they all took advantage of the clear nights and comfortable temperatures of the late summer.

Lighting a lantern, he stared at the interior of the tent, his shock replaced by unreasoning fury. He felt consumed. Picking up a glass pitcher his men had liberated from one of the Union's supply trains, he hurled it with all his considerable strength against one of the tent poles. It shattered, sending shimmering splinters and splashes of water over the dirt floor.

He had never done such a thing before but had wondered if those who spent their violence on inanimate objects received any satisfaction from doing so.

Now he knew.

There was damned little.

Sean disregarded the mess and knew he would be left alone. He was a popular officer who shared both discomforts and victories with his men, but he also had a legendary temper, which, though rare, was to be avoided at all costs.

He brooded silently over Morgan's presence in the camp. There had once been real affection between the two. More than affection. Sean had felt closer to Ben Morgan than to anyone else in his life. But their friendship had ended badly, and the very thought of Morgan through the past years had never failed to provoke both raw anger and bitter regret. Apart from his personal outrage, he knew Morgan to be a very strong danger to him and to his men— and their mission. There had been few more capable men at West Point and certainly none as determined. If Morgan lived, there would be a very intelligent enemy in their midst.

Sean knew he had had uncommonly good luck, but he also realized it could run out at any time. He had personally selected each one of his men, preferring the hard independent Westerners who often did poorly in more disciplined units, and had melded them into a strong disciplined unit.

Although he himself was a product of West Point, Sean had been uncomfortable in the regular army. His independence had repeatedly landed him in trouble and prevented him from advancing in rank. He was recognized as a good officer but a troublesome one, who never bothered to hide his contempt of incompetent senior officers nor his preference for the enlisted men.

It was for exactly those qualities that the Confederate War Department had chosen him to staunch the flow of gold from the West to Washington.

Like many Southern West Pointers, Sean resigned his commission when Texas joined the Confederacy. He had little sympathy for the Deep South's slave states, but he felt Texas had the right to withdraw from the Union. He had joined Jeb Stuart's cavalry in Virginia, served a year, and then was summoned to Richmond.

"You know what we face," General Weels had said, looking sharply at his former student from West Point. "They have the factories, the arms and the men. We have cotton and pride. Not a very good balance," he added ruefully, "regardless of what some of the hotheads say. I personally feel everyone's fooling themselves to think England will come into this war. Cotton's important to them but not that important. And cotton is going to do us precious little good when we run out of guns and food.

"We're going to need money, Wills continued. "There are ways to buy what we need, even from the North, if we have gold. That's going to be your job. I remember when I taught you tactics that one year at West Point. You had some pretty innovative ideas. Hit-and-run. Guerrilla actions. Make one man count for many. I know some of the fools up there disagreed. Honor was better served by sacrificing men uselessly. Well, that's what they're doing. We are seesawing back and forth, spreading blood over the same damn ground over and over again, both sides hesitant to move when they have the advantage. But it's a war of attrition. They can afford it—we can't. We're already short of guns, ammunition and medicines. We're going to have to make the best use of smaller numbers of men if we are to hang on."

With those words Sean had been given his own command and unusual control in selecting his men, his strategy and his targets. There had been only one warning. "Take what you can from the army, but leave civilians alone. We don't want you branded as outlaws. So wear uniforms whenever you attack. You are now officially attached to the Second Corps." Weels had held out his hand. "Good luck, Sean, and good hunting."

Sean interviewed volunteers and found one young man who had hunted the Colorado territory extensively. Jimmy Carne was only eighteen but had been on his own since the age of thirteen. He told Sean about a hidden valley he had discovered, whose only entrance was behind a waterfall and through a narrow gap.

"Are you sure there is no other way out?" Sean had asked.

"If there is, I never found it," the boy had replied. "But there's a hundred places in the rocks where you can see for miles without being seen."

"Can you draw me a map?"

"I don't know, sir," the boy had said. "I know I can take you there."

"Okay, sign yourself up. I'm glad to have you."

Slowly handpicking the rest of the men, he had chosen his officers with particular care. All were Westerners, most of them Texans, and none were West Pointers.

In six weeks they had been ready to move, and in another six, well entrenched in the valley. It wasn't long before Weels was being congratulated for his choice. Sean Mallory had proved to be an extremely competent thief and a thorn in the side of the Union.

The success of the first year, however, faded as new routes were found for the gold shipments. Some were sent by ship from California to Panama, carried overland, then shipped from Panama to Boston. Another route ran north through Wyoming and the Dakotas. Although it crossed dangerous Indian lands, it seemed safer to the gold-hungry Union leaders than the growing surety of Southern raiders. Each of the alternatives, however, were expensive in both manpower and time.

Sean's band continued to attack supply trains, but the resulting blankets, foodstuffs, even medicines seemed unworthy of the treacherous trip through Union territory to Southern lines. Sean had sent Braden, his most trusted lieutenant, to notify Richmond that he planned to leave. Braden's return, his new orders and his unexpected companion had come as a distinct shock....

Braden had returned six months ago. Sean had just ridden in himself when he had heard the first warnings from the sentries. Dirty and unshaved from two days in the saddle, he was tired to the brink of exhaustion, but the raid had been worth it. They had taken a hefty army payroll, which meant not only valuable currency for the South but the added dividend of a disgruntled army post.

Standing in front of his tent, he watched intently as six riders emerged from the valley entrance, Braden at the lead. He studied the others, his strong lean face full of astonishment as his eyes concentrated on a slim rider who rode with the grace of a born horseman. His eyes flickered from the wide brim hat to a slim waist and finally down to dusty split riding skirts as the rider followed Braden to where Sean was standing.

He continued to watch the figure, but her face was hidden by the hat and the bright glare of a noonday sun. All the same, he couldn't dismiss a sudden sense of familiarity.

His face was cold and forbidding when Braden reached him. "What in the hell is going on?"

Before Braden could answer, the slim rider had dismounted and approached him, reaching for her hat. A long golden braid fell as she shook her head free of the encumbrance, and she looked at Sean with great dark eyes.

Her face was controlled, but her mouth trembled slightly. The eyes, however, captured all his attention. They were incredibly alive and expressive . . . full of dancing sparks and undisciplined merriment. He had seen eyes like that only once before. His mother. His mother had had the same glow. And his sister. But she was only a child. . . .

He was mesmerized by the face in front of him. It was almost like looking in a mirror. No wonder he had that brief image of familiarity. She was a feminized version of himself.

A muscle worked in his cheek, and his brows drew together. "Ryan?" he said tentatively, unable to believe the evidence before him. "It can't be Ryan."

Her tense face suddenly dissolved into an eager plea for acceptance.

"Yes," she said softly, "I'm Ryan."

There was a moment of silence while the new troopers and the veterans who had been attracted by the unusual scene watched quietly.

"But how?" Sean's voice faltered as he reached back in time. He had not seen his sister for twelve years, not since a brief visit after his graduation from West Point. But then he realized he didn't care how, or why, when he saw the sudden hurt in her eyes. His two long arms went around her, and he held her tightly to him. He let her rest there and placed his cheek on her head. He felt her arms go around him, and he felt a sudden warmth and protectiveness he hadn't known in years.

After several minutes he gently withdrew from her and held her shoulders at arm's length while he studied her.

"You look just like Ma," he said finally. He touched her face. "But what are you doing here? This is no place for a chi—" He checked himself. Whatever else she was, Ryan was not a child. "A woman," he corrected himself uncomfortably. "Where's Dr. Foster? What was he thinking of . . . letting you come here?"

Tears shone in her eyes, and her mouth trembled again. "He's dead. Both he and his wife. Typhoid."

Sean closed his eyes. *Oh God,* he thought, *not again.*

He was suddenly aware of all the eyes on them. "Come," he said gently, leading her into the tent. At its entrance, he turned and looked at Braden. "I will talk to you later," he said, his voice hard and merciless.

Sean led her to the cot inside and gestured for her to sit, but she declined. "I think I've been sitting forever. Please don't be angry at Lieutenant Braden," she added. "I didn't give him any choice."

He looked at her, aware of an unfamiliar tenderness. She was extremely pretty, and he already sensed much of his own stubbornness about her. He couldn't deny his sudden joy at seeing her, but, at the same time, he knew it was a dangerous place for her to be.

"He had no business bringing you here," he said, a muscle tensing in his cheek.

"And I had no business forcing him?" she said, an undercurrent of sadness and anger in her voice.

He reached for her hand and drew her down next to him on the cot. "You will never know how much it means to me to see you . . . to know that you are well . . . and—" he hesitated "—all grown up. We'll have time to talk and get to know each other again, and then I'll send you back with an escort."

"There's nothing back in Taylor," she said with a quietly determined note in her voice. "The whole town is disappearing. Indians. The war. Then typhoid. Everyone's gone. I have no place to go. The Fosters are gone. My friends are scattered over cemeteries across Texas and Mississippi." One solitary tear wandered down her face, and she angrily wiped it away.

His sister, Sean thought. His brave determined little sister. She had lost two sets of parents, the first to an Apache raid and now the second to typhoid. He touched her face, his hand exploring the strangely familiar planes.

"This is no place for you, Kitten," he said, unintentionally using his old name for her.

"Why not?" she asked. "I can be useful."

"Because, well, because there are more than two hundred men here. It just wouldn't be—" he searched for a word "—safe or . . . proper." He nearly choked on the last word. Propriety had never held much allure for him, and he was quickly coming to the conclusion that it was no more attractive to Ryan.

Her brows knit together. "Safe? Is there any place safe now?" It was a question for which he had no answer.

Sean noted the fatigue in her face. "You need some rest," he said softly. "And so do I. We'll talk about it later." He helped her off with her boots and watched as she lay down on the cot, struggling to stay awake. When her eyes had finally closed, he placed a gentle hand on her face and leaned down to touch her forehead lightly with his lips.

Along with Ryan, Braden had brought new orders from Washington. There were indications that a shipment of the new repeating Spencer rifles would be sent west, and their capture was deemed critical by Richmond. He must stay and wait for them.

Despite his best intentions, Sean continually delayed Ryan's departure. He was amazed to find she knew a great deal about medicine. It was apparently a natural talent that had been nurtured by her foster father. She was also a good cook—something extraordinary in camp—and it wasn't long before thoughts of sending her away were postponed indefinitely.

Despite his initial misgivings about a woman in camp, her rapport with his men was almost instant. She had worn riding skirts into camp, but long before had begged a pair of trousers from Jimmy Carne. Her total lack of self-consciousness and her skills made her accepted immediately, and Sean's troopers became as protective of her as if she were their own kid sister.

After a raid that netted several covered wagons filled with blankets and medical supplies, one wagon remained in camp and was given to Ryan. It was understood that the wagon was off-limits, as it was equally understood that her brief baths in the nearby stream would go unobserved.

With the captured medicines, she started a daily sick call, cautiously dispensing the precious hoard. She doctored the few casualties from the raids and nursed those with fevers. There were no more deaths in camp.

As she became more and more an integral part of the troop, she started asking about the town thirty miles away. The men took turns drifting into Center to pick up supplies and coded telegraph messages from the Confederate intelligence network in Washington and to scout information in town.

"You just can't keep sending men into the telegraph office," she told Sean one day. "It's too unusual to have men going through town who expect a telegraph. Once, yes. Twice, maybe. But you've done it too many times."

"And what, little Kitten, would you suggest?" he asked teasingly.

"Well, there's nothing unusual about a man and his son expecting messages from relatives who plan to join them," she said. "At the same time, they can buy a lot of supplies for the trip."

He stared at her, wondering if she would ever cease to surprise him. "And where, may I ask, are we going to find a young boy?"

"Me." She chuckled, pulling her hair back and setting her mobile face into that of a sullen farm boy.

The proposal made sense. But it also put Ryan in danger. Sean discussed the idea with Braden, who had also worried that they were repeating the same pattern too often. The rifles were much too important for the men to risk creating suspicion now.

The decision was made. Ryan and Braden would go on the next trip and request an approximate arrival date for the shipment. They had made that first trip two weeks earlier, and the answer had come today, on the second one.

Now Sean blamed himself for that decision. He should never have allowed Ryan to stay. Now there would be hell to pay. The last thing he needed was a prisoner, particularly a colonel whose disappearance would sound an alarm. Particularly Ben Morgan.

Sean's thoughts were interrupted by a light tapping on the tent pole outside.

"Come in," he said.

Braden entered cautiously.

"What is it?" Sean's tone was abrupt.

"We brought in the Yank's horse," Braden said. "I started to go through his saddlebags and found some papers. I thought you might want to read them first."

Braden passed him the well-worn saddlebags. He had pulled out a leather pouch, which obviously contained orders.

"Should I leave, sir?" The words came hesitantly as Braden remembered Sean's earlier anger.

"No, stay here." Sean opened the pouch and took out some sealed papers. He quickly tore them open and read rapidly. His face visibly tightened.

"I think you did the right thing after all, Braden," he said. "It looks as if the colonel was sent specifically after us. To hang us."

"Sir?"

"We've been labeled outlaws.... It would appear we've been a bit too troublesome."

"But sir, we're a regular unit.... We've only attacked military targets."

"I know that. You know that. And they probably know that. But they apparently want to make an example of us, and our colonel was the man dispatched to do that. This gives him the authority to commandeer as many troops as he needs from Fort Myers and search until he finds us." He looked at the orders again. "We're all to be executed. My men are to be held at Fort Myers, and I'm to be taken back for public trial . . . and public hanging, I suppose."

Despite his outrage, Braden's mouth twisted into a skeptical smile. "If they catch us, that is. Personally, I would gamble on you any day. At least you can stay on your horse."

Sean didn't return the smile. "Don't underestimate him, Tom. I know him. He's dangerous. Very dangerous."

Braden sensed his commander's dismay, and the smile disappeared. "Should I tell the other men?"

"No, not just yet. With luck, we'll be gone before they know he's missing. Once we get back to Texas, there's no way to identify us."

"Except for him," Braden replied bitterly.

"Except for him," Sean confirmed, his expression thoughtful.

Braden started to leave but turned at Sean's voice.

"Tom?"

"Sir?"

"Forget what I told you earlier. You did the only thing you could have. No one knows my sister better than I do. She would have dragged him back here by herself if you hadn't helped."

Braden just nodded.

"What did you find out at the telegraph office?"

Braden caught himself. In the confusion he had almost forgotten. "The shipment is due through here in three weeks. It left Washington on the fifteenth and left Chicago a few days ago."

"Did he have the route?"

"No, not yet. He said to check again in two weeks."

"That means you and Ryan will have to go back. Did they accept your story?"

"No reason not to. Settlers are pouring through town every day."

"Where did you tell them you were camping?"

"A little stream six miles to the north. I left it vague enough no one could pinpoint it."

"Good. Thank you, Tom."

Braden nodded and left, relieved that Sean's swift anger disappeared as rapidly as it came.

Sean sat down and went through Morgan's saddlebags. On one side he found a white linen shirt, an extra pair of uniform trousers, some fine-smelling cigars and a book. Sean permitted himself a wry smile. The Ben he had known had seldom been without the latter two items. The other side contained a well-worn deerskin jacket and a photo of a young boy—a younger version of Morgan. As he dug deeper, his hand encountered metal, and he pulled out a pair of handcuffs and leg irons.

Sean looked at them a moment. Anger rushed through him as he realized that they were meant for him. He put everything back into Ben's saddlebags, pushed them under the cot and quickly left the tent.

He walked over to Ryan's makeshift hospital. Ryan, with Jimmy Carne's help, was tending Morgan. She had cleaned the open wounds and covered them with moss, a trick learned from an old medicine man to draw out infection. She quickly wrapped white cloth over the moss, binding it firmly to the deep cuts.

"How is he?" Sean asked, glancing at the injured man's pale face and shivering body.

She looked up at him, impatient to get back to work. "Not good. I was able to get some of the poison out, but too much got through. I don't know if it was enough to kill him. He also has a bad head wound and a broken leg. He'll be very lucky to live."

"He's nearly indestructible," Sean said, studying the man who was once his friend. "Tom said he had two snakebites."

Ryan nodded, her hands busy wiping the dampness from Morgan's face.

"I've never heard of anyone surviving two bites," he said slowly.

She looked up angrily. "Is that wishful thinking?"

He shook his head. "I don't know, Ryan. I really don't know." Then he added with some anger himself, "Don't forget, he's the enemy."

"He can't do much right now," she said, continuing to bathe her patient.

Sean turned to leave. "Let me know if there's any change," he said shortly, "particularly if he wakes up."

"It won't be for a long time," she said, "if he ever does. The fever from the bites is just beginning. It's going to be a long fight."

Sean turned to Jimmy. "Make sure she gets some rest. You can spell her some, can't you?"

"Yes sir, I will."

Chapter Four

Please don't let him die. Please God, don't let him die.

It was a plea that Ryan made frequently during the next few days as the Yankee colonel hovered between life and death.

His fever raged and so did his ramblings. Left without any defenses by the illness, Ben Morgan's personal hidden agonies ripped open with the fever and took root in Ryan's natural sympathy.

She had always, she realized ruefully, taken on the sorrows and joys of others as if they were her own. It was one reason she had such an aptitude for medicine. She often knew what her patients were thinking and feeling before they themselves were fully conscious of it. It was sometimes a joyless gift.

But never had she merged so fully with a person as she did now with Ben Morgan. She felt his loneliness, knew his despair and trembled with his rage. It was that combination that penetrated Ryan's open heart. That and his apparent indifference to life. He seemed not to fight the fever that attacked him so viciously. Life appeared to hold little value for him. She had sensed it before in others and recognized it, though she didn't understand why some gave in so easily to death while others fought so bitterly against it.

As the fever intensified and her patient grew weaker, Ryan willed some of her own strength into him. She touched him continually, pressing on him her own determination and energy. As she washed the sweat from his face and body, she talked to him, urging him to fight back, to stop taking the coward's way out. She knew he couldn't hear, but she felt that somehow the message would take hold.

He talked incessantly through the fever. She heard the name "Melody" over and over again—sometimes softly, as if in love, other times with a cold deadly anger, and finally, with a terrible curse. There were other names that quickly came and went with the flow of the illness. One time, as she wiped the sweat dripping from his face, she heard his voice crack. "So many dead...so many...boys...only boys...."

And then there was her brother's name. There was nothing else for a while and, for a time, she thought she must have been mistaken. But it was there again, later. This time, the voice pressed on, growing wilder.

"Sean...it's not true, damn you. Not true.... You're a liar. Not Melody...." The words were agonized, and Ryan flinched at the pain in them. The man was in a hell of his own, and she couldn't help but wonder at her brother's role in it. She knew Sean had heard the Yank's words, and when he asked later about Morgan's progress, she couldn't restrain her questions.

"What is he saying? What does he mean?"

Sean's face became granite, and his eyes glittered with anger. A muscle twitched in his jaw and his whole manner told her not to pry. She had never seen him that way before. They did not mention it again, but the questions hovered uncomfortably between them.

Two days went by, then three, and the fever was still in control. At times his eyes would open and look at her blankly, and she was transfixed at the dark blue color of them. They swirled with angry emotions and images only he could see. Ryan wanted to grab his face in her hands and take away the anger and the loneliness that were so apparent.

Sean often watched at a distance, worrying about the intensity that so obviously linked the two of them. He watched as she seemed to pass some of her strength into Morgan, and he noted the fatigue and desperation that replaced the delightful optimism that was usually so much a part of her. When he urged her to rest, she refused to leave the colonel's side.

Ryan came to know Morgan's body well. The fever kept him in a sweat, and she washed him repeatedly, leaving only the care of his most intimate parts to Jimmy. His well-developed muscles rippled in his unconscious struggling. He was a large man, as tall as her brother and broader in build. Every part of him seemed as hard and solid as a piece of fine oak. It was a nearly perfect body, marred only by a large ugly scar that covered his left shoulder.

Even now, as he lay there unconscious, the merest contact with him sent currents of heat through her body. Of all the men she had previously nursed, she had never felt the intense emotions that flooded her when she touched Colonel Morgan.

She would not, she vowed, let him die.

It took three and a half days of constant attention before the fever subsided. At Sean's insistence and his promise to remain by Morgan's side, Ryan finally consented to rest and freshen up.

Bennett Morgan woke to immense pain. One wave cascaded over another, bringing new spasms to torment him. There was no space between the onslaughts, just one agonizing swell after another.

His head felt as if it were about to explode, but worst of all was the incredible thirst that racked his body.

"Water," he whispered almost soundlessly, and felt his head being lifted, sending yet another fiercer agony through him. Then he felt the drops of water on his tongue and instinctively, greedily, reached for more.

"Take it slowly." He heard the low voice, but his overwhelming need for relief disregarded it. Back somewhere in his fevered mind, he recognized a certain familiarity about it but abandoned any attempt to search his memory for it. He sucked greedily at the water allowed him.

Again he heard the man's soft voice. "Drink slowly or you'll throw it back up." But the words meant nothing to him; his only understanding was his consuming need for the water.

Morgan, in his half consciousness, heard, or thought he heard a new voice. A woman's voice. "That's enough ... I'll give him some laudanum. He'll rest easier."

Morgan tried to argue. Water. That was the only important thing. Water and more water. His body, almost completely dehydrated from the fever, begged for it. He tried to tell them that, but his mouth wouldn't work. He felt a gentler hand lifting his head, and he tasted the cool bitter liquid invading his mouth. The pain slowly receded as he fell back into a fitful blackness.

Ryan looked at her brother. She had gone to fetch some water when Morgan first stirred. Sean had been nearby and responded to the first low whispers.

"He should be all right now," she said, "but he's going to be in a lot of pain for a while. He's also going to be very weak."

Sean looked down at Morgan. "I told you he was indestructible," he said as he quirked an eyebrow at her, a hint of affectionate mischief in his eyes. "But I didn't think even you could save him, this time," he admitted softly.

She smiled tiredly. "Are you pleased? Or disappointed?"

"I'll have to think about that," he said wryly. "I don't know what in the hell we'll do with him, but I guess we'll think of something. Now," he said sternly, "you get some rest. I'll watch him for a while."

Ryan agreed wearily. She had spent most of the past three and a half days next to her patient. She felt she could sleep for days.

After she left, Captain Mallory stared down at the wounded Yank colonel. He fought the anger and bitterness that competed with the odd sense of relief that Ben would, indeed, live.

There was much he remembered about the man who had been his roommate and friend at West Point fourteen years earlier. The body, always firm, appeared even stronger, and Sean noted the fairly recent scar on his shoulder. The black hair, always unruly despite Ben's best efforts, was cropped short and thick ends curled in the disarray he remembered so well.

His eyes traveled quickly over the splinted leg and the thick bandages covering the area above the knee. Only Ben would have lived through two rattler bites and a host of other injuries, Sean admitted ruefully to himself. But he knew how difficult and awkward the coming days would be. Ben would not take easily to being a prisoner, and especially to being his prisoner.

When next Morgan woke, it was twenty-four hours later. He first felt a gentle licking on his fingers, and, as he slowly opened his eyes, again to pain but this time not so intense, he saw a small nondescript dog. It lay next to him, its tongue systematically washing each finger.

"You should be honored," he heard a soft voice say. "He doesn't give his attentions lightly."

He turned his head and looked upward. A girl stood there, an uncommonly pretty one. Her hair was the color of rich burnished gold; it was confined in one long braid, which twisted back across her shoulder. Her large dark brown eyes regarded him with gentle humor as a small smile played around her wide full mouth. Her face was dark with the sun, making the glorious hair even more startling.

Morgan closed his eyes, then opened them, thinking she would be gone. It was the fever, he thought. It had to be. Either that or a dream. But she was still there when he opened them again. She was dressed in a pair of britches and a boy's shirt. Strangely enough, he thought through a haze of pain, they made her look very feminine. The rough clothes accented her fine slender body and graceful movements.

"Well, Colonel," she said in that same soft voice that sounded almost like music, "do you like dogs? If not, I'll tell him to go away. It will hurt his feelings immensely, but he will survive."

Morgan didn't answer immediately. The pain kept pounding at him and nothing seemed real, certainly not the girl or the dog. His mind refused to accept them. He let his eyes wander to a group of men some distance away, immediately noting the scraps of gray clothing they wore. The physical pain was suddenly forgotten with the mental anguish that assaulted him. He couldn't stop the overwhelming feeling of failure nor stifle the groan that escaped his throat.

The girl knelt quickly next to him. "Don't try to move," she said, the laughter in her voice replaced by concern.

He shook his head to clear it, but the movement only sharpened the constant throb of pain, and he winced.

The girl touched his forehead gently and felt the heat that lingered there. Filling a cup from the nearby bucket, she held it to his lips. "Slowly," she said. "Very slowly."

This time he understood. He drank slowly but steadily, his eyes watching her face. She was even prettier than he had first thought. Her eyes with their strange amber lights were somehow familiar, and a few tendrils of her hair had escaped the braid and framed her face. For one incomprehensible moment, he wondered how it would feel in his fingers.

"Who *are* you?" he asked instead, trying to chase the fleeting thought from his traitorous mind. "Where am I? How long have I been here?"

Her mouth curved back into a teasing smile, and he knew from its ease that it came frequently to her. "So many questions, Colonel Morgan. You must indeed be better. As to where you are, you are with the Second Texas Cavalry in Colorado."

The use of his name startled him until he remembered his papers. Whatever had happened, they had apparently recovered his horse. The thought did not give him comfort.

"You have the advantage," he said stiffly, formally. "You know my name. I know neither how I came to be here or your name."

"You remember nothing?"

"I was riding," he recalled. "I don't remember anything else. Except a voice I'd heard before, which I knew well. But I couldn't recall where."

"It was my brother," she said quietly, the smile gone from her face. She felt his uncertainty, and she unconsciously responded to it. Here was a man unused to weakness or being without control. That he was in severe pain was obvious by his inability to concentrate on any one question. "Your horse," she continued, "must have stumbled onto some rattlesnakes and thrown you. You had two bites. That's what caused the fever."

"But how did I get here?" he asked, still bewildered.

"We—a friend and I—saw your horse bolting from the woods. We found you almost immediately after you had been bitten," she said simply. "You almost died. I thought you would several times."

He started to move and flinched as renewed waves of pain hit him. She put a hand on his shoulder. "Don't try to move," she said. "Your leg is broken, and you have a bump the size of a boulder on your head. You must stay still and rest."

Ben Morgan fell back, his eyes meeting hers. His were a very dark blue, almost black with concentration. Pain, weakness and confusion were all reflected there, and she suddenly, unwillingly, felt a sympathetic echo of them in herself.

"I still don't understand," he said slowly. "The snakebites..." The question trailed off.

"Something we learn early in Texas," she said. "I cut the veins just above the bites and sucked out most of the poison before it got in the bloodstream. Some did."

"You?" The surprise was evident, his voice suddenly sharp and disbelieving. His experience with women made it almost impossible for him to accept the statement.

Ryan smiled at the bewilderment and disbelief in his voice. "Would you rather I hadn't?" she answered, her voice only slightly amused.

His mouth twisted into a tight disciplined smile. It was more a grimace, Ryan thought sadly.

"No.... I'm just surprised. I suppose I'm in your debt." He sounded anything but grateful.

He tried to sit up again but fell back, the muscles in his face tightening with the effort. He closed his eyes. God, he felt terrible. He was unaccustomed to the overwhelming weakness that confined his body so completely. When the pain receded slightly, he opened his eyes again and saw the girl watching him, her face soft with sympathy. It made him unaccountably angry.

"Where's the commanding officer?" he demanded, suddenly arrogant. He wanted the girl away. She was unsettling...the way she looked at him...the warm way a part of him wanted to respond. And he wanted to know his position. Or lack of it. He had made an unholy mess of everything.

"He's not here right now," she replied in the same quiet soft voice, obviously unperturbed by his sudden hostility.

"How long have I been here?" he asked shortly.

"Nearly five days now," she answered, noting his dismay as he absorbed the news and realized without question that he was a prisoner. Despite his weakness, Ryan caught a fleeting impression of control and power as his eyes grew blank and a curtain settled over his face.

"Get some rest," she urged. "That's the best medicine now." She got up to go.

"Wait," he said almost involuntarily. "What's your name?"

"Ryan. It's Ryan Mallory." And she walked away.

Mallory. The name shook him. Mallory. Sean Mallory. It had to be the same. She had mentioned a brother. Sean. That was the voice he had heard earlier.

Unwelcome thoughts tumbled in his mind. Sean had once been his closest friend, more like a brother than his own brothers, until one terrible anger-filled night, which had haunted him for years.

One thought led logically to the next. He had been sent to track and capture a band of Southern guerrillas operating in the Colorado territory. At West Point Sean had been fascinated with the early American partisan leaders and had frequently argued with their instructors on the value of guerrilla warfare. The conclusion could not be avoided. Sean was the one he had been sent after. As much as he wanted to reject the idea, he couldn't shake the growing certainty.

He laughed—a sardonic mirthless soundless laugh—at the irony of his situation. Sean, his quarry, had instead found him. Sean, with whom his last encounter had been so bitter and had ended so violently, was now responsible for his still being alive. Morgan wished fleetingly that he had not been found, that he had been allowed the oblivion that had never frightened him.

He closed his eyes, willing back the blankness of sleep. He was tired of thinking.

Chapter Five

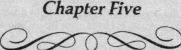

The music came from the camp fire some five hundred yards away. Morgan was awake but kept his eyes closed, letting the sounds fall gently around him.

He recognized the sound of Sean's guitar. There was a plaintiveness about it that he remembered from West Point. He had never heard anyone play it quite that way again.

He also remembered the song from West Point. It was one of his roommate's favorites.... He played it whenever he felt trapped—which was often. Sean had not, he recalled, liked the military academy.

Morgan listened to the strings, when suddenly the girl's voice joined it. It was clear and honest, almost bell-like in its simplicity.

The mood changed abruptly as a fiddle took over and swung into an Irish country dance. He could hear the hands clap and even the feet tap in unison in the hard dirt.

He opened his eyes reluctantly. The dog was next to him, lying there contentedly. A young soldier with rumpled straw-colored hair was on the other side, his eyes and attention turned toward the music. Morgan's slight movement startled the man, and he quickly reached for his holstered pistol before he realized the source of the noise. He turned toward the Yank somewhat sheepishly. Instinct had made him wary.

"I didn't realize you were awake," he mumbled. He hadn't particularly liked being nursemaid to an enemy.

Morgan studied him carefully. He seemed very young, yet the speed with which he had reached for his pistol spoke eloquently of his battle experience.

"I was listening," he said softly. "Do they do this every night?"

"Almost. The cap'n loves music, particularly that guitar." His face opened with a sudden grin, wide and boyish. "I think he chose most of them," he said, nodding toward the soldiers gathered around the fire, "'cause they make good music...not because they can fight. Everyone but me, that is." He immediately flushed, realizing what he had said. "Not that they ain't good soldiers, too," he added quickly.

Morgan almost smiled but caught himself. "How long have you been here?" he asked, instead.

Jimmy Carne gave him a reproving look. "No questions, Yank. The cap'n will tell you what he wants you to know."

Sharply reminded of his status, Morgan's face tightened, and his fists curled in frustration.

Jimmy's expression softened a little. "Ryan said I was to ask if you could eat something. She's kept some broth hot."

All of a sudden, Morgan was overwhelmed with hunger. He nodded curtly as he recognized his need while hating to ask anything of his captors.

When he returned with a steaming bowl, Jimmy looked at the patient. "Can you sit up a little? I'll move a saddle over."

Morgan nodded, not really sure if he could or not. He leaned slightly forward as the boy quickly inserted a saddle behind him. Even that small effort exhausted him. He closed his eyes, trying to gather what little strength he had.

The young Texan watched as Morgan tried to lift his arm. His right hand trembled as it tried to clasp the spoon.

"Never mind," he said. "I'll do it."

Morgan leaned back against the saddle as the young soldier spooned the hot broth into his mouth. He didn't think anything ever tasted so good. It was light and flavorful with tiny pieces of potato giving it substance. He felt some small trace of strength as the soup warmed him.

All too soon he felt he could eat no more. He shook his head as the young trooper started to refill the spoon. The boy, seeing the Yank's exhaustion, removed the saddle, and Morgan sank back down on the blanket. Cursing the weakness that made him so helpless, he struggled against surrendering to it. He had to think, had to plan some action, had to recover some control over his situation. But nothing came to him, and he yielded to the deadly weariness. As sleep came, he heard Sean's fingers wander again over the guitar strings in an endless melancholy tune.

Ryan rose early as usual and with the same enthusiasm with which she met every day. She loved to rise before the sun and watch as the first colors pierced the night sky and spread across the horizon. This morning presented a special incentive. She had gone to sleep the night before thinking of the Yankee colonel. He was still very much in her mind when she woke up.

She dressed hurriedly but with more care than usual. She chose a better-fitting pair of britches and one of her few blouses. While not tight, it showed her slender figure to much better advantage than one of her brother's or Jimmy's shirts. She tucked it in and tied a scarf loosely around her slim waist.

Ryan was one of the first up, although Cook was already preparing biscuits and refilling one of the large coffeepots that were always left on the fire. Coffee was always available, mainly for the various troopers who maintained watch over the valley walls. She wished him a good morning and received a wide smile in return. Ryan was always one of his first customers in the morning, and he enjoyed her cheerful greeting.

He handed her a cup of coffee, and she asked for a second one. He looked at her curiously but did as she asked without comment and watched as she walked over to her makeshift hospital carrying both cups.

She moved carefully, not wanting to wake the Yankee if he was still asleep, but she had a feeling he would be awake. There was no guard. He was still obviously too ill and weak to present any problem, yet improved enough not to need constant nursing.

As she approached she noted a small movement and saw in the first glimmers of light that his eyes were open and watching her.

She sat down cross-legged beside him.

"Would you like some coffee?"

He nodded slowly, his eyes following her every move.

She put the coffee down and reached for some extra blankets she had left beside him. Helping him sit up partially, she packed the blankets behind him, then handed him one of the steaming cups.

Ben's hand was steadier than the night before, but he still had to focus all his attention on holding the cup. It seemed incredible to him that he was still so weak.

Ryan watched quietly as he very carefully used both hands to lift the cup to his mouth. She felt, rather than saw, the control he needed to do the simple task. Colonel Morgan took several sips, then lowered the cup and rested it on the ground.

"How do you feel?" she asked, regretting the question as soon as she uttered the words. He was obviously not well at all.

His eyes were a fierce brooding blue; they still held a glittering light from the fever that continued to punish his body. He shrugged, unwilling to admit his weakness.

"That doesn't tell me much," Ryan said companionably, her face breaking into an almost irresistible smile. It was so full of goodwill and infectious happiness that he had difficulty not responding to it. But the deep black hole that had settled inside him yesterday after learning of Sean's identity kept his face an indifferent mask. He turned away.

A cool hand touched his forehead, then both his cheeks, and the gentleness was unexpectedly soothing. He looked back at her.

"You were the one who nursed me," he said. "I remember your voice . . . insistent. You wouldn't let me go."

"No," she said softly. "I wouldn't."

"You did me no favor," he said, glowering at her, even as he realized he was doing so for his own protection. Protection against her warmth.

"That's not something you should decide right now," she replied with a touch of impatience. "I know this is not where you want to be. I know there's something troubling between you and my brother. Something other than the war. But there's a long life out there ahead of you, and this is just a small piece of it."

"A philosopher as well as a doctor," he said sarcastically. "How many other talents do you claim?" He wanted her to go away. She disturbed him in a strange disquieting way.

"No," she said simply.

He looked at her again, his face a dark cloud. "No what?"

"No, I'm not going away. And I'm not easily bullied. It's been tried by the best, and you aren't even in the running."

The latter observation brought an unwilling quirk to his mouth. "There are many who would be surprised by that," he noted wryly.

Despite his best efforts, his dimple grew deeper, and he looked, Ryan thought, like a disappointed boy whose teacher had not been frightened by the frog in her desk.

Ryan was charmed by the momentary lapse, but all too soon the moment was gone and the glower was back. She wondered if she had imagined that brief whimsy. Her voice became softer. "Are you hungry?"

Morgan nodded. He needed his strength back, and food would help him get it. He could do nothing until he conquered the weakness that so debilitated him.

He lay there, his hand on the small dog as Ryan disappeared. He didn't completely understand his enmity toward her, wouldn't admit that perhaps he feared the warmth she seemed to offer so freely.

She returned with fresh coffee and a tin plate of biscuits and beans. "Do you need some help?"

"No," he growled.

"I guess you don't if you have the energy to be so angry," she said tartly. She handed him the plate and watched as he ate.

It was good. And he was hungry. He ate slowly, feeling some strength returning.

When the tin was empty, he handed it back to Ryan. "Thank you," he said simply. It was almost an apology.

She was encouraged by it. "Do you have any more pain? You wouldn't tell me before."

"Some," he said, his hostility temporarily gone. "The headaches keep coming back, and the leg hurts when I move. All to be expected, I guess."

"I have some laudanum if you need it."

"No," he said sharply. "I don't like it."

"Is there anything you do like, Colonel?"

He considered the question. "Freedom," he said finally, "and I find that gone."

"There's not much freedom in being dead," she retorted. "It is rather confining."

He shrugged. "Perhaps," he answered, "but that should be my choice, not yours." He was surprised to find he was halfway enjoying the exchange.

"You couldn't choose at the time," she said. "I had to make that decision for you. I'm sorry if you're unhappy with it." There was a challenge in the last words.

"And Captain Mallory... How does he feel about having an unexpected guest?" The question was out before he could stop it. He was curious—and puzzled—that Sean seemed to be avoiding him.

The girl studied him solemnly. She had wondered the same thing. "Well," she said finally, "I don't think he's any happier to have you here than you are to be here."

Morgan's face twisted into a slight sardonic smile as he realized how little he knew of the Pandora's box she had opened. Dark as it was, the smile broke the angles of his face and hinted at something finer. There was a trace of bitter humor in his blue eyes, but it was gone as quickly as it came.

"How *is* Sean?" he asked without warning, and Ryan detected real interest in the question.

She regarded him carefully. "He's tired. And now that you're here, he's something else, and I don't quite know what. Troubled, even hostile where you're concerned."

He turned his head away. There was so much regret there. "Did he ever marry?" he asked in a low voice.

"No," she said softly. Then hesitantly, she continued. "He used to write me about you...when you were both at West Point. I kept all his letters. He said you were his friend, that I would like you very much. And then he graduated, and he never mentioned it again. Now in the past days—since we brought you in—he's changed. There's a reserve I haven't seen before. Can you tell me why?"

He stared at her now, knowing he had opened the door. And all he could do was slam it shut again. "No," he said shortly. "I can't." *Not can't. Won't. How do you explain betrayal?*

She heard the pain in his short answer, but his face remained impassive, and she wondered again at the iron control that kept it so. "All right," she said, knowing she would receive no further information. "Is there anything else I can get you?"

"A razor," he said, running his hand over his stubbled face. "I feel so dirty."

"I don't think you're quite up to that yet," she answered. "You don't need any more wounds. But if you like, I'll do it for you. I'm quite good at it, and I promise not to inflict any more damage."

The quirk in his mouth came back. "Doctor... philosopher...barber. I wait with bated breath for other revelations," he replied, but the sarcasm was hidden in a small smile that transformed his face. She had been right. It was really quite overpowering. "I would be grateful," he added stiffly, as if unaccustomed to the words.

She gathered a razor and went to work. Any doubts he had were removed by her efficiency. There was no question that she had done it before, probably many times. She was gentle and thorough, and he was surprised at how much he enjoyed her touch.

He thanked her and was startled at his feelings when she left. He didn't want her to go.

Chapter Six

The heat of the sun woke Ben as it penetrated the canvas above him. He could see the bright round ball just beyond the cover. Unfettered by clouds, it was sending glittering splashes of gold to dance among the slightly swaying trees.

He was alone; even the dog had disappeared on some errand of its own. He had lost track of time but thought it had probably been a week since his injury. His strength was returning, although he chafed at the slowness of his recovery. The fever had finally given up its last hold on him, but his head still ached, and he couldn't move his leg without pain.

He looked around the camp, his eyes guarded and watchful. Some men were busy with the horses, hobbling them so they could graze at will in the rich valley. Ryan was nowhere to be seen. Neither was the young soldier who had relieved her during the past several days in caring for him.

Ben remained puzzled by Ryan. He had served in Virginia and hadn't forgotten the hostility of its women. They would much sooner have shot him than nurse him. One had actually tried, and failed only when one of his sergeants had grabbed the antique musket in midair.

But there was none of that in Ryan Mallory. Instead, she had tended him with a certain unspoken understanding, if not sympathy. She seemed to know he would accept the first and reject the second. In return, he granted her a respect that was entirely new to him.

Indeed, he mused, his opinion of women had not been high in past years. He had been cloistered during his teen years at military schools, then sent to sea. After that came West Point, and his experience was limited to occasional nights on the town—brief hurried events that left him empty. Then came Melody, and his deep unmet need for love and a warm family life had blinded him to all else. Since that time, his involvement with women had been restricted to brief affairs.

He had never had problems finding women and was constantly amazed that his indifference seemed to attract them. His very ease with them had only increased his contempt and birthed a longing in him for something more. He recognized it but was afraid to give any part of himself again. Instead, he had built a barrier around himself and ignored the pain within it.

But Ryan was already penetrating the shield. She had a warmth that intrigued him and drew him to her as surely as a moth to flame. Yet he couldn't get her eyes out of his mind . . . eyes that laughed and probed and penetrated; they missed little and he knew they read his moods as no one else had ever done. He thought he had become a master at hiding his thoughts—but he knew that Ryan already deciphered them easily. It was, he thought, disconcerting at the very least . . . a form of invasion that he both resented and challenged.

His thoughts were interrupted as a rider neared his bedding. He watched silently, his expression guarded, as Sean dismounted in front of him in one fluid movement. Ben had often envied Sean's effortless horsemanship; he had unquestionably been the best rider at West Point.

Sean gave his reins to a nearby soldier. "Rub him down, we've been a fair distance." He turned and strode over to Morgan.

The two men regarded each other intently, both searching for things they'd remembered and things that had been added through the years. So many ghosts stood between them.

Sean was the first to speak. He had avoided Morgan since he had offered him water nearly four days earlier, gone on about his business, unable to face his own churning contradictory feelings. He had taken a long ride today to sort them out and come to a decision about his prisoner.

"How do you feel?" he said now, his voice abrupt.

Morgan carefully searched Sean's face. In many ways it was much like Ryan's—a wide generous mouth, dark eyes, strong white teeth and golden eyebrows. But the face was stronger than he remembered. It was creased by the sun and years of command.

He answered slowly. "I'm alive. I can't ask for much more than that. I suppose I should thank you."

·Sean looked at him with anger. "But you don't, do you?" His voice grew even harder. "You've created a number of problems for me."

Morgan nodded with understanding. He was now certain that Sean's troop was the one he had been sent to find, and he realized how precarious their position had become. There would be an extensive search when he failed to appear.

Sean hunched down, balancing himself on the balls of his feet, his eyes never leaving Morgan's.

Morgan met them directly. "It's been a long time, Sean," he said finally, unable to tolerate the silence.

"Not long enough, Ben, not nearly long enough," Sean retorted, his anger close to the surface. "I think never would have been too soon."

Morgan nodded. He had been the one who betrayed the friendship, and no words could ever repair the wounds, especially now that he was Sean's prisoner. He clenched his fists, his thoughts instantly back at West Point.

Sean had been the first to call him Ben. He had always been Bennett to his friends and family. At first he had resented the Western informality, but he had grown used to it. After his graduation, he had discouraged the use of the nickname, wanting no reminders of a time he wished to forget.

"You found my horse," he finally said quietly, wondering if Sean had seen his orders.

"Yes." The reply was short, but there was fury in it.

"I didn't know it was you," Morgan said, almost involuntarily.

"And if you had? If I were the one lying there and you stood here?"

"I don't know," Ben replied bluntly, refusing the easy answer.

"Well now we'll never know, will we?" Sean said bitterly. "And what if it had been someone else? Would you have even that slight compunction?"

Ben flinched at the rage in Sean's voice. He hadn't liked the orders, but he had agreed to follow them.

Sean pulled the leather pouch from his pocket and threw it next to Ben. "We've never attacked a civilian, never so much as taken a loaf of bread from one. That's a hell of a lot more than I can say for Sherman and your army of looters."

"It is war. Destruction is what war is all about, or are you so isolated here you don't know anymore? There aren't any rules, not ones that mean anything." Ben's words were bitter and flung with a challenge.

Sean's voice was suddenly quiet, almost gentle. "You don't really mean that," he said. "I can't believe you've changed that much."

"We've both changed," Ben said wearily. "West Point is a thousand miles and a million years away. The one thing that doesn't change is we both follow orders—despite how we may feel about them."

"Not always," Sean disagreed. "My lieutenant disobeyed orders when he brought you in."

Ben laughed, but there was no amusement in the sound, only self-mockery. "And so here I am, saved by the men I was supposed to take. There's quite a bit of irony in that, isn't there, Sean."

"It was Ryan who saved your life," Sean said quietly. "I merely spared it. Mainly because of her." There was a thoughtful pause. "Don't," he added, "make me regret it. I consider my debt to you paid. You are my enemy now, and I won't hesitate to kill you if it becomes necessary." He spun to his feet and left without another word.

Morgan's eyes held a glint of deep regret. Sean had changed greatly in the more than a decade since they had seen each other. He was more confident now; command, it seemed, came easily to him. The affection his men had for him was obvious, yet there appeared to be no lapse in discipline. Morgan knew that although he had the feared respect of his men, he had never commanded the same type of loyalty. He was only too aware of the difference.

His thoughts became increasingly dark. He turned, grimacing at the pain created by the sudden move. The loneliness that he had denied for so long became an almost unbearable agony, dwarfing the physical pain by comparison.

The bitterness was still there when Ryan changed the bandages the next day. The drainage had stopped, and there was no sign of infection. She washed the crusted cuts gently and smiled up at him.

"In a few days I can take out those stitches. We don't have to worry about blood poisoning anymore. As soon as you get some strength back, we'll have you walking."

She tipped her head to one side. "No hint of a smile at that? No enthusiasm? Can't I have even a little tug at your mouth, a tiny little light in those frowning eyes?"

His look chilled her. His eyes were bleak, his face grim and shuttered. "It might have been better for everyone," he said finally, "if you had left me there."

"Oh no, you don't," she said sternly, her smile gone. "I've seen too many people who would give anything for even a few more days of life. Sean said he thought you had a son. What about him? How would he feel?

"Besides," she added with a twinkle, "I've spent much too much time on you to see it go unappreciated. I've also incurred the wrath of my brother, along with several of my hotheaded friends. Don't tell me it's all been for naught."

Remorse hit him. He had never been a quitter. He wasn't about to start now. He nodded, his eyes clearing, and allowed himself a slight abashed smile that deepened the dimple and made him look—once more—like a naughty boy.

"When," he said, "did you say I can start walking?"

Her smile widened and her eyes glowed. "Next week," she said. "If you behave."

"Now," she commanded as she sat down, "tell me about Boston. I've never seen an ocean," she added wistfully.

The question distracted him, and he welcomed the impersonality of it. "The sea is a lot like the prairie," he said, "endless, constant. Always the same, yet always changing." The slightly self-conscious smile returned, and he added somewhat impishly, "All you have to do is paint your Texas blue, and you have the sea. I'm sure you must be a painter, too." The glint in his eyes told her he couldn't resist the last observation.

"Why didn't you go to sea?" she asked curiously, not wanting him to stop.

Sean, he thought immediately. Sean's been talking to her. How much, he wondered, had his former friend said?

"I did," he answered honestly. "My father forced me to when I was seventeen. I was gone a year, and I hated it. I hated the confinement. I hated the total authority a captain has over the lives of the men who sail with him. Even when he's wrong, there's no appeal. Even the army gives you that. I think my father hoped it would give me a love for the sea—and the business. It did the opposite. I couldn't wait to get away. I think that's why I went to West Point—to get as far away from the sea as possible. Colorado," he added with the strangely attractive wry humor, "is pretty damn far." The dark blue eyes, which had been so bleak, softened for a minute, then retreated behind the old enigma.

"At least I know you can smile," she said teasingly. "I shall try to explore how far you will allow it to go. Right now I must go and help with supper. Fortune will keep you company."

She started to leave, then turned back suddenly. "Did you ever decide?"

He looked at her questioningly.

"Have you decided whether you like dogs or not?"

"Well, Fortune, anyway," he answered, again with the tiniest of smiles. "I think we have a lot in common. No one seems to like us very much."

"Well—" she smiled "—you both have been a lot of trouble, and neither of you seems very appreciative. Poor Jimmy rescued Fortune from a trap and got bit for his trouble. I think Sean feels somewhat the same wariness about you."

She started to turn again, then stopped as his hand clasped her wrist. Despite his illness his hold felt like a steel clamp.

"Why," he said, "are you doing this?"

Her face creased in puzzlement. "Doing what?"

"Taking care of me like this?"

She regarded him sadly. "If you have to ask, Colonel, then I have no answer you would understand."

He let go suddenly, his hand feeling as if it had been burned. He had not expected the rush of heat that ran through his body when he touched her. His blood was suddenly like a river of fire, and when his eyes met hers again, he knew she shared the same sensation.

She stared at him, confused by the quickening of her blood and the desire that flooded her. Unable to move she remained still until she heard his low voice.

"You're right," he said roughly. "I don't understand it. I don't know if I ever will."

Ryan fled.

Ryan had squeezed every bit of information she could from Sean, piece by unwilling piece. He was unusually taciturn about Morgan, and even more so as he noticed her increasing interest in the Yank. He wished the problem of Morgan would just disappear, but he knew it wouldn't.

The night before he had fended Ryan off as well as he could, briefly outlining the history as he knew it: Ben's Boston origins; his large but apparently cold family; his assignment in the West. He would say no more. Unmoved by the plea in her eyes, he volunteered only one thing: a warning.

"Stay away from him, Ryan. All other considerations aside, he is our enemy."

"He was your friend. You used to write me about him."

It was his turn to be startled. "You remember that?"

"I kept all of your letters. I used to read them over and over again."

"That was a long time ago." His voice was sharp, his patience near an end.

"Tell me," she begged. "What happened? Something did. It's not just the war."

"Maybe not. But the war is enough right now." He put a hand on her shoulder. "Just trust me, Ryan."

She said good-night and went to the wagon, puzzled with Sean, puzzled with herself. She didn't understand why she was so drawn to Morgan. At first his initial indifference to everything around him, even to whether he lived or died, had been a challenge. He was, she admitted, one of the most attractive men she had met, but there were others, including Tom Braden, who were more traditionally handsome and who, she thought, lacked his prickly nature. But they had never stirred the inexplicable yearning and sudden warmth that she felt whenever she thought of the Yankee colonel.

Ryan pushed the disturbing feelings from her mind, undressed quickly and slid onto the small mattress Sean had produced from somewhere.

She lay there for a long time, thinking of Sean and Ben, wondering over the antagonism that was so apparent between them.

They seemed, in nature, opposites, and she questioned whether that had always been so or if each was molded by time and experience. Sean was easy to be with, his feelings usually close to the surface. He was quick with affection and blessed with a ready laugh and gentle wit. Most people liked him instantly, drawn by the natural warmth in his eyes. He had a fierce temper—Ryan had seen it explode several times—but while it was quick to come, it was just as quick to go, often leaving him repentant. Ryan had never known him to hold a grudge, which made his attitude toward Colonel Morgan all the more bewildering.

Morgan, on the other hand, was guarded and unfriendly. She could almost feel the barely restrained violence and energy that was so much a part of the man despite his weakened condition, and she wondered if the mask he usually wore would ever slip and reveal his true feelings.

She sensed the deep anger that always hovered near the surface, and she knew, for the first time, fear of a man. It was not a physical fear but a sudden realization that Colonel Bennett Morgan would exact a heavy toll from anyone who cared for him. There was no ease in him, no acceptance of weakness—for himself or for anyone else.

She explored Sean's words again for more understanding of the bitterness that squirmed like a live thing between them. But there were no answers.

Ryan tried to sleep, but Morgan continued to haunt her, his distant blue eyes staying fixed in her mind. She tried to chase them away and was strangely relieved when they refused to go.

Chapter Seven

In the next several days, Morgan's fever disappeared completely, and his natural color returned. Ryan found herself spending more and more time with him. Sometimes she would sit and share breakfast or the evening meal with him. Fortune would often intrude, placing himself beside them, demanding only their company. The dog limped badly but still managed to get around. Morgan asked about the injury.

She told him how Jimmy Carne had found the little dog, who had wandered into an animal trap and nearly chewed his leg in half trying to get free.

Jimmy had released him, getting bitten for his trouble, and, after carefully wrapping the half-crazed pup in a blanket, brought him to Ryan. The dog immediately recognized Ryan as a friend—a fact that still gave the young soldier some pain. As much as Jimmy tried, he could not tempt Fortune into accepting food or affection from him. Fortune was decidedly a one-person dog and had remained so until Morgan. Jimmy was incensed. A damned Yankee, for God's sake.

"Perhaps," Morgan commented, "Fortune believes there's comfort in shared misfortune."

Ryan looked at him thoughtfully. She had been intrigued by Fortune's unusual attachment to her patient. Morgan had certainly done nothing to encourage it other than an occasional light touch, yet they seemed content in each other's company. "Maybe," she said slowly, "he associates pain with Jimmy, and it's made him wary of uniforms."

"I'm wearing a uniform."

Her smile was mischievous. "Not much of one. I did a pretty good job of tearing it up."

He turned rueful attention to his clothing. The jacket was long gone; the shirt was open to midchest because of the heat. One legging was tattered from his fall, the other cut above the knee where she had found the snakebites. His lower left leg was encased in a makeshift splint. "I would hardly pass muster now," he agreed, with a bitter half twist of his mouth.

"Sean can probably help out there," she said with a wicked look in her eyes. "Sean has a knack for finding anything and everything."

"Then Fortune would probably reject me, too," he said, a rare flash of humor in his eyes. "I don't know if I'd risk that."

"You and Sean," she began, changing the subject abruptly. "Tell me about it."

The veil dropped back over his eyes. "There's not much to tell."

Ryan's eyes were piercing, waiting for him to continue, demanding that he do so. "There's something between you two. Sean hasn't been the same since you came here. His face tenses every time your name is mentioned. It's not just the inconvenience of you being here—it's deeper than that. I want to know what it is." Her voice was suddenly haughty, exasperated at his silence. "I have the right," she said. "I'm the one who brought you here."

"Maybe you would have done everyone a favor if you hadn't," he said rudely.

"Damn you," she exploded suddenly, unexpectedly. "You can go to hell, Colonel," she said succinctly. Her voice was colder than he had thought possible, and her brown eyes were suddenly as hard as agates. "And I have no doubt you will." She whirled around and left.

He was too stunned to retort. The flash of temper reminded him of Sean, but he had not expected it of her. It was yet another new dimension to this strange girl, who kept surprising him. Somehow, he liked her even more for it.

Morgan closed his eyes, his hand fondling the dog, who had stayed with him. He had tried to ease Sean from his memory for the past thirteen years. He would never forget the raw agony on his roommate's face that night when he, Morgan, had accused Sean of attacking his fiancée. He had called Sean a liar and a cheat and worse. Sean had stood there, taking it, until Ben had swung wildly at him, and then Sean's own anger had erupted.

It took half the barracks to tear him off Sean, and less than six months later, he knew that everything Sean had said was true and recognized how hard it had been for Sean to come to him. He had thought about seeking him out and apologizing, but could not bring himself to admit such a terrible misjudgment. Instead, he had retreated into a private world of his own.

Morgan's fists clenched as he remembered Sean doubled over on the floor, his face convulsed with pain as he tried to breathe. It was the last time they had seen each other until now. He suddenly wished he was anyplace but here. Anyplace at all.

Ryan's temper cooled as quickly as it had exploded. She knew she was being unfair. Why, after all, should Colonel Morgan tell her any more than Sean had? She had let her frustration take over, and she was immediately chagrined, but her pride prevented her from returning. She thought about the two of them, wondering anew what could have torn them so far apart.

She even now had several of Sean's letters. They had meant everything to her that first year after her parents' death. She pulled them out and read one passage over and over again, hunting for a clue. There was none. Sean had described Ben in an affectionate tone tinged with respect. "You would like him, Kitten," he had written. "He is good at everything and, like you, has a funny whimsical sense of humor. I think I would have left West Point long ago if he hadn't been here to make it tolerable."

Ryan shook her head. What had changed both of them so much?

She swallowed her pride that evening and took two dinners and two cups of coffee over to Morgan. Jimmy had earlier propped a saddle behind him, allowing him to sit up.

"Like some company?" She asked him gingerly, partly expecting a refusal.

Caught by surprise, he merely nodded.

"I'm sorry," she said. "I had no right to pry this morning."

Morgan looked at her thoughtfully, some of his bleakness disappearing. "You're the first woman who's ever apologized to me for that," he replied with an edge of self-defensiveness. "I thought they considered it a God-given right."

"You don't like women very much, do you." Her question was soft, more like a statement.

Morgan took a sip of the hot bitter coffee before looking up. "I like you." Despite his words, the tone was flat, his face unsmiling. It was more an unwilling admission than a compliment.

"That must be quite a concession," Ryan said with a smile. "I'm flattered . . . I think."

A slightly sardonic grin appeared on his lips. "I don't think your brother would agree."

She decided to change the subject before the water got any deeper.

"Tell me about the picture in your saddlebags," she asked unexpectedly. "Sean supposed it was your son."

Morgan's mouth grew taut at the admitted invasion, then relaxed slightly. What could he expect? Of course Sean went through his belongings. But he had to fight his resentment at Sean's sharing them with Ryan.

Ryan understood immediately. "He didn't show me," she said. "I just happened to see it and asked. The boy in the picture looked like you."

Morgan nodded, his expression suddenly unguarded, even wistful. "He does." Morgan ran a hand through his thick dark hair. "His hair is just about as unmanageable as mine. It usually sticks out in a dozen places." His voice was unexpectedly warm.

Ryan was struck by the change in his face. The lines smoothed out and the dimple in his cheek became more prominent.

"He must be very special," she said, quietly urging him on.

"He is." Morgan looked up at her, his face puzzled. "Very much like you, in fact. He has the same curiosity, the same compulsion to rescue strays. I keep telling him it's going to get him in trouble." His tone was grimly amused. "He doesn't listen to me any more than you apparently listen to your brother."

Ryan noted the frequency with which he mentioned Sean—consciously or unconsciously. Sean did the same thing. Whether either of them realized it, there was obviously still a strong bond between them. Somehow she would get them back together again.

Her brief reverie was broken by his voice.

"You two would like each other.... He wants to be a doctor. He's been helping at a hospital in Washington...."

"He's lucky," Ryan said. "He has you."

"Not so lucky," Ben Morgan said, and she hated the return of that deep bitterness that never stayed hidden long.

"I didn't know him very well until this year. I was never able to spend any time with him." Morgan closed his eyes, knowing the statement for the lie it was. It wasn't, he knew, that he wasn't able. It was that he hadn't chosen to. How he wished he could change that, change so many things.

"At least you will have time now," Ryan said. "That's just as important. I lost my parents when I was seven, and I've missed them all my life."

Morgan looked up at her. It was the first sign of sadness he had seen in her. She was usually so vibrant, so incredibly alive it was difficult to reconcile the two.

"Indians," he said flatly, remembering the day Sean had been notified. Ben had tried to comfort him then. He had listened for hours as his roommate and friend had talked about the small Texas ranch and the mother and father who had loved each other so much. Sean had blamed himself for not being there and had worried about his little sister. She had apparently been hidden in a fruit cellar during the raid and was found wandering in the hills three days later. A week after Sean's notification, another letter had arrived from the doctor and his wife, asking to adopt the seven-year-old. Sean and Ben had gone out and gotten very drunk. Finally Sean had agreed to the adoption, and later he had shared some of his sister's letters. Even at seven she could read and write, and they were full of fanciful drawings. Ben remembered his fascination with the merry little soul who must have written them.

He looked at her now, recalling them and wondering how he had forgotten.

"How did you happen to come here?" he asked finally, curiosity overtaking his self-protective urge to keep his distance.

Her eyes clouded again, the light fading from her face. "My adoptive mother and father died from typhoid," she said. "There was no one left, no one but Sean."

His heart twisted for her . . . the heart he thought dead. "I'm sorry," he said softly as he watched the pain cross her face.

"The doctor," he said finally. "He taught you medicine?"

"Not by choice," she said, a tiny smile easing her sorrow. "Not in the beginning, anyway. They didn't have any other children, and he used to take me on rounds for company. I would usually wait outside, but one day he needed help, and there was no one else. A woman was in labor, and her husband was completely useless. He called me, and I helped. I think he was shocked that I didn't faint or something worse. After that, he often asked me to assist. He said I had a natural aptitude and taught me everything he could. Mother Foster was horrified." She smiled wider, remembering the recriminations between the doctor and his wife and the tug of war over her activities. They had gradually faded as the relationship between Ryan and the doctor grew stronger. Mary Foster had loved them both and finally admitted reluctantly that Ryan had more talent for nursing than needlework. Ryan's attempts to please Mrs. Foster, however, did give her some skill at the latter, and Dr. Foster delighted in her fine stitchery on his patients.

She hesitated a moment before continuing. "He finally took me to a nearby Apache reservation. Most of the Indians were old and sick, and he helped them as much as he could despite the feeling in town against them. He used to sit and visit for hours with the old medicine man, learning his herbal remedies. 'Never close your mind,' he would tell me. He showed me we were equally guilty for the wars between us. We had forced them off land they had lived on for hundreds of years."

Morgan couldn't take his eyes from her constantly changing face. It was incredibly mobile and reflected every thought, every emotion. He had never met anyone so open.

She tipped her head to one side, her face serious. "In a way, I was very lucky. I had two sets of parents, both loving, both giving me something special. The first a love of life and music, the second a love of books and knowledge . . . and an obligation to others. And then—" she brightened "—there's Sean."

"You're very close to him, aren't you," Ben said slowly, his heart churning with unfamiliar pain.

"We're all each other has," she said simply. "I don't know what I would have done if I hadn't found him. He chases all my nightmares away."

She saw the question in his eyes. "I still dream, sometimes, of that Indian raid." There was a glint of tears in her eyes as she remembered the most recent nightmare . . . and Sean's comforting presence.

Morgan could think of nothing to say. He couldn't imagine the horrors she had faced; even less did he understand how she had emerged as unscathed emotionally as she appeared.

Morgan thought how different their lives had been. His own had been rich materially, but not in love. His parents had been religious and strict; they took no joy in their four children. They had been produced of duty and raised in duty. His mother had died at the birth of his sister twenty-four years ago, but there had been no real mourning. It seemed he had never known her, only governesses and tutors and then military schools chosen, mainly, to strip him of his rebellious nature. It was ironic that they had, instead, instilled in him a fascination for things military. He had later won his father's support of a West Point appointment by threatening to enlist as a private.

But until his marriage, his life had been relatively uncomplicated. Everything came easily, even the year at sea his father had demanded, and he accepted his advantages and wealth with graceful detachment. Melody had systematically destroyed that protective cloak. She had made him care desperately about another person and then had betrayed him in the worst way possible. He had vowed then to never again allow another person even a small piece of his life.

And now there was Ryan, who touched him as no woman ever had before, not even Melody. He liked her strength, her humor, even her stubbornness, in pursuit of what she wanted. And though he was loath to admit it, he liked the way she made him feel, the way he came alive every time he saw her, the way his blood quickened and awakened the passion and hope he thought gone forever. He was also aware of a special tenderness. It struck him like a fist, unexpected, unwanted.

He looked at her and she met his eyes. There was a sudden strong current between them, a shared intimacy that surprised them both. She lowered her head as the overwhelming impact of pure want flooded her. ''No,'' she whispered. ''No.'' And then she was gone.

He heard them again that night. The brother and sister. The guitar was plaintive, Ryan's voice tinged with new feeling. The poignant sounds of ''Aura Lee'' and ''Someone's Darling'' drifted back to him, but neither Mallory ventured near him. The vast clear sky of jeweled stars only accentuated his aloneness.

Chapter Eight

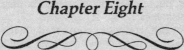

Ryan woke the next morning, knowing something had changed inside her. A new excitement pulsed through her body.

She took her time in dressing. As though denying that special shared moment last night, she started to clad herself once more in a worn pair of pants and shirt. She hesitated, then threw them to the flooring of the wagon and went instead to her one blouse and skirt. It was a riding skirt, plain, but a rich dark brown that complemented her dark eyes. She tied a gold sash around her slender waist.

Ryan took particular care with her hair. Instead of the usual convenient braid, she brushed it until the copper highlights sparkled. She then tied it loosely with a dark brown ribbon, letting it tumble around her face and down her back.

She reluctantly, even shyly, left the safety of the wagon. She knew her appearance would surprise her brother and the others. She had, she knew, carried convenience and comfort to the extreme. It had been a long time since she had worn a skirt or her hair unbound.

Ryan joined the group of men at the morning fire. She gratefully took an offered cup of coffee and ignored the stares as nonchalantly as she could. Sean just arched a golden eyebrow, adding to her growing embarrassment.

It was one of the hardest things she had ever done, but she kept her eyes away from the area behind them where Ben Morgan lay, alone with his thoughts. She could feel his eyes on her. They bore into her back, demanding her attention.

Sean seemed to sense her confusion. He took her by the shoulder and guided her into his tent.

"I'll get your breakfast," he said. "Let's eat together this morning."

She nodded her agreement, unsure whether she was grateful or resentful. She was totally confused by the conflicting emotions that assaulted her. More than anything else, she wanted to see Ben, to be with him, to test all these new feelings that were playing games with her senses. But fear kept bubbling up. The time and place were wrong, and she knew it.

Sean brought two servings of corn bread, bacon and bitter coffee. He set one down in front of her on the small camp stool and held his in his lap. He ate indifferently, more out of necessity than any real hunger.

Ryan didn't touch the food. She had never felt less hungry. Her stomach churned and her thoughts were on the other side of the camp.

"It won't work, Ryan," her brother said softly. "I know Ben. He's not for you. I don't think he's good for any woman anymore. Look at his eyes. They're dead."

"No," she denied. "They're not with me. They're alive and caring. Look at him with Fortune. He's the only person Fortune will have anything to do with except me."

"Because they're both mavericks," he retorted. He stopped her from saying anything. "Neither of them are totally able to trust again. Fortune will take your care and your food, but that's it. Ben's the same way." Sean hesitated a moment, then plunged on. "You asked me about Ben. The man I knew isn't there any longer." Sean's face grew pensive. "He used to regard the world with a sort of humor. But for all that he had a fine sense of justice and compassion. It's gone now. There's only bitterness and distrust left. You can see it in his face. The scars are there, and they're not the kind that heal."

His voice became harder. "I don't want you hurt, Ryan. Don't make me regret keeping him here. I told him that. Now I'm telling you. Leave it alone."

She shoved her plate aside. "I'm not hungry."

"I mean it, Ryan. Stay away from Morgan."

"I need to change his bandages," she said stubbornly. "He's far from well yet."

"Jimmy can do that. You taught him well."

"No. It's my responsibility. He's my patient."

"And he's my prisoner," Sean retorted. "And you're both here on sufferance. You forget that. I should have sent you back a long time ago. As for Morgan, he should never have been brought here in the first place."

They glared at each other, each one refusing to retreat. Sean watched as tiny tears gathered in her rebellious eyes. She had never seemed more vulnerable.

He gave in first, realizing that his opposition was making her more intractable.

"All right, you are going to do what you want to do. But remember, Ryan, I may not be able to influence you, but I sure as hell can control his future."

She looked at him with disbelief. "Is that a threat?"

"Take it any way you wish. He's our enemy." His voice was suddenly harsh. "He came here to find us, to hunt us, me specifically. He came to see us hang. Every one of us."

Ryan's face paled. "What do you mean?"

"He came with orders, Ryan. Written orders. He was sent to find us and to take me back to Washington for trial and hanging. The others—Tom, Jimmy, Justis, Smithy, all of them—are to be executed."

"No," she whispered.

"Yes, Ryan. Do you want to see the papers?"

"No." She was silent a moment, thinking about the implications of his statement. "Why, Sean? They must know you're a part of the Confederate army."

He shrugged. "They don't care. We've been too successful. They want us out of the way. We've being accused of every robbery and killing in the territory. Hanging would put a nice neat ending to it all."

She rose from the cot and stood over him. She put her arms gently around his neck and lowered her head to his. "I'm sorry, Sean. I didn't know."

"Of course you didn't. I didn't want you to. I thought we would be gone in another few weeks and none of it would matter. I just didn't figure you to fall in love with a Yank."

"Is that what it is?" The question came softly. "I don't know. I've never felt this way before. I feel so strange, so expectant. I want something so badly, but I don't know what. I do know that I like him and I trust him, even if you don't."

Sean stood up. He put his hand on her hair, caressing it lightly, letting it fall through his hands. *God,* he thought to himself, *she is so vulnerable.*

He took her chin and tipped it upward. "My little sister. You're not so little anymore. I keep forgetting that. But promise me...you will think about what I said."

She nodded, her eyes huge and lost in their uncertainty. "I have to find out, Sean. I have to discover for myself. Don't you see? But I'll be careful." She reached up on tiptoe and kissed his forehead. "I'll be careful for all of us."

Ryan didn't go to Morgan immediately. Instead, she found excuses to stay away. She helped one young private repair the rips in his shirt and fussed over a trooper who had been wounded weeks before. Finally, she helped prepare the midday meal.

When she couldn't find anything more to do, she gathered some fresh bandages and water and walked over to Morgan. He watched her approach, her slender body beautiful in the swaying skirt and simple blouse.

Their eyes met in sudden mutual understanding tinged with wariness.

"I was afraid you wouldn't come," he said in a soft low voice, "that I had offended you in some way." His next words were an almost painful admission. "I've missed you."

Ryan couldn't answer him, but her eyes revealed her fear, joy and confusion.

She tried to make some sense of what was happening. In her muddle she knelt beside him and started to remove the bandages. Her hands were remarkably gentle, and he felt pleasure from the touch of them on his leg. "I'm going to take out those stitches," she said, taking a tiny pair of sewing scissors out of a small bag. He watched her as she bent over his leg, the scissors carefully snipping the tiny scraps of thread. When she finished, she poured some alcohol over the slightly bleeding wound.

She finally looked up at him, avoiding his searching eyes. He bent over, one of his hands touching hers. His fingers wandered over it, exploring, and then he brought it to his mouth. His lips touched it lightly, and then he folded the hand into a ball and gave it back to her.

"You're so damned pretty," he said almost accusingly.

She looked at him then. His dark blue eyes were almost black. The mussed, slightly curling dark hair barely hit his neck, shorter than fashion. His face *was* hard, the lines etched there not from laughter but from his private and not so private wars.

"Ben," she said slowly, savoring the sound. "Bennett Morgan. I don't understand what's happening." Her voice was more than a little frightened, her confidence gone.

"Then," he replied, his own voice almost a sigh, "that's two of us." He closed his eyes, feeling the same bittersweet bewilderment. *This is no time to start caring for someone,* he thought, *especially with all the entanglements between the two of us.* "God," he whispered, not realizing he spoke aloud. "What a mess."

"Is it true that you came looking for Sean?" she asked softly.

He wanted to deny it, to wipe away the hurt on her face. But he simply nodded. There was nothing to say. No excuses to make. "Does it make a difference?"

"It should," she answered quite honestly. But the denial never made it to her face. "It should," she repeated, trying to convince herself. But her face softened as she looked at his handsome features, and their eyes locked.

They sat there, lost in a small world of their own making. Morgan's face looked years younger, and Ryan's had the special sparkle of one encountering a new delightful adventure. They were oblivious to everyone around them, oblivious to Sean, who watched them silently with real fear.

They spent more and more time together in the week that followed. Sean had still not placed guards on Morgan, realizing he was still far too weak to try an escape. Ryan gave up any pretense that she was only attending to his medical needs.

There was some initial resentment among the Texans, a feeling that soon cooled when Jimmy pointed out it was nobody's business but Sean and Ryan's. They all considered Ryan their little sister and needful of their protection, but they heeded Jimmy and adopted a wait-and-see attitude.

Not so Sean, who quietly raged. It was all he could do to keep a rein on his temper and his mouth. He knew that the more he opposed the growing relationship between the two, the faster it would progress. He couldn't take that chance. Ryan with all her apparent softness was extremely independent and stubborn. He found comfort only in the fact that their time there was limited. There would be one more trip to Center. With luck, the repeating rifles would be through within a week. And then they would be gone.

* * *

Out of growing fear for her safety, Sean decided that Ryan would not go back to Center. Morgan's orders had made very clear what kind of danger they all faced. His men were trained for it and fully aware of the risks. Ryan was not.

And he wanted a break in the monotonous routine. The mere presence of Ben Morgan stifled him. He needed both the excuse to get away and the exhilaration that danger always brought him. Braden would go again in his guise as a farmer, and he would accompany him as a saddle tramp to keep an eye out for him. He always sent his people out in pairs, one as a backup, in case of trouble.

He told Ryan at dinner, noting the quick relief that fluttered over her face and then the growing concern that quickly replaced it.

"But isn't it dangerous for you?"

"No more so than for you or Tom or anyone else. It's a weekday. I don't expect any soldiers from the fort to be there. Even if they were, it's unlikely any would recognize me." He gave her a crooked grin. "I was always getting into trouble and being sent to isolated places."

Ryan didn't share the smile. "I don't think you should. Counting West Point, you've been in the army nearly eighteen years. There are too many people who know you, who would know you joined the South. If not me, send someone else."

He looked down at her serious face. "I've already decided, Kitten."

She knew from his voice it would be useless to argue. "You will take care?"

"You should know me that well, by now. I always take care. Now you get some dinner while I talk to Braden."

Ryan didn't miss the lilt in his voice. She suspected what was driving him, and she was afraid that it would make him careless. An involuntary shudder ran through her body.

Ryan brought Morgan's dinner over to him and sat down, her legs crossed carelessly. She only picked at the food.

"You aren't going to eat?" he asked. She had lost some of her usual sparkle; her eyes were serious and her mouth twisted into an unusual frown.

She shook her head. "I'm not hungry."

"What's wrong?"

"Sean's going into Center tomorrow. I'm worried about him. He shouldn't be going. I should. No one knows me. Certainly no one suspects the boy I become, and if anything went wrong, they wouldn't hurt a woman."

A muscle in Ben's jaw twitched as he thought about Ryan arrested and jailed. "I wouldn't count on that," he answered stiffly. "Several women have already been imprisoned for spying."

"But they wouldn't hang me, and they would Sean."

His leaden silence eloquently told her she was probably right. She closed her eyes, her face a study in misery.

He took her right hand in his and held it tightly. "I've never seen anyone as capable of taking care of himself as Sean," he said. "He's indestructible. He'll be fine."

She opened her eyes and stared at him with amazement. "That's exactly what he said about you," she said slowly, "just after I brought you in."

"Maybe we're both right. We seem to be survivors," he said with an unexpected smile. It was the first real one she had seen, and it reminded her of a sunburst after a heavy rain. It lighted his face and softened the harsh lines around his eyes and mouth. Even his eyes were warmed by it.

The smile threw her off balance, and all she could think of at the moment was preserving it. He had been handsome before in his dark brooding way, but now he radiated irresistible charm. It was such a complete change, it took her breath away.

It was gone all too soon, but so was some of the deep bitterness that usually clung to him.

He tightened his grip on her hand again. "I'm glad you're not going," he said, his voice low. He had heard of the circumstances behind his rescue and thought Sean wrong in permitting her trips.

"He will be all right," Ben said again. In a voice so low she halfway thought she imagined it, he added, "I don't think he and I are through yet."

She gave him a puzzled smile and leaned over toward him. She touched his cheek gently and held her hand there. She shivered, consumed with the need to let the hand wander, to twist it in the thick hair, to bask in that wonderful smile again.

Sean suddenly interrupted them. He held out his hand to Ryan and pulled her up. "Leave us, Kitten," he said gently. "I want to talk to Ben."

Ryan looked from one to another. The two men regarded each other with animosity. It was as if she were watching two dogs circle before going at each other's throats, she thought hopelessly. "Sean . . ."

"Go for a walk. Talk to Jimmy. I don't care. But leave us, now."
This time, it was a command. She didn't have the heart to argue.
Not when he was going to make the dangerous trip to Center in the
morning. She gave both of them a pleading look and obediently
turned toward the wagon. She looked back. "Good night, Ben,
Sean," she whispered softly, not waiting for, nor expecting, answers.

Sean continued to stand there, looking at Ben. "I once asked you
not to make me regret sparing your life. I already am. I don't want
her around you." He turned and stalked away, taking with him the
warmth that Ben had so recently felt.

Chapter Nine

Sean and Tom Braden left early the next day. Tom was dressed in his rough farmer's garb and drove the dilapidated wagon. Sean had chosen the lighter clothes of the itinerant cowhand. He thought momentarily about taking his guitar; it had become his good luck charm.

He dismissed the thought as quickly as it came. He needed nothing to single him out from the other restless wanderers who came and went. With that thought, he chose a nondescript chestnut, which he knew to be much faster than he looked, rather than Zeus, the big bay stallion he usually rode. He strapped on his gun belt and checked the Colt revolver he had liberated from a Yank patrol. The gun had become intensely popular throughout the West, and he felt little attention would be paid it.

He and Braden traveled together for several miles before Sean turned his horse in an easterly direction. He would circle the town, watch for any army patrols and go in alone. The two would stay apart unless there was some kind of trouble.

Center stood astride the main route to the west. Established as a trading post, it had started to grow at the onset of the Civil War to serve the increased traffic. An army post had been built forty miles west of town to protect the trail and gold shipments, adding to the demand for services.

It was a raw ugly town. Most of the buildings had been hastily constructed with little concern for aesthetics. Each seemed to balloon forth from the earth with no relationship to the one next to it. Only the general store had any kind of porch, and that flooring was uneven and apt to cave in under heavy loads.

Sean guided his horse to the one large sprawling saloon. He knew he had plenty of time before Braden would arrive. A beer would taste damn good, and maybe he could pick up some information at the same time. He walked in and saw a group of men arguing in a corner. He didn't like their looks at all. There was one in particular who bothered him. There was something familiar about him, but he couldn't place it. He went to the opposite end of the bar and ordered his beer....

Braden drove in an hour later. He went quickly to the telegraph office and collected the message there. The telegraph operator was friendly, too friendly for Braden, and he merely grunted when the man asked about his son.

"Good news, I hope," the man tried again hopefully. "Your kin better git here soon if you want to beat that weather in the mountains."

Braden just shrugged and grunted again. He wasn't going to encourage the man. He left the office and started to board his wagon, when he heard a commotion from inside the saloon.

"Git the sheriff!" someone yelled. "We got us a Reb here."

Braden played with the harness and looked toward the saloon. The noise had alerted the sheriff, and he was already on his way from his office. Braden hesitated. He had a rifle in the wagon, but Sean's orders had been explicit. "If there's a crowd, go for help. Don't risk capture yourself. We would both be out of luck."

Braden was weighing the alternatives, when he saw Sean hustled out the door. He was followed by the sheriff, who had a gun pressed into his back. The group stopped briefly at Sean's horse, the sheriff obviously looking for something. There was a loud argument, and then Sean was pushed forward again. He saw Sean's eyes search the street for him, and he noted the slight nod in the direction of the camp as Sean caught sight of him. Braden lowered his head in agreement.

After Sean disappeared, Braden sauntered into the saloon and up to the barkeep. "Looks like some excitement?"

The barkeeper winked. "Someone thought he recognized the fellow they just hustled out of here. They're all seeing Rebs under their beds."

"He didn't look like no Reb to me," Braden said, fighting to keep the Southern drawl out of his voice.

"He probably isn't. Rafe's always stirring up trouble. He doesn't like anybody. But the sheriff thought he better check with the army just to make sure. He's sending a deputy to check at the fort, see if they want to send someone to take a look-see."

Braden gulped down his beer and tossed a coin to the man, waiting for his change. He hated to take the few extra seconds, but he knew a farmer wouldn't throw away hard-earned money. He collected his change and forced himself to saunter out. He quickly climbed aboard the wagon and whipped the horse into a fast pace.

Once well outside the town, he drove into some woods, unhitched the horse, cut its reins short and leaped onto its bare back, kicking it into a gallop.

Sean was led into the one cell at the tiny jail, cursing himself for his stupidity. He should have recognized Rafe Brown immediately, but it had been a number of years since he had charged the man with theft and saw him court-martialed. It had been an unpleasant incident, and he had quickly forgotten it. Obviously Rafe had not.

He turned back toward the sheriff. "That man's crazy as well as drunk. You can't hold me on his say."

The sheriff locked the door. "I can do anything I want to," he said curtly. "The Rebs have been real active in these parts, and the army told me to hold anyone who even looks suspicious."

"But even he admitted that the fellow he says I was always carried a guitar. I ain't never had one."

"Perhaps not," the sheriff said, "but I still have to hold you. If you're who you say you are, you'll be out of here by morning."

"But I have a job waiting for me up north. If I'm not there, I'll lose it."

"That's your hard luck," the sheriff retorted. "You shouldn't have taken time for a drink."

Sean realized talking would do little good. But he also knew it would look strange if he didn't keep protesting.

"Look here, sheriff, I need that job. I ain't no Reb. I'm from Montana and don't have no stake in this war."

"We all have a stake in it," the sheriff said. "Now shut up."

Sean sat down on the filth-encrusted cot and wished Braden a very quick trip back.

Ryan was sitting with Ben when she heard the first signals of incoming riders. Ben saw the tension in the way she arched her back and the piercing look she gave the valley entrance.

Braden came galloping in and bounded from his horse, calling to the nearest trooper. "Get Justis and Lieutenant Marion. And at least fifty men ready to ride."

Then Ryan was in front of him, her face creased in fear. "Sean?"

"Someone recognized him. They're holding him in the jail until the army comes for him. We have to get there first."

"I'm coming with you." Her voice brooked no argument, and Braden knew that even if he forbade it, she would be right behind them.

"You can't go like that," he said, looking at her blouse and riding skirt. "You're too distinctive."

"I'll get my boy's clothes," she said, dashing away as others gathered at the tent.

She ran by Ben, stopping only when he called.

"Ryan, what is it? Where's Sean?"

"The sheriff in Center is holding him for the army. We have to get there first." She whirled around toward the tent.

"You aren't going?"

"Of course I am. I can shoot as well as anyone here."

"Ryan!" His voice was now a command. She looked back with surprise and saw the muscles in his jaw tense.

"God help me," he said in a low voice before looking back up at her. When his eyes met hers, she could see his indecision. Then it was gone, replaced by determination.

"Get Braden over here."

Her face reflected her puzzlement. "He's busy. I'm supposed to be changing clothes."

"I can't believe he's agreed to take you. I can't believe you think you can just storm the town without getting half of you killed."

Her fear over Sean's safety erupted into anger. "Damn it, *you* know better than anyone what his capture means. Does it bother you that someone else might do the job?"

Her angry taunt struck him like a physical blow. "Just listen to me. There's a better way. Get Braden."

"Why would you help?"

"Because, damn it, I don't want anything to happen to you or Sean. You don't have much time. Please get Braden." His voice was now desperate.

It was his pleading note that decided her. "I'll see if he'll come."

Braden was talking to Justis and a fellow lieutenant, when she returned. He looked at her questioningly.

"Colonel Morgan wants to talk to you. I think you should."

"So he can delay us. Hell, no," Braden retorted.

"No, I don't think so. It will just take a second. Tom, he used to be Sean's best friend. Please listen to him."

The last statement came as a surprise to Braden. He had sensed that there was something between Sean and the Union officer, but he hadn't guessed at this.

"Then why was he after Sean?"

"He didn't know it was Sean," Ryan answered quickly. "Talk to him."

Braden ran his fingers through his hair in frustration, then nodded. "It had better be good."

Ben was waiting impatiently, a dozen thoughts running through his mind. He hoped against hope that Braden would listen.

He didn't mince words. "Do you have Union uniforms here?" he asked, positive that they did.

Braden hesitated, and Ben exploded. "Damn it, man, there's no time!"

Braden nodded.

"You've seen my orders?" Ben questioned again, noting the quick anger in the Reb lieutenant's face as he nodded once more.

"The timing would have to be perfect," Ben continued, "but three or four of you, dressed in Union blue, could get him out a lot safer than raiding the town. You can use the insignia from my uniform and show my orders. No one knows me out here. No one would question it. But you have to get there before the army detachment."

Braden stared at him, knowing immediately that Ben's proposal was far better than his own. He also knew it would have been Sean's choice. In fact, he thought, it sounded exactly like something Sean would have planned. Why hadn't he thought of it? He was honest enough not to resent the idea, although he greatly resented its author.

"Why are you doing this?"

"I have reasons of my own," Ben answered curtly. "And, Lieutenant, I would shave that beard and cut your hair. You don't look very military at the moment." He couldn't resist the gibe and enjoyed the irritation that passed over Braden's face.

Braden disappeared into Sean's tent, stopping only to tell one of the Texans to fetch four Union uniforms, the size of himself, Justis and two others he named.

While Braden shaved, Ryan found Ben's uniform jacket and retrieved the rank insignia. With pin and thread in hand, she hurried over to Sean's tent.

When Braden and three others emerged, they were clad in the hated blue. They had worn it previously, on occasion, but none of them liked it. Ben's clearly marked U.S. Cavalry saddle, along with his well-traveled saddlebags, had been placed on Braden's horse.

One of the troopers was holding Braden's horse, waiting for him to mount. Instead, he went to Ben's side. "Any other suggestions, Colonel?"

"When you get there, be quick about leaving. From what I understand, you won't have much time. The army post is about forty miles away?"

Braden nodded.

"And Colonel," Ben added acidly, recognizing the Reb's newly achieved rank, "try to hide that Southern accent. If anyone asks, you're from Maryland."

Braden grinned. "I'll do that, Yank."

They were only gone a few minutes before Ryan came out of her wagon. She was still dressed in the riding skirt, but she obviously had taken great care with her hair. It was brushed to a sheen and pulled back into a modest knot.

She called to Jimmy. "Let's go for a ride."

The young soldier immediately read her mind. "Oh no, you don't."

"Either with you or without you," she said.

"Darn it, Ryan. You're going to get both of us in trouble. If not in town, then with Lieutenant Braden and your brother."

Ryan looked at Ben, who had been listening with dismay to the conversation. "If the soldiers come while Tom's in town, maybe I can distract them for a few minutes. No one knows who I am. They certainly wouldn't know I was that smelly obnoxious boy." She wrinkled her nose as she said it. "If anyone asks we could say we're visiting a nearby homestead. Jimmy?" She was pleading now.

Jimmy couldn't resist any longer, particularly when he knew it wouldn't do any good. Besides, he wanted to be there in case of trouble. He hadn't liked being left behind.

Ben remained silent. He knew better than to argue that one of the reasons he had presented his plan was to keep her out of danger. And he knew it wasn't the entire reason. He had also wanted, in some way, to protect Sean. There had to be another way to stop his raids.

As Ryan turned toward the corral, she stopped when she heard Ben's low voice. "Be careful." He hesitated, as if he wanted to say more but was afraid to do so. "Just be careful." The words were so soft she thought she might have imagined them.

Ben lay there and watched her go, frustrated and angry at his helplessness. The evil little game master had outdone himself this time, he thought bitterly.

Because Tom Braden and his men had to circle town and come in from the side nearest the fort, Ryan and Jimmy arrived first. They hitched their horses in front of the general store and went inside. Ryan had tossed a quick glance at the jail, but it seemed quiet.

Ryan told the storekeeper she wanted to look at dress goods, knowing it would give her an excuse to linger. The storekeeper was only too eager to help. It wasn't often he had such a pretty young customer. She found it hard not to giggle when she thought how surprised he would be if he knew she was the same young boy he had ejected a few weeks earlier. Instead, she favored him with a smile he thought came straight from heaven.

He stayed by her side, modestly complaining that nothing in his small stock would do justice to such a beautiful lady. He glanced at the young man who had entered with her. "Perhaps . . . your husband . . ."

He delighted in her laugh, which seemed directed solely at him. "Oh, he's my brother."

The storekeeper grew even more attentive, and when Ryan agreed that none of the material was really suitable, he went into the storeroom.

At that moment Jimmy motioned to her. She went over to the window and watched as Tom Braden and the others dismounted in front of the sheriff's office. She gave Jimmy a little sign of victory and watched as four riders entered the jail. She was pulled back to the counter by the storekeeper's voice.

He held a big hatbox in his hand. As she watched he carefully opened it and pulled out one of the loveliest hats she had ever seen. It was a misty blue and decorated simply by a wide bow of dark blue silk ribbon. But what delighted her most was the rakish feather that combined the two shades of blue in an intricate pattern only nature could create.

"Oh," she exclaimed, her mission momentarily forgotten, "it's beautiful." Her face saddened. "But I don't have enough money for a hat."

The storekeeper's face fell, then lighted. "Don't worry about that," he said unexpectedly, even to himself. "A drummer talked me into this, and I've had it a long time. I've never even shown it to anyone before. I would be pleasured if you would try it on, miss.''

Ryan looked at Jimmy, and he indicated with a nod that all was still well. With a little dance step of anticipation, Ryan turned to the mirror. She undid the ribbon holding her hair back and carefully pulled the hat on, tying the wide bow under her chin. "It's wonderful," Ryan said with a sigh, wanting the hat desperately.

The storekeeper agreed. He thought he had never seen anything so pretty. The blues in the hat contrasted with the rich dark gold of her hair and the amber lights sparkling in her wide eyes. If his wife had looked like this only once he would have been a happy man.

He was moved to do something he had never done before. "It would give me great joy," he said, "if you would take the hat. It was made for you." He was taken back by his own gallantry, but he was determined that this lovely young woman would have the hat.

Ryan looked at Jimmy, who glanced from the window long enough to grin with approval. He nodded, then returned to his vigil.

"Thank you," she said, taking off the hat. "But I insist on paying you something." She took a small purse from her skirt and emptied it. She knew it was not nearly enough for the hat, but she offered it to the storekeeper.

"Just right," he said, a rare twinkle in his eyes.

Her smile more than repaid the difference between her payment and the actual price of the hat.

Ryan insisted on carrying the hatbox despite Jimmy's attempt to take it. She had never had anything so pretty, and she was going to hold on to it.

They went outside. Tom's horse was still there, but now they saw that someone had fetched the horse Sean had taken earlier. The chestnut was standing quietly with the other horses.

They heard the hoofbeats striking the packed dirt before they saw the incoming riders. Five Union troopers were coming from the direction of the fort and heading directly for the sheriff's office.

Ryan didn't even have time to think, she just reacted. Hoping that she hadn't waited too long, she caught her foot in a loose plank and went diving into the middle of the road, the hatbox landing next to her and spilling its precious contents.

The scream wasn't planned. It simply came rippling from her throat as she caught a glimpse of hooves boring down on her.

Everything had gone well at the sheriff's office. Too well, Tom Braden thought. It was just too damn easy.

He had shown Morgan's credentials to the sheriff and was accepted immediately. The sheriff was particularly impressed that a colonel had made the trip, so impressed that he missed the distinctive softness in Braden's accent.

"So you really think he might be one of those Rebs," the sheriff said.

"Perhaps," Braden said stiffly. "You did right in holding him. The army appreciates your diligence. I'll see that you're commended," he added, avoiding the laughter in Sean's face. Sean was standing just behind the sheriff, his hands tied in front of him by Justis.

"I would appreciate knowing if he turns out to be one of those damn raiders," the sheriff said hopefully.

"Oh, you will be notified," Braden said with a straight face. He glanced out the window and stiffened as he saw the Yankee troopers. He started to reach for his pistol, then saw the soldiers dismount in a hurry. He hesitated, his eyes and expression warning the others.

Making sure his body blocked the sheriff's view, Braden kept looking out the window and saw one of the Yankees carrying something inside the store across the street. They were soon all out of sight.

Braden turned quickly. "I think we should be on our way." He turned to Justis. "Hustle that prisoner outside," he commanded, his words warning the others to hurry.

They all mounted quickly and cantered to the edge of town, where they spurred their horses to a gallop.

For a moment Ryan thought she had badly misjudged the speed of the oncoming horses. They were just inches away when the lead rider frantically pulled back his mount, causing the horse to turn into the path of the horse behind him. Both horses fell, their riders just barely clearing their saddles in time to avoid being crushed. Total confusion reigned. The spooked horses required every bit of skill their riders possessed to be brought back under control.

Jimmy was instantly leaning over her, his face tight with concern. It relaxed only when he saw the quick wink just before her face turned into a mask of pain. She moaned softly. If he hadn't seen the wink, he would have been convinced she was dying.

The officer who was leading the detail joined him at Ryan's side. His face blanched when he saw her glorious hair tangled in the dirt and her pretty oval face contorted by pain. He looked up at Jimmy. "She just fell in front of us.... There wasn't anything we could do."

Jimmy pointed at a loose board in the porch. "She tripped over that. I thought for sure you had killed her."

At those accusing words, the Union officer looked even more wretched. "Is there a doctor in this damned town?" he asked, using a hand to brush the golden hair from the girl's face. She looked up at him piteously before closing her eyes and going limp.

The officer leaned down and listened to her soft breathing. "She's alive. I think she's fainted." He turned to Jimmy. "Who are you?" he suddenly challenged.

"Her brother, and she shouldn't be lying out here." He started to tug at her and was pushed aside by the officer, who leaned down and picked her up. The officer looked over at the hatbox and the now dusty hat on the ground. "Sergeant, retrieve that hat."

He looked around, still holding Ryan, wondering where to take her, when the storekeeper came rushing out. His face darkened when he saw the officer holding Ryan and another soldier gingerly holding the hat. "Upstairs," he said, indicating stairs at the side of the store. He rushed up and opened the door, waiting as the Yank officer carried the girl inside and the other troopers followed, each one anxious about the girl's welfare.

The one room was dominated by a large bed. The officer gently lowered Ryan onto it, his hand lingering on hers.

The brief trip upstairs had been agony for Ryan. It was not easy to go completely limp. The body had a tendency to tense at every bump. Once on the bed, she gave up the effort and allowed a low moan to escape her lips. As her eyes fluttered open, she noted that every one of the Yankees had followed her upstairs as she had hoped.

"What happened?" she asked in a confused little-girl voice.

"You fell, but I don't think anything's broken." The Yank's voice was worried but comforting, and she felt a momentary flash of guilt.

The Yankee officer turned to the storekeeper. "Is there a doctor in town?"

"No," the man replied, "but we have a vet, and he sometimes helps in an emergency."

Ryan groaned inwardly. That's all she needed now. A horse doctor.

"Captain," she said pleadingly, "I'll be all right. Truly I will. I just need to rest for a few minutes. Those horses coming at me—" She shuddered.

"Lieutenant, Miss. I'm just a lieutenant. I know it must have been a frightful experience."

"May I have some water?" she asked.

Every one of the men jumped for a pitcher in the corner. The storekeeper got there first and carried the glass over to Ryan, holding it as she finished it slowly.

"Jimmy," she said suddenly. "Is my brother all right?"

Jimmy moved to the front and grinned at her. "I'm fine, sis."

The lieutenant reluctantly stirred, remembering his mission. "Are you sure we shouldn't call that vet, miss, or maybe you should go back to the fort with us. We have a doctor there."

Ryan shook her head. "I'm feeling much better, thank you. My people will be worried if we don't get home. She sat up on the bed and put one foot on the floor and then another. She tried to stand, crying out with pain as she did and falling back on the bed.

"I think I must have twisted my ankle. Lieutenant, could I trouble you just a minute more to bind it tight? I can show you how."

He nodded and smiled at her, thinking how pretty and brave she was. He wondered where she lived.

The storekeeper went downstairs to his store and brought back some bandages. Ryan instructed the Union officer on tying her ankle. "No, no. That's too loose. Just a little too tight. Ah, that's perfect. You should have been a doctor, not a soldier." Her smile brightened the room, and not one man was unaffected by it. "Thank you," she said. "I thank all of you."

She sighed as she stood unsteadily. Ryan looked at the officer again. "May I ask one more favor? We really have to get home, and I don't think I can manage those stairs. Will you help me down?"

He almost drowned in Ryan's large brown eyes. At that moment he would have carried her all the way across Colorado.

"Miss . . . I didn't get your name?"

"Melissa," she said. "Melissa Darcy. And you, Lieutenant? I should know the name of my Good Samaritan."

"The one who almost ran you down," he said ruefully, and Ryan found herself liking the blue-clad soldier. "I'm Bill Davies."

"And these other gentlemen," she said, prolonging their stay as much as possible.

She gave each a special smile as the lieutenant named them. "You all have my gratitude," she said. "And now, Lieutenant..."

He picked her up easily and carried her down the stairs. She pointed out her horse, and he swung her up onto it.

"Are you sure you can ride?" he asked anxiously, hoping against hope she would change her mind and ride to the fort with them.

She nodded bravely.

"I would like to see you again," he said. "Where do you live?"

Ryan looked at him with real regret. "I'm sorry, Lieutenant Davies. We're just visiting on our way west. We're leaving in the morning."

He looked crestfallen. "Just my luck," he muttered, then recovered. "Maybe we'll meet again. I shall hope for it, anyway. Goodbye, miss."

"Goodbye, Lieutenant. And thank you."

He watched as she and Jimmy slowly walked their horses down the road.

"Miss Darcy."

Ryan turned and saw the sergeant catching up with her, dangling the mangled hatbox.

Stopping, she walked her horse around and took the box. "Thank you again," she said, hugging it to her. When she caught up with Jimmy once more, they both struggled to withhold their laughter.

The lieutenant turned back to his men. "Come on," he said. "Let's pick up that Reb."

There were so many tracks in and out of town that Braden and Sean didn't worry about their own trail. They just rode fast until they were well away from Center. When they felt comfortable with the distance, they stopped and rested the horses. Sean climbed off his mount, his hands still tied in front of him.

He went over to Justis and smiled ruefully. "You really didn't have to be so dutiful about it."

Justis returned the smile. "It was a once-in-a-lifetime chance, Captain. You can't expect me to do less than my best."

"Damn it, Justis, cut me loose."

Justis took out his knife and quickly sliced the ropes. As Sean rubbed his wrists someone yelled, "Riders."

They all scattered for shelter. Then Braden called out in surprise. "It's Ryan and Jimmy."

Sean stepped out onto the road, and the pair reined in their horses.

"What," he said, "are you two doing here?"

Braden joined Sean. "Yes, Jimmy," he said in a hard voice. "What *are* you doing?"

Jimmy and Ryan looked at each other, and she held out the hatbox.

"I needed a hat," she said innocently.

Jimmy couldn't contain his mirth. He laughed until he almost fell off his horse.

"Captain, your sister is the best liar I've ever seen," he said with pride for his friend's accomplishments.

Ryan blushed and tried to look modest.

"Will someone tell me what's going on," Sean demanded.

Jimmy dismounted and told the story. Both Braden and Sean looked at Ryan with astonishment; neither had had any idea she was the one who had created the diversion.

"I'll be damned," Braden said.

"And I could tan both of your hides," Sean added, his severity tempered by the hint of laughter in his eyes. "Jimmy, the next time you disobey orders, I'll send you back to Texas. And Ryan, I'll put a twenty-four-hour guard on you if I have to.

"However," he added, "I don't think I'll complain too much this time."

He turned to Braden. "By the way, that was good thinking."

Braden went red. "It wasn't mine, I'm sorry to say."

"Then whose was it?"

"Colonel Morgan's."

Sean couldn't hide his surprise. "Morgan?"

Braden shrugged. "I was going to shoot our way in. Morgan convinced me otherwise. Damned if I know why." He looked sheepish. "I hate like hell for a Yank telling me my business. I should have thought of it myself. You would have."

Sean released a long sigh. "You listened, Tom, and for that I'm grateful."

"Ryan said you used to be friends . . . otherwise I don't think I would have."

A cloud came over Sean's face. "That was gone a long time ago," he answered slowly. Suddenly impatient, he moved quickly toward his horse. "This day has been full of surprises. Let's get back. There are a few questions that I want answers to."

Ben waited as anxiously as the others during the long afternoon. He heard the signal for incoming riders and watched as all
seven rode in. The tension seeped from him, but he knew he didn't
want to talk to anyone. He turned his head away from the main
corral and closed his eyes. They remained closed as he heard footsteps approach, stop and then turn away. He willed himself to
sleep.

When he woke he knew Sean was there before he opened his
eyes. He could smell the tobacco, and his senses did the rest. He
couldn't feign sleep forever, and he lazily stretched out and slowly
opened his eyes. Sean was sitting on the ground, regarding him
with amused concentration.

"You always could sleep anyplace, anytime, particularly when
you wanted to avoid something," Sean said, his wide mouth crinkling into a smile.

"There's nothing to avoid," Ben said curtly.

"My thanks, I think," Sean said. "In any event, I do thank
you."

"Don't," Ben said harshly. "It had nothing to do with you.
Those damn fool men of yours were ready to shoot up the town and
take Ryan with them. Someone had to talk some sense into them.
How in the hell can you let her do these things?"

Sean laughed. "You haven't ever tried to stop her. She does exactly what she wants, and no one—not me, not Tom Braden and
probably not you—can change her mind once she's set on something. This time, I was glad she was there."

Ben's curiosity overcame his reluctance to continue the conversation. "Why?"

"Your plan worked beautifully, until we were ready to leave.
Then the real escort came along. Ryan stumbled in its path and
distracted them long enough for us to get out of town." He decided not to elaborate on how close Ryan had come to real injury.

Ben was not mollified. "Your luck is going to run out one of
these days. And Ryan could be hurt along with you."

Sean sighed, his laughter gone. "I know, but aside from tying
her hand and foot, there's nothing I can do. Until recently I felt
there was comparatively little danger, but now..." His voice trailed
off.

Ben knew Sean referred to his orders and the threat they contained for all of his command. The emptiness welled up inside him
again, and his voice was sharp when he spoke. "Why don't you get
out of here—go back to Texas. Surely you know it's getting too
dangerous for you now."

"There's one thing I have to do first," Sean said slowly. He pulled out some tobacco and paper and offered the makings to Ben, who took them without thanks and carefully rolled a cigarette. Sean lit it for him and made one of his own.

"In any event," Sean continued, "I appreciate what you did today, even if I don't understand exactly why."

Ben's mouth curled up at the edges. "Let's just say I can't break the habit of giving orders."

"Not good enough," Sean replied.

Ben's face hardened. "It wasn't for you and certainly not for your bunch of cutthroats. Your sister's been good to me, and I don't want to see her dead or in prison. A lot of innocents could have been hurt today, including Ryan. Your lieutenant is a fool. I would have expected better."

A muscle twitched in Sean's jaw. "Tom's anything but a fool. He's courageous and loyal, and most of all, he's honest. Too honest to have the same Machiavellian streak we both seem to share," he said, his voice rising in anger. "Damn, why am I justifying myself to you?"

"Why, indeed, Captain?" Ben mocked. "Unless there's truth in it."

"I don't think you're in any position to judge who's a fool and who's not," Sean retorted angrily.

"You're right," Ben said wryly. "I'm certainly not." Now the mockery was for himself.

Sean's anger fled. "Damn it, Ben, I'm trying to thank you."

"Don't. It doesn't change anything between us. I think you have to be stopped, and if I get the opportunity, I'll do just that."

Sean rose carefully, his eyes never leaving his antagonist's face. "I understand," he said, his voice now cool and distant. "So be it."

Morgan couldn't help hearing more about Ryan's activities in Center. Jimmy gave a minute-by-minute account to anyone who would listen, reveling in Ryan's courage and cleverness. The hat was produced and cleaned, and Ryan agreeably modeled it, much to everyone's amusement. The poor feather was somewhat the worse for wear and gave the hat a special jauntiness.

She wore it over to where Ben was sitting, leaning against a saddle. His eyes were watchful, his face tight and withdrawn.

"What do you think?" she said.

"You don't want to know what I think," he replied, his voice grimly serious.

"Yes, I do," she insisted.

"I think both you and your brother are fools," he said rudely, an internal devil urging him on. "Both of you could easily have been killed today. And for what? An adventure?" His bitter words masked the anxiety and fear that had haunted him all afternoon.

He watched as the laughter and joy drained from her eyes. He hated himself for saying the words, but he had to make her understand the danger she had courted. He also wanted her to understand that he had played a very unwilling part in the day's events.

"It was very difficult for you, wasn't it?" she said in a gentle voice.

His next words were said softly, but they obviously carried pain. "It was a betrayal . . . a small one, perhaps, but still a betrayal. To my uniform. To my country."

Her heart suddenly ached for him. "I'm sorry," she said, "and I'm grateful. So is Sean."

"I don't want your damn gratitude, even less his," Ben snarled. "All I want is to be left alone."

There was nothing more to say. Ryan nodded and retreated, but not before Ben saw the hurt in her eyes.

Braden and Sean conferred after a late dinner. The lieutenant had not had time earlier to discuss the telegram he had received in Center.

He made his report simple. The wagon train had been delayed again while additional troops were found to escort it. There were probably more than two hundred guards now, all equipped with the new rifles.

"Two more weeks," Sean swore softly. "And another two weeks after that to let the search die down. It's too damned long. We need to get the hell out of here."

Braden stared at his superior. It was the first time he had ever seen Sean visibly worried.

"Let's stop all the other activities," he said. "Maybe after the close call today, they will think we've skedaddled. Maybe they'll get tired of looking for us."

"They'll never get tired of looking for us," Sean said bitterly. "But you're right. We'll lie quiet for the next two weeks. It's going to be hard on the men, though. I think inactivity is worse than anything for them. This valley can be a prison sometimes." He spoke as much for himself as for the others.

They were interrupted by Ryan, who knocked on the post outside and entered looking tired and discouraged.

Sean turned to his lieutenant. "Get some sleep, Tom. You've earned it. Thanks for your help today."

Braden nodded and cast a quick encouraging smile at Ryan before leaving.

Sean turned to Ryan. "He's sweet on you, you know."

"He's a friend," Ryan said, emphasizing the word *friend*.

"And Ben Morgan?"

"Right now, he doesn't want anything to do with either of us."

"It's mutual," Sean retorted.

"Don't you understand what it took for him to do what he did?"

"He's dangerous and he's unpredictable," Sean said. "He made it very clear today that nothing has changed. He will still try to take us, if he can."

"No," Ryan said. "I don't care what he says. He's trying to protect you as much as me."

"It doesn't make any difference," Sean said wearily. "I can't take the chance of trusting him." His voice changed as he looked at her tired face. "I haven't thanked you yet, Kitten, though I'm still tempted to take you over my knee."

She smiled back. "Don't worry. After seeing those horses bearing down on me, I won't try it again."

"I'll never understand you, Kitten," he said. "You keep surprising me. But please, no more. I'm not used to worrying about someone like this."

Ryan leaned over and kissed his cheek lightly. "I'm fine, truly I am."

"I'll take your word on that." Sean took her hat off and freed her hair. He felt a surge of tenderness in him as he looked at her face, tired and defenseless. "I'll take you to the wagon."

He intentionally made a wide berth around Ben. When they arrived, he leaned down and kissed her forehead. "Sleep well," he said, and left.

Ryan undressed, putting on one of Sean's old shirts. She lay down and listened to the night sounds, too tired at first to even sleep. She had refused to admit her fear today, but it had been there. She couldn't forget Ben's orders. She couldn't forget those hooves coming toward her. Before Ben came, Center had been an adventure. It wasn't anymore. Now everything was a very real matter of life and death.

And Ben Morgan? The sudden image was unwelcome. She wasn't prepared to cope with that tonight. She realized only too clearly the distance between them, the danger he brought to her brother. And yet today he had helped save Sean's life.

Ryan heard Sean's guitar. "Lorelei." It was one of his favorites, and she had always loved the sweet sad strains of it. She wondered, not for the first time, about Sean's personal life. Had he ever been in love? They had never talked about it. She was still thinking about it when sleep finally came.

Chapter Ten

It was late when she woke the next morning. All the sounds of a busy camp were there. Clanking dishes, horses whinnying for water and the faintly ominous clicking sound of rifles being cleaned.

Ryan lay for a few luxurious moments, thinking about what she might do with the day. She stretched and enjoyed the cool morning air filtering through the canvas cover.

All the fears of last night were gone. It was going to be a good day. It was her birthday, her twenty-first, and she felt a shiver of excitement. She loved birthdays, even though this year she would celebrate it in her own private way.

She had not mentioned it to anyone—not even Sean—and she didn't think he would remember after all these years. It seemed out of place here, and she didn't want a fuss made or her friends to think they had to do something when there was so little that could be done.

It was a delicious secret, she decided, and she would pamper herself wickedly.

Suddenly feeling grimy from yesterday's misadventures, she decided to bathe in the stream before putting on clean clothes. She slipped on a pair of pants under Sean's shirt, and looking out the canvas flap, she asked a trooper to fetch Jimmy.

It was sometimes frightening to realize how much she had come to depend on the steady young Texan. He had become her friend, her protector, her pupil. He had quickly learned some of the more simple medical skills; despite little formal education, he had a keen mind and an insatiable desire to learn. He had become her chaperon when she ventured out for a bath, and he was there when she wanted to talk.

When he appeared, Ryan turned on the full force of her smile. "Is it safe to take a bath?"

"Yes ma'am," he said teasingly. "I was just down there getting some water for the Yank. He uses more water than any one human being I ever saw."

She ignored his comment and sprung lightly from the wagon, carrying a clean pair of jeans and a cotton shirt along with a rough bar of soap. They walked together down to the stream and along the bank until they came to Ryan's favorite spot, a cool deep pool surrounded by trees.

"I'll call when I'm through," she said. Jimmy turned and sauntered up the bank and disappeared just over the top. He had her medical book with him and would put the time to good use.

Ryan quickly undressed and slipped happily into the cool water. The pool was deep enough to swim, and she gratefully stretched into long strokes. She let the water nurture her and rejoiced in the freedom and almost sensual comfort of it. After swimming across the pool several times, she floated in silence, enjoying the solitude. The only sounds were those of the woods: the musical humming of busy insects, the sound of leaves as squirrels chased each other across the branches, the quiet sound of the water rippling around her. She gloried in the peace and harmony they invoked.

Realizing she had stayed longer than usual, she came back to reality. She reached the bank and took the bar of soap, washing herself vigorously, then soaping her hair and rinsing it in the clean water.

She sat on the bank a few minutes, letting the sun dry her body and hair, and thought about Morgan. He would love this special place of hers. Unlike most of the Texans, he had an obsession about cleanliness. In the beginning she had shaved him and let Jimmy bathe him. His gratefulness for the small service had been evident in his eyes. As he'd improved, he had used the wash water greedily, never getting enough.

No, she thought, *I'm not going to let him haunt me. I can't let myself care about him.*

Feeling pleased with herself for reinforcing a decision she had made last night, she dressed quickly and whistled. Jimmy appeared immediately over the bank.

"I was afraid you'd drowned," he said with a grin.

"I just needed some time alone," she said. "You knew that, didn't you?"

Embarrassed, he just shrugged.

"Come," she commanded, "sit with me while I brush my hair." They sat in the woods, Ryan brushing out the wetness with firm sure strokes.

She broke the rules of the camp. They seldom talked about the future. "What are you doing to do when the war's over?"

"Your brother's asked me to help round up some cattle and maybe start a ranch," he said. "Several of us are planning to join him."

Ryan was quiet for a moment, wondering about her own future. "I'm glad," she said slowly. "I would miss you. I don't know if you realize how much both of us have come to depend on you."

He looked at the ground, his face inscrutable. "It's the same with me, Miss Ryan," he said, reverting back to his old address of her. "Your brother's given me a lot. He's treated me more like a brother than a soldier. I've never had much family. I'm grateful to him. And you, too."

"You *are* family," Ryan said fiercely. "Don't ever forget that."

Ben watched as Ryan slipped out of the camp with Jimmy. After his bitter words last night, he had not expected her to share breakfast with him, but he still felt a sharp stab of disappointment.

The thought was interrupted when a tall lanky Texan wandered over to his side. "I'm Justis Davis," he said. "Miss Ryan asked me to make you some crutches. I reckon you're about the captain's length."

Morgan nodded, surprised at the Texan's cordiality. He was startled even further as the man sat next to him and started whittling on a strong branch. He worked without comment, whistling a tuneless song.

Ben made the first move. Despite himself, he was lonely and had found it was much worse to be alone in a crowd than alone by yourself. "Where are you from?" he asked, trying to place the accent.

"Down Austin way," Davis replied. "A far piece from here. Too far. It'll be good to get back to Texas dirt. It may not be much, but it's mine."

"Why are you fighting for the South?" Ben asked, truly curious. "You Texans fought to get into the Union."

"We did," the sergeant said agreeably. "I was one of them. Wanted to get away from Mexico. Thought the United States would leave us alone. It didn't. Too much telling us how to run our lives. Texans are just a naturally ornery people.

"And," he added, warming to his subject, "I guess some of us just plain like to fight. No matter who. Indians, Mexicans, you Yanks. When it ain't people, it's the land. We're always fighting something." A slow grin stretched across his face as he considered his countrymen's peculiarities.

"Is that the way it is with your captain?"

"I don't know," Davis said noncommittally. "I ain't never asked him. Don't plan to. It's none of my business."

There was a certain rebuke in the answer, and Ben fell silent. He watched the steady sure fingers shape first one branch, then another into a pair of rough crutches. It was late morning before he had completed the task, and Ryan had still not appeared.

"Want to try them, Yank?"

Ben nodded, eager for the exercise and the chance to try his strength.

"I'll get some help. Miss Ryan said to be sure you take it easy and not rest any weight on that broken leg." He was the first, Ben noticed, who had prefaced Ryan's name with "Miss." He could feel the affection the older sergeant had for the young woman.

Justis fetched another soldier, and together they helped Ben up. Justis let Ben lean on him as he hopped over to a tree to steady himself. His head felt light, and dizziness overtook him. He stood there for several minutes, standing on his good right leg and leaning on Davis for support.

As some strength slowly returned, he tucked the crutches under his arms and took one unsteady step. He almost fell before the two Rebs caught him. The crutches accepted his weight, and he took several steps, growing more confident each time.

Too confident, he went sprawling on the ground after one uncautious move. Cursing his weakness again, he turned away a proffered hand. "No," he said, "I'll do it myself." He painfully set the crutch upright, leaning on it and his good leg as he slowly pulled himself up.

He looked back at Justis and smiled in triumph, the first smile either Reb had seen on his face.

"I think that's enough, Colonel," the older Southerner drawled. "Miss Ryan would have us both horsewhipped if you hurt yourself any worse. We'll try agin later. Just don't be in so all-fired a hurry."

Ben looked at both the Texans, grateful for their efforts. "Thank you," he said simply. He stumbled back to his makeshift bed, exhausted from the effort. He was frustrated at his continuing weakness, but there had been some small victories, and he took refuge in that fact.

"Here," Justis said, pushing a cup of water at him. "Drink this and get some rest. You'll be getting stronger. It just takes time." He started to walk away, then turned back to Ben. "By the way, Yank, that was a pretty good idea you had yesterday." He turned away again without waiting for a response.

Ben didn't appreciate the half compliment. He just wished everyone would forget it. He decided to take the sergeant's advice. He was much weaker than he had imagined. He sipped the water gratefully and closed his eyes.

Ryan was just returning from the stream when she saw Ben on the crutches. She watched him from the edge of the trees, not wanting to distract him. She knew she had to give him time to solve his internal conflicts. It had hurt yesterday when he struck out at her, but she understood it. She had done much the same thing when she had taunted him about being the one who wanted to hang Sean. They both needed some distance.

When she saw him sink down on the makeshift mattress, she veered over to the camp fire, took a cup of coffee and cold biscuit and sat down.

Sean joined her, pleased to see she was keeping her distance from Morgan. "Let's take a ride," he suggested. "We'll go south and explore the river."

Her face lighted up. She had dreaded the thought of staying in camp. It would be impossible, she realized frankly, to stay away from Morgan for long. "Now," she said. "Let's go now."

He caught her urgency. "I'll saddle the horses. Why don't you pack some food, and we'll make it a picnic."

With Cook's help she packed some fresh bread and cheese and several thick slices of beef. She was ready when Sean rode up, a second horse in tow.

They rode out together, both of them ignoring the Yank colonel, who had opened his eyes at the rhythmic sound of the hoofbeats.

Ben was surprised at his disappointment. He had wanted her to know about his first steps. He had, in the past, experienced little need to share things and had held in some contempt those who did. He realized he was undergoing some changes and wasn't quite certain whether he approved of them. He wanted, no, needed to talk to her, to see the teasing light in her eyes, to hear the laughter in her voice. He tried to dismiss the betrayal such thoughts presented. He should be thinking, instead, just how he could escape. That should be the most important thing in his life. Not a woman. Not Sean's sister.

He tried to sit up, but the saddle had been moved, and he couldn't reach it. He tried to bunch some of the boughs into a pillow but had little success.

He had never felt so helpless. He was as much a prisoner of his own physical weakness as he was of the Rebs. His fists tightened into knots of frustration as he watched Ryan ride from the valley. She had the same natural grace on a horse as her brother. Morgan's eyes followed them as they disappeared from sight, his thoughts dark. He was suddenly afraid of losing her. She had seemed so within reach the other night, the night before Center. His sense of loss was unexpected and crushing. The glimpse of what might have been struck him with a ferocity that shattered all his defenses.

Ryan and her brother rode for more than two hours, following the river. It was wide and full and sheltered by huge cottonwood trees. As they rode they glimpsed a richness of wildlife—rabbits, deer, even scolding squirrels, who voiced their objections at the intrusion.

Finally, Sean slowed the pace and led the way through a narrow path in the scant woods. They both dismounted almost lazily, and Sean led his sister to the bank's edge. The water was so clear they could see trout darting in and out of a deep pool just below them.

"It's too bad you've already taken a swim this morning," he said, "I haven't."

She watched as he took off his shirt and boots and dove into the water.

Why not? Ryan thought, glad she had worn the pants and shirt that morning. She, too, slipped into the cold sparkling water, welcoming the soothing effect it always had on her.

"I'll race you," she called to Sean, and they looked for a finishing line. "That tree down there," she called, immediately starting and taking an advantage.

Despite her few seconds head start, he ended up well ahead of her.

"Ah," he said with a laugh, his eyes full of mischief, "I have you now. Damn shame you're my sister."

He helped her up the bank, and they lay there silently, drying in the sun. He started skipping stones in the water, each one making more skips and wider arcs.

"Remember when I taught you this?" he said. "You were just a little tadpole yourself."

She remembered—painfully. It brought back all the old longings she had felt at losing her first family.

"Yes," she said slowly. "I remember. You weren't very patient."

"Well, you weren't a very quick pupil."

"Slow maybe, but sure," she said, picking up her own stone and sending it skipping in an even more complex pattern than his own.

"Ryan," he said, suddenly serious. "We have to talk. We'll be leaving after this last raid. We've been ordered to deliver the guns to Richmond. The need is the most critical there."

He watched her face closely. "You can't go with us. The trip is too long and dangerous. We'll be splitting up in small groups and traveling through Yankee-controlled land. There's nothing in Richmond now. People are hungry and it's full of refugees. The Yanks are slowly surrounding it."

Ryan looked at him thoughtfully. "Then what do you intend to do with me? You're my only family."

She watched the fight being waged inside him. His intense dark eyes half-closed in concentration. She had seen that look before, more frequently since Ben Morgan had been thrust upon him.

"There's a fort in east Texas," he said finally, carefully watching her expression. "The commander and his wife are friends of mine. It's also a stockade for Yankee officers. I plan to take Morgan there." He hesitated before continuing.

"You know the way I feel about him. And you. I just don't think you belong together. I think a lot of what you feel is a natural result of your nursing him for so long. I know you're attracted to him, and I think I understand that. He's new and different and he's a challenge to you. And I know how much you like a challenge. But I hope that's it. He isn't right for you—he never will be."

He looked at her closely. "I hope you will remember that, because I think Fort Scott is also the best place for you now. There are people there I know will take care of you. It's well enough away from the real battlegrounds to be safe—as safe as anyone can be today."

Ryan couldn't conceal the sudden light in her eyes, and Sean flinched. It had been a decision he did not want to make, but he had searched for alternatives and could find none. He had to be sure she was safe, and he knew she would be with Matt and Anna Andrews. There simply was no other choice. He would have to trust her usually sound instincts.

He didn't realize he was frowning and was startled by her words. "Why didn't you ever marry, Sean?"

Sean looked toward the river for a moment, then glanced back at her, a familiar mocking look in his eyes. "There weren't many marriageable young ladies where I've been for the past years."

"There were some," she persisted.

"Maybe," he admitted. His hand touched her chin lightly, turning it toward him. "You were so young when Ma and Pa died," he said quietly. "They had something special together, something I've rarely seen. There were never two people more in love. They were complete together—friends, partners, lovers. I think sometimes I was jealous. I felt left out. I know now that there was enough love in that house to go around several times over, and I have never forgotten it, or been able to settle for anything less."

"And if you find it," she asked quizzically, "and she happens to be a Yankee?"

His face creased into a slow smile. "I would probably throw her over my horse and tell everyone to go to hell.

"But," he added quickly, amusement in his voice, "that doesn't mean I want you to do the same thing." He suddenly grew serious again. "If it was just that, Ryan, if it were just a difference of loyalties, I wouldn't feel so strongly. But it's so much more. Your backgrounds...the difference in age. He's fifteen years older than you—fifteen very hard years. He's been married—he might still be for all either of us know. More importantly, something's missing. He's an entirely different person from the man I knew. He's hard and he's bitter, and I don't think you could ever be happy with someone like that."

"Did you know his wife?" Ryan had known about the son, but for some reason she never acquainted that idea with a wife. The thought was shattering.

"Yes," Sean said shortly, avoiding the question in her eyes.

"Where do you think she is?" The question was painful.

"I don't know and you don't, either. The point is, you don't know anything about him except he's wounded and he needed you. Just like Fortune. You see something hurt and you immediately want to make everything right. There are some things you can't make right."

"Will you let me find out?"

"Find out what?"

"If I can make it right, of course." She grinned.

"Do I have a choice?"

"Not really." Her face was set as she looked at him. "I've never felt this way about anyone. I don't know if it's love. I don't know if it's like the way you described Mama and Papa. But, Sean, it hurts to be away from him. And," she added softly, "it hurts to be with him."

His smile was gentle. "I can't make your feelings go away, Kitten. I wish I could. I wish I could make the nightmares go away and the bad memories and all the hurts." His face was troubled as he continued slowly. "There are some things you have to do for yourself.... Just promise me you will go slowly...that you will be wise."

"I don't know if I can be wise with Colonel Morgan," Ryan replied honestly. "He sends all my senses tumbling."

Such an admission astounded him. Ryan always took such great pride in being in control of herself. His thoughts darkened.

"For my sake, Kitten," he said finally, "be careful."

Her great dark eyes peered up at him, suspecting a trick. Sean was never afraid of anything.

"He wouldn't hurt us."

"What if he tries to escape?"

"He won't," she repeated confidently. "He's too weak, anyway, but I know he wouldn't do anything to hurt you."

"Don't bet on it," Sean said shortly. "He's a soldier, remember. He's a Yankee officer and a good one. He's not a man to take prison lightly, nor is he one to ignore duty no matter how unpleasant it may be . . . or who he may hurt."

"He won't," she said, again with assurance. "He knows what we risked bringing him in."

Sean sat up suddenly, his face blank. "Come on, sis, let's go. They'll be combing the country for us."

She caught his hand and sprung up. "You're a cynic, brother."

"Maybe," he said. As he steered her toward the horses, a plan started forming in his mind.

As they rode back into camp, Ryan caught a sense of excitement. The men were clustered around the chuck wagon, and there were broad grins on their faces.

She looked at Sean, and he looked back sheepishly, his face crinkled in anticipation. He dismounted quickly and hurried over to her horse. Without ceremony he lifted her down and carried her to the camp fire. "You really didn't think I forgot your birthday?" he teased.

He put her down before a makeshift table loaded with cakes on one side and a number of packages on the other.

She looked from one man to another. Each was wearing a wide smile. Ryan felt a surge of joy and anticipation. It was well enough to celebrate in private, but this . . . this really was much better.

Sean led her over to one package, larger than the others. "This," he said, "is from all of us. Every man chipped in something."

Like a young child, she tore it open and looked with wonder at the dress that lay nestled in the package. It was a lovely blue gingham with a rounded neck and puffed sleeves and a tucked waist. Bewildered, she stared at it.

"But how?"

"Braden got it when you were in town two weeks ago," her brother answered. "He saw you looking at it and bought it when you went after the horse. He just sort of hid it in with the other supplies."

Her eyes were suspiciously wet. She had admired the dress in the store window but had passed by quickly so no one would wonder about a boy's interest. She couldn't believe Braden had caught that brief pause . . . and understood it.

She went over to him and kissed him lightly. "Thank you," she said in a low voice. "Thank you all."

Ryan suddenly clapped her hands with delight. "The hat," she said suddenly. "The hat is perfect for it."

Sean grinned. "We noticed that yesterday."

Ryan whirled around to face Jimmy. "And you knew, too. You wretch."

"If that storekeeper hadn't been so besotted," he said, his eyes bright, "I was going to find some way to get it. He sort of simplified things."

They all laughed; new pride for her in all of them. She had taken real chances yesterday.

"I think there's more, Ryan," her brother said quietly. "Everyone's been working to make presents. And it's been agreed that each is from all of us."

Ryan thought her heart would burst. They had all kept it such a secret. A few happy tears wandered down her cheeks.

The troopers pretended not to notice and urged her to examine the gifts. There was a small carved animal that looked exactly like Fortune. Although it had no name on it, she knew it came from Justis. She kept it clutched in her hand while she looked at the other presents. There was a buckle shaped like a rose; it came, she knew, from Smithy, the blacksmith. There was a bouquet of wild-flowers, some ribbons and a blue scarf. There was also a worn Bible, which, she realized from its worn condition, had been a valued possession.

She turned to them. "This has been the best birthday ever," she said with delight on her face. "Thank you. Thank every one of you. And I will always remember you, and this time, and this place." The tears were coming faster now, and she turned to her brother, who hugged her to him.

"Time to test Cook's cake," one man exclaimed, breaking the solemnity. A number of catcalls joined the chorus, and Ryan started laughing.

She looked at the cook. "Can you really bake a cake?" she teased.

"For you, anything," he said gallantly. "But I'm not promising it will taste as good as yours."

They all watched as she cut the first slice and tasted it. "Ah," she exclaimed. "None better."

Sean rolled his eyes and joined the merriment, taking the second slice and grimacing as he tasted it. Then everyone joined the crowd around the table for their share.

Torn by conflicting emotions, Ben Morgan watched from his bed. He wished he had known it was her birthday, that she had confided in him. But even if she had, he knew, there was nothing to give her and little to say. He watched avidly despite the hurt it brought, and he flinched when he saw the joy in her face as she kissed Braden and hugged her brother.

He tried to turn away but could not. She was so pretty and so full of life. Braden, he observed, also couldn't take his eyes from her.

The men finally started to leave, and Ben watched as Ryan cut a final piece of cake and brought it over to him.

He stubbornly refused to take it. "I don't have anything to give you," he said rudely, unable to keep the bitter words back.

"Oh, but you do," she replied, her face still shining. "In fact, you can give me the best present of all."

He looked at her suspiciously.

"A smile. Like the one the other day." Her eyes were mischievous, and there was challenge in her words.

She looked so expectant, he had difficulty in not giving her what she wanted.

Instead, he said with just a tiny tease in his voice, "I don't think I know how."

"Now why," she answered, "doesn't that surprise me, Colonel?"

Her tart reply and irrepressible mood made it impossible for Ben to restrain a smile any longer. It touched his eyes first, crinkling the edges and filling their blue depths with an unexpected warmth. When it reached his mouth, it was open and gentle, untouched by the usual cynicism. Then it deepened the cleft in his chin and smoothed out the tight lines around his jaw. There was charm and humor and, taken as a whole, Ryan thought, it was really quite wonderful.

"Ah, Colonel, sir," she exclaimed happily, "you really should do that more often."

"There are not that many opportunities," he replied somewhat gently.

"But you're wrong.... You just have to take the time to look for them."

He shook his head at her innocence. "I wish it were that simple," he said carefully, thinking about the past years. They had offered little but death and killing...and more killing. He had become very competent at it. It was a damnable skill but the one he knew best. His smile disappeared. She was confusing him, interfering with what he knew he had to do.

"What do you want from me?" he asked abruptly.

"Something you're not ready to give yet," she replied softly.

"And what's that?"

"It begins with trust," she answered. "Now eat your cake. You've earned it."

He ate it slowly, more for her benefit than his own, watching the delight flickering over her face.

That he was eating it at all was a major victory, Ryan thought, especially after her last statement. It was another tiny chink in his armor, and she regarded him wistfully as he very carefully ate the cake, allowing no crumbs. Everything he did was careful. Just once she wished he would lose that control.

"You've been walking today," she said suddenly. It was a statement, not an inquiry. She had seen his first attempts but wanted to know how he felt about them.

"Not very well," he said, more shortly than he intended. He was still unused to the debilitating confusion that attacked him every time he was with her.

"It won't be long before you're as good—" She stopped, a wicked gleam in her eye. "Well, maybe *good* is not exactly the word. It won't be long," she corrected herself, "before you will be able to walk as well as ever."

Her small attempt at humor didn't help. Ben had spent the past several hours in despair. A trap was closing in on him. A trap of caring again for someone. He was terrified of the prospect of the pain such weakness brought. But he couldn't restrain the quickening of his pulse when she was near, nor the comfort of her touch, nor the hope that kept springing up inside him despite all the grumbling nay-saying devils within him.

Those devils were in his eyes when he looked up at her, and her heart contracted with the anguish she saw there.

He finally found the words he wanted. "Sean wants you to stay away from me. I agree with him."

"I don't," she said, "and I don't think you do, either. Not really."

"A mind reader now?" he said caustically. "Well, you're wrong. I completely agree with him."

"It seems that will be the first time," she countered. "I guess that's some progress."

He sighed, thoroughly frustrated. "Are you always this stubborn?"

Her chin went up. "I'm told so." A sudden puckish smile brightened her face, stabbing his resolve.

He shook his head. "He's right this time. I'm his Jonah. I'm my own Jonah. We should never have come back together again. Sean has no reason to like me. He has, in fact, every reason to hate me." There was a ragged unexpected sorrow in his voice.

"I'm not going to ask you why again. You've both made it clear it's something private between you. But no, Sean doesn't hate you. I know him well enough to know that. But he doesn't trust you, and you're a complication, one he doesn't need right now. I'm another one. Neither of us are doing much for his peace of mind, I'm afraid." The smile was gone now, her tone quietly wistful. "Sometimes I wish I could be what he wants and do as he wishes."

Ben's voice was gentle when he answered her. "I don't think he wants you to be anything other than what you are." For a moment his eyes caressed her, his face unguarded. "You're like a drop of sunlight that filters through whatever obstacle you find.... You nourish everything you touch." He looked away, embarrassed and surprised at his own words, at how much they revealed.

"That's why Sean's right," he continued slowly, preventing her from replying. He put a finger to her mouth as she tried again to speak. "No, Ryan, let me finish.

"I would drain you. I've been a taker too long to change. Sean knows that. He also knows I'll do anything I must to finish what I start. He's right to be cautious. For himself. For you. I've already created tension and discord between the two of you. It can only get worse unless you do what he says and stay away. Because, God help me, I don't want to use you, but I'll end up doing it."

His voice faltered. He felt he was tearing his own heart out.

Ryan was silent, pondering his words, hearing the conviction in them. She had to know what was behind them. "Your wife," she said slowly, carefully. "Is she in Boston?"

Morgan was completely stunned by the question, even more so by the sudden realization that he had not thought of Melody in the past several days. Even the rage at the sound of her name, which had ridden with him all these years, had lessened.

"No, she's dead," came the abrupt painful answer.

Ryan digested the statement, knowing from his expression that she should travel no further on this particular road. "I'm sorry," she said.

"Don't be," he replied curtly. "I'm not."

Her bewilderment was total. Of all the answers she had anticipated, that was not one of them. "I don't understand...."

He had turned entirely hostile, as if the few minutes of warmth between them had never existed. "You don't have to," he said rudely. "I'm tired." It was a curt dismissal.

Ryan's world became suddenly joyless. She turned quickly and left, her legs hurrying toward the wagon.

"Damn," he muttered quietly, knowing he had again hurt someone not deserving of it.

That evening Ryan tried on her new dress, knowing it was expected. She tried to regain some of her happiness, but Ben Morgan's words kept echoing in her mind. *"She's dead.... I would drain you.... Sean's right."*

"No," she said to herself, stamping her foot on the hard flooring of the wagon. "He's not right. I won't let him be. I won't."

"Sean's right.... Sean's right." The refrain was constant. It wouldn't go away. A tear trickled down her face. And then she remembered Ben's eyes, warm and wanting and caressing just hours earlier.

She closed her eyes, throwing her head back. How she wanted him! How much she wanted to put her arms around him and take away the hurt and suspicion and anger!

"Ryan!"

She started at the sound. It was Sean.

"Your presence is desired at dinner," he said in his familiar teasing way.

Ryan stood up in the wagon, smoothing the folds of the new dress and giving her hair one last pat. It took every ounce of her determination to mold her face into a smile.

"I'm ready," she said, forcing a lilt of gaiety into her voice.

The music went on deep into the night. No one asked Ryan to sing that evening; it was her special day, and she was to be serenaded. All her favorites were played, and she was asked repeatedly to dance. She smiled and laughed and whirled. And cried inside.

Only Sean noticed the change in her. Only he saw the undercurrent of sadness under her smile. His gaze continually went to the hospital area as he silently cursed Morgan.

When the last instrument was stilled and the final good-night spoken, he accompanied Ryan to the wagon. His hand touched her hair. "You stole every heart tonight," he said.

"I think not," she answered quietly. "But thank you for a wonderful day." She gave him a quick kiss on his cheek and went inside. Sean couldn't remember ever seeing her so subdued.

Sean knew he couldn't sleep. And he didn't want to see Morgan, or his rage might explode, and he knew that wouldn't help anything at the moment. He lit a cigarette and decided to check on the sentries. Thoughtfully, he started the long climb to the rocks above the valley.

Chapter Eleven

Ben was another who could not sleep. He kept seeing Ryan's stricken face as he so curtly dismissed her. Like Sean, he had seen through her forced gaiety during the evening and hated himself for ruining what should have been a wonderful day. It had not helped to see Sean's malevolent glances directed his way. He knew he deserved each one of them.

He tried to focus his thoughts elsewhere. He didn't understand why they kept going back to that wagon just yards away. Duty had been his only concern for so many years that he was bewildered that he was now pushing it aside. He should never have assisted the Rebs in retrieving Sean. Nor should he even think about not going after Sean if, by some miracle, he could escape. But the thought of doing so was completely abhorrent.

Escape. He must escape before sinking completely in the quicksand that was tugging at him, pulling him down, smothering him. He was so engrossed in his own thoughts, he failed to hear the first whimpers that came from the wagon.

They were light at first, barely audible to even his trained ears, but they grew in intensity. The whimpers changed into moans and then frightened crying. The sorrow and fear in the sound was excruciating, and Ben felt as if someone was pounding nails into his soul.

His eyes went to the wagon. He was closest to it, and he doubted if anyone else could hear. *The dream...the dreams that Ryan had mentioned.* He looked for Sean, but the Reb captain was nowhere to be seen. Frantically he searched until he found the crutches he had used so awkwardly earlier in the day. Using every fiber of his strength, he struggled to his feet, falling back twice before finally finding his balance. Damn the weakness. Damn the leg. He hobbled over to the wagon, placing the crutches against the wheel and lowering the gate. He managed to swing himself up, dragging his splinted leg behind him.

The glow of full moon reached through the opening and revealed Ryan's twisting turning form. Tears were rolling down her cheeks, and he could hear the grief-stricken words, "Mama... mama." Her hands were balled into tight fists.

Ben moved close and leaned over her. "Ryan," he whispered. "Ryan... wake up." His hand touched her face with infinite tenderness, and his heart ached for her. "Hush, baby.... I'm here." His face moved down, and his lips softly touched hers.

At the warm pressure, Ryan woke, her eyes wide and startled and full of fear. Then they saw his face, and the horror disappeared in the wonder of the tender expression she saw there. "Ben?"

A crooked grin spread across his face. "I'm afraid so," he answered. "Your nightmare?"

Ryan looked up at him, the tears still swimming in her eyes, and her breath caught in tiny little sobs. "They won't go away." She held her arms up to him like a hurt child, and he gathered her in his own, feeling her hands winding around his neck. Her head rested against his chest as her frightened sobs subsided. His hands lightly stroked her back, and his lips touched her hair.

Pressed tightly against his broad chest, Ryan felt a warm security she had never known before, not even with Sean. It was as if she had been on a long, long journey and here, in Ben's arms, she had finally come home. She snuggled deeper into the comfort of his body.

Ben continued to soothe her with soft words as he grew conscious of the lightly clad body that hugged his own so trustingly. He was only too aware of every lovely curve under the man's shirt she was wearing and could feel his inevitable response. It took enormous effort to pull back and take her face in his hand.

"Better?" He asked, trying to break the invisible magic cord that was tightening its hold around them.

"Much, much better," she murmured, trying to burrow back against him. Her hand found its way to his face and explored it, and then her face unexpectedly came up and their lips met. He was exceedingly gentle, caressing rather than demanding, his lips like a whisper of wind. But as light as it was, his touch sent a hurricane of sensations through her. She reached for more.

And Ben wanted more. Wanted it more than anything he had ever known. In those few moments, he knew a peace he had never experienced before. A peace mixed with tenderness so great it hurt.

And desire. Oh, what desire! But not here, not like this. Not when she was so vulnerable. Again, he pulled away, his hand touching her face, stroking it with slow loving movements, his blue eyes nearly fathomless in the night.

"Get away from her." Sean's voice was like a whiplash, fury evident in each heavily pronounced word.

Both Ben and Ryan stiffened, but Ryan grabbed Ben's hand and wouldn't let it go.

"I said . . . get away from her, damn you," Sean warned as his lanky form filled the wagon. Ben felt the blow before he saw it, and he went spinning against the side of the wagon.

Ryan stared at Sean in horror. She had never seen him so angry.

"Sean, no. . . . I was having a nightmare—he heard me. He was just trying to comfort me."

Sean's voice was harsh. "I saw how he was comforting you." He turned his attention back to Ben. "I didn't think even you would do this. Damn you. Damn you to hell."

Ben closed his eyes. He knew how it must have looked. There was no reason for him to be there, none that Sean would believe. Not now. Not when he was this angry. He had felt Sean's explosive anger before. Opening his eyes he looked steadily at Sean's rage-filled face.

His silence and impassive stare fueled Sean's anger. Sean's hand went back once more, prepared to strike, but Ryan jumped up between them.

"No! You'll have to hit me first."

Ben moved now, gently pulling Ryan away. "No, Ryan," he said quietly. "This is between your brother and me."

Sean hesitated, then dropped his hand, his face a question as he looked from one to the other.

As if in defiance, Ryan turned back to Ben, her hand traveling up to a tiny trail of blood coming from his split lip. Her hand was gentle but Ben flinched, his eyes watching Sean's reaction to the almost intimate gesture. He took her hand and lowered it. "It's all right," he said. "It's nothing."

Sean's lips compressed, his eyes shooting amber flames. "Get away from him, Ryan. I won't touch him again." He flushed as his sister hesitated, obviously not quite believing him. Slowly, she moved away, not wanting to make things worse.

Sean sighed heavily, aware now that he had struck an injured and weakened man, one who couldn't hit back. The thought did nothing to diminish his anger. "Get down, Ben," he said, his voice softly dangerous.

Ben nodded, his eyes never leaving Sean's as he awkwardly moved across the wagon to the opening. He hesitated, casting a quick glance at Ryan. "I'm sorry," he said. "I'm sorry I ruined your birthday." There was real regret in his voice. Then he touched the ground with his good leg and reached for the crutches.

"Justis," Sean roared, waking nearly the entire camp. In seconds, the sergeant was there.

"Take the colonel back to his bed and set a guard. You're in charge of him from now on. He's to go nowhere outside the hospital area without company. And God help you if he does. Do you understand?"

Justis merely nodded, his eyes curious at the heavy tension that surrounded the wagon. He knew better than to ask questions.

"Come on, Yank," he said impersonally. Without a backward look, Ben moved slowly back to his wall-less prison.

Sean stared at Ryan in the moonlight. "What happened?"

"I tried to tell you," she said in a soft pleading voice. "I had another nightmare. Colonel Morgan knew about them.... I had told him. He just tried to help. I asked him to hold me.... He kept trying to move away...." A tear formed in her eye, joining those already dried on her face. "He didn't do anything." Her voice became defiant. "But I wish he had—I wanted him to. He wouldn't."

Sean believed her. The misery on her face made him wince. So did his recent actions. Though he realized he had accused Ben wrongly, his anger remained. The man may not have been guilty of this particular offense, but his very presence had brought about misery and disruption. He swung down from the wagon, cursing softly to himself.

Ryan sat in the wagon, remembering Ben's touch, the warm tender look on his face, the instinctive knowledge that he had been aroused as greatly as she...even as he had fought it. If only he and Sean would forget the bitterness that hung so heavily between them. She was not comforted by the fact that she had made it worse that night.

Sean went to his tent and fetched several blankets, then went outside to sleep. The night was perfection, with its full silver moon and endless stars. A cool breeze swept the valley floor, quenching some of his anger. He used one blanket for a pillow, another as a cover, and he lay there, his head resting on his crossed hands as he stared at the heavens above him.

His fury was receding, but the problems still remained. He had climbed down from the sentry points to find Ben missing from his bed. A quick look discovered the crutches leaning against Ryan's wagon. And then he had seen his sister in Ben's arms, had watched the kiss before his rage exploded. He had immediately assumed the worst—that Ben had taken advantage of her sympathy... her innocence. But he knew she had not lied.

He had not expected Ben to be able to move so independently this soon. But then he had often underestimated Morgan's strength and determination. It meant he had to take more precautions... and sooner than he'd anticipated. *Oh Ben.... Why you? Why now?* Sean was torn as he had never been before. He would like to turn Morgan loose... for all their sakes. But there was no way he could. Morgan knew too much. The rifles were by far the most important prize they had ever sought, more important, even, than the gold.

Ben's orders had shaken him more than he'd revealed to Braden or Ryan. Each of his men had a death warrant on his head. He couldn't let Morgan go and perhaps seal the fate of every one of his troopers. And Morgan would never agree to forget everything he heard or knew. If Sean knew anything, he knew that. And Ben had confirmed it just yesterday, after his return from Center.

The best he could hope for was Ben's parole while in this camp. But even that was unlikely. Ben, he suspected, would never make even that small concession. He would try to escape and try again. And the only possible recourse was a very distasteful one. *Damn you, Ben.* It was his last thought before his eyes finally closed.

For one of the few times in her life, Ryan Mallory dreaded dawn. She had lain awake all night in sweat-stained blankets, misery eating at her.

Her earlier soft thoughts of Ben bending over her had been quickly banished by recurring pictures of the angry aftermath. What had she wrought?

Sean had been furious, and the fact that he had left so abruptly last night told her he wouldn't easily forget. She had no illusions that she would be well on her way *someplace else* if he had the men to spare.

And Ben. His passive acceptance of Sean's anger and unquestioned obedience to her brother's orders puzzled and disturbed her. He had been unjustly attacked, yet he had said and done nothing in his own defense. It was as if he were agreeing with Sean, that something was indeed wrong. She wondered if he was regretting those few minutes of warmth, that fleeting glimpse of passion. He could have taken her—she been willing—but he would not.

She had never known a more complicated man. He was a mass of contradictions, but she had discovered something last night. She had found a rich vein of gentleness and sensitivity that she knew was rare, and she feared greatly that Sean's interference had cut it off.

Ryan knew she loved Ben Morgan. She knew it last night when she felt so safe in his arms. But she also sensed Ben's reluctance to want, to feel, to love. Something had nearly mortally wounded his heart, and she didn't know if there was enough left to heal. If only she knew more. If only Sean would tell her what festered between the two of them. She loved them both, and she was bitterly afraid she might have to choose between them. And she couldn't.

She wanted to cry, but the tears were frozen inside her. Dawn would come. And Sean's anger. And Ben's carefully restored indifference. She didn't know if she could bear either one.

Chapter Twelve

The day was dour. Sometime during the early morning hours, the pristine open skies were slowly invaded with thunderheads—dark forbidding purple-blue splotches.

The glowering visage matched Ben's mood. Last night had aptly demonstrated the folly of his wayward thoughts. He had been a fool to allow even the slightest feelings for Ryan Mallory. That they weren't slight at all was something he would not consider.

He had not protested Sean's assumptions, because he knew Sean had cause for anger. Ben could easily have called for someone else; instead, he had gone himself, assuming a role to which he had no claim. It did not help to remember Ryan's state of undress, the reaction of his own body to hers nor the warmth that had flooded both his mind and body at the lovely form curved next to his so trustingly. It was the last thing in the world he needed. He wished it was the last thing in the world he wanted.

He was already filled with restlessness . . . even with his weakness. It had always been a vital part of him, and perhaps it had much to do with his choice of profession. He had often thought that nothing could be worse than sitting in an office all day or being surrounded continually by the man-made monstrosities that cities had become. They shut out the light and the wind and left the air polluted by open sewers and filthy streets. He had loved the West, loved the wide unspoiled vistas, the open lands that beckoned to him and made him feel free. He could lose himself in them and know the satisfaction of complete and absolute independence. It had been one of the few places where, oddly enough, he had not felt so alone.

And now, as ever when something weighed heavily on his mind, he was consumed with the need of moving, of using his body and skills in the most elementary ways. It was agony of the worst kind to be confined now, to be betrayed by his own body and thoughts.

He *must* get away. Sean was a trap. Ryan was an even deadlier one. He had thought he was immune to these feelings. How could he ever forget? How could he forget some of Melody's last angry words? *"Stay here with you? With you?"* Her voice had become hysterical. *"Who could ever love you?"*

Who, indeed, for no one ever had. Not his parents...not Melody. Her parting statement had killed something inside him. He had known, of course, that something was desperately wrong with their relationship, but he had not guessed at the depth of her hatred. He had, even then, not truly known until she disappeared just five days later. Ben Morgan had turned to stone; his only pleasures lay in a job well-done or the constant challenge of jousting with nature. He had learned to prefer the honest ferocity of a mountain lion or natural killer instinct of an eagle to the perfidy of human animals.

He must get away.

Everything that Ryan had feared had come true.

When she finally ventured out, she found an ill-humored Sean, who barely acknowledged her presence. She pretended to ignore his anger and clucked unconvincingly about the birthday gifts. She stopped when she suddenly realized how false she sounded and how everyone was looking uncomfortable. She wondered how much of last night's happenings were known.

Almost arrogantly, she stuck her chin up in the air and prepared a plate of breakfast for Ben. Her look challenged Sean to protest, and her every movement proclaimed a conviction of purpose. It was only slightly dimmed by the unhappy bewildered, altogether unfamiliar sullen expression on Sean's face. She had to suppress a sudden feeling of guilt. Sean had been in the wrong last night, she told herself. He had not asked...he had not listened...he had not understood. Her chin tilted higher.

But her reception at Ben's side was no more welcoming. In fact, she would have far preferred the disapproving glare of Sean's to Ben's cold and emotionless mask.

"You show," he said, purposely cruel, "precious little consideration for your brother."

Without quite saying so, he implied that she was as feckless and shallow as she knew he regarded most women. Her eyes grew wide with hurt.

"He was wrong..." She started to defend herself, wondering why he was suddenly concerned over Sean's feelings.

"He was trying to protect you. I had no right being with you in that wagon."

"You had every right.... I wanted you...."

The old bitter laugh was back, and Ryan winced at the sound of it. "You still don't understand, Ryan. Sean does. He knows. He knows me. He knows I'm his enemy, and that makes me yours and you mine. Nothing will change that." His eyes were suddenly glittering. "I don't want your breakfast. I don't want anything from you. I don't want *you*." His face was like granite as he saw her pride crumble into tiny bits.

Better now, he told himself. *It's better now than later.* But he hadn't expected his own anguish as Ryan bowed her head. With great dignity she placed the plate at his side, regarded him levelly then turned and left without a word. He watched her disappear into the woods, then turned to see Sean's eyes on him. He was surprised to see an almost imperceptible flicker of understanding dart across his face.

The day grew worse. A cold wind bent the trees at unnatural angles, and Ben could almost feel nature's hovering anger.

Men were scurrying to strengthen the corral gate and calm some of the more nervous horses. The cook's wagon had been carefully secured, and the usual clutter of blankets and saddles were disappearing up a winding trail.

The first heavy drops had already hit the canvas with the impact of hail when Justis and another man came for him.

"Come on, Yank," the lanky Texas sergeant said. "We're going up in the caves." He helped Ben steady himself on the crutches and remained beside him, his hands ready to assist on the difficult climb ahead.

The rain was coming faster now, turning the trail slippery with mud. He would have fallen several times had not Justis been there, his hands quick and steady as one grabbed a crutch and the other kept his body from falling. It was a nightmare of a walk, and Ben was drenched when he finally reached the mouth of one of several caves. As he slowly entered, he looked around in amazement. Several fires lighted the interior, casting shadows against what seemed to be hundreds of boxes lining the walls. Ben drew a sudden breath at the sight of crates of rifles and ammunition, boxes of blue uniforms, barrels of flour and other foodstuffs and the smaller boxes of medicines. He recognized the shapes of them all.

The cave went deep, beyond his vision, and seemed filled with endless booty. The reports of Sean's success had been greatly underestimated. Ben couldn't comprehend how Sean had been able to do so much damage for so long without detection. He was filled with unwilling admiration for his onetime friend, knowing at the same time that Sean must be stopped.

One of the reasons Ben had been sent west was to stop the guerrillas before they could intercept the planned shipments of repeating rifles that were on the way. The various Indian tribes, encouraged by the strange war between the whites, were growing increasingly bold, and army units in the West needed the new rifles desperately. Washington was extremely fearful of the new weapons falling into enemy hands. And so was Ben. The South was known for its sharpshooters—men who had hunted nearly all their lives. The repeating rifles in those hands would be disastrous. It was equally as frightening, however, to think that the undermanned Western garrisons might lose the West.

Ben slid wearily to a spot on the cave floor designated by his new keeper. It was well back, away from the fire, but Justis soon supplied him with some blankets. The cave was damp and cold, but Ben was grateful for its protection. The wind was howling now, and the rain could be heard pounding outside. Thunder drowned out the voices of the more than two hundred men crowded in the cave.

Ben caught brief glimpses of both Sean and Ryan, but neither approached him, and he leaned against the cold damp wall of the cave, considering his alternatives. Unfortunately, it didn't take long. There were damned few. He had no idea how he could escape, not with a leg that barely carried him the short distance to the cave, not surrounded with hundreds of war-savvy troopers, not under the almost constant eye of Sean Mallory. His deep sigh drew Justis's attention.

"Some food, Yank?"

Ben nodded. He wasn't hungry, but every bit of nourishment made him stronger. He accepted the strong black coffee and some dried beef, forcing himself to eat. After completing the meal, he looked again at the boxes, knowing instantly which carried the revolvers and single-action rifles. He played games in his mind, thinking of the possibilities of reaching a weapon. But then he would have to load it. So close and yet so far.

"I don't think so, Yank," Justis said with his slow deliberate drawl. "Don't even give it the littlest thought. I would hate to kill you tonight, I truly would."

Ben's face reflected his astonishment. Was he really becoming so transparent? It seemed everyone was reading his thoughts . . . or thinking they were. "I'm just exercising my mind, Sergeant."

That brought a smile to Justis's usually laconic face. "Well, just as long as it don't move one inch either way, we understand each other."

Ben raised one eyebrow, and the end of his mouth rose slightly upward. He couldn't help but like the Texan, even as he fought such a troublesome sentiment.

The afternoon turned into night, and the storm persisted, the thunder growing even closer until it seemed to be inside the cave. The inevitable music started, and a fiddler competed against the wild howling of the storm. The troopers clapped their hands, and the echoes resounded against the walls and bounced back at them. It was a cacophony of sound: the music, the clapping, the echoes, the thunder. And then suddenly it was over. All of it. The thunder moved on, the fiddler quit, the men drifted into blankets, the echoes remained only within the ears.

There was quiet, blessed peace. Ben lay down, drawing up several blankets for warmth and to shut out the rest of the world. He had just about managed to go to sleep when he heard the first haunting notes.

It was Sean and his guitar, and it seemed alone in the night.

Sean had a special melody he pursued when troubled. Ben recognized it; so did Sean's men. They had all learned to leave him alone when they heard it. It was a plaintive melody, which came from someplace deep inside him. Sean didn't know its origins or when exactly he had picked it up. It had always just seemed to be there. He explored it now, as he had done so many times before, first slowly, then faster in almost a flamenco style as he embroidered the principal theme, dancing around it, but always returning to the simple haunting theme.

The music didn't have its usual soothing effect on Sean. His mind was much too tangled for an easy form of release. He had come to realize that his vehement opposition to any relationship between Ryan and Ben lay in his own troubled and complex feelings toward Ben.

He knew he'd been wrong when he told Ryan that Ben had become an empty shell. He had glimpsed in the past few days some of his friend's old charm and seen the way his eyes lighted when they fixed on Ryan. He had been surprised at Justis's easy companionship with Morgan and even Jimmy's grudging acceptance. They were men not easily fooled.

But he couldn't rid himself of the deep pain he still felt at the loss of something that had been so much a part of his life at one time. The hurt, the disappointment, the disillusionment had stayed with him through the years. Despite what seemed to be an easy camaraderie with his men and friends, there was always a reserve, a distance that he couldn't—wouldn't—bridge. It was there even with Jimmy, whom he sometimes thought of as almost a younger brother.

The intrusion of Ben Morgan into his camp—and back into his life—had made painful embers flare into bright flames. He couldn't escape the memories, nor could he deny that a bond still existed between them. They had been so close. So important to each other. But these were feelings Sean knew he could no longer afford. He couldn't forget the immediate danger, not only to himself but to his command, and he wouldn't risk himself again.

It was his own resistance to Ben that made him so reluctant to accept the feelings he knew existed between Ben and his sister. He didn't want her hurt, but it was much more complicated than that, and he knew—and accepted—it. There was his own wound and his own fears and his own susceptibility. And there was the debt he owed Morgan, the greatest debt anyone could owe another person. He had told Ben he had considered it repaid. But he hadn't and never would. He, Sean, was here now, today, because of Ben. It was something he could never forget. It interfered with everything, disrupted every rational thought.

Sean was a man who hated confusion, and at the moment he hated Ben for creating that confusion, for being here, for clouding his judgment. He wanted to keep Ben as far away as possible from himself and from those close to him.

His fingers slowed on the strings, and the melody once more emerged in its purest form as it lingered—almost wistfully—in each and every corner of the cave.

Ben listened, reading the music as precisely as he would a book. He knew Sean well enough to detect most of the thoughts behind it, and he tossed and turned as they rekindled his own tangled emotions.

Chapter Thirteen

Ben's strength grew steadily. He was back in the hospital area after three days in the cool damp cave. He had thought the rains would never stop, hating every minute of the closed dark space that quickly became gamy with the scent of too many unwashed men pressed too closely together.

He had been watched constantly, sometimes by Justis, sometimes by others. He learned to appreciate the hours with Justis, who seemed more a companion than a guard though there was always a wariness about him. The sergeant, Ben knew, could seem completely at ease, yet he sensed that Justis was a very dangerous man when provoked. Ben had studied him closely since the man had been placed in charge of him, and he continued to find new depths.

Justis was tall and lanky and seemed almost a straw man the way his body contorted into positions that looked horribly uncomfortable. He could sit for hours in one position, seldom talking, but always, always carving, his fingers practically flying over the wood as he transformed it into an almost breathing wild creature. Bears, prowling mountain lions, playful squirrels, a haughty eagle all jumped to life under the man's skilled fingers. Occasionally he brushed a dark lock of thinning hair back from his forehead, back from the bright blue eyes that missed little. Only rarely did a smile touch his mouth, and that was usually when Ryan was nearby.

Why Ben liked him so much he didn't know. He had steeled himself against such feelings a long time ago. He didn't want to like anyone. They left…they died…they betrayed. It was better to trust yourself and only yourself.

As if sensing his confusion, Fortune sidled up, carefully and comically making his slow way across the treacherous branches and finally reaching a place where he collapsed, his small thin body hugging Ben's and his head on Ben's leg.

"Seems you have a friend," Justis observed, a slow start of a smile on his thin lips. "Jimmy's all out of sorts because of it."

"Damn if I know why," Ben replied. "I never had a dog, never knew much about them."

"Well, it's damned near got everybody confounded. Damned dog's growled or threatened or bitten 'bout everyone." Having made that observation, Justis turned his attention back to the piece of wood and Ben to his own ruminations.

He was stronger now... much stronger. When Justis had taken him for a walk that morning, he had managed twice as many steps as the day before, and he had not grown as tired. Food and rest were performing their magic. So was his determination. He was growing adept at the crutches, swinging easily between them, disregarding the tiny blisters that formed when his hands took his entire weight. He would be ready soon to try an escape.

So his thoughts traveled. He was careful not to think of Ryan, although she was a constant torturous shadow. She had gone out of her way to avoid him since the morning after her nightmare. She checked on his injuries periodically but had been careful to keep it impersonal. She had brought the book he carried in his saddle-bags, the novel by Charles Dickens and another book—a cheap Western penny novel that had been circulating in camp. They had been dropped, rather rudely, in his lap, and she had walked off when he tried to thank her. Her large eyes, which he thought resembled those of a wounded fawn, still reflected the hurt she had suffered those few days ago. He wished his guilt would go away. But it didn't, and neither did the longing inside him. He couldn't forget the warmth of her body against his own nor the contented trusting look she had given him.

He spent the next several days reading the books. Reading and rereading. More often than not, his concentration was not on the pages but on possible escape plans. He could see Sean watching him, particularly when he exercised, and he knew it would not be long before Sean took even stronger measures.

Ben willed his strength to quicken. He ate everything offered him, and he spent hours quietly flexing his leg muscles, forcing them to work despite the pain that accompanied his efforts. His cuts were now only livid scars.

He had been in the valley nearly five weeks when, one evening, he heard Sean and Ryan talking. Realizing that he was the subject of their discussion, he feigned sleep.

"No," he heard her say sharply. "He's still too weak to move far. It's not necessary."

"It *is* necessary," he heard Sean reply in a low even voice. "You've seen how well he gets around. I'm not taking any chances. He's too dangerous."

"Another day," she pleaded. "He needs more exercise."

"Okay," Sean said, his tone yielding and affectionate. "But Friday the leg irons go on unless he gives his parole."

Ben listened as they walked away. He had known he was on borrowed time. He didn't think he, under similar circumstances, would have waited as long. He realized tomorrow night would probably be his one and only chance to escape.

He woke Thursday morning with a sense of excitement. The day started much as any other. He washed, ate a breakfast of beans and bacon and turned in his isolation to his book.

Justis accompanied him on his short morning walk. He had become quite practiced with the crutches and moved with new confidence. They walked to the latrine area, where Ben saw to his personal needs, then back to the hospital area, where he sat propped against a saddle.

The day wore slowly on. He read once more, again his mind on other things. He mentally measured the distance between the woods and corral. It was, he reckoned, about one hundred yards from the trees to the back of the corral. If he could get from the cover to the horses, roll under the fence and take a good fast horse without being noticed, he might have a chance to leave quietly. He would have to disable his guard and gamble that the sentries on the valley walls would not expect the exiting rider to be the injured prisoner.

He cursed the unusual tenseness of the camp, which would keep everyone alert. The mood was sullen and heavy. Sean's men had expected to be gone by now. They were ready to go home, and they were held here...waiting. Ben didn't know exactly what they were waiting for, but he suspected it must be important. He wouldn't let himself think it might be for the repeating rifles.

Justis was replaced by another man, this time a private. It was several long hours later when Sean stopped by, waving the private away.

Morgan and Sean exchanged long measuring looks.

"You're getting around very well," Sean said finally, his eyes carefully watching Ben's face.

Morgan shrugged. "I wouldn't win any footraces."

A wry crooked grin answered him. "I wouldn't bet on it," Sean answered slowly. "I learned the hard way not to underestimate you."

"I wasn't at a decided disadvantage then," Morgan said sourly.

"And just how much are you now?" Sean's voice was very quiet.

"I would think that would be obvious," Morgan replied, wondering the reason for the little cat-and-mouse game. He didn't like playing the part of the mouse, and his eyes reflected his sudden anger.

Sean caught the anger and noted the hardening of Morgan's mouth. He felt a surge of victory and, at the same time, a sense of shame. His tone became very hard, and his eyes glittered with ice.

"You know why we're here. You know what kind of danger you are to me, to us. I want your parole, Ben. I want your promise you won't try to escape. In return, I'll make you as comfortable as possible, see that you're sent somewhere safe."

"In the South?" Ben laughed bitterly. "Is there such a place?"

"Is the North any better?" Sean retorted angrily. "The difference is the South really doesn't have the food, blankets and medicine, and you do. The South does as well as it can with what it has. You're the ones who stopped the prisoner exchanges. You're the ones who starve out of just plain meanness."

Ben was silent. He had been in some of the Northern prison camps. They were pestholes and had nearly the same death rates as many in the South and, as Sean claimed, with less reason. Neither side would ever be commended for their treatment of prisoners, particularly now that all exchanges had been canceled and the camps had to house increasing numbers of men in already strained and inadequate facilities.

"What do you plan to do with me if I don't give you my parole?" Ben asked reluctantly. The question had haunted him. He was less afraid of death than he was of his tolerance for captivity.

"It depends," Sean said. "Will you give me your parole?"

Morgan cocked one heavy dark eyebrow, his eyes black with anger. "Blackmail?"

"Call it what you will. I'm willing to make a bargain with you."

"The answer is no."

Sean shrugged. "I thought so. It was worth a try, for both of us. You're a fool, Ben. A bloody fool. There's no way I'm letting you loose. You're just going to make things more unpleasant for yourself, for Ryan, for me."

Ben merely shrugged, his eyes once more totally blank.

"Don't try it, Ben. I don't want to kill you but, believe me, I will if I have to."

Ben heard the promise in Sean's voice and knew he meant it. He looked up. "That's fair enough." He hesitated, reluctant to say what he wanted to say. "Cowboy," he said finally, referring unconsciously to Sean's nickname at West Point. "I'm sorry. I wish I could do what you ask. I can't. I think you know that."

Sean nodded. "I'm increasing your guard tomorrow. Your movements will be limited. I don't need trouble from you right now."

Morgan's eyes followed Sean as the Rebel captain returned to his tent. He sensed that Sean wanted to say more. He himself had wanted to say more. But it was too late. Much too late.

Morgan willed himself to sleep after a lonely dinner. He would need all his strength. When he woke, all was quiet. The sky was perfect for his purpose; clouds dimmed a nearly full moon, allowing little light to filter down on the silent camp.

Justis was back on guard duty, and Ben cursed that fact. It was, he told himself, the very reason he shouldn't let himself feel anything. It didn't pay. It never did. He tried to dismiss his feelings of guilt.

He sat up suddenly, holding his stomach. The sergeant looked at him; it was a brief glance at first, then more intent. "Something wrong, Yank?"

"I don't know," Ben answered weakly. "I have a bad pain in my stomach...maybe something I ate.... If I can just relieve myself..." He looked at Davis for consent.

Justis Davis looked at his charge thoughtfully. He had grown to like the Yank despite his early misgivings. Like himself, the Yank had little to say, and he had been quietly appreciative of Justis's help. He liked Morgan's steady uncomplaining determination. If Morgan said he was sick, then he probably was.

"Okay," he said finally, reaching out his hand. "I'll help you."

Ben took his hand and straightened himself up on the crutches, one hand still clutching his stomach. The Texan took one of Ben's arms for support and helped him walk over to the latrine area in the woods. All of a sudden, Ben moaned and doubled up. As Justis reached to help him, Ben swung one of the crutches, grazing the Reb's head. Justis went down.

Ben checked the fallen sergeant briefly, reassuring himself that no real damage had been done. He took Justis's shirt and rough gray jacket, and replaced his own tattered blue coat. Then he tore strips from what was left of his shirt and tied and gagged Justis.

He stood up, placing most of his weight on his one good leg, steadying himself on one crutch. He decided to discard the other and, at a half hop, half run, reached the far side of the corral.

Ben was just about ready to slip under it when he heard Sean's mocking voice. "It's not polite to leave without so much as a goodbye or thank you."

Ben was suddenly still. He could barely see Sean in the shadows. He tried to think. Was Sean alone? Could he still slip into the corral, hide among the horses until he could mount one? His hand slipped down the railing.

Sean's voice was very cold. "Move that finger one more fraction of an inch and I'll blow it off."

Ben knew in that instant it was over. There was no chance—if there ever had been. He did not doubt for one moment that Sean would do as he threatened.

"Where's Justis?"

Ben nodded in the direction of the woods. "He's over there. He's not badly hurt."

"He better not be," Sean replied. The voice was ragged. The anger, always close to the surface when dealing with Ben, was very evident.

"What now, Sean?" Ben asked the question quietly, almost indifferently.

"If I had any sense, I would kill you," Sean replied tightly.

"Then go ahead and be done with it," Ben challenged.

The two men stared at each other in the shadows. Sean was the first to drop his eyes.

"Jimmy! Dan!" he called. The two men slowly materialized out of the dark. "It seems our colonel can walk better than he led us to believe. Take him back to his bed."

His eyes still on Sean, Ben took one step, and the crutch hit a dip in the ground. Without the second crutch, he lost his balance and his leg gave way under him. He fell awkwardly, consciously protecting his injured leg the best he could, but he felt a new stabbing pain running the length of it.

"Drag him over there," Sean said unsympathetically. "Jimmy, you stay with him, and Dan, go look for Justis. He's in the woods." He looked back at Ben. "Near the latrine?"

Ben nodded before being jerked toward the hospital area.

A few minutes later, Sean heard a yell, and two men, one of them Justis, came out of the woods together. Justis was rubbing his head.

"What happened?" Sean asked curtly.

"He said he was sick, Cap'n. He sure 'nough looked sick."

Sean gave him a disgusted look. "You're slipping, Justis. I didn't think he would get past you."

Justis searched his captain's face. "Dan said you were waiting for him. How did you know?"

Sean looked uncomfortable. "I just had a feeling.... It's of no matter now. Wake Bobby Wilson and tell him he has guard duty, then get some rest. We'll talk more about this in the morning."

"Wilson?" Justis couldn't hide his surprise. Wilson was one of the camp faction that thought the Yank should have been killed outright. The man felt a deep and abiding hatred for each and every Yankee; his kid brother had been killed in Virginia.

Only Sean's hard stare prevented any further objection. Justis shrugged and did as he was told. A sleepy-looking corporal reported within minutes, accepting the nursemaid assignment with mixed anger and hatred.

Sean disappeared toward his tent, leaving a puzzled Justis, an angry Wilson and a frustrated Morgan. Ben sighed, feeling the fresh pain in his injured leg. He looked at the hostile face of his new guard and knew he would not get a second chance.

When Ryan left the wagon the next morning, it was obvious that something had happened. If the atmosphere had been cool several mornings ago after her nightmare, it was absolutely frigid now. She was afraid to ask for answers when she saw Sean's tightly clinched lips.

She cast a quick glance over to Ben's location, saw he was still there, and also noticed that Justis had been replaced by Bobby Wilson, her least favorite of all of Sean's troop. Her face was puzzled when she looked back at her brother. "Bobby Wilson? Where's Justis?"

Sean's frown deepened. "Your colonel tried to escape last night—hit Justis over the head with the crutch he had made for him. Ironic twist, don't you think?"

"How is he?"

"Your colonel? Or Justis?"

"Justis."

"Other than a sore head and hurt pride, he's probably all right. It's going to be a long time before he lives this one down, though."

"What are you going to do with Ben?"

"I'm going to do what I should have done days ago. Make sure he doesn't try to go anyplace again."

"You were right, then," she said. "You were right about him trying to escape." A stricken look passed over her face. "What if he did get away, Sean? He would have brought soldiers back here."

"Perhaps," Sean replied tersely. "It would have taken him some time to get help. By then, we would be gone. But we would have to leave everything, and it would ruin our plans for the rifles. And we need them, Ryan. We need them badly."

"I'm sorry," she said forlornly. "You were right from the beginning. I should never have brought him here."

"No." His voice was gentle now. "I wasn't right. There was nothing else you could do...not my little Kitten. Now go see about Justis, and you better check Morgan's leg. I think he might have hurt it again."

"I don't care," she said bitterly.

"Yes you do, and you know it."

Justis was fine. His pride was hurt, but he was easygoing by nature and had an accompanying ability to laugh at himself. That saved him from complete humiliation. There was a small bump on his head, but nothing a few hours of sleep wouldn't cure.

After checking on the sergeant, Ryan made her way slowly over to Ben. He was partially sitting, pain etched back into the hard contours of his arresting face. But the lines were the only indication of what he was feeling. His eyes were once more a total mystery, a fathomless blue that revealed nothing—not a hint of warmth or curiosity or hostility or even disappointment. Any emotion was completely hidden by the old armor, but now Ryan had her own: pure undiluted anger.

"Sean said you might have hurt your leg again," she said coldly, her voice chillier than he had ever heard it. All of a sudden her rage came pouring out. "You fool," she said, fear for him and for Sean mixing with her confused disappointment. "Don't you realize you could have permanently crippled that leg by walking on it, much less riding?"

Her hands ran down the makeshift splint that was still there. It had slipped, releasing what little support it had given. She could feel the bone, and she saw him wince with pain as she ran her hands along both sides of his lower leg, gently probing it. The bone had been jarred but apparently had remained in place.

Despite her anger, she breathed easier. He had slowed the healing process but apparently had done no lasting damage.

She quickly splinted the leg again, avoiding his eyes. "It should be all right if you leave it alone...no weight at all on it for a while." She started to leave.

"Ryan?"

She turned. "Yes?" The voice was cool.

"Thank you," he said slowly, searchingly.

She looked at him, her face uncommonly restrained. She turned abruptly and left without another word.

Ben barely touched his breakfast, his appetite gone in the aftermath of his botched plans. He knew he had somehow played into Sean's hands, and that fact, along with the throbbing in his leg and Ryan's obvious unhappiness, combined to leave him dispirited and hopeless. A different guard replaced the glowering corporal and sat fifteen feet away, his hands on a rifle and his eyes rarely leaving Morgan.

During the morning Ben noticed items being moved from Ryan's wagon to Sean's tent. He wondered about it briefly, but his own increasingly difficult predicament kept his mind occupied. He wondered what was coming next, realizing he had not heard the end of last night's episode.

At midday, Jimmy and another man approached him, helping him up on the crutches, one of which had been reclaimed from the woods where he had left Justis the night before. He was guided over to Ryan's wagon and told to sit near one of the wagon wheels. Several blankets were already in place.

And then Sean was there, his face a tightly closed mask. He tossed a pair of leg irons to Morgan.

"Put them on," he said softly, his voice carrying a dangerous edge.

Ben had instinctively caught the metal. He looked at them now, knowing immediately they were the ones he had brought from Washington. He had not wanted to carry the extra weight, but the quartermaster had lost a son in a Western raid and had insisted on adding them to Ben's small store of supplies. "Get those devils for me," he had said, his face dark with loss. Ben had not had the heart to refuse. He had buried them in the bottom of his saddlebags and forgotten about them.

"Put them on," Sean repeated, a little louder. "Or I'll send for Wilson. And believe me, he won't be gentle."

Ben looked at them reluctantly, not quite accepting he had probably lost any chance he had of escaping. He slowly did as he was told, flinching at the feel of the iron around his bootless ankles. The left one encircled his ankle just below the splint. As he closed them, he could hear the lock click, and he couldn't restrain an involuntary shudder.

"Now these," Sean said, this time sending a pair of handcuffs his way. "One to your right wrist, the other to a spoke of the wheel."

Ben held them gingerly, doing nothing.

"What's the matter, Ben?" Sean said derisively. "It's what you had planned for me." His voice hardened. "Do it."

"No," Ben refused flatly. "You'll have to do it yourself, Cowboy."

Sean smiled thinly, then leaned down. Picking up the manacles, he tightened one around Ben's right wrist, the other to a spoke that reached from the wheel's center down to the part of the rim touching the ground.

Ben looked at him bitterly. "Anything else?"

"I think that will do for now," Sean replied. "I'll hold the keys to the leg irons. They won't come off until you're safe in a prison camp. Wilson will have the key to the handcuffs. You can forget about any exercise for a while." He turned to leave, then looked back. "You should have taken my offer, Ben."

Ben leaned back against the wheel, watching Sean disappear into the tent. He couldn't help testing the chains that now confined him. There was perhaps eighteen inches of chain linking the wrist bands, and he saw no weakness. The iron bracelet had been secured snugly around his wrist, and there was no chance of slipping from it.

The leg irons also offered little hope. He had made the ankle shackles as loose as possible, but there was no way of escaping them. The length of the chain between them was perhaps three feet, which would have normally allowed a certain amount of movement, but now his left leg was stretched straight with splints, and that left him with few options.

He sighed heavily, knowing the days ahead would be difficult to bear. He had always taken great satisfaction in physical activity of any kind. And he was restless and impatient by nature; it was difficult, if not impossible, to accept that he was now totally helpless and thoroughly dependent upon Sean for even his smallest needs. That Ryan would be witness to his humiliation galled him beyond acceptance. He didn't even try to stem the flow of despair that was slowly engulfing him.

The day passed slowly. The sun was bright and had warmed the earth, slowly draining the damp and chill from it. The leaves were beginning to change color, the green giving way to bright yellows and flaming reds. The sun's rays bounced against them, and the wind tested their fragility. The combination sent blazing colors waltzing randomly about.

Morgan let himself drift away, trying to recapture the indifference of the old cocoon he had constructed for himself. It no longer shielded him from his own feelings. His son had started chipping away at it, then Ryan and, finally, Sean. Sean, he admitted privately, was probably the most invasive, bringing alive all the feelings of regret and guilt he had thrust aside through the years. They hounded him now, leaving him little peace. He wished he could consider Sean an enemy, but even now he could not. To further complicate everything, he was falling inexorably, fatally and miserably in love with his captor's sister.

He missed Ryan, had missed her lively impudent presence since her birthday, and he still felt the chill of her presence that morning. Her movements had been almost mechanical, reflecting only a trace of the previous gentleness. The beguiling warmth of her eyes had turned to ice, and he knew she had felt betrayed. He wished he could explain the compulsion he had to escape, a need compounded by his altogether bewildering feelings toward Sean. He closed his eyes and remembered those first days when he was still so ill. He recalled her voice, so soft and caring; her eyes full of warmth and concern, her smile wide and open and generous. He had thought then that no one could be so gentle. He was haunted by the teasing laughter that held no malice and lightly mocked his temper, and he resurrected their conversations in their entirety. He swore softly to himself. *Why in the hell couldn't he control his thoughts anymore?*

The wheel cut into his back, and Ben shifted slightly, the movement slicing into his reverie. He had managed most of the day sitting up, but the irons so restricted his movements he was never entirely comfortable. He tried to turn again, but the iron bracelet on his right wrist pulled him back. He noticed that the day was already fading, the sun almost hidden now behind the tall trees, and the various shades of gold and pink and orange had started their battle for dominance of the evening sky.

The beauty made his own emptiness even greater. There was the humiliation of failure, a feeling he had not experienced in years. And there was that instinctive knowledge that Sean had anticipated his every move. He even had the uncomfortable thought that Sean had in some way planned the whole thing. Did Sean really know him that well?

And there was Sean's anger.... Even if he had, as Ben now suspected, set things in motion, Sean's anger had been real—Ben knew that as well as he knew anything. It was totally out of character for Sean to be deliberately cruel, and yet he had seen flashes of it last night and again today. This insane situation was bringing out the worst in both of them.

There was the thought of a prison camp. Certain now. No one knew, not even Sean, the phobia he had about being locked up. One of his governesses had locked him in a dark closet when he was very small. It created a claustrophobia that had been with him since. It was one of the reasons he had hated the sea. He could barely tolerate the confinement of a ship, even with the sun and stars above him. And now...

To hell with it, he thought. To hell with everything. He squirmed his way down into a lying position. The pain in his leg and the bitterness of failure had kept him awake last night. He cradled his head on one of the blankets and drifted off into a listless sleep trying, but not quite succeeding, to keep a number of ghosts from haunting his succession of dreams.

Chapter Fourteen

Sean wished more than ever that he had persuaded his sister to leave several months ago. But he, too, had been hungry for family and had quickly come to treasure the growing relationship with his sister, whom he had thought lost to him. Ryan had been like a beam of sunlight and just as elusive. She could be giggling one moment, curiously adult the next, but always brimming with a joy and generosity that touched everyone. Before Ben's arrival they had talked frequently about their family, Sean telling stories that Ryan had been too young to remember. He would play the guitar his father had made for him and sing the old Irish ballads Michael Mallory used to love. The entire camp, except for the guards up in the valley walls, would sit and listen as the two voices, brother and sister, joined in a wry ditty and then moved on to a sorrowful "Barbara Allen."

But if she had enriched his life, he felt he was cheating Ryan of hers. She was twenty-one now and growing older in a place and time where there was little chance for romance and love. Despite his earlier fears, he halfway hoped she would fall in love with one of his young officers. It hadn't happened. She treated each with a quiet fondness, more like a younger brother than a prospective beau.

And then Morgan was literally dropped in the middle of them. Ben Morgan, whom Sean had loved and hated, and who was now, more than ever, his enemy.

From the first time he saw them together—Ben still unconscious and Ryan gently sponging his face—Sean had felt a nagging fear. He saw the bond that grew rapidly between the two as Ben's strength returned. He watched as they talked for hours; he knew she was telling Ben things she had never before put into words, and he felt a strange jealousy as well as anger. He wanted Ryan to love and be loved, but not by Morgan.

He looked at his sister now. She had, at his insistence, moved her things from the wagon into his tent; he didn't want her close to Morgan. He had transferred his own personal belongings to the wagon. It still amazed him that she always looked so pretty and fresh. He felt a surge of tenderness. Her dark brown eyes, usually sparkling, were blank. The inherent joy within her was missing. He missed the spirit that so often both annoyed and challenged him.

"You feel betrayed, don't you?" he asked unexpectedly.

She sat there for a minute without answering. She knew how he felt about Morgan. He had warned her off from the very beginning. She also knew him well enough to realize there had to be a reason beyond the war. "Yes," she said finally. "I thought he was beginning to care.... I thought I—we—were beginning to understand each other."

"And he disappointed you?"

"Yes." It was a small despairing cry. "He knew he was risking your life, Jimmy's...Justis's. We helped him. We saved his life. We took care of him...and he, he..." She couldn't say the words.

"He kept reminding you, and me, too, that saving him was your idea, not his," he said with a wry smile.

Ryan stared at him, surprised at his reasonableness. Even angered at it. She was not ready to be mollified.

Sean got up slowly and took her hand, easing her up from the chair. "Let's go for a walk."

He put his arm around her shoulders and they left the tent, walking to a clearing above the stream. She sat, staring blankly at the water, which reflected the soft golden hue of a setting sun.

"What is it between you two?" She had asked the question before without results, but she knew, somehow, that tonight would be different.

He hesitated a moment. It seemed important, suddenly, that she understand the peculiar relationship between Ben and himself. He realized that everything had gone too far, that she would keep probing until she had her answer.

"It's a long story," he said slowly. "I guess it really started in Texas. There wasn't much of a school where we lived, and Pa wanted, more than anything else, for me to have an education. They didn't have any money, not enough to send me away. He tutored me himself, but he wanted more for me. And I did, too. I didn't want to grub all my life on a small ranch, working from sunrise to moonset and past." He looked at her again, his mouth forming that quick ironic smile he sometimes had. "It's funny," he said, "I can't think of anything better now."

After a moment of silent thought, he continued. "He had served under General Houston and was able with his help to get me an appointment to West Point." Sean looked down at the water, remembering his father's pride when Sean had passed the examination and received the letter of acceptance.

"They didn't have any money for store-bought clothes, and Ma spent weeks making me a suit. I was as proud as only an eighteen-year-old can be, embarking on a great new adventure. It was short-lived once I got east and met some of my soon-to-be classmates. There was a group of them on the packet to West Point. I became the object of their amusement when they learned I was going to the Point. My clothes were not exactly fashionable, and they started making loud jokes. I took exception and swung at the leader."

The ironic smile was back again. "The only way I knew how to fight was Texas-style. Anything goes. So," he said, bitter amusement in his voice, "I let everything go. I was quickly informed it was not the gentleman's way and was beaten pretty badly by a gang of them. That was my introduction to West Point.

"It didn't get better," Sean continued, the amusement gone, the voice tense. "I was an oddity, both Irish and Texan, neither of which were held in high regard by either the Easterners or Southerners. They assigned roommates according to alphabetical ranking of the last names. Mallory and Morgan. So there we were—the Boston blue blood and the Texas ruffian.

"Ben tried to be friendly, but I wouldn't have any part of it. By then I didn't trust any of them nor did I care to be a part of what I thought was snobbish arrogance. I rebuffed his every effort at friendship, only accidently discovering that he was heir to a large shipbuilding family in Boston. That made me even more wary.

"As for me, I was a pariah. And I didn't care. I didn't like my classmates any more than they liked me. But they went further. They decided to get me out. My uniforms would be suddenly soiled just before inspection, the boots would be muddied after I spent hours polishing them. Legs would stick out on parade, causing me to trip and fall out of formation. It seems I spent the entire first year on punishment tours. But I was damned if I was going to let the bastards win.

"Ben never took part and even tried, in his own quiet way, to stop it. I once overheard him warning one of his friends that any more 'incidents' against me would be ones against him. I probably should have been grateful, but I wasn't. I was young, and I was proud, and I damn well could take care of myself. I told him to mind his own business.

"From then on, I did everything I could to best him. I boxed better—" Sean's eyes suddenly twinkled. "Yes, I did learn the rules...rode better, studied harder. Everything seemed to become a contest between us. He was never anything but increasingly polite. I hated that politeness more than I hated the taunts from the others."

Sean stopped talking. He stared into the wood beyond the stream, lost for a moment in his own memories. He shook them off and turned back to Ryan. "You see, Kitten, you come by your stubbornness naturally."

"Go on," Ryan said impatiently. "What happened?"

"We were swimming one night across the river—on a wager. It was late October, and the water was like ice. It was a stupid thing to do, but I was always trying to prove something. It was just Ben and I, and everyone in the academy had bets on one of us. Most of the blue-bloods were backing Ben, the mavericks me. Halfway across I got a cramp and started to go under. Ben was just behind me. He dragged me across the lake, almost drowning himself. Someone jumped in and pulled both of us out.

"It's damned hard to hate someone who has just saved your life, particularly at the possible expense of his own. That happened our first year. For the next three we became inseparable. He became the brother I never had. I think I was the same to him. We still competed in almost everything, but it was a friendly kind of competition."

Sean stopped, wanting to find the right words. He no longer smiled.

"In our senior year, we met Melody Bryan. She had just moved up from South Carolina with her mother. She was beautiful. Coal-black hair and eyes like perfect emeralds. They were very low on funds, although they seemed like they once had money. Their clothes, though well mended, were stylish, and they wore them like royalty. Before long, every cadet at West Point was pounding on the door, but the only two she encouraged were Ben and myself. It took me a while to realize it, but she delighted in playing each of us against the other. I suppose it gave her a sense of power to watch us fight over her.

"And we did...for several months. She had eyes that begged for affection and lips made for kissing. She had a way of making you feel like the most wonderful person on earth. Ben and I finally discussed it and decided not to let it interfere in our friendship. We would let her decide. The other would step out gracefully.

"Melody didn't want it that way. She wanted both of us, and she wanted us at each other's throats. She lied constantly, telling one of us one thing, the other something else. She would make an engagement with both of us an hour apart and then say she forgot and deliberate on which one she would allow to stay. I finally decided I wanted no more of it.

"I was lucky, Ryan. I had a good example. Ma and Pa. They taught me that love is based on giving, not taking. Ben didn't have that. He had never had much love from his family... and he hungered for it like a starving man. It made him easy prey for Melody. He was in love, totally, completely in love for the first time, and that was all that mattered. He and Melody were engaged and were to be married the week after graduation. I had misgivings but Ben was so damn happy I just left it alone. Then two days before graduation, she sent someone for me, said it was urgent, that it concerned Ben. When I arrived at her rooming house, her mother was gone and Melody was, well, not exactly dressed for male company.

"She told me she loved me, that she would go away with me. She didn't really love Ben, she said, she just wanted the security he represented—a big house, money, position. But she would give it all up for me." Sean laughed, a tight unamused sound. "By then, you couldn't pay me to take her. She couldn't stand the fact that someone saw through her, didn't want her. It was...I don't know, some kind of sickness. I tried to leave, and she asked me to make love to her. I slapped her then, called her what I thought she was and left.

"I was going to tell Ben that night, but he had pulled special duty and apparently left to see Melody from there. Melody gave him her version of our meeting. She said I came uninvited, that I raped her. She showed him a torn dress and a bruise on her face. I can see those tears now, flooding huge helpless eyes." Sean's voice was full of disgust.

"It worked. Ben came back to the room and demanded an explanation. I tried to talk to him, to tell him what had happened, but it was too late. He had chosen to believe her. He called me every name there is, and then hit me. I hit back and suddenly everything was out of control. We had boxed together and were usually evenly matched, but not that night. He was possessed with a fury I had never seen before. I really think he would have killed me if some of the cadets hadn't pulled him off."

Sean was silent for several minutes. Ryan could hear the anger and rigidity in his voice. She felt his loss and knew with certainty that the emotional cost had been much greater than the physical.

Finally, he continued softly. "I never saw Ben Morgan again, not until you brought him in that day. I was sent to the hospital with several broken ribs and was there during graduation ceremonies. He and Melody were gone by the time I was released. I've heard about him, of course—West Point has an incredibly reliable grapevine. I knew when he was promoted and where he was posted. I knew he had married Melody and that she was with him in Kansas briefly. That's it. I never heard anything else about her. Ben built a reputation for ruthlessness. I ran across more than several officers who actually hated him. I have to admit, though, I didn't care much for most of them. Ben never suffered fools lightly. Apparently he doesn't suffer them at all, anymore."

He turned around and looked at Ryan. "Now my nosy little Kitten, you know everything I do."

But Ryan had slowly sunk to the ground, as if someone had hit her in the stomach. She had realized as her brother spoke how deep the hurt was between himself and Ben. With the reality came unbearable pain, knifing into her heart, tearing at her senses. So much agony caused by one person. And then she hated, hated as she had never hated before, that unknown woman who had caused it all. She had nearly destroyed Ben and had taken much that was dear from Sean. She couldn't halt the rage that flooded her entire being at that person, nor the pity that followed it. Pity for Ben. For Sean.

"Now I know what he meant," she whispered, remembering what Ben had said several days ago. Her voice was so soft Sean had to lean down to hear. "He said his wife was dead, that he wasn't sorry she was. He said it with such bitterness." She shook her head to rid it of the image.

Sean reached his hand to her, pulled her up and wrapped his long arms around her, holding her tightly, feeling her pain. At that moment, he had never felt so close to another person. She was hurting because others were hurting, and he loved her all the more for that compassion and understanding. He said nothing, knowing she needed to work it out herself.

She finally pulled back and looked up at him. "I understand so much I didn't before," she said. "I can guess just a little how you must feel. I'm sorry. I've gone my own thoughtless way and never thought what you might be feeling."

Sean quieted her with a glance. "It's not your fault, Ryan. It's not his. Not mine. We just happened to all come together at a very bad time. It's no easier for him. In fact, I suspect it's much worse. It would be for me."

"He's so lonely, Sean," she said with an insight he hadn't suspected. "He doesn't know it or won't accept it. But he is, and now I know why, and I hate her. Even if she's dead, I hate her."

Sean looked down at the face he knew so well. The eyes were clouded with tears and the face was fierce, as fierce as any mother bear protecting her own. He felt an acute sense of loss. It was obvious now, at least to him, that she was in love with Morgan, and he couldn't help but feel that it would end in tragedy and destroy the three of them.

But he couldn't stand her pain, the anger and confusion that racked the slender body.

He quickly made a decision and tipped her head up so her eyes met his in the moonlight.

"There's something else, Ryan," he said. "I was at the corral last night because I thought Ben would try to escape."

She was puzzled. "I don't understand."

"I was sure he would try it. I knew he was awake when you and I were talking the other night. I hoped it might convince him to give me his parole yesterday. It didn't."

He studied her intently, his eyes willing her to understand what he was trying to say. "I don't think he's for you, Ryan, for a number of reasons, some of which I just tried to explain. But I don't think you should feel betrayed. Ben Morgan's a career soldier, a damn good one. It was his duty to escape, just like it would have been mine. And I certainly wouldn't relish a prison camp any more than he does." Sean hesitated a moment, then continued. "I knew what he was going to do because I would have done the same thing myself."

"Then why," she asked, her voice trembling, "were you so angry this morning?"

Sean's face clouded. She would ask the one question he couldn't answer. "I don't know," he said thoughtfully. "I wish I could tell you. Perhaps I was hoping against hope he wouldn't try it, but I had to find out and I had to find out when I was expecting it."

He looked straight into her eyes. "Maybe it was because of what he did to Justis. Maybe it was because he was forcing me to do something I didn't want to do. I didn't want to use the chains. I know how proud he is, and how he treasures his freedom. But I can't let him go. Every man here has a rope with his name on it now. I can't give them less than everything I have. The only thing I can do," he said tightly, "is make escape so impossible that he'll give me his parole."

"And if he doesn't?"

Sean's face was bleak. "There's no other choice. He's not leaving me any."

"There's still something strong between you two, isn't there?" she said suddenly.

"There are some things that can never be erased," Sean replied. "No matter how much you want them gone. I told him I considered my debt to him paid. I don't. I never will. I'm standing here now, tonight, because of him. I can't forget that, not for a moment.

"But then," he added, "I also can't forget that night before graduation. My friend, my best friend, the person I thought knew me better than I did myself called me a rapist and almost killed me."

He looked away from her, to the water's edge. "Those two images keep clashing. I can't separate them anymore. I guess that's really why I was angry. I can't be logical about him."

Sean felt her arm go around him, and she leaned her head against his shoulder. He felt her unspoken understanding and appreciated her silence. There was really no way she could help, nothing she could say that would make things better.

After several minutes he broke the silence. "I will tell you this," he said. "I don't think he would have gone straight to the authorities. I think he would have been 'lost' for a while and then had trouble finding his way back. He would have eventually led them back here, make no mistake about that, but not before we had ample time to pack up and leave.

"Now," he said with a small smile, "does that make you feel better?"

"Does it you?"

He shook his head. "You're much too perceptive," he said. "Let's go back."

She went in front of him. She didn't want him to see the tears that wouldn't stop coming.

It was late when they walked back. Most of the camp was already asleep. There were a few restless soldiers still awake, one playing a harmonica softly, another two crouched near the fire playing cards. Sean took Ryan to the tent and left her.

The sky was clear, and Sean sniffed the clean fresh air appreciatively. It would be cool again tonight, but he was ready for it and knew they would be gone before the weather worsened. He lit a cigar and, feeling a need for a drink, walked over to the wagon, where Ryan still kept the medicinal supplies. He was startled to see Morgan awake and sitting up.

Sean started for the back of the wagon without saying anything when something pulled him back. Perhaps, he thought, it was the memories he had invoked tonight, perhaps curiosity. Whatever it was, it had a stranglehold on him, and he stood for a moment, uncertain about what to do as Ben watched him, his dark eyes carefully blank.

Sean remained there awkwardly, considering the man who was once his best friend. For some inexplicable reason, he found himself unable to leave. "Cigar?" he asked finally.

Ben nodded, accepting the cigar Sean pulled from his shirt pocket, and he sniffed it with interest and appreciation. His face didn't change expression as he noted evenly, "One of mine."

"The spoils of war," Sean answered with a small smile.

The irony of the statement did not escape Ben. They had sometimes argued, years ago, the practical and ethical aspects of war, of sacking—the practice of ancient armies to plunder captured cities.

Ben had defended the practice, pointing out that it had left the defeated peoples demoralized and unable to mount new attacks. Sean, on the other hand, took the ethical argument—the basic right of civilians to protection. The arguments had sometimes continued long into the night, neither altogether convinced by the other.

Ben's mouth twisted into a small grimace. It had been easy enough to argue then. Now it would not be so simple. He had seen too much misery, too many farms laid to waste, too many people hungry, too many good animals slaughtered. He chewed hard on the tip of the cigar and waited patiently as Sean leaned down and lit it. He took a long draw and returned his eyes to Sean, looking for answers.

Sean eyed him with suspicion, his glance traveling over the hard face, the strong compact body resting against the wheel, the right wrist held closely to the spoke and finally to Ben's legs. The left was stretched straight by the splints, the right was bent at the knee as far as the ankle chain would allow. He looked tired, and Sean felt a momentary surge of sympathy. It was not a feeling he welcomed.

"Why don't you get some sleep?" he said suddenly.

Ben laughed, a short bitter sound. "Your hospitality and accommodations lack something in comfort," he answered, his eyes now veiled.

"Deserving when a guest tries to sneak off in the middle of the night without paying the bill," Sean retorted.

The moonlight played on an unwilling smile that pulled at Morgan's mouth. "You, at least, haven't changed. Never without an answer."

Sean eyed him coldly. "I would enjoy what few comforts you have now if I were you," he said, suddenly vicious. "It's going to get worse." He turned to leave but was stopped by Ben's low voice. "Sean . . ." There was a silence. Reluctantly, Ben started again. "Sean . . ."

The Reb captain turned and studied his prisoner. In that moment, the good memories, unbidden, flooded him: the two of them drinking together after passing exams, the nights they had explored their masculinity at sporting houses, the night Ben had saved his life, the easy companionship they had shared.

"How's your leg?" he asked suddenly, surprising even himself.

"Complaining bitterly about my mistreatment of it," Ben said grimly. "It's getting even."

There was a pause. "Would a drink help?"

"Like old times?" Ben's voice was mocking, yet Sean knew instinctively that the same memories that troubled him were there with Ben.

"No," Sean replied bluntly. "Not like old times. It will never be like old times. There is only here and now. You know that better than I."

The mockery was gone when Ben answered. "Yes," he said slowly, surprising Sean, "a drink would help."

Sean climbed into the back of the wagon and reappeared in several minutes with a bottle of Ryan's medicinal whiskey and two tin cups. Morgan noted instantly that his gun was gone from its holster.

Sean saw his quick measuring glance, and his eyes flared. "Forget it," he said. "I'm not making the mistake of underestimating you. The key to the leg irons is also inside."

Sean called the guard over. "Bobby, get our guest here some more blankets, then you're relieved. I'll wake your relief when I'm ready."

Wilson scowled and left, returning almost immediately with several blankets, throwing them beside Morgan with no little anger.

Ben looked at Sean, a question on his face.

"His kid brother was killed in Virginia," Sean said curtly. "I understand you were there."

Ben sat silently as Sean sank to the ground and sprawled out. The Reb opened the bottle and poured healthy amounts into each cup, handing one to Morgan. They sat there quietly, savoring the fiery drink and thinking their own thoughts. Each was reminded of the years when they used to drink together, never feeling the need to talk. It was different now. They were both wary of the other, and anger and regret leadened the silence.

Both finished the first cup almost at the same time. Sean poured another, then asked softly, "What happened to Melody?"

Morgan's eyes, visible from the bright moon, turned empty. His hand tightened around the cup. When he looked at Sean, his face was ravaged.

"I owe you that, anyway. She's dead. She died trying to abort a child. It wasn't mine."

Despite himself, Sean felt a stab of pain for his old friend. He, more than anyone, knew the intensity with which Ben had loved Melody. He knew Ben's pride, as deep as his own, and knew that last betrayal had robbed him of it. He was beginning to understand how and why Bennett Morgan had changed so much, and how he had earned the merciless reputation that followed him from command to command.

Ben was continuing, almost unaware of Sean's presence. He remembered the days he first courted Melody, the joy he felt when she agreed to be his wife. How quickly, he thought, he had been drained of it.

"I thought I was the luckiest man alive," he said, his voice low and ragged. "It turned out you were.

"Melody never wanted anything from me but money, a life she conjured in her mind. I took her to my first posting in Kansas. I was so damned foolishly happy that they had family quarters. She resisted, but I just thought it was fear of the unknown. I thought once we arrived, she would settle in and be happy. After we were there two months, I came back from patrol one day and found her, her clothes and all my money missing. A sergeant was missing with her."

Ben was unable to tell Sean of those two months. The ugly scenes, the accusations, the final taunt she had thrown at him the night before she left. *"You could never make any woman happy."* It had been money, always money she wanted. And Boston and a big house. When she couldn't have that, she didn't want him.

He continued slowly. "She just seemed to disappear for several months, then ended up at my family's home in Boston. She was six months pregnant. She told my father about the 'hardships' in Kansas and begged to stay. She charmed him just as she always charmed everyone—when she wanted to. She stayed until the baby was born, and then she disappeared again, leaving the baby behind. She turned up a year later to claim the baby. My father paid her ten thousand dollars to leave young Avery with him.

"He didn't hear anything else until he received a call from a hospital where she was dying of gangrene from a botched abortion. They found his name among her belongings. He had been a substantial benefactor to the hospital. She was already dead when he arrived there. My father hired a private detective and found out she had been the mistress of a highly regarded businessman. He shut off the inquiry." Ben's bitterness was open. "I even think he enjoyed telling me about it."

Sean looked at Morgan dispassionately, seeing him objectively for the first time since his early days in camp. Deep hard lines were etched across his face, and there was no trace of that wry unexpected humor that used to startle people and draw them, almost unconsciously, to him. Morgan's eyes were still penetrating, searching, but the compassion, which had once been their most interesting quality, was gone. Sean could easily imagine how Ben Morgan had reached colonel so rapidly. He had simply poured all his considerable fury and energy into war.

"And your son?"

Ben's face lightened for the first time. "He is the one good thing that came out of that marriage. He stayed with me in Washington this spring, and we finally got to know each other. I think part of me rejected him over the years because of his mother. That's another regret. I have more than a few of those," he said, glancing at Sean.

"Avery was really raised by my sister, Charlotte, although she was just a kid herself when he was born. Thank God, he got some love when he was growing up. He got none from me, and except for Charlotte there was precious little in that house."

Ben was talking more to himself than to Sean; words poured out that had not been spoken before. Sean realized it was a kind of cleansing, partly brought on by the whiskey, and he remained silent. This was no time to let his feelings about Ben become any more complicated than they already were. He wondered what had prompted him to offer Morgan a drink and to invite his confidences. He couldn't afford to relax his guard; he didn't want to renew a friendship that had proved so fragile, yet here he was, partially doing just that. He didn't understand it but couldn't deny the compulsion that kept drawing him to Morgan. He cursed himself for a fool.

Sean was startled when Ben changed the subject abruptly. He looked over at him, his eyebrows arched in a question.

Ben repeated himself. "You knew what I was going to do last night." It was more a statement than a question.

"Yes," Sean said simply.

"You planned it that way. Because of Ryan."

"Partly."

"You bastard," Ben said, but there was little rancor in his voice, only acceptance.

"I took no pleasure in it. You should know that. But Ryan doesn't realize the stakes, not altogether. She knows about your orders, but I don't think she totally accepts what they mean. When you turned down my offer of parole, I knew it was only a matter of time. I knew you would try to escape—I had to be here when you did. I just sped things up a little." He looked off into the woods. "And she would never have accepted those irons if you hadn't proved they were necessary."

Ben leaned back with a small mirthless laugh. "You *have* changed, Cowboy. You never used to be this devious. Tell me, could you always read me this well?"

Sean was silent, not willing to tell Ben that it was because they were so much alike in some ways.

Instead, he refilled the cups. Both were beginning to feel the effects of the whiskey as well as the personal battles in which they were engaged.

Ben broke the silence. "Ryan isn't nearly as naive as you would like to think. I think she realizes very well what's happening, what's going to happen. She just doesn't choose to let you know she knows it. She knows you want to protect her. She's letting you do it."

Sean thought to himself that Ben was probably right. He had consistently underestimated his sister. He couldn't shake the image of her as a seven-year-old child. He still couldn't quite accept the grown-up version as real.

Sean suddenly asked the question that was so much on his mind. "What do you think of Ryan?"

Morgan looked at him thoughtfully, then said with care, "She's a very unusual girl. I think everyone here is in love with her."

"Do you put yourself in that category?" Sean pressed.

"I don't have any right to," Ben answered.

"I'm glad you understand that," Sean said, hostility creeping back into his voice. "Surprised, maybe, but thoroughly in agreement."

The edge in Sean's voice irritated Ben. "You wouldn't approve?" he baited his adversary.

"No." The answer was explosively angry.

Ben was silent. He couldn't blame Sean for his anger. There wasn't much to commend him as a contender for Ryan's future. He took another sip and leaned his head against the wagon rim.

Sean searched his face, finding the mask tightly back in place. "Ryan," he said finally, "doesn't see a thunderstorm, she sees the life that springs from it and the rainbow that follows. She delights in a desert flower no one else sees, and she can find beauty in the plainest of objects. There's a joy in her I never want to see wounded or killed."

"And you think I could . . . would do that?"

"Hell, you already have. You've changed, Ben. There's the professional soldier and not much else."

"You're a soldier," Ben retorted.

"But I don't take pleasure in it, and I think you do—at least you take a perverse pleasure in being good at it."

"Perhaps you're right," Ben said wearily. "There's been little else these past years."

Sean braced himself against his increasing empathy. He, too, was sick of the fighting and killing that was so much a part of his profession.

"What in the hell would you do with her, anyway?" he said. "How do you think your family—and friends—would welcome a Texas girl, an Irish one at that, who rode with a Confederate troop? One," he added ironically, "that you were charged with capturing and hanging? I've had a taste of Northern hospitality, remember."

Ben let several minutes go without answering. He wondered why he was even bothering. There was little chance of any kind of future with Ryan. He knew that better than Sean. But the old combativeness that he had always enjoyed with Sean kept him from saying so.

"I don't give a damn what anyone thinks," he answered finally. "You know that as well as anyone. And I burned my bridges in Boston a long time ago. If I ever go back, it will be only long enough to get my son."

Sean jumped at the last sentence. "Your son, then... What will he think?"

Ben leaned back and closed his eyes briefly. When he opened them, there was a sad wistfulness there, a look Sean had never seen before.

"You mentioned Ryan and rainbows. Avery's a lot like that. He and Ryan are so similar it's almost frightening. Neither of them see the ugly things in the world, or, if they do, they let the good eclipse them."

He looked at Sean, willing him to believe his next words. "I hurt Avery. I hurt him badly for many years. I won't do that to Ryan."

"You might not mean to," Sean answered quietly. "But she's very vulnerable right now. She's lost not one family, but two. Her home is gone, and everything she's known or loved."

"There's you."

"I'm afraid that's not enough," Sean said. "Not now." He was quiet for a moment, weighing his own thoughts, considering the problem that Ben's presence had created.

He suddenly wanted to hurt Ben. "Besides," he said coldly, "your immediate future is rather bleak. You're going to be a prisoner for the rest of the war—and there's a lot of fight left in the South."

"That's if you get back," Ben said just as roughly. "There's a hell of a lot of Union troops between you and your lines."

"Oh, we will get back, Ben," Sean retorted softly. "You can bet on it."

"And then what?" Ben asked cautiously. "Andersonville?"

Sean's eyes met his steadily. "No," he said. "Fort Scott in Texas."

Ben recalled the name. It had been a military prison before the war, holding most of the deserters and other military prisoners from throughout the West. The Rebs had taken it over when Texas seceded, and a year later it had been converted into a prison camp for Northern officers. It did not have the fearsome reputation of other prisons in the South; it was, however, located in Indian country and considered nearly escapeproof.

"The commander there is a friend of mine," Sean said. "Matt Andrews is a good officer and a fair man. You'll be safe enough there, but you'll be out of the war. For good. No one escapes from Scott."

He poured the last of the whiskey into the two glasses. Both were silent now; the talk of Scott had emphasized the division between them.

Ben had unconsciously changed the cup from his left hand to the right, forgetting the chain. As he started to raise the cup, the chain abruptly ended the movement, and the whiskey splashed on the ground.

Sean looked at him with a mocking smile. "It's not like you to waste good whiskey."

Ben felt sudden anger. He reached his chained wrist to its limit. "Is this really necessary?" he challenged Sean. He looked down toward his legs and the bands around them. "I'm obviously not going anyplace."

"I'm going to make quite sure you don't," Sean retorted. Then, softly, "You can always give me your parole."

Ben thought about it seriously for the first time. It was unexpectedly tempting. His body was already sore from the lack of movement imposed by the physical restrictions. It was also obvious to him now that he had little or no chance to escape with the chains. Yet . . . giving his parole meant surrender, meant giving up any chance at all. It meant being docilely led to prison. And he couldn't quite force himself to do it. Not yet. And not to Sean.

He looked at Sean. "No," he said quietly.

"Then you stay as you are. I'm not taking any chances with you. I know you too well and you can do too much damage to my plans." Sean stood up, took the two cups and threw them into the back of the wagon. He looked over again at Ben. "The offer's open. Anytime." He woke the relief guard who silently trod over and took up his vigil.

Sean climbed into the back of the wagon and stretched out; sleep, aided by the whiskey, came almost immediately. Outside, Ben Morgan remained seated as he watched the few clouds chase each other across the star-studded sky, each one briefly shading the moon and casting oddly shaped shadows across the now silent camp.

Chapter Fifteen

The coolness of the night was gone the next morning. Morgan woke to find a pink haze framing the valley wall and the sun a bright fireball as it began its ascent. His head felt dull, his mouth dry and his stomach unsettled by the whiskey of the night before. The smells from the main camp fire drifted over to him and, despite the disquiet lingering from the conversation with Sean, he felt the first stirrings of hunger. He had eaten little the day before.

More than anything, though, he wanted some cold water. His mouth felt like cotton, and he could almost feel the stubble on his face from two days without shaving. Just getting clean again would help immensely. He looked over to his morning guard. He had seen the soldier before, but he was not one who had previously guarded him. It was impossible to tell his rank; the uniforms were all pieced together, many of them in tatters. There were few insignias of any kind.

"Water?" he asked finally. It was a question he hated, an admission of his dependence. He said it with a growl.

The guard, who had been seated, rose lazily to his feet. "You can have some to drink, not to wash," he answered. He called over to another soldier and asked him to fetch a cup of drinking water.

Morgan looked at him with surprise mixed with anger. He had never before been refused water for washing or shaving. They had, in fact, been obliging about providing whatever he needed.

"I don't understand," he said. It was a question.

"Cap'n's orders," the man said. "You'll have to ask him."

"I'll do that," Morgan muttered bitterly under his breath. He felt the painful disappointment rising; he had thought he and Sean had reached a certain understanding—if not a renewal of friendship—last night. Apparently they had not.

He took the offered cup of water, sipped at it thirstily but saved a few drops to splash on his face. It felt cool and refreshing, but he rubbed the stubble of his growing beard with distaste.

He gave the cup back and watched the movement in camp. It was busier than usual; an aura of anticipation was alive in the air.

Morgan looked for Ryan, but neither she nor her dog were visible. He wondered if she had taken an early morning ride or whether she was continuing to avoid him. Then he saw her standing at the camp fire and watched as she carried two plates and cups toward him. He was immediately aware of his appearance: unkempt and dirty... and chained like a disobedient dog. He turned his face away, the muscles tightening in his cheeks.

She seemed not to notice as she stooped down and waited until his glowering face turned back toward her. Ignoring his hostile expression, she held out a plate patiently until he finally, reluctantly, decided to take it. She sat next to him, her legs crossed, her hands balancing her own breakfast.

"May I join you?"

He looked at her, a scowl still in place. "No."

It was immediately apparent that his answer meant little. Ryan stayed, her slight smile warming him with unexpected impact. "I told you before I wasn't easily bullied."

"Or discouraged," he muttered under his breath.

Ryan caught the words and grinned. "Not that, either," she retorted.

"Where's Fortune?" he said abruptly, changing the subject.

"I think he went to catch his own breakfast. He likes to prove to himself he can."

A muscle in his jaw twitched. He identified with the dog's independence.

His thought was quickly interrupted. "Sean told me you saved his life at West Point," she said abruptly. "I want to thank you. I don't think I could have borne losing him, too."

"What else did he tell you?"

She shrugged. "Not much."

He visibly winced, knowing she lied. He realized she probably knew much of the story, including Melody and that painful night before graduation. He didn't know if she knew the full bitter ending. Probably not. Even Sean had not known until late last night. He had thought the memory of Melody and the pain she had caused, would lessen in time, but it had remained a nagging ache that never entirely left him.

Ryan watched his face as his eyes clouded and his jaw tightened.

"Is it so hard to talk about?" she asked gently. "I'm a good listener."

He forced a small smile, trying to keep the old images at bay. "It was a long time ago, Ryan." His smile suddenly became real as he repeated her name slowly. "Ryan." He savored the sound of it. "It's an unusual name."

"It was my mother's family name," Ryan replied, holding mixed feelings about the change of subject. She was disappointed he still didn't trust her but relieved at his lightning change of mood. "She was Margaret Ryan, and she was the last of her family. It was decided to pass the name on through me."

They stopped talking then, both of them paying attention to their breakfast of biscuits and steaks. Sean had ordered the slaughter of several cattle he kept in the valley. It was a welcome break from the usual corn bread and bacon. The coffee was very strong and bitter, and Ben welcomed the taste on his still thick tongue.

Frustration came, however, when he tried to cut the steak. The plains cattle was tough, and his chained right wrist didn't have the flexibility to cut it. When he tried, the plate went skidding out of reach.

Ryan couldn't miss the shame and anger that flickered over his face before it went blank again.

She ached for him but knew she couldn't show it. Pity was the last thing he needed, or wanted, now.

"I think," she said slowly, very carefully, "Cook did not do a very good job. It still seems to be kicking."

She was rewarded with a small rueful smile. "It might do with a bit more taming," he replied. "How are you with mavericks?"

Ryan grinned. "Between Sean and you and this whole bunch here, I'm an expert."

She reached over and took the plate, quickly cutting the tough beef into small pieces, ignoring the frustration that was so obvious on his face.

"I've never realized how clumsy one can be with only a left hand," he said softly, thinking of those men he had seen on the battlefield and in field hospitals who had lost a leg or arm permanently.

"It's so damn frustrating," he continued, unexpectedly putting his feelings into words. "I keep reaching out with it only to find it jerked back." There was a certain black humor in the words.

"At least it's not permanent," she said, again giving him the uncanny feeling that she had read his thoughts. She let a moment lapse, then added quietly, "We'll be moving out of here before long. Have patience."

The thought did nothing to lighten Ben's mood. Leaving here would probably mean losing Ryan. Would she be going with Sean?

He just nodded, but Ryan sensed his reluctance.

"It seems you were in an all-fire hurry to leave the other night."

"It just seemed a good idea at the time," he said noncommittally. "It obviously wasn't."

She studied him intently. "Would you have headed for the Fort and brought troops back?"

"What did Sean say?"

"He said you would probably have given us time to get away."

Ben's face showed his surprise. He hadn't expected Sean to admit such a thing to Ryan, not with his adamant opposition to any relationship between the two of them. He took a bite of biscuit and chewed it thoughtfully. "Don't ask me questions I can't answer," he said finally. "I don't know what I would have done. I really didn't think that far ahead."

"I don't believe you," Ryan said. "I think you always know what you're doing and that you're always several steps ahead of yourself and most everyone else."

"Obviously not Sean," he replied. He was angry, more at himself than anyone else. He was increasingly troubled by his growing attachment to the girl next to him. "All right," he said bitingly. "You want to know. I'll tell you. I have my orders. I would have ridden like the Furies to Fort Wilson, and I would have gotten every man I could find to come back with me." He turned back to his breakfast without looking at her.

Her eyes didn't change, but a smile played around her lips. "You expect me to stamp off in horror."

He turned back to her, his face a study in confusion. "Something like that," he finally admitted wryly. "It obviously didn't work. Would you mind telling me why?"

"It just wasn't that convincing," she replied tartly.

Their eyes met and held. His were lighter than usual and much like the intense velvet blue of a vivid sky at twilight, she thought fancifully. They were surprisingly expressive, full of startled perception at the strong currents that flowed so easily between them.

It was Ryan who broke the spell. She dropped her eyes, trying to rid herself of the swelling waves of emotion that threatened to engulf her. When she finally spoke, her voice was cool.

"Let me check your leg. How does it feel?"

He shrugged, confused and even disappointed at the sudden detachment in her voice. "It still aches a little. Not bad. Just enough to remind me it's there."

It was painful to feel her touch on his leg. He ached to touch her, to hold her, to feel her next to him. His body was rigid as her fingers prodded the leg, feeling the bone gently. Ryan looked at him and smiled.

She started to take his plate and coffee tin but sat down again when his question came. It was sharp, throwing her off balance.

"What's happening?"

"What do you mean?" she answered, deliberately misunderstanding.

"Something's happened or is going to happen. There's so much activity. Is Sean ready to leave?"

Ryan avoided his eyes. "I don't think so, not yet."

"Then what's going on?" He was impatient now. "For God's sake, Ryan, I'm not going anywhere."

"It's none of your affair," she said shortly, her temper rising at the question. It had ruined the mood between them, and she felt strong resentment and quickened apprehension. The coming raid on the Union shipment of rifles would be the most dangerous Sean had made. She couldn't still her fear for him. It had nagged at her for several days.

Morgan's expression went blank, frustrated by the rebuke and the sudden chill that passed over her face. He shrugged, but his eyes showed his anger. He turned away and heard her footsteps move away from him.

It was more and more obvious during the day that something was in progress. He watched as the Westerners slipped from the camp in twos and threes. They had replaced their uniforms with clothing more suitable for hunters or settlers. He never ceased to be amazed at the wide variety of clothing the Texans seemed to have at hand. His admiration for Sean's unique abilities had grown daily; he appeared to have a bottomless hat of rabbits.

Morgan rested his back against the wagon wheel. His guard, he noted, was more alert than usual. He could feel the excitement that ran through the camp. He pulled his right hand away from the wheel and winced as the metal bit into his wrist, silently damning the world around him.

Bobby Wilson hated his guard duty. He felt it a waste of his not inconsiderable talents with the rifle. And he deeply resented the mollycoddling of a damn Yankee.

As far as he was concerned, the Yank colonel should have been left to die. Since he hadn't been, he should have been shot. No prisoners. Those were Captain Mallory's orders, and Wilson lost any respect he had for the captain when he violated his own rules.

His disgust grew as he watched Ryan and the Yank together. Bitch. Slobbering over a Yank the way she was. She hadn't given *him* the time of day, and now she had plenty of time for that blue belly. The only thing that gave him any satisfaction was the ability now to make life as miserable as possible for his prisoner. And he knew how to do that through small humiliations.

Bobby Wilson had never had anyone other than his kid brother. They had grown up in a small Tennessee valley, the only survivors among twelve children born to Caleb and Annie Wilson. The others had been stillborn or had died of neglect or malnutrition during their first year. Wilson had never quite understood how he and his brother had survived.

Their father was a preacher whose gospel was fire and brimstone. There was no mercy or forgiveness in his religion, and there was none in his spirit. He hated everyone and everything and took the worst of it out on his wife and children. They were beaten regularly to cleanse them of the devil. The two boys learned to dread the days he was home from the circuit and would often hide in the woods until he was gone. Their absence, however, made their mother the main scapegoat. Almost always pregnant, she bore her scars with dronelike forbearance. There was no place to go; Caleb would find her.

Caleb was a poor provider. And Bobby and his brother, Jamie, learned early to find their own food. They became expert fishermen, and when they were twelve and ten, Bobby stole a rifle from some travelers going west. He became, out of necessity, an expert hunter and could shoot a squirrel from a distance of two hundred yards.

They would often stay out in the woods for weeks during the summer weather. They came back one day to the sound of screaming. Bobby ran into the cabin and found his father leaning over his mother. Without thinking he had pointed his rifle at the father he hated and fired.

His mother was dead. He and Jamie buried their mother and left their father for scavengers. He didn't deserve their efforts. They left the cabin and Tennessee without a backward look. Bobby was fifteen, Jamie thirteen.

The two boys set out for Texas, far from any law that might be after them, robbing isolated cabins as they went. They joined a group of hunters, but neither had ever learned to get along with others, and they were soon told to leave despite their prowess with firearms.

So they continued on across Texas, rustling a steer now and then, robbing a lone traveler, starting fights in saloons. They never felt the need of company other than themselves.

It ended suddenly when they were arrested in Austin. A man was killed in a fight they'd started, and the two brothers were charged with manslaughter. Now in their early twenties, they were given a choice, prison or enlistment in the new Confederate army. They chose enlistment.

They had found a new purpose in war. Shooting was their one talent. Killing bothered them not at all. For the first time in their lives, they had the respect of other men. Bobby even won the rank of corporal after one battle in which he showed conspicuous bravery. He had no noble motives; he had just enjoyed the killing.

And then came the second battle at Manassas, and Jamie was hit by a minié ball. He took several days to die; Bobby never left his side.

Afterward, Bobby's hatred accelerated. He hated every Yankee, and his courage and marksmanship became legendary. But he was constantly in trouble with authority. He left his unit when he felt like it. He stole from others. He was a constant thorn in the side of his officers.

When Sean's inquiry about men for his new troop reached the army, they quickly recommended Wilson, and Wilson, chafing under what he considered unfair treatment, applied.

Sean's first instinct had been to deny the request, but Wilson's ability with a rifle and his unquestioned courage swayed him.

Bobby was a loner, and made no friends among the others, yet Sean had seldom regretted his selection; Wilson was his best marksman, and the commander knew when and how to use him.

Sean had appointed him Ben's custodian in a moment of anger. He knew almost immediately it was a mistake but didn't feel he could backtrack. Perhaps it would work; at least Wilson wouldn't be susceptible to Ben's quiet persuasion...not like Justis. Sean still puzzled over that. It had been the first time he had ever seen anyone get the best of his wary first sergeant.

The day crept by slowly for Ben Morgan. He had alienated Ryan; Sean completely ignored him; his books had not been returned. And Wilson was, as usual, glowering at him as he sat ten feet away with a gun at ready and fingers obviously itching to use it. He was stiff and sore, and his muscles were cramped. Everything looked hopeless.

His only activity was watching . . . watching and wondering and worrying. Sean was up to something, something that bode little good for the Union.

He didn't relax when Justis approached; he had not spoken to the sergeant since the aborted escape. He still felt a twinge of guilt.

But Justis ignored him and climbed into the wagon, reappearing in seconds with maps clutched in his hand. As Justis got back down out of the wagon, Ben called to him quietly, "Sergeant."

Justis turned around and looked at him, his face noncommittal.

"Sergeant, would you share a cup of coffee with me?" he asked in the same low tone.

Justis was about to refuse until he saw the plea in Morgan's eyes. He looked around for cups and saw none. "Is this some peculiar Yankee way of asking me to fetch some coffee?"

He was unprepared for the quick smile of response. The smile was small, granted, but there was real amusement in it.

"I guess it is," Ben said.

Justis looked over at Wilson. "He giving you a hard time?"

Ben shrugged. It was no use to complain, but he noted the look of disdain Justis gave Wilson. There was no love lost there. It seemed to be a common feeling around the camp. He even had the feeling that Sean regretted his choice of Ben's keeper, but felt committed to it.

Justis made his decision quickly. "I'll be back. I have to get these to the cap'n."

As good as his word, he was soon back with two cups of steaming coffee. He handed one to Ben and sat next to him, knowing that Ben had something he wanted to say.

Ben looked down at his coffee, then up at Justis. "I wish like hell it hadn't been you the other night. I just wanted you to know that."

Justis suddenly grinned. "That's probably the strangest apology I've ever had. It *is* an apology, isn't it?"

Ben's mouth crooked up in a slight smile. "I guess it is. I'm not very good at it. I've been told that before."

"Well, it's good enough for me, Yank," Justis said, now understanding Ryan's attraction to this man. He had an immense charm when he smiled, and it was made stronger by the way he husbanded it. There was also a streak of self-mockery that ran through everything he said. It was a trait that particularly attracted Justis. He did not care for people who took themselves too seriously.

"I hope I didn't get you in too much trouble?" Ben continued.

Justis smiled. "Jest some kidding . . . and that's soon gone."

They drank their coffee without additional words until Justis started to rise.

"What did you do before the war?" Ben asked, wanting to prolong the visit. He was miserably bored—and lonely—even if he did have a hard time admitting it.

"I was a foreman on a ranch in west Texas," Justis replied. "I joined Gen'l Sibley when he went into New Mexico. So did the ranch owner. He was killed at Glorieta Pass. When I got back, the ranch was gone, sold for taxes. I rejoined Sibley when he went east, heard about Cap'n Mallory recruiting Texans for a special unit and volunteered." It was the longest speech he had made about himself in a long time. He wondered why he was making it to Morgan.

"What is it like in West Texas?"

"Dry. Hot. Not very good for cattle. Takes too much land to feed them, near an acre a head. Even without the war, my boss would have been hard-set to last long." He stood, feeling he had already given away too much of himself.

"Thank you, Sergeant," Ben said. "Thank you for the coffee. Thank you for the time."

Justis stepped away quickly, realizing that the Yank's thanks were rare. Damn if he didn't like the man.

Sean was bent over the maps in his tent when Braden came in. Justis had just delivered them.

"The last two men just left," he told his captain. Ten pairs had been sent out to scout the Union supply train: first, to find it, second, to report its progress, and third, to find a place to attack. A pattern of rendezvous sites had been established among the teams. "It's just a matter of waiting now."

Sean nodded. "Keep a particularly alert eye on the prisoner," he told his lieutenant. "We can't afford to lose him now."

"Sam said he's already complaining vocally about not being allowed any water for washing."

"Let him complain," Sean answered shortly. "Just make sure he stays where he is."

"When we leave for the attack . . . ?"

"We'll just have to leave enough troopers here to watch him," Sean replied. "Start thinking about it. It won't be popular. I think every man here wants a chance at that supply train—we've been idle too long."

"What about Wilson? He won't like staying behind."

"No, and we'll probably need him," Sean answered wearily. "Get someone else. Damn. There's no end to it, is there?"

Braden looked at Sean's tired face and wished there was something he could do to lighten the load. "No sir, it doesn't seem so," he said finally, knowing it inadequate. "But at least we'll be heading south again. That's something I think every man here will be glad of."

It was two days later before the first rider reported in. The supply train had been spotted seventy miles to the northeast, traveling slowly with a large escort. Another rider came in later that day, reporting that the train appeared headed for a pass that would serve well for an ambush. At their present speed the wagons would be there in three days' time.

Sean, Braden and two other lieutenants met that evening in the tent. Ryan busied herself outside, consciously staying away from Morgan and the wagon. She spent some time teaching one young Texan to read. She mended another's shirt. One of the soldiers pulled out a harmonica and she hummed softly to its tune, finally breaking out in song. It was a sad melody, one that had floated down from the Eastern seacoasts.

As she finished the tune, Ryan's clear voice trailed off, leaving the plaintive sounds to linger in the night air. Everyone had stopped to listen, even Sean and his lieutenants in the tent. Her voice had a new quality to it, a haunting sadness that affected them all. It filled Morgan with an almost unbearable pain. He realized he had never wanted anything so badly as he wanted Ryan. And realizing that, he suddenly felt relieved from the burden of Melody. He knew then that Melody had been an obsession. There had never been the communication between them that he had with Ryan, the contentment of having her nearby, the gentleness that comes with truly caring about another person. Melody had been a fire in his blood, and he had never looked beyond that.

Sean finished with Braden and the others and fetched Ryan back to the tent. The maps were still stretched out over the camp table.

"It's soon?" she asked fearfully.

He nodded, his eyes full of understanding. "We'll be leaving the day after tomorrow. We should be back in two days. Don't worry, Kitten," he added softly. "We've done this many times."

"Not against so large a force." She had heard the talk.

"They don't know we're still here. We have surprise on our side."

"I know," she whispered. "Don't let anything happen to you. Something always happens to people I love."

He scanned her face, realizing for the first time that she really did feel she might be bad luck. "That's nonsense," he said severely. "You couldn't be unlucky for anyone."

He touched her face, tipping her chin upward, meeting her eyes. "I didn't know how much I missed having a sister until you rode up that day. That was one hell of a shock."

She grinned, remembering his expression. "I didn't think you would let me stay the night."

"I almost didn't. Now I don't know what any of us would have done without you."

She smiled. "I've been happy," she said almost shyly.

"Always be that, Ryan. Always be happy. You were made for that." Sean leaned down and pecked her cheek, turned and left. Ryan quickly undressed and lay down, but sleep evaded her, and she passed the night listlessly, afraid to hope, afraid to think.

Chapter Sixteen

Men continued to filter out of the camp for the next two days. There were constant meetings with Sean in the tent before the small groups would pack their horses and ride out.

It was the second morning when Sean, one of the twenty or so men remaining in the valley, prepared to leave. He silently packed his bags with the distinctive Confederate jacket and some food. He had dressed in the cowboy's uniform, jeans and a worn cotton shirt. He disliked carrying the Southern gray, knowing that it would immediately convict him if discovered. But he also understood the need of maintaining the image of a regular unit. There were too many wandering bands of outlaws robbing for their own benefit and calling themselves Southern patriots.

After saddling his horse, he strode over to Morgan. They looked at each other silently for a moment, Ben waiting for the other to speak.

"I'm sorry we met again this way," Sean said with real regret in his voice. He stooped down and held out his hand; Ben hesitated, then clasped it firmly with his own left one.

"No matter what happens tomorrow," Sean said, "you'll be taken care of. My men have orders to take you to Fort Scott."

There was nothing for Ben to say. He only nodded in acknowledgment.

"No good wishes?" Sean's voice had turned harsh again.

Ben regarded him levelly. "Should I?"

Sean laughed mirthlessly. "You never give an inch, do you?" He turned to leave.

"What about Ryan?"

"She'll stay here—along with about ten of my men. None of them are anxious about nursemaiding you, so I wouldn't do anything foolish if I were you."

Sean didn't wait for an answer. He turned away and hurried over to his horse. He mounted in one long smooth movement and gave Ben a brief mocking salute as he cantered toward the valley entrance.

It was a long afternoon for Ben. The tension hung heavy in the air. No one approached him or spoke to him. His new guard watched him silently, eyes narrowed and face unfriendly. As Sean had predicted, he resented being left behind.

But if the afternoon was bad, the evening was worse. His guard had grown increasingly resentful through the day, and the earlier hostility was replaced by real hatred. Ben was given some cold corn bread and water for dinner, and even that was offered grudgingly.

Morgan watched the sun's descent beyond the valley wall. The sunset was a particularly spectacular one, a vast canvas splattered with various hues of pink and gold, all of which finally erupted into a blood-red sky.

Ryan spent a completely miserable day. After Sean left, she took a book, one of those that circulated around the camp, and Fortune, and went down to her favorite place along the bank of the stream.

She couldn't shake the feeling that she brought bad luck to those people she loved the most. She had lost two sets of parents within thirteen years and had seen many of her friends die in the war or of the fever.

She thought of Sean, her tall golden brother, whose eyes were always full of life and humor. His confidence and strength had made her feel safe again, a feeling she had lacked since her adoptive parents had died a year ago. She said a soft prayer for his safety.

She had wanted desperately to talk to Ben Morgan, to feel again that warmth that always seemed to encompass them. But she felt it would be a betrayal of Sean. He was Sean's enemy and should be hers. But, try as she might, she couldn't shake her thoughts of him nor the heat in her body that accompanied them. The book she had brought was of no help. It was a compilation of religious tracts, which had been sent to one of the Texans by his wife. She allowed herself a moment of amusement as she thought of the recipient, a profane lanky fellow whose tales of conquest and drunks were legendary. His wife had obviously thought he needed some guidance. Ryan had not noted any deep change.

She finally discarded the book as hopeless and leaned against a tree. She basked in the hot sun, enjoying the life around her. She could see the rings in the deep pool as trout surfaced to grab an unsuspecting insect and heard the rustle of trees from the carefree play of squirrels. How she would like to be one right now, jumping from branch to branch with wild abandon.

She wished she could stop thinking of Colonel Morgan, but it was quite impossible. It was as if he had already become a part of her. Why did her heart start pounding when she whispered his name, or her body grow warm at the thought of him? *I love you, Ben. But Sean... I can't hurt him. I can't betray him. Be safe, Sean.*

The conflicting loyalties and feelings played havoc with her mind as the day wore on, and she was surprised as the sun's warmth disappeared and a chill replaced it. She felt Fortune snuggling up to her, licking her hand sympathetically, sensing her confusion and doubts. She picked him up and rubbed his stomach absently. "You like him, too," she whispered, creating a new special bond with the dog. Ryan watched as the sun began to fall and saw the same ominous red sky that so fascinated Ben. She shivered with apprehension.

Sean followed the route outlined by his scouts. The terrain was thankfully rough; it would be difficult for the Yanks to find any trace of their trail on the way back.

He enjoyed the sunny day, taking pleasure in the heat radiated by the sun after a cool night. His stallion seemed equally eager to be traveling; his regular smooth gait was broken by little dance steps.

It was half a day's hard ride before he reached the pass. He had sighted some of his men at a distance, but none had passed close to him until he reached the woods at the foot of an incline.

From here the trail went upward more than two miles. There was a similar incline on the other side of the pass. The pass itself was a shortcut through the hills, which would save some twenty miles' distance for the heavily loaded wagons.

Sean met Braden on the way up. "They're still a half day's ride from here," his lieutenant reported. "We think they will stop for the night and be here about midmorning. I sent Jimmy as the courier suggesting the pass."

Sean nodded. They had agreed on using Jimmy as a disguised Union courier. He had less of an accent than many of the others, and his youth would make his role more plausible. Sean didn't like it, but they had to make sure the train moved through the pass and not around it. Jimmy had orders to relay the message and leave immediately, saying he had to report back with the troop's location.

"Let's get to work," Sean said as men joined him along the way.

At the top of the pass, they all began their task. They gathered boulders and brush at both the entrance and exit of the canyon, on both sides. They held the debris back by downed trees anchored by heavy ropes. Once released, the falling rubble would send more boulders down, effectively blocking both ends and preventing any of the Yanks from escaping the canyon.

They worked throughout the evening and into the night. They were all sweat-stained and weary when Sean told them to break off and get a couple of hours' sleep.

There was no sun the next morning. Heavy dark rain clouds cast a pallor over the barren landscape below. Sean said several prayers, hoping for the rain to hold off until after the raid and then come, wiping out any traces of the retreating Southerners. He went over all the details, trusting he had missed nothing. Four men were stationed at each side of the blockades, ready to cut the ropes on signal. His sharpshooters were positioned among the rocks. They would be almost impossible to spot. Other troopers remained outside the perimeter to remove any trace of direction and to plant a false trail. Sean knew the same sick nervousness he always did before battle. Despite his training as a soldier, he hated the killing and death that went with it. After the war, he thought, he would put his gun down forever.

One of the scouts rode over to him. "They're minutes away," he reported.

"Did you see Jimmy?" Sean asked anxiously.

"I saw him go in last night. I didn't see him leave. But they're coming this way, so everything must be fine."

"Damn it," Sean said explosively. "I told him to leave immediately."

"I wouldn't worry," the trooper said. "Jimmy's pretty good about taking care of himself, young as he is."

Sean nodded, his attention diverted by the dust rising from the Yank supply wagon. All of the men fell silent as they watched the slow progress of some forty wagons and an escort of approximately two hundred men. Sean had expected more; perhaps their inactivity in the past weeks had been effective.

The first wagons reached the opening of the pass with twenty soldiers riding in front, twenty behind and the others abreast the wagons. Two scouts rode ahead, apparently completely at ease.

They were full in the canyon pass when Sean signaled, and the men on both sides of the pass cut the ropes. The debris fell simultaneously at both openings. The Yanks were completely caught by surprise, some of them falling from their mounts as they and their horses were struck by falling rocks. An officer at the head of the column understood almost immediately what had happened. He dismounted quickly, calling to his troops to do the same and take firing positions behind the wagons.

Sean signaled again, and his sharpshooters on both sides of the canyon let loose a volley of fire. The Yanks were caught in a cross fire even as they crawled under the wagons. They were unable to see, much less fire at, the gray figures behind the rocks.

Sean waited until a number of bodies lay beside the wagons. There was little, if any, returned rifle fire; the Yanks were still surprised and were unable to see anything but the glint of rifle stocks. The heavy repeating fire made the Southerners' number seem far greater than it was. Sean finally signaled for the firing to stop. He asked one of his men for a white flag and climbed halfway down the cliff.

"Who's the commanding officer?" he yelled.

The officer he had seen earlier slowly rose. Sean slipped down the bank, still holding the flag as the Yank approached him.

When they reached each other, Sean looked the officer over carefully. "We have you in a cross fire, Captain," he said. "We overpower you two to one," he lied. "We don't want to kill any more of your men. Will you surrender?"

The captain, a tall bulky man with intelligent gray eyes, glanced around. He could see the rifle stocks through the rocks and the figures of several of his men sprawled in the dust. They were surrounded on both sides with no place to go.

Sean gave him time to assess his situation. He wanted no more killing than necessary. He felt sympathy for the Yank, who was obviously waging an internal battle.

Finally, the Yank spoke, his voice angry and curt. "Terms?"

"I give you my word none of your men will be hurt. All we want is the wagons. We'll leave you here."

"Our horses?"

"That's asking too much, Captain. Don't worry, you'll be found soon enough. There'll be patrols all over the place when you don't show on time."

"What about my wounded?"

"We have someone who can help them temporarily. Then they will be on their own."

The Yank officer looked at him bitterly. "Do I have any choice?"

"No," Sean said softly. "I'm afraid you don't."

"What do you want?" The surrender was in the Yank's voice.

"Tell your men to put their arms in a pile over there, one at a time." Sean pointed to a spot behind the last wagon, in full sight of all his men.

The Yank walked slowly back to his command, his shoulders sagging. He went along the wagons, calling to his men to come out and drop their weapons where he had been told. Slowly, reluctantly, they crawled from under the wagons and stood silently, seemingly unable to move.

Sean scrambled the rest of the way to the valley floor, calling to several of his men to join him, motioning for others to stay in the rocks where they were.

He approached the Yank officer again. "Your name?"

The man returned his look, dislike strong in his eyes. "Carstairs," he said shortly.

"Well, Carstairs, you go first. First your sidearm, then your sword. Slowly. Very slowly. Then go sit where my lieutenant suggests."

The Yank glared at him but did as he was told.

Sean turned to the next Yank soldier. "Now you, quickly." He urged each of them on as the pile grew higher. At one point he watched as a corporal discarded his weapon and caught the man's brief glance to his pant leg before moving over to the growing circle of disarmed men.

"Wait," Sean called. He strode over and looked at the man hard. "Roll up that pant leg," he commanded.

The man flushed. "There ain't nothing there."

Sean hit him, knocking him to the ground. He hit him again, ignoring the angry cries from the seated Yanks. He needed an example, and his man, unfortunately for him, just happened to be it. Sean reached down and drew a knife from a sheath tied around the man's ankle.

The Yank captain was rising. "I must protest."

"You protest?" Sean said, his anger just barely held in check. "*You* protest? I'll kill the next man I find hiding a weapon. You can count on that, Captain. You can protest all you want."

He nodded to two of his men. "Check them," he said, indicating the prisoners who had already surrendered their weapons. "Make sure they don't have any other little toys."

Sean watched carefully as the rest of the Yanks filed by, adding their weapons to the pile. Several of them pulled out concealed guns or knives, knowing they would be searched and believing the cold promise in the Reb captain's voice.

"What about my wounded?" The Yank captain interrupted Sean's concentration.

Sean dismissed him as if he hadn't spoken. He turned to Braden. "Have you seen Jimmy yet?"

"Yes, sir," Braden replied. "He arrived up the trail just after the fight started."

"Tell him to get down here with the medical bag."

Just minutes later Jimmy scrambled down the cliff and reported to Sean. Carstairs's eyes narrowed as he recognized the man who had sent him into the trap.

Jimmy met his eyes easily. "Sorry, Captain," he said. He had changed back into his Confederate uniform, or what there was of it.

Sean turned to him, now. "They have some injured. See what you can do for them. And then I want to see you."

Sean's troopers had already separated the dead and injured. Jimmy looked them over quickly, recalling the lessons Ryan had taught him. Only one of them, he realized thankfully, was seriously injured. He worked efficiently, taking the bullet from one wound. It was bandaged quickly, and the man was sent over to join the other prisoners. Another was hit twice in the side; he was bleeding badly, but Jimmy thought the bullets had missed any vital parts. He staunched the bleeding with pressure and quickly cleaned both wounds and bandaged them. He made splints for two leg wounds and cleaned and applied alcohol to several superficial wounds.

The eighth man had no chance. He had a bullet in the stomach. Jimmy gave him some laudanum to ease the pain and left several additional doses with the man next to him.

Jimmy reported back to Sean. "I've done what I could," he said, telling him about the man with the stomach wound. Sean in turn told the Yankee captain and allowed him to move over to the dying trooper.

As Sean saw to the prisoners, a number of his men had scurried down from the cliffs and started clearing the entrance into the pass, leaving the exit blocked. All the orders had been given in advance; there was no hesitation.

As part of the debris was cleared, another group gathered up the Yanks' horses and still another checked the wagons. One of the Rebs reported to Sean that the entrance was cleared sufficiently for the wagons, and with a quick order forty of his men quickly discarded their uniforms for the clothes they had worn previously and jumped up into the wagon seats. They pulled out quickly, followed by another eighty men.

Outside the sight of the Yanks, they would stop, empty ten of the wagons and send them in the opposite direction. All the rifles were transferred first to the other wagons or to special packs carried by the horses. The other supplies in the wagons would be discarded and destroyed.

Sean had kept fifty men in the canyon with the Yanks. The extra horses had been herded out. He eased himself to the ground, looking at his watch. He planned to give the wagons several hours' start before leaving the Union soldiers behind. He wanted every advantage possible.

Jimmy was back with the dying man and the Yank captain. He had given him another dose of laudanum and resisted the wounded man's cries for water, knowing it would only make the pain fiercer.

It was late evening when Sean was ready to leave. He walked over to the group of Yanks. "Captain, I'm afraid we're going to have to inconvenience you some more. Take off your boots. The sergeant here," he indicated Justis, "will collect them."

He gestured to his remaining men, who grinned. They went among the Yanks, hurrying the slow ones, taking the boots and throwing them into several large sacks.

The Yanks were obedient with thirty rifles aimed at them. Their faces reflected hatred mixed with humiliation.

"Don't be so glum," Sean said lightly. "The Confederacy will be most grateful for your contributions." He turned to his men. "Take care of the rest of it." His men went among the Yanks, cutting the suspenders of those who wore them, taking the belts of those who did not. They then deftly sliced off the trouser buttons.

The Yank captain glared at Sean. "You won't get away with this. They'll catch you and I hope I'm there to see you hang."

"Maybe," Sean answered agreeably. "Don't worry, Captain. I imagine someone will be looking for you soon. Have a safe journey back." He hesitated, then said slowly as he looked at the badly injured man, "I'm sorry about him."

He mounted and spurred his horse ahead, the rest of his men on his heels.

Sean knew the easy part was behind him. The problem was, and always had been, getting the bulky weapons back to the valley undetected. He felt more confident as he looked for signs, and found none, on the trail they were to follow. His men had done a good job. He welcomed the first drops of rain, knowing they would cover any signs his men had overlooked.

The wagons had moved fast, the horses spurred on by a touch of the whip. It was unusual for the Texans to use a whip on a horse, but speed was essential.

Sean caught up with the wagons several hours away. He had been traveling fast and felt comfortable with the distance they had put between the pass and themselves. The rain started pelting down, and Sean was grateful for the hard terrain they were traveling. At least there shouldn't be any mud. Though he knew it was going to be a long cold night for all of them.

As the wagons and horses moved toward the valley, more of his men joined the troop. They had driven the other ten wagons north, leaving a wide trail. When they had gotten to a streambed, they had driven them down a mile, then dismantled them the best they could, hiding what they could not take. They expected, and hoped, a search party would continue to follow the stream.

It was past daybreak when they sighted the waterfall in the distance. He motioned to several of his men to go ahead, and they did so eagerly, pushing their tired horses to a gallop. They were anxious to tell the news to those who had been left behind—and to finally get some sleep.

Sean stayed back, watching the wagons and horsemen go through the entrance. He then backtracked, looking for any sign of their trail or any strange riders. After several hours, he turned back, feeling as safe as he could at the time. *Now,* he thought to himself, *we only have to get them to Richmond.*

Ryan was sleeping when she heard the first elated shouts of horsemen coming in. She got up quickly, pulled on the breeches next to her cot and tucked in the shirt she had slept in.

One of the men spurred his horse to the tent; it was Justis, his face split into a wide grin.

"Miss Ryan," he said, stuttering with unaccustomed excitement. "We have the rifles." He stopped, then grinned even wider. "That brother of yours, he's one heck of a general. They would be winning down there in Virginia if he were there."

Ryan stopped him with her look. "No one...no one was hurt?"

"Evans was shot in the shoulder. Nothing serious. That's it."

"Where's Sean?"

He went backtracking. You know the captain. He ain't never satisfied. But nothing to worry about. I 'magine they're looking for us a good hundred miles north of here."

"Thank you," she said softly. "Thank you for riding ahead and telling me."

"Ain't nothing, Miss Ryan. Ain't nothing a'tall." He doffed his hat and went over to those who had stayed behind to tell them the story.

Ben, too, had watched the men ride in. He had spent a cold wet night wrapped in a rain poncho Ryan had found for him. His guard had refused to allow him in the wagon when the rain started, and Ben felt a certain satisfaction that the private had to brave the weather himself. He had watched as Justis approached Ryan and had noticed the relief on her face and the way her unnaturally stiff body relaxed. He was surprised at how glad he was for her. And, if he admitted it, relieved at what was apparently Sean's safe return. It had been happening increasingly often, this battle of loyalties.

Ben was still watching as Ryan glanced his way; he couldn't help a nod, acknowledging the obvious success of the mission. She smiled back, recognizing the goodwill he had sent.

She started toward him, her hair still in disarray from a fitful sleep and her shirt wrinkled, but the obvious joy in her jaunty walk made her even more beautiful than ever.

"Thank you," she said softly to him when she reached the wagon. "Thank you for being glad, too."

His left hand rumpled his dark hair in frustration. "Glad is not the word. I didn't want anything to happen to Sean, but glad...about this?" His eyes followed the trail of wagons that had entered the valley. "It's rifles, isn't it? Repeating rifles?"

"Yes," she said defiantly.

Ben closed his eyes. "Dear mother of God," he said. He turned to her angrily. "Don't you know that those rifles could prolong the war? Not change the result . . . just prolong it."

Ryan stared at him, her own joy ebbing. She had caught the contagious excitement of the returning men. "You don't know," she insisted stubbornly. "They could change things. Sean thinks they might."

"He's not that big a fool," Ben said explosively. He leaned back against the wheel, his eyes closed. Preventing the capture of repeating rifles had been the specific reason he had been sent west.

He was shaken from his thoughts by Ryan's voice. "Ben?"

He looked up at Ryan, who was still standing, now bewildered, before him. He tried to smile but couldn't. "Listen to me, Ryan. I don't want anything to happen to Sean, but I can't be happy about those guns."

She studied him for a few more seconds, wanting to erase the bitterness in his eyes. But there was little she could say. There had been a moment—a fleeting moment—when she had felt that rare communion that sometimes bound them. Now they seemed to be enemies again.

There was sadness in his voice. "I'm sorry, Ryan. I'm truly sorry."

Unshed tears shone in her eyes. She nodded and turned. As she walked away, he could hear the loud voices of the returning troopers. He turned his back to the sound of them, his mind rejecting the pieces of scattered conversation. The bitterness was closing in on him again. He could feel its smothering presence. He jerked his right hand against the chain and took a certain satisfaction in the pain.

Never, not even when he received the last letter about Melody, had he felt so hopeless. He realized his feelings for Ryan had grown daily despite the distance they both tried to place between each other. His own physical helplessness, both because of the lingering weakness from his illness and the irons, ate at him, and he knew the same desperation he thought Fortune must have felt in the trap.

As if the small dog read his mind, Fortune crept up to him and settled his head on Morgan's leg.

He absently rubbed the dog's ear with his free hand. Content with this sign of companionship, Fortune snuggled closer and closed his eyes. Ben watched as the troopers put up their small tents against the rain and wearily crawled into them. Despite the daylight hour, he huddled back under the poncho and hoped he, too, would be granted the respite of sleep.

Most of the Texans slept through the day, though some wandered around the camp experiencing an exhilaration and lingering tension that kept them from sleep. Sean had told them on his return that there would be a general celebration that night; it would be the first time in months that he would allow drink to flow freely in camp, although they had captured, and kept, barrels full. He had also ordered two of their small stock of cattle slaughtered and roasted.

He himself had taken the day to sleep. It was the first time in three days he had had more than several hours' rest. When he woke at early evening, there was an air of expectancy in the camp. He asked the few teetotalers to volunteer for watch. Six more were assigned to guard the pass and given the promise they would celebrate the next night.

Ryan tried to enter full-heartedly into the festivities, determined to eject Ben from her mind and, she thought wistfully, from her heart. She was only too aware of his quiet form chained to the wagon and had to use every bit of her will to turn her thoughts from the despair she knew he must be feeling. This celebration for Sean was bitter defeat for Ben. Yet she was set on helping to make this a good night for Sean and the rest of them. They had earned it. She chose her new birthday dress and tied her loose flowing hair back with a matching ribbon.

At the camp fire she accepted a small amount of captured Yankee whiskey. She diluted it with water and sipped companionably.

Ryan was only too willing to sing as the Texans called out their requests. Part of the time, Sean would accompany her on the guitar; at others, several of the troopers volunteered with their harmonica or fiddle. On the fourth request for "She Wore a Yellow Ribbon," she demurred, begging for some rest.

Braden then rose formally, bowed to her and asked for a dance. A fiddler obligingly swung into as much of a waltz as he could master on his handmade instrument, and all eyes, including Morgan's, watched as the two gracefully turned the valley floor into a ballroom. Morgan couldn't restrain his jealousy as he watched Ryan look up at the tall Reb lieutenant, nor as the Reb leaned down and whispered to her.

The spell was ended as the fiddler swung into an Irish dancing tune. Several of the Texans tied ribbons around their arms and played the woman's part in dancing. Before long, half the camp was engaged in a joyful free-for-all. The tension, which had mounted steadily during the past several months, was released in a whirlwind of dancing feet and flinging arms.

The gaiety of the music combined with laughter made Ben's loneliness even more unbearable. He watched for a while as Ryan took turns dancing with his captors. Through the firelight he could see her flushed face and swinging hair. In his mind he could see the sparkle and laughter in her eyes, and he couldn't tear his eyes away, regardless of how hard he tried. He was relieved when the music slowed and its frantic pace was replaced by the soft wistful sounds of Sean's guitar.

Chapter Seventeen

During the next few days the pattern of the camp changed radically. Ben had expected Sean to pull out almost immediately. He didn't. Instead there was frenzied activity, which the prisoner couldn't help but watch with a certain fascination. The Union wagons were dismantled. They had been fairly new with black bases and nearly clean tops despite the wear of several months. The sides were clearly marked U.S. Government.

Teams of the Texans took various parts of the wagons and pulled them apart. The covers were pushed along the ground, washed, then dirtied again. The process was repeated over and over again and, even at his distance, Ben could see the new white canvas cloth turn into a tired gray color of obviously worn material. Dirt was worked into the wagon's base, sanded, then scraped into the cracks again. The color changed from black to reddish brown. The government initials were filled with a clay substance and rubbed repeatedly until all sign of them disappeared. The appearance of the Texans was also changing. Some had shaved their beards clean; others who were normally clean shaved were letting their beards grow out.

Morgan was still denied water for washing or shaving. He could smell his own body now and knew that his face was covered with a black bristly beard. He still asked for additional water; he received the same negative reply, "Cap'n's orders."

He finally asked the guard if he could speak to Sean. He had not spoken to him in the six days since Sean had left for the raid; the Reb captain had slept with the rest of his men and had avoided the wagon.

"I'll ask him when I go off duty," the soldier said grudgingly.

It was several hours later when Sean strode over. He looked at Morgan with a gleam of amusement on his face. "You're coming along nicely," he said. "I doubt if anyone meeting you now would suspect you're a Yank colonel."

It suddenly became clear to Morgan. "So that's it," he said thoughtfully.

"I'm sorry, Ben," Sean said, "but it's necessary. I told you several days ago it would get worse. You can make it easier by giving me your parole."

"You know the answer to that, particularly now I've seen those rifles. Damn it, Sean, all they're going to do is keep the war going a bit longer, meaning more death and mutilation."

"Maybe," Sean replied laconically. "But maybe, just maybe if we can make it too costly, the North will make peace."

"That's a fool's answer," Ben retorted angrily. "It's gone too far. We have you almost whipped. You know that as well as I do."

Sean's look was stubborn. "Do we look whipped? Hell, Ben, I follow orders just like you do. Like you did. I might not like them, but I carry them out."

The shot hit home. Ben sighed wearily. "And in the meantime all the young men die."

"Some of them," Sean replied, "but others will be there to pick up the mess we leave."

"I hope so. I really hope so. But you've been isolated here in the West. You haven't seen how bad it is...the mangled bodies and the rows upon rows of dead so deep you can't see the earth. You haven't heard them screaming to die as their legs and arms are being sawed off."

"I was at Manassas with Stuart," Sean said shortly. "I've seen enough to never want to carry a gun again after this. But that's still a while off. In the meantime, I'll do my job."

Ben changed the subject and asked the question that had been nagging him. "Why did you join the South? I can understand some of the Southerners that went to the Point. They owned property and slaves. They were protecting a way of life. But you?"

"Texas is my state, my home. I had to go with her," Sean said slowly. "It wasn't an easy decision, Ben. But I believe Texas had the right to secede even if I didn't agree with the reasons for it. My father fought for Texas's right of self-determination—I couldn't do less."

Ben couldn't drop it, not now. "But you took an oath when you went to West Point and when you were commissioned. You didn't qualify it."

"It was a voluntary union of states," Sean replied testily, disliking the reminder of his own doubts. "I don't think the North had any right dominating the Union and forcing its views on another economy and culture."

"You never believed in slavery. I know you didn't."

Sean answered thoughtfully. "I don't think any man here does. That's not the point. Texas went willingly into the Union, and it had the right to leave it."

Ben just shook his head. "We're all paying for the stubbornness of both sides. But you, Sean, you of all people, have to know you can't win."

"Perhaps. But we all do what we have to do. Including you."

A muscle twitched in Ben's jaw. "How can I argue with an illogical Irishman? I never could win with you. I don't know why I try now." The brief emotion disappeared as quickly as it had come. "You'll be breaking camp soon?"

"When I'm ready." The answer was curt. "In the meantime, you have your answer about washing. There will be none, and tomorrow you'll get some other clothes. You will do as you are told."

Ben's eyes were curtained, but he couldn't resist a slight taunt. "Or...?"

There was no hesitation in Sean's reply. "Don't press my patience, Ben. I don't have time for it."

Sean turned to Wilson. "If he feels up to it, let him exercise in the morning, but get Jimmy to help you." He turned back to Ben. "The leg irons, however, stay on."

Wilson frowned, obviously displeased at his captain's sudden concession, and nodded reluctantly.

Sean looked hard at Morgan. "That doesn't mean you should push your luck any further. I've warned you several times. There won't be another."

Sean's strategy was obvious during the next several days. He was waiting until the search died down and using the time to good advantage.

In the next two weeks, the wagons were completely transformed. Instead of the well-cared-for army issue, they now resembled the poorest of the poor settler wagons that were flooding the country. Even the wheels had been sanded to reflect hard use. Ben watched as false bottoms were built and set to cover the rifles below.

Morgan had not escaped attention. The day after Sean's visit, he was ordered to change from his own uniform into a dirty shirt and even dirtier dungarees. He flinched as he did so. He could well imagine how he looked now: weeks without a shave, without washing. Dust had been stirred up by the constant activity, and he felt covered with layers of it.

It was yet another week before it became evident that the troop was ready to move. Sean had packed the medicines the Rebs had captured in other raids and systematically destroyed the supplies they couldn't take with them. Some of the men who had shaved earlier were donning dresses; they were all slight in build with hair longer than the others. The other troopers watched with amusement until Sean put a stop to it. It was, Morgan thought, beginning to look more and more like one of the long line of wagon trains traveling west—away from the war.

It was afternoon when Sean came over, unlocked Ben's handcuffs and motioned him over to his tent. Morgan was handed his crutches and he awkwardly followed Sean. He had had several days of practice, but every step had to be measured lest one leg swing too far from the other and get caught short in the leg irons. He had already taken one fall.

Entering the tent, Sean nodded Morgan toward a stool. Ryan was already there, mixing something in a pot. She smiled at him, recognizing his discomfort at his own appearance. He caught the look in her eyes; it told him more than words that his current condition meant little to her. He felt better and let himself wonder for yet another weak moment how she would feel again in his arms.

She came over to him and ordered with a slight smile, "Stay still. We're about ready to make you into a corpse."

He sat there patiently as she rubbed a foul-smelling liquid on his face, blending it in with his skin color. Her fingers were gentle but firm, and he wanted badly to grab them and hold them.

Ryan suddenly shook her head, warning him. It was, he thought, uncanny the way she read his mind and he hers. There was a silent empathy that hovered between them whenever they were close to each other. Which was, he suspected, why she had kept her distance for the past several days.

She finished and stood back, admiring her handiwork. Mischievously she handed him a mirror, and he quickly realized what she had meant. His face was completely unrecognizable. Behind the beard, his skin was nearly white; it looked, he knew, as if he were near death.

Sean also admired her artistry. "That will do," he told his sister. "Thanks."

Ryan felt the dismissal in his tone and left.

"You wanted to know when we were leaving. It's tonight. You'll be traveling in a wagon with Wilson, Justis and my sister. If we run into any Yankee patrols, she'll chloroform you and be the grieving wife. I doubt they'll ask any questions."

Morgan was returned to his wagon wheel but not handcuffed. He watched curiously as the last of the wagons were loaded. The men dressed as women donned sunbonnets, which nearly hid their faces. Several groups of men dressed as cowboys or hunters started on ahead. Some cows were tied to the backs of the wagons.

Fortune wandered restlessly, obviously afraid of being left behind. He finally scurried over to Ben and put his head on his leg trustfully.

It was nearly dark when Sean came back to where Ben sat. "We're ready to leave. Come with me."

Ben struggled up again and followed Sean to one of the middle wagons. A large red cross, signifying a contagious disease, had already been painted on it. There were some blankets covering the false bottom along with a number of items that would ordinarily belong to families going west—pots, pans, a rocking chair. Ben wondered again, but now without surprise, how Sean had found a rocking chair. He had seen too much, however, to be even a little startled.

Sean motioned him over the blankets, then caught his right hand and cuffed it again, securing the other ring to an iron staple attached to the wagon. Wilson climbed in.

"Take good care of him, Bobby," Sean said as he jumped down, reappearing in seconds with Fortune and tossing him into the wagon.

Justis climbed up and he and Sean helped Ryan up beside him. Ryan glanced back at Ben, her face sympathetic.

Morgan felt the wheels move, and he leaned back against the side of the wagon; the unaccustomed exertion of the afternoon had left him drained. He felt the lurching and bounce of the hard boards underneath him and knew with certainty it was going to be a long and painful journey.

Sean had planned to travel straight south at night, turning only slightly to an angle west during the day. He knew the patrols traveled mostly by day; they would question a train going south, not one heading west by a southern trail. He had sixty men with the train, two of them on each of the wagons. Several more rode inside or on horseback, disguised as unmarried farmers or scouts.

Another group was following in pairs at a distance, far enough that no one would recognize them as part of a group but close enough to hear a rifle. Others had been sent on to Richmond. Sean knew his main chance was by guile, not force. The area was dominated by Federal troops.

The first two days were uneventful. They saw no soldiers. The few riders they encountered shied away from the red cross on the wagon. The men on each wagon took turns driving and sleeping, and they rested only long enough to change horses. Sean was everywhere, catnapping in the wagons for an hour at a time before returning to his mount.

It was a nightmare for all of them—particularly Ben, whose body was constantly jolted by the wagon. Unlike the others, who occasionally walked alongside or rode one another's mount for a few hours, he had limited movement and no exercise to reduce the growing stiffness. Wilson was relieved by two other Rebs on a revolving basis, and Justis and Ryan took turns sleeping inside the wagon a few feet from Ben. It had been torture for him when Ryan took her turn, knowing that she was several feet away and he was unable to even touch her.

Every once in a while, he would look at one of his guards and think about escaping. What, he wondered to himself, would he do if he succeeded? He couldn't bring the army back to Ryan. But those damned rifles!

It was the third day when a Union patrol was spotted. A rider reported back to Sean, who rode immediately to Ryan's wagon. He swung up onto the back and told Ryan to chloroform Morgan. Ryan slipped down from her seat and quickly opened a small bottle. Soaking her handkerchief with the liquid, she lowered it to Ben's face. He resisted momentarily until he felt Wilson's pistol on his neck. He couldn't help breathing, sucking in the sweet sickly smell. As his eyes closed and his breath became more regular, Ryan and Wilson turned him over, the rank smell of his unwashed body covered the cloying sweetness of chloroform. A bunched blanket hid the regular rise and fall of his breathing and the irons on his ankles. Wilson quickly unlocked the handcuff on his wrist and pushed it out of sight.

Just minutes later, Braden, accompanied by a Union officer, approached the wagon. Ryan was wearing a dusty brown dress, her hair pinned back in a severe knot. She was leaning over the sick man. Sean stood up in the driver's seat.

The Union officer studied him and the wagon. "I have orders to search all wagons in this part of the territory," he said.

"All you'll find here is illness," Sean replied in a beaten voice. "My brother's near dead of cholera. His wife is in there nursing him."

Sean got down off the seat and started to lift the cover. "You can search all you want, Lieutenant. We've been trying to find a doctor but won't no one let us near."

The Yank officer took one look at the filthy pale man, shuddered and gestured for Sean to replace the cover.

"It's all right," he said. "You take your people on. I wish you luck."

Sean nodded soberly and watched as the officer approached his detail and signaled them on without a backward look.

Ben woke up an hour later, his head throbbing from the unwanted drug. It was obvious that Sean's plan had worked. He could feel the steady pace of the horses.

His hand was again handcuffed to the wagon. He looked over at Wilson. The Southerner was asleep, one of the very few times he had dropped his guard. Ben wondered how long he had been unconscious and how far the Union troops had traveled. He measured the distance between Wilson and himself. The Reb corporal was lying against the back of the wagon, his rifle by his side.

If he could just reach the rifle and discharge it, Ben thought suddenly, he might be able to bring the Union troops back. He started inching forward, when one of the pans fell. The noise woke Wilson, who realized immediately that Ben was creeping toward him.

"Get back where you were," he said with a sneer.

"I just wanted some water," Ben said indifferently, knowing it sounded false.

"You can keep on wantin'," Wilson said.

"No," came Ryan's voice unexpectedly from the front wagon seat. She had needed to get away from the smell of chloroform and her own terrible feeling of guilt at forcing it on Ben. She clambered to the back with a canteen, glaring at the corporal. "He's bound to be thirsty after that chloroform." She held the canteen to Ben's mouth, and he found he was indeed thirsty. The water was a welcome relief to his tongue, which felt fuzzy and dry from the drug.

"I'm sorry I had to do that," Ryan said, her voice low. She touched his hair lightly, and the brief movement sent waves of sensation through him despite the sluggishness he felt.

He reached his free hand up to hers, as if to steady the canteen, but really to touch her. The earlier anger at being drugged was gone, lost in the miserable apology in her eyes.

Their eyes locked, the desire obvious to both of them. "I want you," he whispered, almost under his breath. She nodded, her eyes and face telling him she felt the same.

The wagon came to an abrupt halt, jarring both of them from the intimacy of the moment.

Ryan passed him the canteen. "Keep this," she said, and scrambled back to the front. Sean had ridden up.

"How is he?"

"As well as can be expected," Ryan said. "He's not very happy."

"I didn't suppose he would be," Sean retorted. "It's better than being dead. That was the alternative."

"When will we be stopping again?"

"I want to put a good distance between us and that patrol in case they have second thoughts," Sean said. "We'll travel till dark and see if we can find some water."

Ryan nodded.

"Justis," Sean said, "when we do stop, let Morgan have some exercise."

"Yessir."

Sean turned his horse, urging the bay back into a trot, and disappeared toward the front of the line of wagons.

Justis looked at the girl next to him. "You all right, Miss?" he said, noticing the unusual pallor in her face.

She smiled wearily. "I'm just tired," she said, "like everyone else. It's been a long day."

Justis said nothing. He was only too aware of the obvious attraction between Ryan and the Yank prisoner. He knew her well enough to know how much she had hated to use the chloroform earlier when the Yank patrol had come. She was reluctant to use it even on the sick, preferring the less risky laudanum.

"Why don't you lean back and try to get some shut-eye," he said kindly.

She laughed shortly. "I'm afraid there's not much to lean back on."

"Use me, then."

She looked at the Texan with surprise. He was usually shy and uncomfortable around her. "Why thank you, Justis, but I don't think I could sleep if I tried."

He turned back to the horses. "Well, if you need to, just go ahead."

Ryan looked back, meeting Ben's eyes again. He was sitting up, looking sick.

"I'll check in back," she said, watching Justis's face crease into an understanding smile.

She moved again lightly into the back. "Better?" she asked Ben.

He nodded, not completely sure. He was nauseated from the drug, and his mind still seemed groggy. He moved slightly, and she saw the pain flicker across his face.

"Your leg?"

He looked up, his face tense. "It's nothing, just stiff as hell."

"Sean said you can get some exercise next time we stop. That should help."

"His guilty conscience?" Ben replied bitterly.

She didn't reply for a moment, her own conscience hurting her. "We're all doing things we don't want to," she said finally.

He looked at the hurt in her face, and his anger dissolved. "I don't even know if I could stand," he said, changing the subject and admitting the weakness that had increased in the past three days of being nearly motionless except for the wagon's battering.

"You will," she said with assurance.

"Will he be stopping soon?"

"A few hours. Not long."

Ben nodded, taking another drink from the canteen she had left him. "I never knew water could taste so good."

Ryan searched for a new topic, something to take his mind off the drug and the pain. "Tell me about your son."

He looked at her with surprise. Since that one bitter argument when she had asked about his wife, Ryan had stayed away from personal matters. He found, to his astonishment, that he really wanted to talk to her about Avery.

"He's almost thirteen but he seems much older," Ben said slowly. "He grew up with my father and sister—there weren't many children around—and he's always been more adult than child. Sort of a little wise man," he added wryly. "I think that's one thing I will always regret, never having given him a childhood." Ben was silent, wishing again that he could change the past. Ryan said nothing, letting Ben muse to himself. She was startled when he continued. "I wouldn't have anything to do with him for years. He reminded me too much of Melody. I sent him away and kept him away." Ben's voice broke and sadness darted in waves across his usually impassive face.

He looked at Ryan with intensity, his eyes searching for the censure and disappointment he felt would be there. When he failed to see it, he continued evenly. "Melody was my wife."

It was her turn to nod. She remained silent, afraid of saying anything, afraid it would break this delicate trust he was finally giving her.

"She left me, then she left him. I was just as bad—worse, perhaps." Ben's body had grown rigid as he spoke, every muscle tensing. "Every time I looked at him, I saw her. So I abandoned him to a home I knew had little love...and I escaped. I didn't think about what I was doing to him." His strong face was contorted with pain. "I do that, Ryan. I hurt people. I drive them away...."

Pain branded Ryan's soul. Under his protective mask, Ben was raw with wounds. She marveled that he was permitting her to glimpse even a few of them. Part of it, she thought, was probably the lingering effects of the drug. She hoped he would not regret it later...and retreat again as he so often did.

"But you went back to him," she said softly, comfortingly.

He was painfully direct. "Not willingly. I was posted in Washington after being wounded. My father died and I went up to Boston for the funeral. I found a lonely young man, but even then I was going to leave him there...."

Ben fell silent, remembering the funeral. Avery met him formally, his eyes red but his face tightly controlled, too controlled for a child. "How are you, sir?" the boy had asked him hesitantly. Ben had given a short reply, almost a rebuff, and he could still see the hurt in the boy's eyes.

He could also remember the scorn in his sister's voice. Charlotte was twenty-three then, unsympathetic and caustic.

"Haven't you blamed your son long enough for being born?" she told him after the service. "You did have something to do with it, you know."

Bennett Morgan had been stunned. Char had been his adoring shadow for as long as he could remember. She had only been ten when young Avery was born, and she had more or less taken his mothering on herself.

"He needs a father," she continued. "He needs you. It's time you buried Melody and stopped blaming that boy for your mistake."

Her voice had softened. "You don't know what you've missed, Ben. Despite everything, he is a joy. He's going to make a very fine man, no thanks to you. He needs you, but I think you need him even more. Spend some time with him. Get to know him."

Ben had planned to leave the next day, but he delayed his departure. Char's words had stung him, and he found he was curious about the boy. At breakfast the next morning, he asked his son if he would like to go riding. The boy looked at him with surprise and wariness. It was the first time his father had ever shown him any interest.

"Yes, sir, if you would," he answered politely.

After the horses were saddled, Ben asked him where he would like to go.

A note of enthusiasm crept into the boy's voice. "There's a cave not too far from here. I like to go there and watch the ships come in."

His father looked at him strangely. "About three miles north?"

"How did you know?"

"It was my favorite place when I was a boy...when I needed to get away."

The boy nodded slowly, looking at his father with a new perspective. It was difficult to imagine him as a boy, even more so exploring a cave. Some of the awkwardness left him.

It had been a good day for Bennett Morgan. He finally understood what his sister had been trying to tell him.

His son was marvelously bright and completely without guile. He was interested in everything—from Ben's stories of the West to the tiny sea creatures they found on the beach.

Ben delayed another day, and a third, each day finding new pleasure and surprise in his son. Some of the bitterness with which he had lived—even, he knew, nurtured—drained from him.

He knew he had to leave on the fifth day. He asked Avery to join him at dinner in one of Boston's finer restaurants as a special treat. Finally, he broached the subject carefully, dreading the reply.

"Avery," he started, "I have to go back to Washington tomorrow. I know this is your home now, but I thought that you might stay with me in Washington for a few months. There's a good school there. We could get to know each other better." He waited a moment, then added, "It's your decision."

His son's face broke out in a wide smile. "I should like nothing better," he said.

Ryan watched as the memories played across Ben's face, and listened quietly to the story. She ached for both the man and the boy.

"All those lost years," he said painfully. "And now I'm losing more."

"He'll be there," Ryan said. "He knows you love him now. He won't be alone again."

Ben looked at her gratefully, accepting her understanding as a gift. He noticed the weariness in her eyes and face. "I heard the sergeant tell you to get some sleep."

"What about you?"

"I've already had mine...somewhat unwillingly, I admit." There was a glimmer of a smile.

She smiled back. "No hard feelings?"

He thought about it a moment, then teased. "Maybe one or two, but they're mostly directed at your brother."

She leaned against the corner of the wagon, resting her head on one of the hoops. Ben slipped a blanket from under him and tossed it to her. "Here, use this."

Ryan slipped it under her head and in minutes was asleep.

Ben glanced at his guard over in the corner. Wilson had seemed totally disinterested in the conversation, resenting, if anything, the captain's sister's solicitude for the prisoner. He was obviously lost in some unpleasant thoughts of his own.

Ben kept his eyes on Ryan as she slept. The tight severe knot that had confined her hair had come loose, and it tumbled undisciplined down her back. Golden lashes covered her great dark eyes, which always reflected so much of what she thought.

How completely different she was from Melody or from any woman, for that matter. Melody had hated discomfort and inconvenience. She had loved luxury and thought of no one but herself.

As he looked at Ryan, he could see the little girl who had walked so far to safety, leaving everything she had known in ashes. He could see the young lady who had assisted her adoptive father in sewing wounds and delivering babies. And then there was the woman across from him, participating in a war not hers because she wanted to be near her brother.

"Ryan," he whispered. "What kind of woman are you?"

He answered the question himself, silently. *Mine.* And Ben knew he had to have her. But how? And how long before he could speak to her? He couldn't now...not with all there was between them, not with such a cloudy future. But he knew with certainty that life without her would be no life at all. It would be much worse than ever before because now he had tasted a sweetness, a joy he hadn't known existed. She had brought light back into his life, and he didn't think he could ever face the darkness again.

Chapter Eighteen

Ryan slept until the wagons came to a halt several hours later. Scouts had found a stream where the horses could be watered and the water barrels refilled. They would be entering north Texas soon, and no one was sure how much water they would find. The summer had been hot, and Sean expected dry streambeds.

It was dark before the horses were unhitched and hobbled. Sean still forbade the lighting of fires, and the troopers grumbled as they chewed on beef jerky and hardtack.

Ben was allowed to leave the wagon. Justis and Jimmy helped him get to his feet and steadied him on the crutches while he fought for balance. He took a turn around the camp and gratefully took advantage of some privacy to tend to his personal needs.

Exhaustion still came much too quickly. His legs were weak from lack of exercise; the chains had allowed very little movement. He couldn't help stumbling several times and, all too quickly, he was led back to the wagon. Sean met him there, taking quick stock of the determined but pained lines in his face. "Let him stay outside for a while...the handcuffs aren't necessary," he told Justis. "Just keep an eye on him."

Ben appreciated the fresh air after days in the stuffy confining wagon. He ate the furnished sparse meal quickly and reveled in the cool breeze that ruffled through the woods.

The time was too shortly over. It seemed he had just gone to sleep when he was awakened before dawn and escorted back into the wagon and handcuffed. The wagons moved out and the jolting was worse than ever. The brief respite had lulled his body, and it now objected painfully to the fresh battering.

Five days later they entered Texas. It was still an area controlled by the Yanks, but new spirit flowed into the Texans. They were home at last. Although it was still possible that a stray Union patrol might discover them, most believed they had successfully eluded any forces looking for the rifles. They were, by now, far, far away from any searchers.

There was a new threat now, however. Indians. They were entering Comanche county, and some of the stragglers who had been following the train now joined up. They continued the hard pace, stopping nightly but only for a few hours to rest the horses.

Ryan was spending more and more time in the wagon with Ben, sometimes talking, sometimes in comfortable silence. His main watchdog—Wilson—tolerated the situation only because he feared his captain. He had not been told to prevent the two from talking, and he was not an imaginative man, so he generally turned his thoughts to something else and left them alone. His presence, however, was malevolent, and both Ryan and Ben were silently pleased when he was relieved by a more tolerant guard.

As the main driver, Justis was also constantly present. He was very aware of the growing feelings between Ben and Ryan, but he was not a man to make judgment on others, and he liked the Yank. The incongruity of the situation fascinated him. He knew Sean had kept Ryan in the wagon in case they ran into a Yank patrol. He wondered how soon that would change. Just as Ryan and the Yank could not conceal their attraction for each other, the captain didn't conceal his hostility for either the Yank or the position in which he was placed. Something was bound to give.

Only Fortune seemed immune to the undercurrents. He would sit between Ryan and Ben, obviously content to be with the two people he cared about, and was quietly accepting when one of them would rub his ears or scratch his back. He rarely ventured out, even when the wagons stopped. His usual quest for adventure was apparently temporarily restrained by his fear of being left behind.

In the slow-moving days, Ryan and Morgan cautiously explored each other's lives. Although Ben seldom mentioned his early life and never his married one, he told her about his early days on the plains where various tribes, particularly the Sioux and Blackfoot, made war on each other and the growing number of white settlers. He had a talent for description, and Ryan could visualize the various characters he had met, especially MacKenzie, a half-breed scout who had become his teacher. He had taught Ben to track and hunt, and their respect for each other bonded them. Then, as he did so often, Ben retreated inside himself again, leaving Ryan to wonder what had happened to the scout. The closed expression on Ben's face kept her from asking the question.

It was that way too often. He would seem to relax and trust her and then realize where he was and who he was. It was as if suddenly a door would close between them. It was just that abrupt and that hollow.

When that happened she would try to change the subject and talk about her own life. She told him about Doc and Mary Foster, who had adopted her after the deaths of her own parents.

With that playful mischief of hers, she regaled him with tales of her shooting lessons. Every child was expected to learn the basics of self-protection, whether from the two-legged or four-legged varmints.

"My first victim—" she giggled "—was Doc's long johns. Whenever he got a cold, he blamed it on me and my 'window.'" She also told him about her adoptive mother's mostly unsuccessful attempts to teach her womanly skills.

Occasionally she won a small smile, but then Ben would start to move, and his wrist chain would pull him back. Ryan would watch as his face drew tight and his eyes clouded. She suffered with him each time, wanting to help in some way. She was quick to realize, even if she wanted to commit that ultimate act of disloyalty to her brother and help Ben escape, there was little she could do. The keys to the handcuffs and leg irons were with two different people—she couldn't help but wonder if Sean had worried about her when he divided them—and Morgan's leg was still incapable of carrying him far. She was afraid any additional damage would cripple him for life.

As the train traveled farther south, Ben lapsed more and more into morose silences. Only once did she tempt him into talking about his family when she asked about his sister, Charlotte.

"You would like her," he said. "She's the real rebel in the family. She hates pretense and can have a very sharp tongue. I think all of us have felt it at one time or another, with good reason." Charlotte, he added, had not married. "Not that she hasn't had offers. She's just too bright for most of the pompous asses who have courted her, mainly, she thinks, for her money."

"My brothers, on the other hand," he added with some bitterness, "have always done what was expected of them. They married the proper wives and have carried on the family business admirably. I really can't say I like them very much."

"Why aren't you in the business?" she asked.

"I never wanted it," he answered slowly. "Lord knows there were enough fights about it. But I didn't want to be a part of a business someone else built. And ever since I was a boy, I wanted to be a soldier. It seemed a fine way to see the country."

"And now you are, and now you have," Ryan teased. "And look where you are when you could be sailing from the Boston Harbor."

"There are some benefits," he said, looking at her with watchful eyes.

"Well," she replied seriously, "There's free medical care, free transportation, a grand tour of Texas and the company of a fine dog." She ticked off each with her fingers. A hopeful grin crept over her face. "Am I missing any?"

He refused the hint. "With all that, how could I want for more?" he allowed.

Her face was flushed, and her eyes shone from his brief teasing. Ben nearly groaned aloud with the pain of wanting her. He looked at his guard; a young soldier who had relieved Wilson and who, unlike Wilson, gave him some privacy. He was half-asleep, his face turned away from them.

Ben suddenly pulled her head down with his left arm and brought his mouth hard against hers. Her initial surprise was silenced by his lips as his tongue tempted her mouth open. She did not resist, knowing she had awaited this moment as long as he. Her urgency was as great, as demanding as his own, and she didn't care who knew it. They were drowning in each other, being swept away by a need both had been barely able to hold in check. Ryan felt herself trembling as she sought to tumble deeper into this whirlwind of wonderful blinding feeling.

It was Ben who suddenly realized where they were and drew back, his dark blue eyes full of pain and bewilderment at his own precipitant action and her passionate response. What was he doing? He looked at his guard, still half-asleep as he stared back at the trail, unaware of the intense emotion behind him.

Ben shook his head. Not like this. Never like this. She was staring at him, her eyes huge with wonder, her body tense with need. Her expression didn't change as her hand moved to his face and gently wandered over it, caressing the dark heavy beard, disregarding the layers of dirt and sweat and dye that stained it. She then leaned down, and her lips touched his as lightly as a breeze touches a flower.

There was so much promise, so much acceptance in that one quiet gesture that he felt momentary hope and a flash of intense joy. But it was gone almost as quickly as it came. He had learned to expect little. And the reality of his position could not be forgotten. There was still a war between them, and, before long, hundreds, perhaps thousands of miles. She would be gone, and there would be eager young men who were much more suitable.

Ryan watched his face and saw the brief elation fade as the mask he had perfected settled itself thoroughly back in place.

"I'm sorry," he said, his voice emotionless.

"I'm not," she replied, "and I won't let you be, either." Her voice shook slightly, and the young trooper finally stirred, wondering if he had missed anything.

"Anything wrong, Miss Ryan?" he asked. "He hasn't been bothering you, has he?"

The trooper melted at her slightly trembling smile. "I'm just tired, Johnny. Everything's fine." She looked at Ben's unsmiling face and knew she had to leave. Johnny's horse was tied to the back of the wagon, and she moved toward him. "Can I take your horse?"

He nodded, untying the reins from the back of the wagon for her. The wagon was moving slowly, so he helped her down, thrusting the reins into her hands. He watched with admiration as she leaped into the saddle and urged the horse to a gallop.

She raced the horse ahead, thinking to catch up with Sean. She needed his quiet strength, and right now she also wanted to run with the wind. Why did Ben keep turning away from her?

There were tears in her eyes when she finally caught up with her brother. He turned and watched her approach, sensing the urgency in her movements.

When she stopped, her face was as forlorn as he had ever seen it.

"Ben!" he said bitterly. It wasn't even a question.

"It's not his fault," Ryan said defensively. "He didn't do anything. I guess that's the problem. There's just no way to reach him."

"I've been trying to tell you that, Kitten."

"But it's there, Sean. I know it is. Every once in a while, he'll let his guard down, and he's warm and funny and I know there's so much there, and I, I . . ."

Sean couldn't find anything to say, and they rode silently for a while. He finally turned to her. "We should be safe enough now. I want you to change over to Jimmy's wagon."

She nodded, realizing that after today, she didn't know if she could bear being so close to Ben. It was too tantalizing to want to touch him, too painful to see him turn away from her.

Sean leaned over and touched her shoulder, and the understanding gesture made her straighten her body in determination. She would move to another wagon. For now. But there had to be some way to reach Ben Morgan, to make him trust again. And she would find it.

They were only five days from Fort Scott, according to Sean, and they were stopping for longer periods at night. They were now in Southern-controlled Texas, and the only threat was Indians. Sean felt their party was large enough to discourage any attack.

They had stopped by the Trinity River. Ben had been growing more and more distant from Ryan as he realized how close their destination and how impossible any escape. He would soon be even more a prisoner, and she would go with her brother. And the rifles, the damned rifles, would be headed toward Richmond. The desolation he had carried so long in his soul had returned, thoroughly suffocating the fleeting hopes and glimmers of possible happiness. He retreated into a dark world of his own, leaving Ryan frustrated and angry.

After the wagons had pulled to a stop and the horses were unhitched, Jimmy and Justis helped Morgan down from the wagon and escorted him as he walked slowly around the camp. At least he could feel some strength returning to his leg, and he needed the crutches less and less—more now for balance than support. The splints were gone, and Ryan had warned about putting much weight on the leg yet, but he was gaining confidence as he felt the leg muscles hardening. It was a little more than two months since his accident, five weeks after he'd injured it again.

It was mid-October now. The trees and leaves in Colorado had already changed when they left; the warmer climate in Texas had delayed the annual transformation, and green was still the dominant color.

Ben was handcuffed to the wheel outside, and Wilson assumed his guard duty. Ben watched as dinner was started, and his eyes followed Ryan as she took a pair of britches and shirt down to the river and walked out of sight. Jimmy was with her.

He knew she was going to take a bath. She was wearing the same dark brown dress that had served as her masquerade, and though she had used some water to wash on their headlong flight through Colorado and north Texas, there was never enough to get really clean. The dust stirred by the wagons piled layers and layers on the train's occupants. Ben envied Ryan's freedom to bathe in cool clean water, feeling his own filth even more acutely.

Ryan and Jimmy walked about a quarter of a mile down the riverbank until they found a shaded hidden place at a turn in the river. Jimmy grinned, realizing Ryan's sudden joy over the unexpected privacy and freedom.

"I'll be just over the hill," he said. "Call when you're ready."

She slipped quickly from her dress, tossing it on the bank with disdain. She kept the undergarments on, wanting to wash them at the same time she washed her body. She entered the water, clutching at a small remaining bar of soap.

The water felt wonderful; it was so clear she could see tiny fish dart between her legs as she quickly washed her hair. The water was not deep enough to swim, so she just took pleasure in the cool comfort of it.

After she had washed thoroughly, she took off the undergarments and quickly pulled on a clean set along with the fresh britches and shirt. She leaned down and started washing the dress.

She was so engrossed in removing the dirt that she didn't hear the silent footsteps behind her. A hand suddenly clamped over her mouth and her arms were pinned behind her. She struggled violently until a sharp blow knocked her unconscious. . . .

Jimmy had waited patiently. He knew how much pleasure Ryan took in the few times she had the privacy to bathe. He thought randomly of how much she and her brother had come to mean to him. They had become the family he had always wanted. Sean had taken a special interest in everything he did, always choosing Jimmy as his partner on the various raids and including him in his decisions and his future plans. Sean had talked about his family and shared with Jimmy his joy in Ryan. They had talked frequently about joining up after the war, gathering cattle and starting a ranch.

Ryan had likewise become a close friend, more like a sister than anything else. She had listened to his hopes, had loaned him books and improved his reading and writing. Most importantly, she had patiently shared her knowledge in medicine—an invaluable skill in the West and on the range.

He suddenly realized that she should have called by now. He called to her, listening for an answer. When none came, he called again.

Fear for her safety overwhelmed him. He ran over the hill, looking down at the empty stream. There was nothing there but a dress floating back and forth between some rocks.

He hurried down and looked for footprints. He saw her bare ones immediately, then the large moccasin prints. He ran across the stream, tracing the newly made tracks to a thicket, where they disappeared.

Jimmy ran as fast as he could back to camp, raising the alarm. He headed directly for Sean, who was standing at the center of camp, holding a piece of venison in his hand.

"Captain, it's Ryan. She's gone. There's Indian tracks...about a quarter of a mile down the stream. I was waiting for her and decided she had been gone too long. They must have grabbed her."

Sean whirled around, dropping the meat. "How many do you think?"

"Just a few. It must have been a couple of scouts who just decided to take her...."

Sean turned to Justis. "Sergeant, pick six men to ride with us." He turned to Braden. "Stay here with the rest of the troop until morning. Send a couple of men for help at Fort Scott—request a patrol to meet us. If I'm not back by morning, get the hell out of here. And get those rifles to Richmond."

His horse was already being saddled. He ran across the clearing, stopping only when he heard Ben call out to him. He spun around.

"Take me with you, Sean," Ben said urgently.

"Hell, you can't even walk."

"But I can ride, and I've been fighting Indians for ten years. I can track them as well as any Indian scout. I know how they think. I can help." There was both a command and plea in his voice.

Sean gave him a hard searching look, then tossed Wilson the keys to the leg irons. "Free him."

Jimmy quickly saddled another horse and led it over to Ben. The boy clasped his hands and gestured for Ben to use them as a stepladder. Ben put his leg into them and Jimmy vaulted him up into the saddle.

Jimmy led the small party to the bend in the river and to the thicket beyond. Ben took the lead and quickly found the unshod tracks. There were three horses; one, probably the one carrying Ryan and her captor, trailed slightly.

Ben followed the tracks easily. It was a skill he had painstakingly acquired from MacKenzie. He was one of the few soldiers who had taken the time to learn, but he had never wanted to have to rely completely on the sometimes shifting loyalties of the Indian trackers. He noticed that the tracks changed slightly, indicating that the Indians had slowed their pace.

Sean spurred his horse up to Ben's. "What do you think?"

Ben continued to look at the ground ahead, his voice cautious when he spoke. "I think they thought exactly what you wanted the Union patrols to think. That you're just a settler's train full of farmers and women. They won't expect anyone to come after them. They will probably expect you to head for the nearest military. It's getting dark. I doubt if they'll go far. At least not now."

Sean stared at him. "What do you mean?"

"What you think I mean. They'll stop relatively soon to enjoy what they have."

Sean's face tightened. "Can we go any faster?"

Ben shook his head. "The ground is rough—it's hard to follow. The last thing we want is to lose them."

The sun was spreading the last of its faltering light when they approached some low hills. Ben noticed that the tracks were fresher and closer together, indicating their quarry had slowed to a walk.

He turned to Sean. "They've slowed down. The ponies are tired, not that Indians care much about their horses, at least not as long as they carry them. But they've not backtracked at all. They must feel safe. I think we'll find them soon.

"And Ryan?"

"They haven't had time to do anything yet. They won't," he said, his mouth tight, his eyes cold and hard. Sean felt somehow comforted by Ben's determined expression.

They came to a rise, and Ben stopped the small detail. "Does anyone know this area?" he questioned.

One of the Texans pushed his horse forward. "I've hunted this area pretty well," he said. "There's a stream over this hill, then some more hills before leveling off. The woods are pretty thick."

"Any good camping areas?"

"Right beyond this hill," the Texan answered. "There're some sandy places along the stream. It's good hunting."

"That's probably it, then," Ben said quietly. He looked over to Sean. "I would like two of your best woodsmen to go with this man. See if they can locate them, then report back. I don't want to alarm them and give them a chance to get help."

Sean nodded to Jimmy and another man, who dismounted quietly and filtered through the underbrush. The others waited impatiently, several of them dismounting and resting their horses. Both Sean and Ben remained in their saddles, Sean resting impatiently on the saddle horn, Ben stiff and straight, willing away the discomfort in his leg. It seemed like hours before the men reappeared.

They looked at Ben but reported to Sean. "They're there, sir. Miss Ryan looks okay. She's tied up."

Sean looked at Ben. "Any suggestions?"

"We don't know how close their main camp is or if there are any more wandering around. Try to get them without gunfire."

Sean nodded. He signaled his men to dismount and start for the hill. "What about you?"

"I don't think you need me right now. Thrashing through the brush with this leg, I would hurt more than help." His face tightened. "Don't worry. I won't run. Not now."

"I wasn't worried," Sean said softly, then followed his men into the woods.

Ben watched from horseback as the eight men wove through the trees. He had to respect their skill. He didn't hear a rustle.

Ryan had gained consciousness almost immediately. She had been gagged and her hands tied behind her back. She rode uncomfortably in front of one of the braves.

The stench was overwhelming. She had grown accustomed to the smell of bodies, particularly in the past few weeks, but that smell now was mingled with bear grease. Only fear kept her from getting sick.

They rode for what seemed an interminable time, but she was grateful for every moment despite the extreme discomfort. The Indians couldn't do anything to her as long as they were traveling.

She wondered how long it took Jimmy to discover she was gone, and how far behind them her brother was. She knew her captors had no idea exactly what kind of men they had stolen from. She hoped against hope that they would stop before finding a large camp. She would have a chance then.

Stupid, she thought. It had been so stupid to go off by herself in that country. Her guilt at her own self-indulgence overwhelmed her, her body shuddering involuntarily. She thought of Sean, then Ben. Her mind kept turning from one to the other as she realized each mile took her farther away from them.

When she thought they would never stop, she was suddenly pushed off the horse and fell to the ground. She was only vaguely aware of the Indians tying their horses, then arguing violently. She felt as if every bone in her body ached, but fear made that physical discomfort seem minor. She bunched up her body protectively as one of the braves approached, his face darkened by grease and paint, his eyes shining with lust.

He reached down and tore the buttons from her blouse, then grabbed her hair with one hand and pulled her head back. She was forced to look at him, saw his mouth twist with malevolence and savagery. She felt his hand on her breast, squeezing it with his hard knotted fist until she screamed with pain, then felt her britches being ripped away.

Every time she struggled, he would yank her head, one fist balled up in her hair as the other savaged her body. She closed her eyes, thinking of yesterday and the days before. Her mind started floating away, rejecting the pain and humiliation being inflicted on her body. From a long distance, she knew her legs were being forced apart and she felt a body lowering itself on her.

As she fought against the invasion, her attacker's body jerked and fell as deadweight on her, his pulling grasping hand unwinding from her hair. Suddenly, impossibly, she was free.

Ryan felt gentle hands and heard her name spoken. She slowly floated back, at first thinking it was still part of a terrible dream. Sean's voice came once more, more insistent, and she felt him gather her to him and knew his comforting warmth.

"Ryan." It was another voice, Jimmy's voice. It became sharper. "Ryan, my God, are you all right?"

She opened her eyes reluctantly, afraid Sean would be gone, that the Indians would still be there, that the hand would still be tearing at her.

But it was Sean, really Sean, his face blazing with rage. Her eyes roamed, and she saw Ben slide awkwardly from his horse and drop to her side. He didn't say anything, just searched her face. Only his eyes betrayed his anguish. She moved from Sean and simply held her arms out to Ben.

He gathered her to him, holding her tightly, his mouth caressing her face, whispering to her. "Ryan . . . my beautiful Ryan. It's all right. You're safe." He buried his head in her hair, not wanting to let her go.

Sean stood up and watched silently. He had been wrong. Ben could love again. He did. Sean didn't think he had ever seen such pain on a man's face, nor such tenderness as Ben comforted his sister in a way he could not. There was no longer any doubt that the two were in love.

He sighed, then reached down and touched Ben, attempting to draw him away from Ryan, although she continued to clutch Morgan's hand.

Ben saw the dark bruises on her body, the cuts on her back where she had fallen against rocks. Disregarding the pressure of Sean's hand, Ben took Ryan to him again, smoothing her hair back, wanting to make the pain disappear. "My beautiful little girl," he said. "No one will ever hurt you again."

She clung to him, her body shuddering from the aftermath of pain and fear. He was her harbor, her safety. She didn't want to let go. Not ever.

Ryan finally heard the sounds around her. She pulled away and looked around her. The three Indians were dead, knives in all of them, their mouths and eyes still open in surprise. She recognized Jimmy and Justis and the other men, aware now they were averting their eyes. She looked down, conscious for the first time of her own nakedness. She frantically tried to pull her clothes together.

Ben stopped her with a gentle hand on her shoulder. They were torn beyond repair. He and Sean exchanged looks, and Sean took a blanket from his saddle and wrapped it around her.

Sean reached down for Ryan's hand. "We have to go, Kitten. We have to get back. We don't know where these animals came from or if there's more around. Do you think you can ride?"

She glanced back at Ben, now standing alone with a bleak look. Ryan nodded.

Sean lifted her carefully as Ben, unable to support even her light weight, looked on. Sean put her on his horse and swung up on an Indian pony. Jimmy helped Ben up on his horse, and the others scrambled up on the mounts Ben had brought down with him.

Sean rode over to Ben. "Should we just leave them like this, or should we hide the bodies?"

"I don't think it makes one bit of difference. They're going to come looking as soon as those three don't show up. I think we might just as well get the hell out of here."

Ben looked over at Ryan. She was obviously in pain and trying to hide it. "The sooner we get back, the safer she'll be. She needs someone to look after her." The knowledge that it wouldn't be him was agony. He looked at Sean. "Thank you for letting me come."

Sean nodded. "You were right. We needed you." It was as close to thanks as he could come. He turned to his men. "Let's go."

The entire camp was still awake and on alert when they got back. The horses were saddled, the wagons harnessed and ready to go. The men all grinned when they saw Ryan riding in, bundled up in a blanket. There were no questions. They would, they knew, find out what happened in good time.

Braden hurried over. "Thank God," he said almost reverently. "I've never been so glad to see anyone in my life. Even that damned Yank."

Sean turned his attention to Ben. "What in the hell am I going to do with you now?"

Ben shrugged.

"Will you give me your parole now, for God's sake? We control this entire area."

Ben looked at him stubbornly. "I would say the Indians might disagree with you there."

"You damn fool," Sean exploded. "Okay, if that's the way you want it, get down."

Ben lazily pulled his right leg over the saddle horn and carefully slid down, using the horse for balance.

"Wilson," Sean bellowed, and the corporal was instantly at his elbow. "Put him back on his tether."

Before Ben could move, Ryan was there in front of him, sliding back into his arms. His arms automatically went around her, and he nuzzled her hair, rubbing his lips against the golden strands. He felt her tremble then flinch as his hand touched one of the many bruises.

"I'm sorry," he said, and in reply she just melted closer to him.

He looked up and saw Sean staring at him, a muscle twitching in his cheek. It was the second time Ryan had turned to Ben for comfort rather than him.

Ben recognized the anger building in Sean's face and slowly pulled away from Ryan.

"Get those cuts attended to," he ordered, then he smiled slowly. "And you better get some clothes. That blanket doesn't do any justice at all to you."

She turned and looked at her brother. "Sean?" she pleaded.

He took her hand and urged her away from Ben. "Come, Kitten," he said. "Jimmy's waiting for you. Ben's right. You need to see to those cuts."

Ryan threw a desperate look at Ben but capitulated. Her strength and will were almost gone, and she let Sean guide her to another wagon. When they reached it, she turned and said in a soft voice, "Thank you."

"It was Ben who found you."

"I knew," she said sleepily. "I knew it would be the two of you. Together." And then she crept into the wagon and obediently accepted the draft of laudanum Jimmy had prepared.

Sean stared at the back flap for a moment. He turned and went back to Justis's wagon, where they were holding Ben. Wilson had already locked the handcuffs and was reaching for the leg irons.

"Never mind those," he told Wilson, and was startled at the look of hate that flickered across Wilson's face. He again questioned his wisdom in assigning Wilson to Ben. He would do something about that now.

"Wilson," he said, "we need your eyes and gun someplace else. Get a horse and join Braden. Tell him to get started immediately. I'll stay here with Morgan."

There was a flash of rebellion in Wilson's eyes, but it was gone almost immediately. "Yes, sir," he mumbled.

"And ask Johnny to see to my horse. Tell him to bring him back to me in an hour."

Wilson nodded, sending one quick dark look back at Morgan.

Sean sat down in the back corner of the wagon, stretching his legs out and leaning his head back against the wagon's hoop. "God, I'm tired," he said, his eyes almost closed.

"How is Ryan?" Ben asked.

"I suspect she's asleep by now. Jimmy gave her some laudanum. Thank God we got there in time. It was too damn close. But Ryan's probably the most resilient person I've ever known. She'll be her own stubborn ebullient self again tomorrow, and she'll be telling us all what to do." Sean's eyes closed all the way now, and the steady breathing told Ben he was already asleep.

The first movement of the wagon jarred Ben but had no effect on Sean at all. Ben wondered when the Confederate leader had last slept. He always seemed to be awake, always pushing. Ben stretched his legs out, grateful to be rid of Wilson's malicious presence.

He relaxed and thought about Ryan, treasuring those few moments she had spent in his arms. It had felt so right. She had turned to him for protection, knowing he would be there, trusting him. It was a strange yet very satisfying feeling. He looked over at Sean, remembering the brief anger when Ryan had turned to him when they'd first arrived back at camp, and he wondered if any of their old friendship could be salvaged. Just for a moment, just as Sean was closing his eyes, there had been a flicker of understanding. Or was it simply his own need to see it there?

He leaned back against the taut canvas. Sean had left his pistol in the holster, but Ben knew there was no way to reach it, not with his wrist still chained to the wagon. The knowledge of its close but not close enough proximity depressed him, even as he knew its possession would do him little good. He would never use it against Sean.

Damn. How did he ever get here? How did he ever get caught in such a spider's web? Whichever way he turned, he just seemed to enmesh himself even more firmly.

Sean was still asleep when Johnny appeared, the captain's horse in tow. Johnny and Justis discussed waiting more than the hour to wake him, but both knew better than to disobey. Johnny swung over the seat, and Justis made his way back into the wagon. He touched Sean gently.

"The hour's up, Cap'n. You said to wake you."

Ben watched as Sean was almost immediately fully awake. "Everything all right?"

"Yes, sir, no problems. No sign of Indians."

Sean yawned, then sighed. "Tie Zeus to the back of the wagon. Tell Johnny I'll relieve Braden in a few minutes."

Justis disappeared, and Sean looked over at Ben, the first gray light of dawn revealing a brief grin. "You look like hell, Ben."

"You don't look too great yourself."

"I feel better, though. You know, I think I envy you. Getting out of this damn war. I think I'll sleep forever when it's over."

Ben didn't answer. It reminded him only too well of his destination.

Sean hunched up on his knees and prepared to leave the wagon. He reached for the reins of his horse and guided him alongside before climbing easily onto his back, leaving Ben alone to brood.

Wilson had reluctantly left the wagon. He had decided to kill Morgan but had been thwarted as long as Ryan remained in the wagon. He had to be alone with the Yankee, as he planned to goad the prisoner into attacking him. Or if he couldn't push him into making a move, he would shoot him anyway and say Morgan tried to jump him. Justis was too busy with the wagon to notice anything.

In his narrow mind, he had already decided Morgan was responsible for his brother's death. The blue belly had been in Virginia; he might even had been the one to fire the bullet. Even if he wasn't, Wilson held him personally accountable.

When Captain Mallory sent the girl to another wagon and told him to rechain Morgan, Wilson thought his chance had come. And then, by the devil's own work, his superior had given him other duty and thrown away the leg irons. More mollycoddling. It just went to show how soft his commander had gone; he was no longer worthy of Wilson's obedience. Wilson swore he wouldn't be denied his revenge as he headed up toward the lead horses. He would get a chance in the next few days, and by God, he would take it.

Chapter Nineteen

They moved fast, all of them aware of their vulnerability. The Texans pushed the horses even harder than before. Those disguised as women remained that way, though the threat of Union patrols was gone. Sean thought it could work in their favor in the event of an Indian attack. An apparent easy mark would turn out far more costly for attackers and might discourage a small war party.

Braden had sent men ahead to seek help from Fort Scott. They could be expected within two days or so.

The wagon train didn't stop at all the next day except to water the horses and change those under harness to some more rested. They had gathered a fairly large herd during the months of raiding and had kept the best, sending the others south. But on the second morning they started seeing Indian signs: smoke signals in the distance, riders in the hills, unshod pony tracks crisscrossing the trail in front of them.

Sean kept the wagons tight and issued repeating rifles and ammunition to all the men. He wished he had not sent nearly half his troop on to Richmond, taking comfort only in the fact that the Indians would have one hell of a surprise if they attacked what seemed to be a helpless train of settlers and farmers.

The expected attack came late the second day. At first there was nothing but empty prairie, and then it was suddenly dotted with horses and men.

Ryan had insisted on moving back to Ben's wagon and was riding next to Justis. She had spent much of the morning with Ben, savoring his closeness. But then as Indian signs became more numerous, she moved to the front. They needed all available eyes.

She had searched the plains as carefully as the others, wondering when and if an attack would come. She saw the onrushing Comanche just seconds after the first warning shots.

Sean quickly ordered the wagons to circle, completing the ring just before the first wave hit. The repeating rifles were deadly, the Texans all being excellent marksmen. The instant the wagons had stopped, the soldiers were stretched on the ground, Ryan, herself a fair shot, with them.

It had happened so quickly, Ben, still handcuffed to the wagon, was forgotten. After dismissing Wilson the day earlier, Sean had left Morgan unguarded except for Justis. There simply wasn't anyplace for him to go.

The gunfire was heavy, the noise uncommonly loud and harsh to Ben. He was used to being a part of battle, and the sound, he now realized, had probably been lost in his concentration on the fight at hand. Now there was only the sense of being a blind stranger who had somehow wandered into a hell he could not see. He could hear the Indians, their first jubilant battle yells, and then the death cries. Combined with them were the mixed sounds of pain and triumph coming from within the radius of wagons.

He held a struggling enraged Fortune, who was begging to join the fray, when his attention was drawn to the back canvas flap. He saw Wilson's face, his eyes glittering with hate, and his own eyes followed the man's hand as it leveled a pistol at his heart....

Wilson had awaited his chance, and now during the midst of battle saw it. He didn't care about the Indians. He didn't care about anything but his consuming hatred for the Yank. He had emptied his rifle at the redskins, then approached Morgan's wagon as if seeking more ammunition. He glanced around; no one had noticed him. Their attention was completely on the action in front of them. He pulled his pistol, thinking gleefully that this was a superb opportunity. Everyone would think the Yankee had been killed by stray fire.

He pulled back the wagon flap and aimed his gun.

Sean had also emptied his rifle and turned around to reload it. His eyes caught the stealthy suspicious movement of Wilson, and he saw the gun leveled. He didn't stop to think; there was no time to reach Wilson, and no one could hear a shout in the now-deafening noise. He stuffed a shell into the rifle and fired, watching as the gun flew from Wilson's hand along with flesh and bone.

Wilson whirled, clutching his hand, shock and pain disfiguring his face.

Sean glanced around. No one had noticed the split-second movements. He stuffed a few more shells into the rifle and turned his attention once more to the Indians, leaving Wilson to sink to the ground, moaning in agony.

Ben Morgan let go of the long breath that had caught in his lungs. He had not wanted to die. Not now. Not after Ryan. And not this way. He didn't know what had happened, only that Wilson's hand had dissolved in blood and tissue and disappeared from sight. He forced himself to breathe normally again, and his tense body slowly relaxed.

He heard a ragged cheer and guessed that the Indians had been temporarily repulsed. Then he heard Sean's angry voice.

"Damn you! What did you think you were doing?"

Then he heard Wilson's low curse. "I'm going to kill you. I'm going to kill you both."

"You won't kill anybody with that hand for a long time to come," Sean retorted. "I'm going to do you a favor.... I'm doing it because you've served me well until now. I'm not going to tell anyone about this. I'll ask for a medical discharge for you. But, by God, if I ever see you again, I'll shoot, and I won't aim for your hand. Now get out of my sight."

The cover at the back of the wagon lifted. Sean's lean body filled the entrance. "Are you all right?"

Ben nodded, his eyes questioning.

Sean tossed him the keys to the handcuffs. "I think they'll be back. They're not quite sure what happened, and they'll probably regroup and test us again." He took a rope and tied a complaining Fortune to the inside of the wagon. "We don't need him chasing across the plains. Ryan would make us all go after him," he finished wryly, then turned back to Ben.

Ben unlocked the handcuffs, rubbing his sore wrist. "Wilson?"

"He won't be pointing a gun at anything for a long time."

"You?"

Sean shrugged. "I'm afraid so. It's too bad. He was a good soldier. Until now."

"Another debt I owe you."

"You owe me nothing," Sean said harshly. "I would have done it for any helpless prisoner. That kind of thing isn't going to happen, not in my command. Now get down and make yourself useful."

Ben quickly did just that and was surprised when Sean tossed him a rifle. "Just be sure you point it in the right direction," Sean said with a touch of grim humor.

Ben took his place between Ryan and Justis and waited. He saw that Sean's men had done their work well. There were at least thirty still or slightly moving forms in front of him.

They heard the yells first, then the pounding of hoofbeats. The number was greater this time; some of the braves had obviously been held back on the first charge.

The fire from the wagon circle was intense and steady. The position of the defenders made it easy to pick a target and fire, while the Indians, who had single-action rifles, were hindered by their own speed and the small targets protected by the wagons.

Only a few reached the circle. One jumped his horse between two wagons and aimed his tomahawk at Sean's head. Ben jerked around and fired, watching as the brave fell from the horse, the edge of the tomahawk grazing Sean's shoulder. A slightly crooked smile thanked Ben.

A few others breached the tight circle but were almost immediately brought down. The remaining braves retreated beyond rifle range.

Sean took a quick tally. They had several men injured, including Wilson, and three dead. Ryan had the injured moved to one side and had already started tending their wounds. When she had spied Sean's bloody shirt, she started toward him, but he waved her away to the more seriously wounded.

Sean huddled next to Ben. "What do you think?"

"They've probably had enough of rushing us. They'll sit back and wait for us to move."

"Braden sent some men on to Fort Scott. I think we can expect some help shortly."

Ben leaned on the gun. "You'll be better off staying here, then. You start moving and you'll be an open target."

Sean nodded and moved off to the area where Ryan had established a small hospital.

"How are they?"

"Sandy, here—" she smiled down at the young Texan she was bandaging "—is going to hurt for a while, but he'll be just fine. He'll have a nice scar to show all the girls."

Sean grinned at the sudden blush on the boy's face. "She's right, boy." He turned back to Ryan. "And the others?"

"Just flesh wounds, except for Corporal Wilson. His hand's pretty bad. How did it happen."

Sean shrugged. "A lucky shot, I guess." He hesitated, then leaned over. "Take care of him," he said in a low voice, "but be careful. Stay away from him as much as possible."

She looked puzzled but nodded. She had never liked the man. "What about the Indians out there?" she asked, motioning to the killing ground outside the wagon.

"They'll sneak down tonight and get their own. Ben doesn't think they'll trouble us again today."

He allowed her to quickly bandage his shoulder, then left, checking at each wagon to see whether every trooper had ammunition, water and food. He explained patiently to each group that they would stay in place and wait for a relief party. It could come at any time. If it didn't arrive by evening, they would make a run for it.

He completed his rounds and turned back to Ben, who was now sitting, the rifle still in his hands, when one of Sean's men yelled to him. "The Comanche, sir. They seem to be leaving."

Sean walked over. They were indeed riding off. He stood there silently as he heard a distant bugle and then watched as gray-clad troopers approached. He heard the cheers from his men as he turned back to Ben and slid down next to him.

The second lieutenant leading the relief party came directly into the circle. He looked bewildered for a moment, searching for uniforms and the ranking officer. He leaned down and asked one of the Texans, who pointed over to Sean.

The officer, conspicuous in his neat uniform, slowly guided the horse over to where Sean, Jimmy and Justis were rising. Ben remained seated, his rifle lying carelessly over his legs.

By then, Sean's men were feeling the euphoria of being, at last, with their own kind. The "women" among them shed the bonnets and threw them up in the air with happy shouts. Their long cavalryman's stride belied their dresses. The rest were shouting greetings, seemingly unaware of their irregular garb. All semblance of discipline was gone.

The newly arrived Reb officer surveyed the camp with astonishment and not a little disapproval. It took him several minutes to assimilate what he was seeing. He had been told to assist a Confederate unit bringing in rifles. It seemed, he thought, most improbable that this ill-clad unruly group could be part of his army.

He finally approached Sean. "Captain Mallory?"

His voice was doubtful as he eyed the now-bearded scruffy-looking farmer. He then spied the red cross on the wagon and caught sight of Ben lounging nearby, looking like a man more dead than alive despite the rifle he was holding.

He backed his horse gingerly, looking again at Sean, whose face by now was twitching with amusement.

"Lieutenant," Sean answered. "We appreciate your assistance. I'm Captain Mallory." His eyes moved to Morgan. "Don't worry about our friend here. He's a lot healthier than he looks. He just killed that Indian behind you, saving my neck in the process."

Sean's eyes met Morgan's, and he was surprised to see Morgan's face almost convulsed with laughter. Then he turned back to the young officer. "Let me present Colonel Bennett Morgan... of the Union army."

The lieutenant's eyes went to Morgan and traveled down to the rifle he was fondling. His face was rigid with disbelief. "This is," he finally stuttered, "most irregular."

At that, Sean and Morgan couldn't contain their mirth. They looked at each other and doubled up with laughter, both realizing that much of it came from the tension and fatigue that had been with them for the past several days.

Sean finally stopped long enough to say, somewhat caustically, "Well, Lieutenant, this has been a slightly irregular situation."

The young officer's face bent into a deeper frown. "I fail to see the humor," he said stiffly.

Sean straightened up, his face still creased in amusement. "I'm sorry, Lieutenant. It isn't you. From your view we must look a pretty motley bunch."

The lieutenant let a tiny smile escape. "I think that would be a mild way of putting it."

He dismounted stiffly just as Ryan came from the wounded. Despite the blood on her shirt and britches, she looked as pretty as ever. Her hair was tied at the nape of her neck with a blue ribbon, and her eyes were bright with excitement at their rescue.

The lieutenant's shock returned, sending Sean and Morgan off again. Ryan glanced their way, both surprised and delighted at their joint laughter. She was particularly fascinated with Ben; it was the first time she had ever seen him laugh. His face, even through the dye and dirt, looked relaxed, and his dark blue eyes were alight with mischief.

Her enchantment was interrupted by the suddenly attentive lieutenant. He bowed formally. "Lieutenant Barry Maynard at your service, Miss...?" He looked at Sean quizzically.

Sean straightened his face as much as possible and said with amused formality, "Lieutenant, let me present my sister, Ryan Mallory."

The lieutenant couldn't take his eyes from Ryan. "If there's anything I or any of my men can do for you, I would consider it an honor, Miss Mallory."

Ryan glanced from the lieutenant, whose stiffness had only slightly melted, to her brother and Morgan, understanding the laughter they could barely hide. Jimmy and Justis were also having difficulty maintaining their composure.

She turned to the lieutenant with a dazzling smile. "I hope my brother thanked you properly."

Lieutenant Maynard couldn't take his eyes from her. "No thanks are necessary, Miss Mallory. It's my very great pleasure."

Ryan lowered her eyes. "You must forgive our appearance," she said with mischief. "We've been traveling for days, trying to avoid those mean old Yankees."

The lieutenant was so intent on making a good impression he completely missed the new wave of laughter that assaulted the men behind him.

"You're safe now," he said comfortingly. "I'll personally see to your welfare."

He turned back to Sean, who struggled to keep his face straight. "I think we should get moving, Captain. I doubt if they will attack again, not with this many men, but you never know about Comanche."

Sean nodded, suddenly very much in command again, the laughter gone as he assumed leadership. "I think you're right, Lieutenant. We'll be ready to leave in a few moments."

He turned to Ben. "I'll take that rifle now," he said and caught it as Ben hesitated a second before tossing it to him.

"Ryan," Sean continued, "put the wounded in your wagon. We'll put Ben back on a horse. I don't think he'll object." He cast a quick smile at his prisoner, the past hostility gone and a shadow of the old affection replacing it.

"Jimmy," he said, "get the colonel a horse, a very slow horse." The amusement was back, the quicksilver humor softening the words. "And Justis, you ride along with him. I don't think you'll make the same mistake twice."

"No, sir," the sergeant said. "I'll take care of him like he was a baby chick. Won't let him git into no trouble at all."

Sean had considerable difficulty thinking of Ben as a baby chick, but restrained himself from saying so. Ryan couldn't do the same. She broke out into laughter, the merry sound of it turning the heads of both Sean's men and the newly arrived troopers.

Lieutenant Maynard broke the spell as he returned after giving brief orders to his men. "We're ready, Captain, anytime you are."

Sean and Ryan, suddenly sobered, supervised the loading of the most seriously injured men into the wagon. Sean helped her inside, and Jimmy joined her after bringing over a saddled mare that had obviously seen better days.

Ben winced but climbed on with some assistance from Justis. Justis swung up onto his own mount and urged Ben over to the center of the mounted men. They pulled out minutes later.

Chapter Twenty

The ride to Fort Scott was a nightmare for everyone. It took the entire evening and much of the next day because of the heavily loaded wagons. Time became a blur to Ben as he slept on and off in the saddle. Ryan tended to the wounded in the jolting wagon, relieving pain with laudanum and grabbing short periods of rest. Sean took short catnaps in the wagons, but he was restless and worried about his reception at Fort Scott. He would be asking much.

It was late afternoon the second day when the wagons neared the fort. Sean had ridden ahead; he wanted to talk with Major Matt Andrews before the fort commander was confronted with the ragtag Confederate band, an unexpected prisoner and an uninvited houseguest, not to mention the red cross on one of the wagons.

The gates opened before them. Braden and the Confederate lieutenant rode at the head of the wagons and guided them inside. They were directed to the stable area, the main body of riders following behind them.

Sean had arrived an hour earlier, talked briefly with Major Andrews and gone to clean up. As his weary men approached, he appeared in a fresh uniform and directed Justis to take Ben to the fort headquarters. Ben was exhausted beyond caring. He had at first been happy to have a horse under him, but the miles had consumed what little strength he had, and the dull aching pain in his leg had intensified steadily as the weak muscles rebelled at the unexpected demands placed on them. There was little mutiny in him.

Major Andrews came out the headquarters door, watching as Ben slid from the saddle and then stumbled, his leg failing him. The man was incredibly dirty, his face smeared with sweat and dirt and dye. Andrews looked at Sean, censure flickering across his face. "This is your prisoner?"

Sean nodded.

Andrews called to two of his men. "Raynor and McBride, help him."

Ben's face was perfectly still, his eyes dark and secret. He took an assisting hand, then shook it off as he straightened, still unsteady but defiantly standing on his own.

"Can you walk?" Andrews asked, surprised from the Yank's appearance that he was even standing. It had to take amazing concentration and will.

"With a cane or stick," Ben answered, his voice surprisingly strong.

"Raynor, go to Doc's office and get a cane. Fast."

The man obediently trotted off. Morgan swayed with the effort to keep on his feet, beads of sweat breaking out on his forehead.

The Reb trooper came back, holding a cane. Ben took it, leaning on it gratefully.

Andrews looked around and found a lieutenant. "Take a trooper with you to the officers' quarters and get this man cleaned up. Then bring him to my office." He turned to Sean. "I want to see you. In my office. Now." He turned and went inside.

Sean took Ryan's hand and pulled her inside. She had left the wagon of wounded to others, who had carried them into the fort infirmary. She had been about to follow them when she noticed Ben falling from the horse. She had wanted to go to him, but Sean's hand had stopped her. "He wouldn't thank you now," he whispered, and she watched helplessly as Ben was led away. She followed her brother inside Major Andrews's office.

Sean introduced her to Andrews, whose angry expression relaxed only a little.

"I'm glad to have you with us, Ryan," he said. "And my wife is delighted. Our one daughter is in Austin, and she is dearly missed." He went to the door and called his wife. "Anna. She's here."

A pretty graying woman came bustling in. Noting Ryan's dusty appearance and exhausted look, she took Ryan's two hands in her own. "I'm so glad you're staying with us. You just come with me, and we'll get you fixed up." Ryan looked at her brother briefly, then followed the major's wife out the door.

"Sit down, Sean," Andrews said testily. "You didn't quite warn me about that Yank's condition. What in the hell did you do to him?"

Sean told him the story he had neglected earlier: how Ben was found, his attempted escape, the capture of the guns and the elaborate charade to escape the Yankee patrols. "We had no choice. We needed a reason for him to be unconscious. We were searched once, and Ryan chloroformed him. The threat of cholera made them look us over rather casually."

Andrews's severe face lightened, and he allowed himself a chuckle. "Well, he certainly looks the part of a dead man. I'll admit that readily enough."

Sean searched his friend's face and said finally, "I had a reason for bringing him here. Ben Morgan was my roommate at West Point. I couldn't send him to that hellhole at Andersonville."

"So that's why you came so far out of your way?"

"That and Ryan. She has no one. I couldn't think of anyplace else where she might have some measure of care and protection."

"She'll have that here," Andrews said warmly. "My wife has been lonely without Bette. She'll make a daughter out of her in no time."

"I know," Sean answered with affection. "I depended on it. I know Anna."

Sean had thought carefully about what he was to say next. He had debated even mentioning it but knew the problem existed and wouldn't go away. It was better that Andrews knew exactly the situation. He outlined Ben's military history, stressing his Western experience and his old roommate's ability. "I think," he concluded, "you can expect him to try to escape. Repeatedly. He never gives up."

Andrews nodded. "Most of the Yanks here have that kind of record. That's why they're sent to Scott."

"There's something else I should tell you," Sean said slowly.

Andrews closed his eyes and leaned back. He didn't like Sean's soft approach. It meant trouble.

"Ryan nursed Ben back to health. She's in love with him."

Andrews opened his eyes and sat straight up. "And you approve?"

"No," Sean replied abruptly. "But that's not the point. I don't have much to say about it." He hesitated. "I want to ask a favor. I want you to let them see each other—privately. Now."

Andrews looked at him quizzically. "Am I allowed to ask why... particularly if you're unhappy about it?"

Sean sighed, still trying to sort out his conflicting emotions. Even he didn't know why he was doing this.

"I wish they weren't so close geographically, but they are. There can be only misery unless they face each other and resolve something. And I'll tell you this, Morgan would be a lot easier to handle."

"Are you willing to accept the consequences?"

Sean laughed suddenly. "You don't know my sister yet. I won't have any choice."

Andrews shook his head. "I don't know if you're crazy or if it's just that damned romantic Irish in you."

"Will you do it?"

"Why didn't you?" Andrews persisted. "Why me?"

"I thought about it," Sean admitted. "But that might indicate approval or acceptance. And God knows I have neither. But Ryan will make up her own mind, and I'm afraid keeping them apart will only make her more determined."

Andrews looked thoughtful. Sean didn't want to press the point. He had already asked enough. More than enough. He knew he was stretching their friendship to its limits.

"If I do," Andrews said slowly, "it will be only the one time. This is a prison camp and a tightly controlled one because of the people we're sent."

Sean nodded. "There's one more thing."

Andrews arched an eyebrow in question, his expression long-suffering at this point.

"One of the wounded—a man called Wilson—tried to kill Morgan in cold blood. I shot him. Because of his past record, I told him I wouldn't report it. But he's vicious and I would get him out of here as soon as possible."

Andrews looked at Sean with astonishment. "Why don't you come visiting more often?" he said sarcastically. "I'm beginning to wonder how I occupied my days before you wandered in."

Sean just grinned. "You know you enjoy a challenge."

Matt Andrews shook his head. "You give the word new meaning. What about you? What are your plans?"

"I've been ordered to Richmond with the rifles. I'm already late. I'll have to make up the time along the way. We'll be leaving at sunrise."

"Will you have dinner with us tonight?"

Sean smiled. "I would be delighted. Thank you. And Morgan?"

Andrews shook his head. "You win. They can see each other today after he's cleaned up."

Sean stood up. "Thank you, Matt. I owe you."

"No thanks necessary. Just get those guns to Lee."

Sean was given a bed in the officers' quarters. He quickly undressed and slid between the clean sheets. It was pure luxury after
eighteen months in the saddle and on the ground. He thought
briefly about Morgan, but sleep claimed him almost immediately.

Just two doors down, Ben Morgan was taking his first bath in
months. The lieutenant and trooper had guided him—at as much
distance as possible—to the bath area. They called an orderly to fill
the one bathtub there and told Ben to strip. The trooper kicked the
discarded clothes in a corner; when the orderly appeared with hot
water, he was told to burn the discarded rags.

Ben sank into the hot water in the tub. God, he thought, nothing had ever felt so good. He scoured himself with lye soap, and the
water turned black with dirt. He turned toward the two Rebs
watching him silently. "Some more water?"

The officer nodded. The smell of the prisoner was still strong in
the room. The tub was drained, then filled again. This time, Ben
washed his hair and then scrubbed his body once more. He felt he
would like to stay immersed forever.

His guards finally became impatient. "That's enough, Yank."

Ben rose reluctantly. The heat had helped soothe his leg, and he
felt strength seeping back into his body.

"A shave?" Damn, he hated to ask favors.

The lieutenant recalled his orders: "Get this man cleaned up."
He nodded. "You can use my razor, but be careful. . . . No sudden
moves."

Ben just nodded curtly, a ball of frustration growing inside him
as he realized even so small a thing as shaving was dependent on the
goodwill of his captors. He quickly shaved the beard that had
grown so thick on his cheeks, then trimmed his hair in back. A
quick glance in a mirror told him he looked halfway human again.

The Reb lieutenant threw him some saddlebags Ben recognized
as his own. "The captain who came in with you said there's some
clothes in there."

Ben opened them. Expressionless, he took out his spare pair of
uniform pants, the linen shirt and deerskin jacket. The book was
also there; so was his son's picture and a few of his cigars. A
shadow of a smile touched his lips. So not all of them were "spoils
of war."

There was also something unexpected—a pair of boots, which Ben knew didn't belong there. They were worn but soft and supple, and he regarded them with pleasure. He had been without anything but socks and a kind of covering made from a blanket since his fall months earlier.

As he pulled them on, he felt an obstruction in the toe of the left boot. He ignored it and stood, stretching, feeling whole and clean again for the first time in a very long series of days. His curiosity was pricked by the mound in his boot, but he kept it to himself, guessing that it was meant to be removed privately.

After dressing, he ran a comb through his thick hair then stood, this time more steadily.

The lieutenant looked at him with something akin to amazement. "I would never have thought it," he mumbled. The tall handsome arrogant-looking officer bore little trace to the man they had led inside the building.

"Let's go," the Southerner ordered. "The major wants to see you." He opened the door and nodded for Ben to lead. Ben took the cane and limped to the opening.

Andrews was in his office when the knock came. He called for them to enter, then asked his men to wait outside.

He leaned back in his chair and studied the Yank colonel. "That's one hell of a transformation," he said. "Sit down."

"I would rather stand," Ben replied stiffly.

"It wasn't a suggestion. It was an order. You'd better start learning to take them."

Ben started to protest, then sat down wearily. It wasn't worth it. Not now. *Save it,* he told himself.

Andrews noticed the expression on his face change from defiance to unwilling capitulation. He let several minutes lapse, taking the time to study the colonel. The man's hostility was clear.

"Captain Mallory," he said finally, "and I had a long discussion about you."

"Nothing good, I expect," Morgan said with careless indifference.

"On the contrary," Andrews said, surprising Ben. "You have a better friend there than you will probably ever appreciate. He disobeyed orders and came hundreds of miles out of his way, mainly to keep you out of Andersonville."

"One prison is as bad as another," Ben replied bitterly.

"You're wrong there, Colonel," Andrews said. "But I'm not going to argue with you."

Ben was silent. Waiting.

"Let me tell you something about Fort Scott, Colonel. We get the troublemakers here. We get them because we're completely secure. If by some chance you escaped from the compound, there's no place to go. Any man alone ends up on an Indian roasting fire. You've already had a taste of our Indian hospitality in this country." He was silent for a moment before he continued. "The prisoners here are treated as well as possible. But try to escape and you'll stay in irons for the rest of the war. Do you understand?"

Ben nodded slowly.

"Sean asked me a favor," Andrews added. "I said yes against my better judgment."

Before Ben could comprehend what the Reb major had said, Andrews stood up and opened the office door going into his private quarters. "Just stay seated," he commanded.

Ben sat there, completely puzzled. He glanced around the room, wondering briefly if there were any weapons.

The door opened, and he found himself staring at Ryan. She had changed into one of the dresses young Bette Andrews had left behind when she was sent to safety in Austin. It was a copper color, almost matching her hair and accentuating her dark brown eyes, which were, right now, shining with what appeared to be hundreds of lights.

He rose slowly. "Ryan." It was a soft whisper, almost inaudible.

Her eyes met his dark blue troubled ones. She feasted on them, letting her gaze dip deep within. She couldn't miss the sudden joy in their depths, and the want, and the need, and then the confusion and, finally, the mask. That damned mask. She was going to rip it from him if it was the last thing she did. She let her eyes wander over the rest of him. He was so beautiful. She had almost forgotten exactly how handsome he was. Rough whiskers no longer hid the cleft in his chin nor the strong fine bones that screamed strength and masculinity. His spotless uniform trousers and shirt fit the hard-muscled frame superbly, and the deerskin jacket added a taste of dash and adventure. He stood there tall and proud, and she thought she would die with want.

She finally glided toward him, completely unaware of anything but his mesmerizing presence. She felt his touch as hands gently played with a curl, then moved to her face so lightly they might have been a whisper of wind. They were tentative, as if afraid a touch might make her disappear.

And then his mouth came down and Ryan trembled as his lips caressed her eyes, her cheeks and finally her lips, first gently as they clung together and then with desperate need. His mouth felt so warm, so wonderfully warm as his lips played against hers, fondling, loving, teasing and finally demanding. She felt every part of her body ache and quiver and strain toward him as she met kiss for kiss, loving the taste of him as his tongue entered her mouth and played games with every sense she knew she had and some she didn't. Until now. How could anything be so totally glorious?

Ryan could feel him growing hard against her, and her body responded by pressing closer to him and melting more and more into his. She cried out softly. She had never felt such a longing before, never believed possible the wild urges running rampant within her.

Ben suddenly groaned. "Ryan, I want you so much." He drew his head down to where her breasts swelled gently above the fabric of the dress. With quick deft accomplished movements, he unhooked the material and freed them. His hands touched them with wonder as he thought how absolutely perfect they were. He couldn't stop his lips from seeking their softness, from tasting the sweetness,

When he lifted his head, he saw the glazed look of awe on her face, a mixture of reverence and fear and astonishment as she felt her body come alive in so many new and different ways.

Her expression was so open, so innocent yet so full of yearning that Ben went tense with frustration. He was bringing them both to a place where there would be no turning back. He could let it go no further, not now. Abruptly, he pushed her away.

Ryan muttered an unladylike oath and added another when she saw Ben's slight wry smile.

"Ryan." The sound of her name on his lips was like music. She couldn't stay angry. She threw herself back into his arms, her eyes filling with tears of her own confusion.

She felt her head being cradled against him then slowly tilted up by two strong insistent hands until she was looking directly into his eyes. He kissed her again, this time gently, his eyes memorizing her face. When he let her go, a hand remained touching her face as if he couldn't bear to lose contact.

"Ryan, we don't have much time. We must talk."

A tear wandered down her cheek. "I love you," she said simply.

"I can't ask you to wait for me. I don't know how long this damnable war is going to last."

Ryan couldn't tear her gaze from him. He looked so incredibly handsome. His face without the grime of the past few weeks seemed so strong. So strong and yet so gentle. It was that way now. Gentle and tender and wistful. "I think I've been waiting for you all my life," Ryan said slowly. "And if I have to, I'll wait the rest of it."

There was a slight hesitation in his voice, an unusual note of fear. "Where will you be?"

Ryan's heart was in her eyes. "Didn't you know? Didn't Sean tell you? I'm staying here. The Andrewses have asked me to live with them. Sean's going to Richmond. He thinks it's too dangerous for me."

"Thank God for that," he said. And the realization hit him. It was going to be hell, he knew immediately. She would be so close, yet there would be walls and fences—and not all physical—keeping them apart. But at least she wouldn't be trailing behind Sean across enemy lines.

He couldn't keep his eyes from her. She looked so pretty, so vividly alive, her face reflecting a range of emotions as she searched his. He wanted to tell her he loved her, but he couldn't. Not yet. He was in no position to do so, not physically or emotionally. He had nothing to offer now, absolutely nothing. He was not free to protect her or take care of her, nor was he entirely free of Melody and the distrust she had so completely planted within him.

Ben took one of her hands. It was hard and callused from riding, but he thought nothing was quite as lovely. He couldn't resist lifting it to his mouth and kissing it.

"I won't ask you to wait for me," he said again.

"You don't have to ask," she replied with no little frustration. "You don't really have a choice. I'll wait whether or not you want me to. There's absolutely no way you're going to get rid of me."

He touched her hair again. It was impossibly silky. He pulled her head back, his lips on hers again, more and more demanding. She responded with all the energy she had, her mouth eagerly exploring his.

There was a knock. Ryan pulled back, straightening her skirt, her suddenly clumsy fingers frantically trying to rehook the dress. Ben calmed her with a steady look, and his hands competently took over the task, completing it just as the door opened. Ryan's hand sought Ben's and locked it within her own.

Andrews came into the room. He looked from one to the other. Ben's face was somber and forbidding, Ryan's bright and eager. The major turned to her, his eyebrows raised. "My wife would like to see you," he said. "She wants to talk to you about dinner to-night."

Ryan smiled, her face glowing. She had received far more from Ben this day than he realized. His gentleness and obvious need said more than the words he still couldn't force himself to utter. But he would. They were there. Inside him. She knew it now. She let go of his hand, reached up and kissed him without embarrassment, then walked over to Andrews. She pecked him on the cheek, and he surprised himself by blushing.

"Thank you, Major," she said softly. "Thank you very much."

She started for the door, then turned around. "I love you, Ben. I'll always love you." She didn't wait for an answer; she knew there wouldn't be one.

Andrews looked at the now-glittering brilliance of Morgan's eyes and the compressed line of his lips. He couldn't even guess at what had happened—why Ryan seemed happy, why the Yank seemed angry. He only knew from Morgan's frustrated expression that Sean had handed him a plateful of trouble.

He went to the front door, opened it and summoned the two soldiers outside. "Take the colonel over to the compound. Tell Lieutenant Frazier to put him in A Barracks."

Sean was permitted to sleep until just before eight. A young corporal touched him gently, and his quick reflexes did the rest.

"Major Andrews sent me to wake you, sir," the young trooper said. "He said it's time for dinner."

Sean dressed quickly and ran a comb through his dark gold hair eagerly. A civilized meal, at last.

He walked swiftly across the fort's parade ground to the major's quarters, meeting a fellow officer on the porch. They almost crashed, both of them being late and in a hurry. They stepped back and started apologizing at the same time. They stopped, laughed, and Sean motioned the other man to speak first.

"I'm Wyeth Seldon. You must be Captain Mallory. I've heard of nothing else today. There isn't much excitement except Indians, and we would rather do without that."

Sean nodded. "And you?" he asked curiously. The officer had no insignia on his jacket but exuded an air of command.

"I'm the doctor here," Seldon said, "There's not much need for military trappings in a hospital."

Sean looked at him closer. The doctor was tall and wiry, almost thin. His face was strong but pale, as if he had been sick. His eyes were a smoky gray, friendly yet conveying a sense of determination and purpose. His accent was pleasant, faintly lilting. Sean liked him instantly.

"Are you from Texas?"

"No, Louisiana. The bayous. I think we better go inside, Captain. We're already late."

Sean nodded, turned toward the door and knocked. It opened almost instantly.

"Come in, gentlemen," Major Andrews said. "I see you've already met." He turned toward Sean. "My wife asked Captain Seldon to join us tonight after she learned how interested your sister is in medicine."

Wyeth turned toward Sean questioningly.

"My sister's been taking care of all of us for the past several months," Sean said proudly. "Her father was a doctor, and I don't think you will find anyone more competent."

Andrews poured the three of them a drink, and they talked briefly about Sean's raid on the Union supply train. "I wish I could keep some of those rifles here," Andrews said wistfully, "but I know how much they're needed in Richmond."

"I might just happen to lose a few," Sean said. "It will be a miracle if we get them all back, anyway."

"I'll take you up on that, Sean."

They were interrupted by Mrs. Andrews. "Dinner is ready, gentlemen."

They followed her into a dining room. Sean looked across the room and saw Ryan, who was bringing in some bread. It was the first time he had seen her in a party dress. The dark copper silk made her eyes even more luminous, catching their amber lights. Her hair fell softly down her back, pulled back gently by two slender braids, which met at the top of her head. They were interlaced with delicate small flowers. Her slender body radiated with energy and excitement. He had never seen her look so alive and beautiful. *So,* he thought to himself, *the meeting with Ben went well.*

Wyeth Seldon had stopped moving, his eyes transfixed on the girl in front of him. He knew, of course, that a girl had arrived with Sean's troops, but no one had really noticed her in the confusion of the arrival; the dust and dirt had coated her, and she had disappeared quickly into the major's home.

Wyeth had never seen a more lovely girl. Her eyes flashed with quick humor and intelligence, and she seemed quite unaware of the effect she was having.

He heard the introductions as if from afar and jerked back to reality only when he heard her voice. It was clear and melodic, a hint of delightful mischief very much a part of it.

"I'm very pleased, Doctor," she said softly. "I'm afraid you will find me a nuisance. I can't seem to stay away from hospitals."

"Never," he said gallantly, meaning it though he was finding it difficult to reconcile this very pretty girl with the sights he encountered in his often unpleasant work.

"You might regret those words," Sean broke in, his voice amused.

"Please sit down," the major's wife said. "Ryan, you sit between Captain Seldon and your brother."

Sean winked at Major Andrews as Wyeth Seldon hurried to hold out the chair for Ryan and awkwardly settled in his own. The doctor was hard-pressed not to stare at his dinner companion and was bewildered by his own sudden lack of speech.

The food was already steaming on the table, and both Ryan and Sean eyed it hungrily as a blessing was said. There were vegetables from the major's garden, platters of fried chicken and potatoes covered with butter. In the center of the table was an apple pie.

Ryan forgot the doctor next to her as she submerged herself in the food. It had been at least ten months since she had seen such a full meal and nearly that long since she had sat at a table. She couldn't remember a better meal. It had been even longer for Sean, and he attacked the food ferociously as the Andrewses watched both of them with amusement.

Wyeth, on the other hand, had completely lost his appetite and nibbled only politely. As Ryan finished, she eyed his still full plate. "Doctor," she said lightly, her eyes sparkling, "that's a sin, an absolute total unforgivable sin."

He had never before found himself at a loss for words. "I was too busy watching you," he finally blurted honestly. "I don't think I've ever seen anyone enjoy a meal as much."

She looked up at him, the mischief back in her voice. "Not very ladylike, is it? I'm afraid I'm the despair of everyone, including my brother."

"On the contrary," Wyeth said, "it's refreshing."

Ryan looked at him with new interest, and Sean sat back with a small smile. "Don't encourage her, Doctor. But you have to realize what we've been eating lately. Hardtack and jerky can get mighty old.''

Mrs. Andrews broke in, watching Ryan and Wyeth with troubled eyes. Her husband had told her about the Yankee officer and Ryan after she had invited Wyeth. She had in her usual romantic way thought what a wonderful match her visitor and the doctor would make. She liked Wyeth, had nursed him through several bouts of malaria and had worked with him at the hospital. She didn't want to see him hurt.

"I understand Ryan saved the life of the Yankee officer you brought in today," she said to Sean.

Sean nodded noncommittally, but Wyeth's attention was caught. He looked at Sean questioningly. "What happened?"

"You tell him, Ryan," Mrs. Andrews persisted, hoping that the doctor would see the sudden light in her eyes and catch the message there.

"His horse apparently stumbled into a rattlesnake nest," Ryan said, her tone even but her eyes bright and intense. "He was bitten twice, had a blow to the head and a broken leg. We were just lucky to find him in time."

It was Wyeth's turn to stare. "Two snakebites? No one's lived through that."

She shrugged. "He did."

Sean finally interrupted. "Ryan has a way with medicines. She learned a lot from her father and an old Indian medicine man. I've seen her herbs and roots cure wounds and fevers after traditional medicines failed. She knows both. After she came to us, we never lost another man to sickness or wounds. It's almost as though she wills them to live."

"Tell me more about the Union officer," Wyeth said, sensing the undercurrents in the room.

"He's almost recovered," she said, misunderstanding. "He's still a little weak, and his leg isn't entirely healed yet, but he's doing well."

"I'll check on him tomorrow," Wyeth said. "The other injured you brought in are all in good shape. They had excellent care." His words were obviously meant as a compliment, and Ryan acknowledged it with a slight smile.

They all turned their attention to the apple pie, even Wyeth. It was a special treat. Apples were hard to come by, rarely brought in by supply trains and then only by special request.

The party ended early. Ryan was obviously exhausted despite the brightness of her eyes, and Sean planned to leave at daybreak.

Wyeth complimented Mrs. Andrews on the dinner and quietly said good-night to Ryan, bowing slightly. "I'm delighted you're staying," he said. "I hope to see you quite often."

"Oh, you will, Captain," she said, again misunderstanding his intent, thinking instead of the hospital.

After he left, Matt and Anna quickly cleaned up and went to bed, leaving Ryan with Sean.

He looked at her closely. "I won't see you in the morning, Ryan. I don't like goodbyes. Just take care of yourself. Take very good care."

"And you, Sean." She leaned against him for a moment, then gave him a quick hug. "You're too darn cantankerous to get hurt."

"Look who's talking," he retorted. He hesitated, then said slowly, "About Ben . . . Matt said you two met?" It was a question.

"Your doing, wasn't it?"

He looked guilty.

"You don't look like Cupid," she said with a laugh. "You usually don't sound like him. But you did a fair job." She turned suddenly serious. "I love him, Sean. I know that now. I told him I would wait for him, no matter how long."

"And Ben?"

"He'll come around. I know he loves me. He's just too darn proud and stubborn to admit it right now. Was he always this muleheaded?" she asked.

"Yes, and he probably always will be. You better understand that."

He pulled back. "God be with you, Ryan."

"And with you," she whispered as he turned out the door and closed it quietly behind him.

Chapter Twenty-one

Like an angry tiger, Ben Morgan paced the small confines of his cage. He could think of it in no other terms. He had been there a month now, and it seemed to grow smaller with each slow-passing day. Smaller and deadlier, for it sapped at the freedom-loving core of his soul.

His imprisonment had been bad from the beginning, but it grew worse—along with his towering frustration and jealousy. One of the agonies of his presence here had been Ryan. Ryan and Dr. Wyeth Seldon. He would often glimpse them through the small barred window that looked out over the officers' quarters and infirmary. Ryan was usually at the hospital most of the day, and he deliberately crucified himself by watching as the doctor walked her back to the Andrews' home, often staying for long periods of time. It hurt. God, how it hurt. The cool tall doctor seemed so perfect for her, and he was free to court her, to laugh with her, to touch her.

Thinking of her also brought back thoughts of Sean. The morning after their arrival at Scott, he had asked to see Sean. Andrews's words had sunk in during the night, and he realized what chances Sean had taken for him. He had wanted desperately to talk to his old friend, to set things right. But he was informed that Sean had left at sunrise. That left another chapter of unfinished business. Lord, but he was accumulating them.

Ben knew his bitterness over Melody's desertion had changed him, and not for the better. He had grown to expect the worst from life. In the past few months, he had envied Sean's easy control of himself and his men. There wasn't one, except for Wilson, who would not die willingly for him. He knew he couldn't say the same about his own commands. Even his new relationship with his son had not changed his basic outlook nor his firm distrust of life. The fact that Ryan and Sean had intruded into his closed world had made him defensive and even bewildered. They were uncommon feelings for him, and he alternately damned and welcomed the new feelings and hope they brought him. But the endless hours and days were now slowly suffocating him, and he could feel the explosion building up inside.

Ryan had tried to help. The prisoners had two hours a day outside when the weather so permitted, and she would wait and watch and come to talk to him. But there was a six-foot wire fence and a deadline four feet within it. The fence was not the obstacle; it could easily be breached. It was for this simple fact that the deadline was taken very seriously by the guards. One step outside invited rifle fire . . . without warning. It also meant that Ben and Ryan had little or no privacy. He couldn't stand seeing her without touching. He had finally asked her not to come anymore. Her consent, though reluctant, meant it had been every bit as difficult for her. After that she sent him books and cards. Ben had asked the guards to thank her, and he had shared them with the others. They all had so very little.

"Still torturing yourself, Ben?" Sam Forster asked. Sam was his cellmate and an old acquaintance from West Point and the frontier. They had never been friends, but Ben had respected him as a good officer. Now in the close confines of the cell, they had come to understand each other.

In the past month, Sam had learned much about Ben, a limited amount from the man himself but more from just observing him. There was no disguising the anguish Ben felt when he watched the pretty young guest of the fort commander, nor his quick anger at the Reb doctor.

He had made the mistake of asking once. It had been just after Ben was brought in, and Sam had watched his hands clench into tight fists as he looked out the window. Sam's interest was piqued enough to look also, and his eyebrows lifted at the lovely young girl watching the prison area so intently. He had looked swiftly at Ben and saw the tightly compressed lips and hurting eyes.

"She wouldn't mean anything to you?"

"How could she?" Ben answered in a distant icy voice, his eyes once more guarded. "She's over there. I'm here. There's a world separating us." His tone warned against further intrusion.

And then the next day, Dr. Seldon visited. . . .

Ben had been asking questions. He wanted to know everything about Scott: its strengths, its weaknesses, whether anyone had ever escaped, what had been attempted.

The door to the cell area opened, and one of the guards came forward, followed by a tall man in a white coat and gray Confederate trousers, who stopped at Ben's cell. The guard opened the door, allowed the other man in, then locked it again. "Just call when you're ready, Doc," the guard said.

The man turned and nodded, then gave his full attention to Bennett Morgan. Ben returned the silent inquisition, noting quickly the calm, steady, gray eyes and pleasant smile. It was nonetheless a face that also reflected pain in tiny etched lines around the eyes and mouth.

"Colonel Morgan?" The voice was low and soft, courteous. There was almost a European accent.

Ben nodded, leaning languidly against the wall.

"I'm Dr. Seldon. I understand you've had some trouble with your leg. Would you roll up the trousers?"

Ben did as he was asked, his interest in the newcomer instantly veiled as he felt a sudden inexplicable antagonism rising in him. Just as quickly, he realized the reason why. Ryan would be thrown together with the man, and he couldn't restrain a fierce jealousy.

He knew Seldon felt the change. There was an undeniable menace in the air between the two men—a tension so strong it could almost be seen.

The doctor said nothing but ran his sensitive fingers down the injured leg. It felt straight and strong, the only weakness being in the muscles, which had had little exercise.

Ben saw the man's eyes study the still visible scars from the knife wounds, and he tensed even more as the doctor said softly, "She did a fine job."

"You've met her?" Bennett asked just as softly.

Seldon didn't have to ask who. He just nodded. "I couldn't have done any better. The only thing you need now is exercise. You can get some right here on the cot. "Just lift that leg up and down, keep it straight, make those muscles work. When you're outside, walk on it as much as possible. Don't worry about hurting it—it's just about healed. Throw away the cane as soon as possible."

Ben's eyes never left the doctor's face. He was a handsome man, the type most women would admire. Ben was also quite aware of Seldon's own interest in him.

"Any other problems, Colonel?" the doctor finally asked quietly.

"No." The answer was extremely hostile. Flat and hard.

Wyeth nodded, his face noncommittal, and turned to Forster. "And you, Captain, how are you feeling?"

"Like getting out of here," Forster said lightly. "Anything you can do about that?"

"No," Seldon answered cheerfully. "But if you Yanks would just stop making so much work for me, maybe all our lives would improve some."

He leaned over and checked Forster's leg. Just before Ben's arrival, Sam had thought he had found a blind spot in the fence and had tried to slip out. He had been shot for his trouble. Not only shot but quickly fitted with leg irons.

Seldon quickly examined Sam's gunshot wound and proclaimed it free from infection. "You, too, Sam. Give it some exercise."

"You know I'm on restriction, and I can't do much here with these damn irons."

Seldon looked at him carefully. "I can't do anything about that, Sam. You know the rules. But I'll see if I can get the restriction lifted."

The Reb doctor went over to the door and clanged a cup against it. The guard was back almost immediately. Wyeth went up and down the aisle asking if there were any other complaints. He was met with a chorus of them, none physical.

On his way out, he stopped back in front of Morgan's cell and looked at him again, his gaze intent. Then he nodded briefly and followed the guard out the door.

Ben questioned Forster. "What about him?"

"Seldon? Oh, he's all right. He seems to be a good doctor. He got the bullet out of my leg, and cured Marcus down there when he had pneumonia. He's pretty sick himself, I understand. Malaria. He's been down a couple of times since I've been here."

Ben groaned inwardly. Only too well did he understand Ryan's protective streak for those hurt or sick.

"Is he married?"

Forster looked at Morgan with surprise. "That's one hell of a question. I don't know. I've never seen him with anyone, but that doesn't mean anything. Most of them have sent their families away. There's precious few females here, and they don't have anything to do with us. They look at us like we're poison. All but the major's wife. She's been pretty decent. Why are you so interested?"

Ben clamped his lips together and said nothing. It was only later that Sam pieced some of the story together—Sean and Ryan and Ben.

"Still torturing yourself, Ben?" Sam's words echoed in Ben's brain. There was no way he could rid himself of the images . . . of Melody, of Ryan, of Seldon. They haunted him at night and mocked him during the day. He knew he had to get away.

His determination grew stronger later in the day when he and the others were allowed out for their daily exercise.

He was walking slowly in the yard when he suddenly saw Ryan emerging from the door. She looked over to the prison yard and saw him standing there. Fortune was with her and excitedly bounded over to the fence, crawled under it and jumped up on Ben.

Ben took Fortune up, fondled him roughly for a moment, then looked at one of the Rebel guards. Ryan started toward him, and he felt himself stiffen and almost unconsciously move forward. He realized the number of eyes on him, but he didn't care. She was as beautiful as ever, this time wearing the brown riding skirt and tan blouse he remembered so well.

It was as if time stopped. He forgot the deadline and had almost reached it, his feet continuing forward as one of the guards lifted his rifle.

The spell was suddenly broken when Seldon emerged from his office and immediately grasped what was happening. Ben Morgan was already on the deadline and moving toward the fence, his eyes steady on Ryan.

Wyeth reached Ryan and put a restraining arm on her. "I'll get him," he said softly. He strode over to the fence, shouting to the guards not to fire. His hands reached up over the fence for the dog.

Ben looked at him coldly and only reluctantly released the dog over the wire. A muscle twitched in his jaw, but he said nothing. He looked at Ryan, then back to the doctor, his eyes hooded, giving nothing away.

"I would step back if I were you," Wyeth said quietly. "They are quite serious about that line."

Ben looked around him. Two rifles were trained on him; all the other prisoners were silently watching. He shrugged carelessly and turned slowly toward the barracks. Despite the relaxed gesture, Wyeth saw the curtain drop from his eyes and couldn't miss the rage in them.

Back in the doctor's office, Ryan shivered. Wyeth put a hand on her shoulder. "You want to tell me about it yet?"

"He could have been shot, couldn't he?"

Wyeth nodded.

"Thank you," she said.

"There's no need for that," he said gently. "You love him, don't you?"

She gave a wistful little smile that touched and saddened him with its obvious unhappiness. "For all the good it does me, yes."

His gray eyes were expressionless. "I'll see if I can't help you see him."

There was sudden hope in her face. "Could you? Matt told me it wasn't allowed."

"You're my assistant, aren't you? I'll find a reason."

She thought about Wyeth later, as she tried to sleep that night.

She liked Wyeth Seldon. She liked him very much. He was, indeed, everything she once thought she wanted in a man: kind, gentle, intelligent. She watched him with his patients, noted his unfailing kindness and total absorption with their particular problem. When once she had suggested a poultice for a very stubborn infection, he had listened, helped her gather the fungus and was genuinely appreciative when it worked. He was, all things considered, a highly unusual man.

Though she *liked* Wyeth, she *loved* Ben, and if she knew little else in her life, she knew that nothing would change that. She missed Ben with every fiber of her being. She was never without the thought of him. His very evident need for freedom had made her as much a prisoner as he was himself.

She liked Wyeth, but for Ben she wasn't above using him....

She knew Wyeth had often studied her as she watched out the window of the infirmary, looking at the prisoners as they walked or talked or played cards in the brief time allotted them outside. She did it often, her eyes following the tallest one, her face intent on his every move, her lips slightly moist as she tried to control her outward expression. How she loved him.... How she loved that sometimes arrogant, sometimes boyish man, who seemed, even now, to dominate his surroundings.

That same night, Ben turned to Sam Forster. "There has to be a way of getting out of here."

"I was wondering when you were going to get around to that," Sam replied. "If there is one, we haven't found it yet ... not in the two years some of us have been here. And then getting out is only the beginning."

"There's a way," Ben insisted. "I want everyone thinking about it. I'll be damned if I'm going to stay in here for the rest of the war."

Wyeth met John Frazier, the lieutenant in charge of the prisoners, the next morning. The two were fast friends and often shared meals together. Frazier and Wyeth were of an age, older than most of the other soldiers. Frazier's face was lined and a scar ran along one side of his face from his eye to his mouth. Strangely enough, it didn't detract from his looks but added a perpetually sardonic expression to them. He had been with General Sibley in the abortive mission across New Mexico and spent two hellish years in a prison at Fort Douglas before being exchanged. He had been given command of Scott's prison compound for that very fact. The experience, instead of hardening Frazier, had made him sympathetic to the plight of his charges. He disliked the duty intensely, but he was quite good at it.

Wyeth made his request in a matter-of-fact tone. "Would it be possible to bring Colonel Morgan to my office in the next several days? There's not enough room to properly examine his leg in the cell."

"It seems fine to me," Frazier said. "He's barely limping anymore."

"I know," Wyeth answered. "But there was a lot of muscle weakness, and it was a bad break. I would just like to check it thoroughly."

The lieutenant glanced at the doctor closely. He and every other officer on the post knew he was sweet on Ryan Mallory. There had also been rumors about her and the Yank colonel.

"Any ulterior motives?"

Wyeth kept his gaze steady. "No," he said.

"Okay, you can have him tomorrow. He's not allowed in the yard because of that little episode yesterday. What time?"

"Afternoon, about two."

"He'll be there."

"Thanks, John."

"Just be careful. I understand he tried to escape on the way here. I don't need anything like that now."

Ben was rereading Sean's note. He did that sometimes when he was alone. It cut the loneliness.

The others were outside, including Sam, who had finally been allowed back out. Ben realized now just how strong the threat of rescinding that small privilege was. Andrews needed few other punishments. The cells, originally meant for one man, were so small they threatened to smother and destroy even the most stable of their inhabitants.

The note, which he had found in those boots weeks earlier, was in Sean's undisciplined free scrawl.

Ben,

I remembered we shared similar boot sizes, and your lack of suitable footwear was so out of character I decided I must share my humble belongings.

Since I recently liberated a new pair of boots from a fellow countryman of yours, I felt this a fair exchange.

Ben stopped reading for a moment, envisioning Sean's grin and the amused look in his eyes as he wrote the note. But then the note turned serious.

It has been a difficult several months for both of us ... but I want you to know I wish you well. We have shared too much for it to be otherwise.

A trace of humor returned.

I warned Matt Andrews you would be trouble. I don't expect you will belie that prediction—it will, at least, keep Fort Scott alert.

I'm leaving your black horse with Matt for safekeeping. He's much too grand for my poor Texans.

If anything happens to me, I am asking you now to take care of Ryan, to make sure she's safe. This I ask without reservation.

Sean

The last somber paragraph moved Ben as little else had in the past years. It suggested a trust that had been missing for so long. It also revealed Sean's fear that he might not live through the war, a prospect unbearable to Morgan. Now, more than ever before, he wanted to renew the rare friendship they had once shared. That he may not have a chance to do so was unthinkable.

When he heard the outer door open, he quickly stuffed the note back into his boot just as two guards entered the cell area. He paid little attention as one of them approached.

"Come on, Morgan, we're going for a little walk."

Ben rose lazily. "May I ask where?"

"No," the guard said. "Put your hands out here." Ben looked at him curiously but held out his wrists, and the guard put handcuffs on him. Ben followed the guard out, passing Lieutenant Frazier's desk, through the door and across the parade ground. His face tightened as he noticed he was being led to the infirmary. "Do I have any choice in this?"

"No. The Doc wants to see you. That's all I know."

They entered Wyeth's office without knocking, and the doctor rose quickly. "Thank you, Corporal. Wait outside. I'll call if I need you." The guard nodded.

The two men studied each other. Ben's eyes were icy, his mouth compressed in a tight straight line. Wyeth seemed relaxed, but he was intent on finding out what there was about this man that had so captured Ryan. He saw little to like.

He finally spoke. "You don't like me much, do you, Colonel?"

"No," Ben said shortly, his voice rough. "But I don't have much say over my company these days."

"That's direct enough," Wyeth replied. "I'll be just as direct."

Ben raised his eyebrows.

"I'm not your enemy, Morgan. I'm not even your competition, though I wish I were. Ryan thinks of nothing but you. I'm trying to figure out why."

"Is that what this is all about?" Ben snarled. "Then you've wasted your time and mine." He started for the door.

"I don't think I've wasted yours, Colonel. Mine, maybe. Sit down." The command was in his voice. Ben, surprised, sat.

"How's your leg?"

"It's there," Ben answered coldly.

"I want to look at it." Ben thought about refusing, then changed his mind. It was obvious the Reb doctor had something on his mind, and it wasn't Ben's leg. He pulled up his trouser leg. The snakebites had faded almost entirely. The cuts had left deep scars, but the muscles in his leg had tightened and the bone felt straight and strong.

"I would say you were very lucky, Colonel."

"You knew what you were going to see. Why go to the trouble?"

"Because I didn't want to lie to a friend, and there's someone who wants to see you."

He opened the door to the hospital area and called Ryan. With a trace of sorrow on his face, he turned back to Ben. "You have thirty minutes. I'll be in the back."

As Ben stood up, Ryan slid quickly toward him. He put his handcuffed wrists over her head and around her, pulling her tightly against him, cherishing the warm contact of her body with his. He buried his head in her hair, smelling its sweet fragrance and relishing the feel of the silky strands against his face.

"God, you feel good," he whispered. "I've missed you. Oh, how I've missed you."

She clung to him just as tightly as he did her, her hands touching, exploring the strong muscled body now welded to hers. Almost with a will of their own, her hands climbed upward, from his corded back to his neck and then entwined with his hair.

At first the comfort of their bodies was enough. Ben reveled in her closeness, and Ryan again had the curious feeling of belonging, of coming home. But then need emerged. Need and desire.

He moved his mouth to hers with fierce urgency. It seemed as if he would devour her, bruising her with the violence of a kiss that grew in intensity. His tongue found its way into her mouth, probing, caressing, demanding.

When he thought he could stand its sweetness no longer without drowning in it, his lips disengaged and he groaned. "It's been so long...so very long."

Ryan felt the coiled tension in his body, saw the taut line of his lips as he fought for restraint. She touched his face tenderly, brought it down to hers, and this time it was she who kissed him. She started gently, her lips barely touching and then growing stronger until her demands were as great as his had been.

And then the blaze started. It began deep inside her, in some mysterious place she hadn't even realized existed until a few months ago. Like a plains fire she had once watched in terrified fascination, it spread with great greedy bursts of flame until everything seemed enveloped in a raging inferno.

Ben felt her body tremble, saw the amber in her eyes turn to molten gold, and the fire jumped again, encompassing him in its wild hungry fury.

He felt consumed by the mixed pain and joy of it. His manhood surged to its fullest, straining against his clothes, straining toward Ryan, his Ryan. His in every way.

He slipped his hands back over her head, silently cursing the handcuffs, which made his movements so awkward. His hands fumbled with the buttons of her blouse and the chemise under it until her breasts were completely free. He kissed each one, slowly, lingeringly, igniting tiny new fires throughout her body. "You are so beautiful, so very, very beautiful," he said with no little wonder.

His hands moved down, his lips still caressing the hardening breasts, and to Ryan his fingers were like burning brands, scorching wherever they touched. Unable to stand any more, she tore herself away from him.

She stared at him, amazed and confused at all the new responses in her body, marveling at the wild things happening inside her. "Bennett Morgan," she said finally, loving the sound of his name on her lips. "What have you done to me?"

He stepped back and cupped her face in his strong hands, the long fingers touching and feeling her face almost desperately, memorizing it both by touch and by sight. Desire flooded him anew, and his loins ached with wanting. He throbbed with need for her, and he couldn't stifle a low moan as his hands went around her once more, pinning her to him as he moved slowly against her, seeking to alleviate the craving inside him. Her breathing stopped and held as she felt the incredible answering response even through the layers of clothes—and the need for more.

As his movements became more urgent, his hands moved, and she couldn't help a small cry as the chain linking his wrists bit viciously into her back.

The involuntary sound brought him back to reality with stunning, painful impact. He shuddered, his face full of strain as he struggled for control. Ryan felt the tightly drawn chain against her back slacken and then disappear as he lifted his arms and whirled around, turning his back to her. He took a deep breath, then another to escape the frustration that was pounding in him like a hammer on an anvil. Ryan touched him, feeling the angry tautness, the trembling her touch inspired.

"Ben . . ."

He turned around, his face suddenly cruel with his need to protect himself.

"You seem to have cast a spell I can't break," he said roughly. "Have you done the same with the good Rebel doctor? Have you cast your spell on him, too? Is that why I'm here? Do you enjoy torturing both of us?'' Each word was designed to hurt, to somehow break that hold that was so agonizing to him.

His bound hands seized hers and pulled her once more to him. As if to exorcize his demons, he kissed her roughly, cruelly, all trace of gentleness gone. There was only undisciplined raw want now.

"Let me go!" She pushed against him suddenly, and he released her just as quickly. Thrown off balance, she went spinning against a wall and slid to the floor.

He rushed over, devastated, and reached his hands down for her. She refused them as hurt and anger clashed on her face. "Damn you," she whispered.

Ryan slowly got to her feet. Confused by his sudden icy violence, she stepped back from him, looking both miserable and defiant at the same time.

A rare uncertainty flashed across his face as Ben stretched his cuffed hands again toward her in an oddly supplicating gesture.

Ryan's outrage faded as she watched pain and self-disgust flicker across his face. She moved toward him, leaning her head against his heart, hearing its beat and feeling its warmth.

He made no effort to put his arms around her. He had forfeited that right. "I'm sorry, Ryan," he said softly. "I just can't bear the thought of losing you.... I'm afraid every breeze will carry you away...."

"I'm not a tumbleweed," Ryan said quietly. "I'm not a leaf to easily fall. Are you never going to understand? Are you never going to be able to accept?"

His face was full of torment. "I don't know," he answered with a hurting honesty.

"I love you, Ben. I'll always love you. No matter where you are, no matter how long I have to wait to be with you."

Ryan wanted desperately to kiss him again, to wipe that sad uncharacteristically lost look from his face. But it was up to him now. She had said all she could.

After several seconds he put his arms around her and touched his cheek to hers. "I seem to keep apologizing to you."

She snuggled inside the circle of his arms, and her lips silenced his words. She never wanted him to apologize...never.

They heard a bugle outside and were immediately aware of how little time they had.

"Ben," Ryan started carefully, reluctant to ruin the moment, but she knew she must. She had to try. "Ben...I know from Major Andrews the war is nearly over. It will be just a few months, maybe not that long." She looked at him, a plea bright in her eyes. "Please don't try to escape."

She was used to his abrupt change of moods, and one came now. The barely contained violence returned. "That's a promise I won't make."

He lifted his chained wrists from around her and held them out for her to see. "You have no idea what it's like. Caged like animals. Nothing to do but stare out the windows. The worst is you. So close and yet so far. And then seeing you with *him*." He nearly spat out the word as he nodded toward the infirmary door. "And these chains. God, I hate them. I keep wondering what it would be like, just you and me. No one waiting behind a door, no shackles, no cell to return to."

"Just a little while," she begged.

He shook his head. "Not that promise, but another one. If I can get away, I'll be back for you. No matter where I go, or for how long, I'll be back. Remember that." And then he heard himself say the words he had vowed he would never say again. They came hard, almost unwilling, as if he couldn't hold them back. "I love you, Ryan...." His lips twisted with the effort.

Sudden joy leaped in Ryan's heart, but she merely nodded. She didn't even try to argue with his expressed intent to escape. It was something she had expected and knew she couldn't change.

"I'll be here," she said quietly, wanting to say nothing to spoil his unexpected declaration—painful for him as it apparently was. She would, instead, treasure it deep inside.

They heard a slight knock on the door. Ryan quickly tried to repair herself. She buttoned her blouse and smoothed back her hair, her eyes intent on Ben's face, watching as it changed back into the cold indifferent mask. Only the flicker of pain in his eyes betrayed him.

She went and opened the door, staring silently at Wyeth, recalling what Ben had said. Was she really hurting him—torturing him—as Ben had accused? Unhappily, she noticed his drawn face. Why was everything so complicated? So hurtful?

Ryan turned back to Ben, her expression pleading with him to be careful.

He nodded, understanding. She went out the door, not seeing the change in his eyes, not seeing the returned anger.

Wyeth closed the door. He turned to Ben, noticed the suspicion on his face. "You don't trust anyone, do you, Colonel?"

"I've not had much reason to," Ben replied, suspecting Wyeth's motives, believing he was his rival, a free rival, and that he had arranged the meeting to curry Ryan's favor.

Wyeth's patience ended, ire boiling up inside him. "Your anger will destroy her," he said. "You're not good enough for her."

He didn't move as Ben clenched his fists and walked toward him. "Go ahead, Morgan. Make more trouble for yourself."

Ben swung, his attack awkward with the handcuffs, and Wyeth ducked easily. He spun around and moved quickly to the door, opened it and called the guard.

"You can take the prisoner back now," he said, his eyes fastened on Ben. Ben dropped his fists, realizing the futility of continuing the attack. He looked at Wyeth with cold anger and a wordless but easily understood vow that there would be another time.

"Anytime," Wyeth said softly, loud enough for only Ben to hear. Ben nodded and obediently fell in next to his guard.

Chapter Twenty-two

Ben made his plans carefully. He was not going to wait. It could be months yet. He wouldn't underestimate the South's stubbornness.

Forster had talked to each of the men in his barracks during the time outside. "You might as well forget about me and the others in leg irons," he told Ben. "We don't have a chance. I don't know where they keep the keys, and we obviously can't ride. Some others think the war will end soon. There's about ten who want to go."

Ben nodded. It was what he expected. They knew, as Ryan did, that the war was nearing its end. There was little sense in risking their necks for what might be only a matter of weeks. He ate his evening meal with disinterest, completing it only because he knew he would need the strength. He passed his empty plate through the bars and concentrated solely on the problem at hand.

He knew it would be nearly impossible. Frazier was extraordinarily careful. The guards never carried guns into the cell area, and rules demanded that there always be two guards together at one time. If one guard was overwhelmed, another could quickly slam the cell door shut. Without a gun or sharp instrument, there was no effective weapon with which to threaten.

They were all watched carefully, their cells searched frequently. They were given razors to shave but those were taken away immediately after use. They were allowed no knives or forks, and the spoons were all counted.

This barracks had been the original army prison. Another, across the exercise area, had been built specifically to house Union prisoners and was an open dormitory, much preferred to the close confinement of the older building. The two groups were kept apart, Frazier not wanting the constant rebellion of Ben's section infecting the others. Ben had earlier asked each man to inspect their cells for crumbling brick; none had discovered any weakness. There was no way, he realized quickly, to escape from the yard during daytime hours. Forster proved that. It was always well covered with a number of guards, their rifles ready.

It had to be at night. They had to be able to obtain rifles and horses when most of the post was asleep. It was their only chance.

The prisoner at the end of the barracks started playing his harmonica. Ben continued to sit morosely as some of the others joined in a song, then a second. It was one way to drive away the almost overwhelming loneliness.

Any type of plan still eluded him when sleep finally invaded his mind and he drifted off, Ryan a constant presence in his dreams. Every time he reached for her, she faded farther and farther away.

When, at week's end, he was finally permitted outside again, he arranged a poker game with those interested in escaping.

Ben and Forster left the barracks building together, Ben heading to the far side of the yard and Forster settling down near the guards. A small crowd slowly gathered when Ben, Campbell and three others sat down with a deck of cards.

Ben shuffled the deck as two more sat down to join the game and four others squatted to look on. Ben searched each face carefully. Four he knew well; they were in the next several cells. The other six he knew by voice and face but little of their background or character.

"First of all," he said quietly, "I want to make sure you really want to go. We could be released shortly. And there's a damn good chance some of us—or all of us—will die."

He continued to study each one as they nodded. One was only a youngster, younger even than Jimmy. He couldn't be more than seventeen. "Lieutenant?" Ben questioned.

The others grinned. The boy was Lieutenant Ty Donaldson, and he had come in for a lot of teasing because of his youth.

Campbell answered. "Young Ty, here," he said, "received a battlefield commission after killing a mess of Rebs at Vicksburg. All his officers were killed. And," he added, his eyes twinkling, "he's had more experience at escaping than any of us. He's tried three times. The last time they sent him here. He just plain has rabbit in him."

Ben looked at Ty intently. Despite his youth, Donaldson's eyes were dangerously cold and hard. *I wouldn't like him as an enemy,* Ben thought, a glimpse of forewarning crossing his thoughts. He shook it off. "Okay."

He turned to the others. "Anyone have an idea?"

Ty spoke up. "Yes sir. Two times in the past six weeks, they seemed to be shorthanded...maybe someone's sick or on leave or something. My mate was sick one night, and only one guard came in. Apparently there wasn't anyone in the front because he had to leave to get another Reb before opening the cell door. If we can make someone seem ill enough that the guard will go ahead and open a cell without getting help, we can jump him, get the keys and take the uniform. With one uniform, we can get others."

They all stared at him. None of the others had noticed the lapse at night. "From the mouths of babes..." uttered one bearded veteran.

"I think you might have it, Ty," Ben said. "We'll start testing them. Think of things you can ask for late at night. We'll see who comes in and when. Who's careless and who's not. And finally, who would be likelier to open a cell if he thinks someone is really ill."

They nodded. "We'll talk again tomorrow." He addressed the four who were not taking part in the game. "You better move on. Tomorrow we'll start rotating those who play. We don't want the guards to get suspicious."

One by one, the four drifted away. The others started playing poker in earnest, all talk of escape gone as a guard approached. He gave a brief nod of approval as Ben took the hand on a wild bluff.

The eleven continued to meet on and off during the next ten days. They had disturbed the night watch six times with various excuses. Campbell, in particular, had been magnificent in faking a nightmare. His yells could be heard throughout the fort. Of those six times, only once did a lone man enter the cell area, and that was in the early morning hours. None of the guards would open the cell doors.

Out in the yard, they discussed the guards who had the early morning watches. Of the eight who rotated, only one seemed sympathetic enough to break the rules and open a door alone. They would concentrate on a night they knew he was on duty.

Ryan had her own hands full. Several days after Wyeth had arranged the meeting between Ben and herself, he fell ill. He had said nothing to her about the meeting, and they had continued as friends, although there was a new note of reserve about him that bothered her. When she went over to help with a newly injured man, she found Wyeth shivering at his desk.

She touched his forehead, felt the intense heat and noted the misery in his gray eyes. "Malaria?" she asked, already knowing the answer.

He nodded.

"Come on," she said, helping him up and to the back. "You're going to bed."

"The trooper..."

"I'll take care of him. Now do as you're told, Doctor."

He assented, too weak and sick to protest. He leaned on her as they went into the back. She helped him down on a bed and pulled his boots off.

She quickly checked the trooper in the next bed. He had taken an arrow in his side. She removed the bandage and saw that the wound looked clean and without infection. She rebandaged it and looked down at the trooper. "You're doing fine, soldier."

"What wrong with the doc?"

She looked down at Wyeth. His face was soaking with perspiration. "Malaria," she answered.

Ryan fetched a wet cloth and sat down next to Wyeth, wiping his hot forehead with cool water and holding his hand as he sunk into the fever.

Ryan heard him call her name, but when she answered he was incoherent. There was still a touch of quinine in his medical stores, and she spooned it into his mouth. She was still there at dinnertime and was startled when Anna knocked and came in.

"We were worried. Is anything wrong?" She glanced down at the bed and Wyeth. "Oh no. It's been so much longer than usual since his last attack. We had hoped he was getting better."

Ryan turned her attention back to Wyeth. "How long do these attacks usually last?"

"Three to four days, when we have enough quinine. Longer, sometimes ten days or more without it. And then he's weak for days after."

Anna took the cloth from Ryan. "You get something to eat. I'll stay with him and eat later." Ryan agreed, remembering the close relationship between the two.

As she went out the door, she turned back to Anna. "I'll be here after dinner. Let me know if you need anything."

Anna had already prepared dinner. Ryan quickly dished it up for Matt and herself. When she called the major to the table, he asked about his wife.

"She's with Wyeth. He's had another attack of malaria. I'll spell her after dinner."

Matt sat back in his chair. "Damn," he said. He looked at Ryan and reddened.

"I'm sorry, Ryan. It slipped out. Both Anna and I like that boy. He's had more than his share of grief, but he's never let it bother him."

Ryan looked at him questioningly. "The malaria, you mean?"

"That and his family. His mother, father and sister were all killed in a riverboat on the Mississippi in '62. His father was pilot and thought the family would be safer in northern Louisiana because of the fever. The boat was attacked by a Yankee gunboat and sunk. There were no survivors."

Ryan shook her head. "There's no end to the grief of this war. I keep thinking I've heard it all and then I hear another story, and I hate it even more." The grief was evident in her voice as she thought about Wyeth's loss and how she would feel if she now lost Sean. "He seems so untouched by it . . . the way it treats the prisoners."

Andrews looked at her. "He's a doctor. He never lets himself forget that. I think in the beginning, when he first came here, he had reservations, but the first time one of the prisoners became ill, he put all his personal feelings aside. He's a good man, Ryan."

"I know," she said softly. "And he's a very good doctor. He cares so much about them all."

His eyes suddenly twinkled. "And how's your Yankee colonel?"

She looked at him in astonishment. "How did you know . . . ?"

"It's my job to know everything, my dear. It really wasn't difficult to guess when John Frazier told me Wyeth had asked permission for Morgan to be brought over to his office."

"You didn't stop him?"

"No, I figured it's something for the three of you to work out. Wyeth's in love with you, you know."

"I didn't," she said slowly. "But Ben said the same thing, and I started wondering. Wyeth's never said anything."

"He wouldn't. He knows the way you feel about Morgan."

"You've talked to him about it?" she said, a little angered.

"Wyeth asked what I knew. I thought it only fair to tell him that you're serious about Morgan. That's all, Ryan, and I'm not apologizing for it. You may have been unaware of his feelings, but you're the only one."

Ryan said nothing else. Eating quickly, she cleaned the dishes and left.

Anna had undressed Wyeth and bathed him in cool water. His skin was like fire, and yet he shivered uncontrollably. Ryan touched Anna's shoulder. "You get some dinner and rest. I'll sit with him over the night."

Anna nodded. She knew Ryan's skill was far superior to her own. Before she left she watched as Ryan gently pushed back the light brown hair and continued to sponge Wyeth's fevered body.

Ryan stayed with him all night, administering the small doses of quinine that were left, continually sponging his body as the fever raged and covering him when he was gripped by icy shivers. He called her name several times, and she heard him yell, "You don't deserve her." It didn't make any sense, but neither did his other mumblings.

She fed him water, drop by drop. Once, toward morning, he shook himself free from unconsciousness. His eyes were dulled by fever, but a slight smile formed on his lips.

"You didn't bargain for this when you offered to help."

She placed a cool hand on his forehead. The fever was still high. "I needed the practice. You wouldn't let me do anything."

"Ah, what I won't do to give someone experience." He slid back into a deep sleep.

Anna was there in the morning. "How is he?"

"A little better, I think. He regained consciousness for several minutes last night."

"It comes and goes. Thank you for being here."

"I owe him a lot." Ryan gathered her shawl and wearily trudged back to her house and bedroom, her small dog following behind her.

Ben was eating breakfast when Campbell called to him urgently from the next cell. "The window."

Ben quickly got up and took three steps to the window. He saw Ryan, her shoulders sagging with exhaustion, leaving the infirmary. The sun was rising.

"The major's wife just went over there," Campbell whispered. "Something's happening."

They found out later. One of the prisoners complained of stomach pains; he received little sympathy from Evans, one of the more belligerent guards.

"The doc's down with malaria again. The girl that's been helping him sat with him all night, and I ain't going to call her."

The news went up and down the cells like wildfire. Campbell whispered to Morgan, "That's perfect. If the guard does fetch someone before opening the door, it'll more than likely be the girl."

Morgan looked thoughtful. He didn't want Ryan involved; yet Campbell was right. It would be easier. And he would see that she wasn't hurt.

He nodded, giving his assent.

They discussed the final plans in the yard later that day. "Owens is on duty tomorrow night," Ben said, referring to the guard they thought most cooperative. "We'll try it then. Ty, you'll be the one to get sick."

Ben had carefully chosen Ty because of his youth. He looked even younger than his seventeen years—until you looked at the eyes. He could appear very vulnerable, and his uncomplaining nature had made him a favorite among the guards. They had not realized it was because he simply hated them too much to ask for anything. He had kept his feelings strictly to himself, waiting for his chance.

Ben slept uneasily that night. He didn't want to use Ryan but saw no way to avoid it. Two of the prisoners could certainly subdue a man and a woman quickly—particularly an unprotesting woman— and all his instincts told him that Ryan would cooperate. He wasn't sure about two well-bodied Rebs. One sound, and the whole attempt would be ruined.

The day went slowly and the evening even slower. Hart, the lieutenant with the harmonica, started playing, but Ben could feel the tenseness in the response. They all joined in, even Ben. Each man there knew about the imminent escape; the ones who declined to go wanted the others to succeed despite the punishment that was sure to follow.

The music stopped only when they were silenced by the guards. Ben tried to get some sleep; Ty had planned his sudden illness for the first hours after midnight.

He woke several hours later. No one was sleeping. The minutes and hours seemed to creep by before Forster, who had been stationed at the window, told them the guard had changed. There was only one man, the one they wanted.

Ben let another hour slide by, time enough for the departing guards to get to their quarters and, hopefully, fall asleep.

At 3:00 a.m., he gave the signal. Ty cried out suddenly, doubling over. His screams of agony sounded real enough, and the prisoners started hitting the cell doors with their tin cups.

The outer door into the cell area opened. Sergeant Owens, his face still flushed with sleep, hesitated just inside the cell area.

"Shut up!" he yelled. "You'll wake up the whole fort."

Morgan was standing at his cell door. "Sergeant, that boy down there is real sick. Can you do something?"

Owens went down to Ty's cell. "What's the matter with him?" He turned the question to Ty's cellmate, his voice annoyed and rough.

"Don't know. It started about an hour ago, and it's been getting worse and worse. He's near about ready to die. Can't you get the doctor?"

"The doctor's sick!"

"You've got to do something. He'll die."

The man in the next cell nodded. "It could be the fever," he offered helpfully.

Owens stood there uncertainly, but another shriek of agony decided him. "I'll go get Miss Ryan. She's over at the doc's office, taking care of him."

He hurriedly left the area, locking the outer door behind him. Morgan lifted his eyes in gratitude, and the others chuckled at Ty's masterful performance.

"They're coming," Forster reported.

The outer door opened again, and Owens and Ryan rushed in. Ryan glanced up and down the cells, found Ben and smiled wearily, then caught up with the sergeant as he unlocked Ty's cell.

Owens ordered Ty's mate to the back of the cell, and Ryan pushed her way between the two cots. Ty was still doubled over, moaning softly. He cried out suddenly, and Owens's attention left Ty's cellmate just long enough for the man to rush the guard and hit him on the side of the head. At the same time, Ty sprung up and put his hand over Ryan's mouth.

"I'm sorry, miss," he said softly. "Please don't yell."

She nodded and he released her. She stood in stunned silence as Ty took off his shirt and quickly bound the Reb sergeant, tearing pieces of the cloth and using them as rope. He took the guard's keys and tossed them to his cellmate, who hurried down the aisle, releasing those who would escape. Ty stayed with Ryan, his hand ready to gag her if she made a sound.

In just a moment Ben was there. "It's okay, Ty. I'll take care of her. You change into his uniform. See what you can find in the front office."

Ben drew Ryan to him. "I didn't want to involve you, darling. But I had to try." He studied her face. "Do you understand?"

She reached up and kissed him, completely oblivious to the stares of the men around her. The act was wild and defiant and something else: a pledge. Ben thought he had never loved her as much as he did at that minute. When she finished, she looked up at him. "Be careful, Ben," she said softly, "and come back to me."

He returned her kiss, hard and quick, but with his own promise. "I will, and now I have to tie you up, or they'll wonder why you didn't sound an alarm."

She nodded, pointing to the medical bag she had brought. "There are some bandages in there."

Ben shook his head, laughter in his eyes. "You'll never cease to amaze me, Miss Mallory," he said. His eyes were more alive, more brilliant than Ryan had ever seen them. They told her, more than any words, how very important this escape was to him.

He took the bandages and tied her hands loosely. She shook her head, a slight wry smile on her face. "They'll never believe that!"

He made them more secure but took great care not to let them bite into her skin. He took another piece of cloth and gagged her, then lifted her slender body and placed it on one of the cots, swiftly tying her feet. When he was finished with her, he turned his attention to the unconscious Reb on the other cot and tied the man's feet, roping them to the end of the cell so he couldn't reach the window.

Ben leaned down and kissed Ryan again. "I love you," he whispered, and was surprised at how much easier the words came this time. And then he was gone.

Ty had dressed in the Reb's uniform and started out to find additional uniforms for the rest of them. He quickly surprised and disabled one sentry guarding the door of his barracks and pulled him inside for another man to take his uniform and bind him. He then sauntered across the parade ground, practically under the eye of sentries at the gate. Making his way to the laundry where Reb troopers deposited their dirty clothes, he opened the unlocked door and rummaged through the piles, finding bits and pieces of nine Confederate uniforms. He strode back to the prison barracks, noticing that one of their own had taken the place of the Reb sentry. The others quickly changed clothes and slipped out one by one, taking several Reb sentries by surprise, including the two at the front gate. Each was firmly tied and gagged and secured to rings in different stalls of the stable. They wouldn't be able to help each other get free.

Morgan supervised the binding of the Reb sentries, and he and Ty chose and saddled horses while others broke into the armory and took handguns, ammunition and rifles. Among them were several of the repeating rifles Sean had left. Morgan silently blessed Sean's unintentional generosity.

The men led the horses out, holding a hand to their muzzles. They had come too far to have a nickering horse wake a light sleeper. The two who had taken the guards at the front gate unbarred the huge doors and waited as the horses passed before closing them as tightly as possible. There was no way to close the bar inside, but they hoped the shut gates would keep any sleepless soldier from noticing the absence of the guards.

The last two Yanks mounted and, after walking their horses several hundred feet to maintain the silence, the eleven men spurred their mounts into a run, each one taking deep satisfaction in having a horse under him again and a dark sky above.

Chapter Twenty-three

It was several hours before one of the sentries had worked himself free from the ropes. He sounded an alarm, and within minutes the fort was crawling with sleepy soldiers.

Lieutenant Frazier was jarred from sleep by another officer.

"There's been an escape," he was told. Frazier quickly drew on his trousers and hurried over to the prison barracks. It had been surrounded by soldiers.

Frazier turned to the other officer. "Sorta like locking the barn after the horses are out," he said regretfully. "How many are gone?"

"We don't know yet. No one's gone inside. They were waiting for you."

"Damn fools," Frazier said under his breath.

He strode into his office and found the door to the cells locked. He took out his extra key and opened it. Morgan was gone. He had known that even before he'd entered. Campbell. He noticed several others gone from the cells, when he heard a cry down the corridor and hurried to the sound. The last cell was locked, the key gone. Owens was conscious but hog-tied. Ryan Mallory was tied and gagged, struggling to sit up.

He went back to the office for keys but found the master set gone. He uttered a curse. Morgan again. He quickly returned, cut the rope binding the sergeant to the bars and then the other bonds as the man scooted up to the cell door. He then gave Owens the knife to cut Ryan free.

"What in hell happened?"

Owens shook his head, knowing he could expect to be busted back to private. "He acted like he was dying. I went over to get Miss Ryan. They jumped me in the cell."

Frazier's voice was tight with anger. "You know you're never to open a cell without another man with you."

Owens nodded miserably. "He just seemed so sick...."

Frazier shook his head. "The keys to the cells are gone. There's an extra set at the major's. My friend," he said to Owens, "both you and I are going to have our tails kicked from here to Richmond." He turned to Ryan. "Are you all right, miss?"

She nodded. "But I'm worried about Dr. Seldon. Someone should check on him."

Frazier nodded assent. "I'll send someone and I'll have you out of here in minutes."

As he walked down the aisle, the remaining Yanks burst into the "Battle Hymn of the Republic."

Frazier allowed himself a small bitter smile. He would have done the same.

Frazier had never seen Andrews so angry.

"You lost them. You find them. Take as many men as you need. I want them back. If we lose those eleven, it will be open season. We'll have trouble holding the others." He reached in his desk and found the extra set of keys and tossed them to Frazier. "As soon as you release Owens and Miss Mallory, get going. And don't come back without them."

Frazier turned to leave, stopping only when he heard his major's voice add, "And tell the girl I want to see her. Immediately."

Frazier stopped at the noncommissioned officers' quarters long enough to order out 150 troopers. He would, he figured, divide them into two parties, each large enough to repel most Indian attacks. He didn't particularly envy the Yanks out there; the number of attacks on small parties had been increasing rapidly.

The man he had sent to check on Dr. Seldon was waiting for him in his office. "The doc is all right, sir, still feverish but conscious."

Frazier went back into the cell area and unlocked the cell holding Owens and the girl. Just the short hours there had made Ryan appreciate Ben's compulsion to escape. The tiny cell had been smothering, even with the prospect of being set free within hours.

"Captain Seldon is fine, miss," Frazier told her. "You don't know how much I regret this...inconvenience."

"At least I don't have to live here," she said tartly.

"Miss, this is a war. I don't like it, either. I particularly don't like being a jailer. But there's a lot worse places, both in the South and North." His voice held both impatience and anger.

"I'm sorry, Lieutenant," she said, truly contrite. "Thank you for being kind." Then she looked at him. "Are you going after them?"

"Of course," he said. "And we'll get them . . . if the Indians don't. They don't understand this country. And now I have to be going. Oh, Major Andrews wants to talk to you." He touched his forehead and walked toward the stable.

Ryan walked out with him. There were men mounting everywhere. She looked at the number and shivered. "Be careful, Ben," she whispered to herself.

Andrews was waiting for her in his office, his eyes suspicious and angry.

"Did you know about this, Ryan? Did you help them?"

She returned his look honestly. "No," she said truthfully. "When I saw Colonel Morgan two weeks ago, I tried to tell him the war was nearly over, that I hoped he wouldn't try to escape. I knew he didn't agree, but I didn't know anything about tonight until that young soldier grabbed me."

"Could you have warned us?"

"Tonight?"

"Yes."

"No," she said, again honestly. "But," she added, "I don't think I would have even if I had a chance."

Andrews's face creased into a smile. "At least you're honest. Get some sleep, Ryan. Anna went over to see about Wyeth."

Ryan agreed, wanting to be alone. She doubted if she could sleep, knowing Ben was being hunted both by her own government and in all probability by Indians. She sunk into bed, not bothering to change into nightclothes, wanting to be ready immediately if there was any news. She remembered his look earlier tonight as he kissed her and recalled the flash of admiration in his eyes. His eyes had been so blue, the vivid excitement making them more vibrant than she had seen them before. Her body grew warm as she thought about his hard lean body, and she ached to touch it again. "Ben," she whispered to herself, teasing herself with the sound of it. "Ben. I love you. Be careful for me."

Ben and his men had made good time. They had selected their horses quickly but carefully. All strong, sturdy animals, chosen for their apparent endurance. They turned north, hoping to run into Union patrols sooner that way.

They had been riding six hours when Campbell noted the Indian signs. The cool dawn had given way to midmorning. The day was gloomy and overcast with a sharp edge in the wind.

The eleven were beginning to feel the first heady taste of freedom. Time had increased their confidence; they felt they were well ahead of any pursuit. They could see no telltale trails of dust behind them.

Morgan stopped his horse, resting him, and looked out into the horizon. Ty rode up, graceful and relaxed in the saddle. It seemed that nothing ever bothered him.

"What do you think?" he asked Ben easily, without concern.

"Indians are out there someplace," Ben replied. "Something's stirring them up—you can tell by the tracks. They are moving fast, crossing each other. Tell the others to get ready to run like hell."

Then the sounds came to them. Rifle fire in the distance. Morgan stood up in his stirrups and strained to see. It seemed to be coming from the south of them, beyond a rise. He knew it couldn't be the pursuit from the fort; they would be coming from the west. The gunfire sounded thinner, and he looked toward the trail north—and freedom—then back toward the men following him.

Ty moved up next to him, his own face questioning. "If it's Indians attacking someplace, it means we have a clear trail."

"You go on," Morgan said. "All of you. I'm going to see what's happening."

He kicked his mount into a gallop, ignoring the confusion behind him. The others watched him go, looked at the trail north, then followed him. He reached the rise before he realized all of them were still with him. "Damn." He turned to Ty with surprise. "Don't you ever follow orders?" He didn't wait for an answer but stretched forward in the saddle and studied the scene below him.

Four wagons had been pulled into a square. There was some firing from behind them, but it seemed weak, as if every shot were husbanded. Ben watched as some thirty or forty Indians circled the wagons. Another group was over to the left, waiting.

Campbell approached him. "Well, Colonel, what now?"

Ben looked at him somberly. "I'm going down. You go ahead and get out of here. Head home."

Campbell stared at him. "The Rebs can't be far behind, and we're in their damned uniforms. Besides, Frazier will be here soon to help, and that will give us more time…" His voice trailed off as he realized Ben wasn't listening. "What in the hell can one man do, anyway?" Campbell added angrily.

"One man with a repeating rifle. And there's no telling where Frazier is. Or even if they're coming. They might just decide to leave us to the Indians." Campbell looked at him with disbelief. Ben couldn't blame him. Frazier would, indeed, be close on their heels. But it might well be too late for the people down below.

Campbell shook his head. "We're both damn fools, but I'm coming with you."

"I've been mighty bored lately," Ty Donaldson added.

The other eight gray-clad figures nodded as Ben looked from one to another. "Okay," he said finally. "Let's make them think we're a regiment. Make as much noise as possible, and go straight into the square."

They came down from the rise as if chased by the very bats of hell, each one yelling with as much volume as he had in him. The attacking Indians fell back from the circle, confused by the rush and noise. It seemed as if there were many more than eleven as Ben's small army raced toward the wagons.

Ben was the first to reach the square, and he jumped his horse over furniture piled between the wagons. The others followed right behind, each pulling his horse up quickly to avoid crashing into a wagon. One figure didn't make it and lay still a hundred yards from the wagon. Ben watched as the Indians retreated, apparently to discuss the new development.

He quickly looked around him. Two men stood up and approached him. One stood tall, an old handgun in his right hand. His left sleeve was empty. The other man held a rifle as he limped slowly toward Ben. Both wore gray Confederate trousers. "Thank God," the first man said. "We were down to just enough bullets for them." He looked achingly at two women, both holding rifles, and three children. The youngest, a girl, was kneeling next to a still figure, her small hands clutching a dead one. The other two were teenage boys, both also holding rifles.

"Is this all of you?" Ben questioned, his eyes on the small girl.

The first man nodded, then looked anxiously beyond the wagons. "What about you? Are there more?"

Ben looked at Ty and smiled grimly. "I think I could safely say we'll have company shortly."

"How long? How far behind is the main troop?"

But Ben had stopped paying attention. His eyes were riveted on the little girl. He kneeled and looked at her solemnly. He looked back at one of the men. "Her father?"

The man sighed and nodded. "Bethany's mother died a week ago. Fever."

Ben closed his eyes in pain. For some reason the little girl reminded him of Ryan, although her coloring was different. She had great blue eyes and hair the color of wheat, but there was something in her face that caught at Ben's heart. There had been the same desolation on Ryan's face when she had told him about her own parents' death. He reached a hand out and touched the girl's cheek with infinite tenderness. She looked at him with large eyes, tearless but full of uncomprehending tragedy. Almost without thinking, he held out his arms to her, and she came into them, finally releasing the hand of her dead father. He gathered her to him, and she rested there, her small body shivering.

"I'll be damned," one of the Southerners said. "She wouldn't let any of us touch her."

Ben nodded toward the dead man. "Get him inside one of the wagons," he told Ty.

Slowly, still holding the little girl, he looked out from the wagons, watching as the Indians gathered for another attack. He disentangled himself from the child, but still held one of her hands. He gestured to his horse. "There's another rifle there," he told the man with the limp. He looked around, telling his men to share their ammunition with the others. The man with the empty sleeve looked at him curiously. All the newcomers wore the uniforms of enlisted Southern troops, but they all, particularly the leader, exuded an air of authority. Nothing about the men seemed to add up, but for now, survival was all that mattered.

Ben took his place behind one of the wagons and told the little girl to stay behind him. They all sat there together. Waiting.

Frazier's group found the trail of the escaping Yanks and sent a courier for the other seventy-five men. They joined up together fifty miles north of the fort.

The trail was easy enough to follow. Ben and the others were more concerned with speed than stealth. Frazier thought he was probably some two to three hours behind them. His men were moving fast, and they knew the area well, but the lieutenant was beginning to think it was an impossible chase. The Yanks had too much of a lead. He spurred his horse to a faster pace, ignoring the groans behind him.

Ben had emptied the repeating rifle he had stolen from Fort Scott's stores and switched to a handgun one of his men had thrown him. There was a growing number of bodies circling the wagon, but the attacks kept coming. The Indians used mainly bows and arrows, although some had single-action rifles. Neither were very efficient under the circumstances, but the sheer weight of their numbers was turning the odds. Ben's men were running low on ammunition.

There was a sudden lull as the Indians regrouped at the rise. The small group within the wagon square had used the few minutes to trade guns and divide the last remaining ammunition. Some was to be saved, if it became necessary, for the women and children.

The man with the empty sleeve looked over at Ben. "I thought you said some help was coming."

"It seems," Ben said with a wry smile, "they're a little slower than I thought." He shrugged. "My usual luck."

The man reached his hand over. "My name's Jarrett. I want to thank you, anyway."

Ben took it, then put his arm around the little girl, who snuggled up against it. He wanted, badly, to keep her safe. "How did you happen to be here, anyway?" he said. "Didn't you know how dangerous it is?"

Jarrett looked down at the ground, his face defeated. "The Yankees," he said. "The damn Yankees. We had to get away."

He looked up at Ben, his eyes full of hatred. "They took my arm, the use of my brother's leg. But that wasn't enough. They burned our plantation, confiscated the land. There was nothing left, no way to survive." The fire left his eyes, replaced by failure. "My cousin has a freight line in California—he promised us jobs. We don't have much food. We had to travel as fast as possible."

Ben looked at the little girl. "And her?"

Jarrett's face saddened. "Beth's father was our overseer. A damn good farmer. He and his wife decided to go with us, see if they couldn't find some good land. Mary died a week ago of some fever. Mitch caught a bullet when we were trying to square the wagons."

"Colonel!"

Ben's attention was diverted to Ty, but he noted the sudden confusion that spread over Jarrett's face. He had no time to worry about it.

"They're getting ready to attack again," Ty said.

Ben pushed the girl behind him, whispering softly for her to stay there. He checked his gun and waited, reminding himself to save one bullet.

Frazier was reconciling himself to turning back when one of his scouts stopped, looked puzzled, then cantered back to meet him.

"Something strange, sir," he said.

"Out with it," Frazier said impatiently. He was sick of this patrol, sick of the fruitlessness of it.

"They seem to have turned, headed south. Fast. It doesn't make any sense."

Frazier halted the troop and sat there, thinking. Then he heard shots. He lifted his hand, pointing south, and spurred his horse in that direction.

Campbell crawled over to Ben. "My ammunition is almost gone," he said. "I don't think," he added dryly, "this was one of your better ideas, Colonel."

Morgan turned around. "Maybe next time you'll listen when a superior officer gives an order." His face relaxed only slightly. "It's too late to change your mind now."

"Who's changing their mind? It's still better than that Reb prison. By the way, Colonel, that's one exceptional lady back there."

A quick grin acknowledged the comment, and Campbell was surprised at how much it changed Morgan's face. It was the first time he had seen the colonel permit even a hint of a smile. Not that there had been much to smile about.

He had no time to ponder it. The Indians were attacking again. The small group of defenders fired quickly, but they now had to conserve ammunition. They repulsed the attack, but three of their number were wounded.

"One more attack and we've had it," Campbell said, looking at the sky, which was now clearing. Although it seemed like minutes, they had been under attack several hours and the sun, now visible between the clouds, had reached its pinnacle and was already starting its climb down. After each attack, the Indians had taken time to argue and reassess the situation.

Jarrett moved close to Ben. "How far behind did you say the others were?"

Ben glanced over at Campbell. It had apparently taken a lot longer to discover their absence than either had thought. Perhaps there hadn't been a chase; perhaps the Rebs had thought the Indians would finish them. He didn't think it likely, however. Neither Frazier nor Andrews seemed the type to give up that easily.

Ben's reply was slow in coming. The two families needed all the encouragement they could get, but he himself was wondering now if the Southern troops would come this far. "They should be here anytime now," he finally said, falsely inserting confidence into his voice. He looked at the girl, who stubbornly stayed at his side, and said a small prayer to himself. It was the first in a very long time.

"They're coming again, sir," Ty announced.

Morgan turned around and saw the painted braves lining up for an attack. "Okay," he said. "Make every bullet count. At least we'll take a bunch of them with us."

The attack seemed slow to the men and women lying behind the protective wagons. Each carefully sighted the rifle or handgun, restraining himself from firing until the Indians were nearly on top of them. Some of the Indians reined their horses as they approached the wagons; four others jumped between the wagons and turned back toward the men.

Ben took his now almost empty rifle and used it as a club against one of the attackers. He saw Campbell go down and an arrow aimed at the child next to him. He pushed her down, covering her, and felt intense pain rip through his shoulder. Through a red haze, his senses picked up another sound—a chorus of almost unearthly yells, a sound he remembered well from Virginia.

The Indians heard it, too, and quickly retreated. The four who had jumped the wagons were dead, but they had taken two of Ben's small band with them, including the sardonic Campbell. Ben's physical pain was almost forgotten in the regret and loss he felt. He slumped against one of the wagons and watched a column of Reb soldiers swing toward them.

Ty Donaldson, who had escaped injury, turned toward him. "I never thought I would be glad to hear that yell," he said with resignation.

Ben straightened up painfully and examined the little girl. There was blood coming from a wound in her arm. She regarded him with her big solemn eyes, but still no tears came. She touched his shoulder where an arrow protruded but withdrew her hand quickly when he flinched.

Ben took inventory of the rest. One man had been lost coming in, two lay dead in the square. Four others, himself included, were wounded. Apart from the child, none of the other Southerners appeared hurt.

He leaned back against one of the wagons and waited for the arriving Rebs. His left hand was around the child, who settled beside him; the other was limp, made useless by the fiery pain in his shoulder.

Jarrett and his family pulled one of the wagons ajar, leaving room for the incoming riders. He moved ahead to greet them.

Frazier rode at the head of the column. He ignored Jarrett and rode into the square, his eyes immediately drawn to the dead and wounded men in gray uniforms.

His eyes turned slowly to Ben Morgan. "You could have been long gone, Colonel."

Ben sighed, a slightly crooked smile on his lips. "Probably," he replied agreeably.

"It seems a damn fool thing to do... stopping to help four wagons of Southerners." His eyes had already taken in the gray Confederate trousers of the two men who greeted them.

Ben merely nodded again, this time pain flickering across his face as his hand convulsively tightened around the girl.

"Why?" Frazier asked. "You must have known we were behind you."

Ben grimaced painfully. "It might surprise you to know I was counting on it, Frazier. You were late." The last words were almost an accusation.

Frazier smiled. "No one discovered you missing until almost daylight. Then there was hell to pay before we got going."

"Miss Mallory. She's all right?"

"Well enough to give me a scolding about the accommodations." His smile disappeared. "You know I have to take you back."

Ben closed his eyes, and for a moment Frazier thought he had lost consciousness. But then they opened again, a haze of pain clouding the usual cold blue. "I didn't expect anything else, Frazier," he finally said. "You would be a poor soldier if you didn't. Not," he added with a wry twist of his lips, "that I would object if you turned out that way."

Frazier lifted an eyebrow. "'Fraid not, Colonel, though I think this time I halfway wish I were." He told a sergeant to collect the weapons from the remaining Yanks, turning back to Ben when he heard the deep voice.

"The men with me... they made the decision to come to these people's assistance knowing they were wearing the wrong uniforms...and that you were close behind." The implication was left unsaid.

Frazier swore to himself. Being caught in enemy uniforms could mean hanging. "I can't speak for the major," he said slowly, "but I think it will be forgiven—considering the circumstances."

Jarrett had listened in total confusion. "What's going on?" he finally demanded of Frazier. "These men saved our lives. Aren't they with you?"

"These men," Frazier said slowly, distinctly, "are escaped Yankee officers from Fort Scott. They were far enough ahead of me to get away altogether if they hadn't stopped to help you and your party."

Jarrett blanched. He remembered his earlier words to Morgan. "You let me believe..." he said, his voice trailing off.

"I didn't think it wise to distract you at the time," Morgan said softly. "You might have turned the rifle my way."

Jarrett's face reflected his inward struggle. He had lived with a fierce hatred for Yankees for three years. Now they had saved his family and himself. It didn't make sense, none at all. "But they risked their lives..."

"They risked something more important to them than that," Frazier said. "Their freedom."

He dismounted and went over to Ben, who had broken off the end of the arrow in his shoulder. The arrowhead had remained lodged firmly inside. Frazier took the scarf from around his own neck and made it into a sling, flinching at the pain that flickered over Morgan's face as his shoulder was jolted.

Frazier checked the other wounded men; none of the three seemed serious. He turned back to Jarrett and Ben. "Can you take the dead in your wagon?" he asked Jarrett, who, still stunned, merely nodded.

"And you, Colonel, can you ride?"

Ben nodded, but Jarrett interrupted. "Perhaps he would be more comfortable in my wagon, along with the little girl." He said it reluctantly, his eyes avoiding Ben Morgan's.

Frazier looked at the child still holding on to Ben's hand. He kneeled, noticing the blood on her dress.

"What's your name, honey?" he said gently.

Jarrett answered. "Beth hasn't spoken at all since her mother died a week ago. Her father was killed today. She wouldn't let go of his body until this...officer...joined us. She hasn't left his side since."

Frazier rubbed his head with his hand. He didn't understand any of it, but he didn't like the look of Morgan's wound.

"If he can ride, he'll be better off with us," he said finally. "We'll make better time back to the fort than those wagons. I'll leave half my men to escort you."

Jarrett nodded. "Whatever you say. But I don't think Beth will leave him."

"She needs medical attention, too," Frazier said. "She can ride with me." Frazier had a horse brought around for Morgan and watched as the Yank slowly mounted, his face white with the effort. The little girl wanted to join him, but Frazier whispered that it would hurt the man, and she reluctantly allowed Frazier to lift her onto his own horse.

It was a painfully bitter ride back for Morgan. He knew he would do the same thing again, but it didn't decrease the dread he felt at returning nor the dull pain of losing Campbell and the other two men. His blue eyes were darker than usual, and his face was taut with the effort of staying on the horse.

Ty rode next to him, recognizing his despair but unable to summon any words of comfort. Far from blaming the colonel, he felt only regret that they were going back. He had learned to take death in stride a long time ago and had become indifferent to it. His three dead companions had been soldiers. They had known the dangers and elected to take the risks. They had died. That was it.

He looked over at the colonel and noticed him slumping in the saddle, blood spreading over the gray jacket. They had been riding several hours now and were, he guessed, fairly close to the fort.

Ty called over to one of the sergeants riding as escort to the prisoners. "The colonel's pretty bad. Can you ask the lieutenant to stop?"

The sergeant motioned for another man to take his place alongside the Yanks, then spurred his horse to the front of the column. Ty watched as he spoke briefly with Frazier, who halted the troop and rode back.

Frazier stopped in front of Morgan. The Yank was near unconsciousness, just barely holding on to his saddle, his face pale and drawn. Frazier sighed, weighing the alternatives. The fort was only an hour away, but Morgan was bleeding badly; the arrowhead had apparently worked itself farther in.

He nodded to Ty. "Get him down and see if you can stop the bleeding."

Ty dismounted quickly and he and one of the Reb escorts eased Morgan from his horse. Ty opened Morgan's jacket and shirt, tearing the latter into strips. "Water," he asked of a nearby Reb and was tossed a canteen. He wet one of the strips and pressed it hard on the open wound. He then tied another strip around Ben's shoulder, binding the wet cloth tightly around his chest.

Ty looked at Frazier. "I don't know if he can make it on horseback."

"The faster we get him there, the faster he'll have attention," Frazier replied curtly, holding tightly on to the girl, who was struggling to get down. "Tie him to the saddle."

Ty hesitated, then, hating to ask a favor of a despised enemy, stopped Frazier. "I could ride behind him, hold him up. It would be less jarring."

Frazier nodded, wanting to get back as quickly as possible. He watched as the young Yank swung up in the saddle and, with the help of two soldiers, eased Morgan's body in front of him.

Frazier returned to the head of the column, increasing the pace of the horses.

They arrived at Scott less than an hour later. Frazier directed two of his men to take Morgan and the other wounded to the doctor's office, and others to return the remaining Yanks to the prison barracks. He lifted the girl down and carried her inside the infirmary.

Ryan was back with Wyeth when she heard the troops ride in. She met the men half carrying Ben at the front door and flinched when she saw his white strained face. There was blood on the bandage wrapping his shoulder and chest, but he was alive. Gloriously, wonderfully alive. She reached out and touched him to reassure herself that he was really here.

A small "ahem" interrupted her careful scrutiny, and she turned to see Lieutenant Frazier with a small blood-covered girl in his arms. Ryan was immediately reminded of her duties now that Wyeth was still ill.

"Take Colonel Morgan to the back," she told the men, and then took the girl from Lieutenant Frazier. She was startled at the child's control and gave her a small hug. She turned to Frazier. "What happened?"

"Indians, miss. Apparently Morgan and his men went to the assistance of a small wagon train. This little girl was shot. Morgan has an arrowhead still in his shoulder."

The child struggled to get free. When Ryan put her down, Beth followed the men who had taken Ben into the hospital area. She went to Ben's side, took his hand and stood there defiantly, daring anyone to make her move.

Ryan looked at Frazier, who had followed her back. Frazier shrugged. "She seems to have a real attachment to Morgan. I don't know why."

Ryan smiled, a secret knowing smile. "Dogs and children," she whispered to herself. Frazier stared at her as if she were mad.

"Don't even try to understand, Lieutenant," she said. "I don't think I do myself."

Chapter Twenty-four

Everything had changed. Nothing had changed.

Ryan considered the paradox of this as she helped Anna prepare the evening meal.

It was late February now, and days continued to move agonizingly slowly, although she knew she was fortunate. She had the hospital to keep her busy. Ben had nothing, and she knew what seemed long to her must seem an eternity to him.

And yet something had changed inside him. It was as if the escape attempt had rid him of his demons, or perhaps the week of nursing him had finally convinced him that he could believe again. He and Wyeth had even made a tentative stab at peace after several days of pure antagonism. Sick as they both had been, they had, at first, acted like gladiators in a Roman circus. A few stern words from Anna Andrews had finally defused them both and even brought a reluctant charming smile from Ben. Ryan knew that Anna, from that moment, had herself been caught in Ben's mesmerizing magic. She had never again questioned Ryan's choice.

The Yanks' rescue of the small wagon train had also changed some of the hardened attitudes of the garrison. At Fort Scott there had never been the deprivation and cruelty found in many of the prison camps, both in the North and South. Texas had been in the backwash of the war and had not experienced its full horrors. The hostility of the Confederate troops at Scott was directed more toward the Indians than the Yank prisoners, most of which had come from faraway battlefields.

Their attitude had softened even more after the return of Morgan and his small band of survivors. For two days the rescued Southerners sang the praises of their saviors. There was also Bethany, the silent little girl. No one could miss her devotion to the tall, taciturn Yankee commander. Beth haunted the infirmary and spent hours with Ben, who was infinitely patient and kind with her. Everyone noted this strange relationship with something akin to amazement. The arrogant, hostile colonel was turning out to be something else altogether.

When Jarrett and his party pulled out—this time with a healthy escort—he left Beth behind. She needed medical attention, and both Wyeth and Ryan were afraid of infection on a long trip. She would be sent on to them later. Anna and Ryan agreed to care for her until arrangements could be made.

All too soon, Ben was back in the barracks. At Jarrett's fervent request and Frazier's recommendation, there was no punishment meted out for the escape. The loss of three men and the wounding of others seemed punishment enough after Jarrett's rescue.

Once again the seemingly endless hurting need in Ryan and Ben flared anew. Rules were relaxed to a certain degree, and Ben was permitted to see little Beth and Ryan on occasion, but always under guard.

Yet Ryan noticed a new calm in Ben. Hope now flared frequently in his eyes, and the hot anger was reduced to a controlled simmering. He still hated his confinement, but he no longer raged against it. He knew it wouldn't be long and that Ryan and now Beth were waiting.

Plans to send Beth on to the Jarretts had been first postponed and then discarded. She was no relation to the family, and Ryan knew from talking to the elder Jarrett that, although they would take her out of obligation, it would be an added hardship for them. In the meantime the girl had captured every heart in the fort, but her own belonged to Ben. In the first few days she frequently sneaked over to Ben's hospital bed and sat, watching with fearful eyes, afraid that he, too, would go away. When he was moved over to the barracks, Beth would sit and wait until the prisoners were allowed outside. The guards ignored the deadline, and Ben would fashion whimsical stories for her, conjuring up tales of fairy princesses and unicorns and magic as he had once done for Charlotte so very many years before. He was amazed he still remembered how, but no more so than Ryan, who often listened with fascinated wonder.

For a long time, Beth didn't speak at all, and only her huge blue eyes told of the tragedies she had experienced. But then Ryan gave her the small carved replica of Fortune. Beth loved Fortune, who tolerated her affection with resigned forbearance. On a visit to Ben in Frazier's office, Beth took both Fortunes and showed the new treasure to her tall friend.

Ben studied the small carving and lifted an eyebrow in mock wonder. "It's magic, you know," he said quite seriously.

Her widened eyes regarded him solemnly as the ever watchful Frazier fought to stifle a smile.

"It brings good luck to anyone who has it," Ben continued. "Do you know it brought me good luck?"

Beth shook her head.

"Well, it did. It helped bring Miss Ryan to me." It was only a little exaggeration. He would always feel the real Fortune had had a hand in events, and his fingers found the dog next to him.

"All you have to do," he said in a grave tone, "is rub him and say his name, and your wish should come true."

Beth's face creased in concentration. Her hands reached for the carving, and she rubbed it. Long and hard.

Ben's gently amused voice interrupted her. "I think that's just about right.... Now you have to say his name."

Her lips trembled with the effort; she had a wish and she wanted it more than anything in the world.

"F-F-Fortune," she finally said.

Ben's arms went around her, and he hugged her. Frazier was embarrassed to feel wetness in his eyes.

After Ben disengaged Beth, he looked at her again with gravity. "Do you want to tell me what it is? What you wished for?"

"To... to be with you... always."

"And you will, darling," Ben said. "Someway, you will." He hugged her again, feeling that his heart was inexplicably becoming quite crowded.

Several days later he had a chance to talk to Ryan. She was alone at the fence when he went outside; Beth had run to get him a cookie.

"It seems," Ryan said, "you performed a small miracle."

"It was Fortune's doing," Ben said modestly.

"I know," Ryan said. "Magic."

Ben smiled at the enigmatic reply. She was so pretty today. But then, she was pretty every day. That treacherous warmth started growing again inside him.

"Beth said she could stay with you someday?" It was a question.

"Is that all right with you?" he asked, and her heart jumped. It was the closest he had come to mentioning a future.

She could merely nod.

Beth came then with her special treat, and the subject was not discussed again. Ryan knew Ben was reluctant to commit to anything until he was free again. But there was now a silent understanding between them, a wordless agreement that somehow they would keep small Beth....

And so everything had changed. Ben's attitude, his capacity for trust and loving, their hopes for the future. Yet nothing had changed: their loneliness, their separation and the constant ache that never seemed to go away....

As Beth tugged at Ryan's dress, Ryan smiled down at the little girl she had learned to love dearly. The child looked toward the door, and Ryan knew Matt was on his way. She started putting the dishes on the table.

Her fingers stilled when the door opened and she saw his face. It was white and strained, and he held a letter in his hands.

He looked at Ryan carefully and saw the sudden fear in her eyes. He handed her the note.

"It's Sean, isn't it?" she said quietly, her hands unsteady.

"He's been wounded, Ryan," Matt said softly. "The letter is from one of his men. God knows how he got it here."

Ryan's eyes wouldn't focus at first. She took a long breath and started to read.

"I have to go to him," she said.

He stared at her. "Do you know how many lines you have to cross? The South is in chaos."

"I don't care," she replied, and he knew he wouldn't change her mind. "He needs me."

He didn't want to say it, but he had to; he had to try. "It will take you weeks, possibly months. Anything could happen in that time."

Dead. That's what he means, Ryan thought. Sean would be dead in that time. No. She wouldn't let it. Never again would she let someone close to her die...not if she could do something about it. "I'm going. With your help or without it."

He shrugged helplessly. Sean had told him about her stubbornness, and he had seen it repeatedly in regards to Morgan. She would do exactly as she said.

"There's someone in Scottdale. We buy cattle from him. He sells to both sides, but he's trustworthy in his own way. I'll see if he will accompany you part of the way. There's a patrol going to town tomorrow morning. We'll go with them."

"May I see Colonel Morgan?"

He sighed heavily. "In the morning. And when you reach Sean, tell him to stay alive. I want a chance to punch him for deviling me with Morgan."

The latter statement drew a weak smile from Ryan. "I'll tell him that."

Ryan didn't eat dinner. She was no longer hungry, and the thought of food made her sick. She went, instead, to see Wyeth and tell him she was leaving.

He was still inside the infirmary and, at the sight of her tight pinched face, led her into the office. "What's wrong, Ryan?"

Wyeth's concern broke her control. The words came out in little bursts of agony. It was grief beyond imagining, and Wyeth took her trembling body in his arms, feeling the first small river of tears and then the hurricane of huge shaking sobs. He held her tight, feeling the moisture spread over his shirt until the sobs subsided into tiny whimpering noises. His hand touched her chin and lifted it up so he could see her face.

"I have to go to him," she said through the tears.

"Of course you do," he soothed. "Your brother will be fine. He'll have the best look after him." A small smile played around his lips. "*You* won't let anything happen to him."

"Ben..." It was a tenuous word. No one knew better than Ryan her colonel's fragile hold on faith.

Wyeth sighed. Ben. It was always Ben. He hadn't understood her devotion until the escape. And then he had seen the man with the little girl and started to comprehend. A little. And not altogether willingly.

"I'll take care of your Ben," he said slowly.

Her eyes were still swimming with tears as she met his reluctant ones. She knew how much that promise cost him. She stood on tiptoe, and her lips touched his cheek gratefully. She didn't see the raw pain in his eyes.

"Beth?" he questioned.

"Anna will take care of her, and she has..." She stopped, now seeing his expression.

"I know," he said in a tone tinged with bitterness. "And she has Ben."

"Thank you, Wyeth," she whispered. "Thank you for being my friend."

He smiled ruefully. "You're entirely welcome, little one. And now you'd better get some rest."

She hated to leave the protective kindness of his arms, but she was aware of how much she was hurting him. She straightened and offered a small tentative smile before leaving.

Ben's restlessness had returned. More and more the men were picking up signs from the guards. There was a new melancholy among them, a hovering tension that had not been there before. Their food had been cut again, and when Ben complained on behalf of them all he was abruptly told that rations for all, including the Confederates, had been sharply reduced.

He paced back and forth, trying to ignore the hunger. Going to the small barred window, he looked out, his eyes eagerly searching the grounds for Ryan. Even a glimpse of her would help tonight.

It was all beginning to seem so possible. Ryan. A lifetime with Ryan. With laughter and teasing and love. So much love. And then there was Avery and now Beth. It wouldn't be long now. Not long at all. He could wait.

His eyes traveled from Major Andrews's home to the infirmary, and his hands suddenly clenched the bars so tightly that the blood drained from his fingers. The quick pain in them was nothing compared to the lightning stab in his heart. He stood there, rooted in shock, as he saw Ryan and Dr. Seldon silhouetted in the infirmary window, their bodies locked together.

An animallike moan ripped from his throat as he saw Ryan's lips reach up and kiss the doctor, saw them whisper to each other. Anguish crawled through every inch of him, clawing at his brain, hammering on his heart, slowly replaced by an icy rage. The violence in him, subdued and harnessed since the escape, flickered in his eyes as every muscle in his body went taut with fury.

What a fool he'd been. What a total fool to believe that Ryan was different, that any woman was different. She was simply a better actress than Melody, better at prolonging the deception. *"What woman would want you? What woman..."* Melody's words were still a singsong chant in his brain. *Ryan. Why you? Damn you to hell. Why?*

His eyes found the only movable object in the cell, the water cup. Suddenly, it became a signal. His freedom and dignity and independence had been trampled on and destroyed and mocked.

He sent the cup, like a bullet from a pistol, clamoring against the floor, ricocheting between the bars, raising an unholy din.

Forster stared at him as if he had gone mad, and Ben was suddenly aware of other eyes drawn intently to him. Then the outer door opened and two guards rushed in, one seeing the still-spinning cup and reaching for it.

He reached too close. Ben's arm extended outside the cell, grabbed him around the neck and held him close to the bars.

"Open this door," he said to the other guard, still raging. "Open it before I break his neck." His arm tightened around the man's throat.

Then Frazier walked in, immediately comprehending everything, including the new bright fury in Morgan's eyes. He knew his prisoner was a very dangerous man at that moment.

"No," he said calmly. "Private Simons is a soldier. He knows the risks. And," he said softly, "you *will* hang this time."

"I don't care," Ben said, his eyes clashing with Frazier's. So intent was he on winning the match, he didn't hear Forster's steps behind him nor anticipate the blow that felled him.

He woke several minutes later. Forster worriedly stared down at him. Everything came back, flash after terrible flash. Ryan and Seldon. The guard. Frazier.

His head ached and he put a hand back and felt the growing lump. His accusing eyes pierced Forster. "You?"

Sam Forster nodded miserably. "We're too close to freedom," he said slowly, "for you to die at the end of a rope. They weren't going to release you."

Ben closed his eyes and turned toward the wall. "You should have minded your own business, Sam."

Forster felt a sickness wash over him. Ben had told the guard he didn't care whether he died. He knew now that Ben had meant every word of it. He looked hopelessly at Morgan, wondering what had changed so radically in the past few hours. Morgan had been so different these past months, so much more at ease with himself. Forster shook his head and moved over to his own cot. It was this damned prison. It did strange things to everyone.

Ben's night was sleepless. He was choking on his drowning hopes and dying dreams. He had never felt such desolation, not even when Melody disappeared. Perhaps he had halfway expected that desertion. But Ryan . . . ? She had taught him to trust, and to what end? During the cold bitter night, his heart hardened. All the emerging new feelings were encompassed in a shroud of defeat. He had been right to distrust others, so very right. He vowed never again to leave himself open. And he wrapped himself tighter and tighter in the cocoon he had weaved so long ago.

Ryan also was sleepless. She kept seeing Sean, wounded and untended, and Ben...the new hopeful Ben. She didn't want to leave him now when there was so much between them. She was being forced to choose between Sean and Ben, but right now, Sean needed her more. She knew Ben would understand. He loved Sean, too, in his own way. They had both shown it repeatedly if, sometimes, reluctantly. She would find Sean, and they would come back, and she and Ben would start a life together. With that hopeful thought, she finally went to sleep.

She woke with the first light of morning. Matt Andrews had said he wanted to leave early, and she had to see Ben first. She hurriedly dressed and dashed down for a quick breakfast with the Andrewses. She was warned that they would be leaving in a few moments.

Ryan almost flew over to the barracks and accosted Frazier, who was also up early. For reasons even he couldn't explain, the lieutenant had chosen not to report Ben's violence of the night before. He had even gained the unwilling conspiracy of the guards themselves. When he saw Ryan and accepted her note from Major Andrews, he consented readily enough. Perhaps, he thought, it was just what Morgan needed. There was no denying the feeling between the two.

He opened the outer door and, after making sure everyone was decently attired, allowed Ryan to enter. Frazier was not, however, ready to open the cell gate. Instead, he stepped away, trying to give some semblance of privacy.

Ben was awake, had been for hours. His eyes followed the opening of the door and watched carefully as Ryan entered and approached his cell. Only a twitch in his cheek betrayed any emotion. He remained where he was, half upright against the wall, his face completely impassive, his dark blue eyes chilling.

Ryan looked at him in disbelief. Not since the earliest days in Sean's camp had he looked so unapproachable. The fact that he remained indifferently relaxed against the wall told her something was very, very wrong.

"Ben...?" she started.

He did not help. He continued to act as if she didn't exist. She tried again. "Ben...I have to go—"

He interrupted her. "I know...I know all about it."

She stared now. How could he? But then there was a very active grapevine.

"Then you understand...he—he needs me...." She was stuttering in hurt confusion. If he knew, why was he acting this way?

Why didn't he care? Anger started bubbling up inside her. Anger and pain.

"You don't need to explain anything," he said, studied contempt in every word. "It's all quite clear. You prefer him. Well, go to him. I don't ever want to see you again."

Ryan felt her heart shatter. She couldn't take her eyes from the cold, dispassionate look, the cruel lips that were saying such things, the hard body she loved to touch and that, now, was tense and coiled to strike. Tears sprang from her eyes.

"Spare me, Miss Mallory," he said. "I don't want your tears or your pity. I just want you out of here." His lips clenched and he looked at Frazier. "I know I don't have any choice . . . but can't I at least be spared this?"

The cruelty of his words stunned her. She stepped closer to the bars, her hand outstretched. "Ben . . ."

"Get the hell out of here." His words were ground out between clenched teeth, each one carrying more rage.

Just then the outer door opened and a trooper came in. He looked at Ryan. "Major Andrews said if you are going with him, you'd better come. They're leaving."

Ryan looked around desperately. Sean. Ben. Why didn't he understand?

"Miss Ryan . . ."

"Ben . . ." It was a cry of grief.

"Miss Ryan . . ."

She whirled around. "I'll be right there." She looked back at Ben. She wanted to say she loved him, but she couldn't. Not with that empty forbidding mask answering her cry for help, not with that icy contempt rejecting her need for comfort. With tears racing down her cheeks, she almost ran for her horse.

Ben heard the horses leave. Ryan and Seldon. He wondered where they were going. Good riddance. He didn't need anyone. He never had. He tried to summon a feeling of relief but felt only a yawning emptiness.

The enormity of his mistake was not clear until two days later . . . partly because he had deliberately distanced himself from the rest of the world. He heard nothing; he listened to nothing. He declined to go out during the exercise time. He declined, in fact, to do anything but simply exist.

Forster became increasingly concerned. He still didn't know what had started it all. He had been napping the evening Ben had watched Seldon and Ryan and had roused only at the sound of the cup against the iron bars. He finally asked Frazier to fetch Dr. Seldon.

When Wyeth entered Ben's cell, Morgan's eyes flew open with shock. "You!" He said the word with complete loathing. The hatred was so strong that Wyeth flinched.

Then confusion entered Ben's mind and sent it spinning. Ryan had left with Seldon? Hadn't she?

He lifted his head, his eyes suddenly filled with doubt. "Ryan?"

There was puzzlement in Wyeth's eyes. Ryan had told him she would tell Ben. "Gone to Richmond two days ago . . . to see about Sean."

"Sean . . . ?" The sudden appeal in Ben's voice was unmistakable.

"Didn't she tell you? She said she was going to. Captain Mallory was badly wounded in Virginia."

Ben's eyes closed. My God, what had he done? "But I saw you . . . you and Ryan together."

Wyeth suddenly comprehended. His office was directly across from Ben's cell. The man had seen them together that night.

"You're an even bigger fool than I first imagined," he said, his voice cold. "She came to tell me she was leaving. She was sick about her brother and just as worried about you and what her absence might do to you. She was torn apart. I would give anything in the world to have someone love me as much as she loves you."

Every word was a hammer blow. Ben tried to remember exactly what he had said to Ryan that morning, but his mind was mercifully blank. He knew he had said unforgivable things. He buried his head in his hand.

His obvious agony softened Wyeth. "Ryan loves you, Morgan. God knows why. At this moment, I sure as hell don't." His smile was more than a little bitter. "She'll be back. She never gives up. Not on anyone, especially people she loves."

Ben's eyes met his. "I don't understand why you're telling me this."

Wyeth's expression was comical as he searched for an answer himself. "I don't, either. Except, perhaps, you're important to her, and she's important to me. She asked me to look after you."

Ben stood up, his face tortured. "Sean . . . How bad is he?"

Wyeth couldn't quite meet his eyes. He knew from Ryan how close the two men had been.

"It's bad," he said finally. "Arm and chest."

Ben recoiled. Chest wounds were nearly always fatal, particularly in army hospitals. Infection and pneumonia were only two of the problems. He knew then how badly Ryan had needed him and how terribly he had failed her.

His hands clenched. Why did he always throw everyone important away? Why did he inevitably cause so much pain to those who tried to love him? Avery. His sister. Sean. And now the finest person he had ever known. Ryan.

When Wyeth looked back at him, he thought he had never seen so much hell in one man's eyes.

Chapter Twenty-five

$\mathcal{A}$s Ryan approached Richmond under a flag of truce, she could hardly recognize the city she had visited earlier.

Signs of death were everywhere. Death and ruin and destruction. Chimneys stood like lonely sentinels where homes had once housed families. The horrible scent of death rose from decaying animal carcasses, which lay twisted and torn on every road. The wounded and homeless were everywhere—walking, stumbling, begging—their eyes glazed with the horrors they had seen.

She turned to her Union escort. Her voice was tight with pity. "It's worse than anything I ever imagined."

The officer turned to his pretty black-clad companion. He had been asked to escort the young widow across enemy lines to tend to her brother's wounds. He scanned the scene, the site of the most recent attempt to take Richmond, and saw it from her eyes. His had grown so used to the destruction that it no longer made an impact. Now he looked at it anew and understood her reaction.

"Don't think about it, ma'am," he said.

"How can anyone not think about it? What are we doing to each other?"

He shook his head. There was no answer. He turned his attention back to the road. They would soon be reaching Reb lines, and he didn't trust them. There was too much hatred and bitterness now. And all the rules were gone. His body tensed as he approached the almost impenetrable fortifications leading into the heart of Richmond, his eyes steady on the white flag carried by a private who accompanied them.

"You will please remain here, ma'am," he said, spurring his horse ahead to where a Reb officer was emerging. They talked for several minutes before the blue-uniformed officer gestured her forward.

"It's all right," he said, "you can go on in. I hope your brother recovers." He didn't wait for a thank-you but turned his horse toward his own lines, his mind still wondering about the very pretty woman. He had been told she was the widow of a Union officer and the sister of a wounded Reb. What an insane war this was....

He didn't ponder it long. As soon as he reached his own lines, he was told to prepare for another attack.

He looked at the small calendar he always carried. It was the fifteenth of March.

Ryan tried to remember the gaiety and hope of Richmond as she rode through its crowded streets. The smell of defeat was everywhere. Milling troops mixed with carriages and wagons filled with people trying to leave the city. All feared the same fate as Columbia, South Carolina, and Atlanta, Georgia. Both cities had been burned to the ground. There was panic now...a panic that fed on itself and grew in intensity day by day.

Lee was faced by an army more than double the size of his own, and Sherman was approaching rapidly from his harsh victories in the Carolinas and Georgia. The Union ring was closing tighter and tighter on the doomed cities of Petersburg and Richmond. Not even the most foolish optimist held out any hope.

Wrung out by the repeated tragedies she had seen on her long journey, Ryan tried to prepare herself for the worst. It had been three weeks since she received the message about Sean, and that had been two or three weeks after his injuries. Her fist tightened on the reins of the borrowed horse as she sought out the address in Jimmy's letter.

The journey had been so very slow. She had ridden by horseback, then coach and finally train. But the trains were slow or late or nonexistent because of guerrilla raids.

Because she had to cross lines, she had prepared her story carefully. She had borrowed a black dress from a woman at the fort and often played the grieving widow. Her story of conflicting loyalties—a dead Union husband, a wounded Reb brother—usually won sympathy and a place when others were denied. It had not been a difficult part to play. There was undeniable sadness in her eyes, and for the first time in her life, her tears fell easily. There were few not eager to help.

She found the street and stiffened. Sean had to be alive. He had to be. She had willed it.

Nonetheless, her swimming eyes had difficulty in finding the house and then she sat there, afraid to dismount. She finally left the safety of her perch and slowly climbed the stairs.

The door opened before she could knock, and she stared at a kindly looking older woman. "Mrs. Osborne?" Ryan wanted to rush on with words, but her mouth was dry, and she couldn't seem to control it.

She tried again. "My brother . . . Sean Mallory?" Her eyes were full of fear. She reached out her hand in supplication. "Is he . . . ?"

The woman's tired face split into a wide smile. "Captain Mallory? He's doing just fine, Miss, or is it Mrs? He told me he had a sister."

A tremulous smile started on Ryan's face. "He's alive!"

"It would take a few more bullets to kill that one," the woman said, "though for a while it was touch and go. He's been awfully sick."

Ryan could hardly control herself. "Is he here? Can I see him?"

The woman nodded. "He's still very weak. He's had a case of pneumonia that would have killed any other man," she said with a smile. "He's very, very stubborn. He said he had someone he had to take care of."

"May I see him?"

"I have to go see about some more medicines. Someone inside will show you where the captain is." The woman squeezed her hand reassuringly, then hurried on.

Ryan went into a hallway and looked into what must have once been a parlor. Now it was filled with row upon row of wounded men. She scanned each face, then hurried to another room. Still more men lay there, some on cots, some on mattresses on the floor.

A woman was coming down the steps, her arms full of bandages. She looked at Ryan curiously.

"I'm looking for Captain Mallory."

"Upstairs, first room on the left." Before she had finished the words, Ryan was mounting the steps two at a time. She opened the door, and her eyes searched the room, finally resting on a thin figure turning restlessly on a cot.

"Sean."

He turned at the sound of her voice, and his eyes leaped with sudden joy. He struggled to sit up, every movement an effort.

"You never stay put, do you, Kitten?" Despite his words, the softness in his eyes told Ryan how glad he was to see her.

Her own eyes filled with tears, and she put a fist to her mouth, trying to hold them back. She didn't want him to see how afraid she had been.

"Come here, Kitten." He held out his hand, and she grasped it and held it tight.

"I knew you would be all right. I knew it."

His mouth turned upward in a crooked smile. "Is that why you came all this way? To see if you were right?"

She ignored the slight tease in his voice. "You're so thin."

"There isn't much food in Richmond," he replied, suddenly very serious. "You shouldn't have come."

In answer, she just pressed his hand.

"How's Ben?" he asked carefully.

An uncharacteristic shadow crossed her face. She knew the question was coming, and she didn't know how to answer it. During the past three weeks, she had tried to sort out what had happened that day she left, but no possible explanation made sense. She saw Sean's eyes narrow as he watched her.

"As you predicted," she finally said, forcing a light note into her voice. "Major Andrews said to tell you to get well. He wants a chance to pay you back for leaving Colonel Morgan with him."

His dark look demanded that she continue, and she told him of Ben's escape and his rescue of the wagon train.

Sean's face lighted at the tale, and he smiled weakly. "I told you he was unpredictable."

Ryan could only nod in agreement, and Sean in his weakened state missed the sharp pain in her eyes. When she looked back, his eyes were half-closed with exhaustion.

"Go to sleep," she whispered. "I'll be here when you wake up."

"Pretty little Kitten," he said sleepily. "I've missed you."

Those in Richmond had grown used to the sound of cannon fire. Ryan had not. Nor did she think she ever would. It was like terrible endless rolls of thunder, but instead of rain, it spewed death and agony. New wounded poured into Richmond daily as the Union forces tightened their hold on the city.

Food, when it could be found, was impossibly expensive. A handful of crackers cost one hundred Confederate dollars. Meat was practically nonexistent. Ryan had a few gold coins remaining from a small hoard left by Sean, which had been stitched carefully into her clothes for the trip to Virginia. She shared some now with Mrs. Osborne for her hospital, keeping only enough to see them back to Texas. She also shared her skills. Every pair of hands was desperately needed as more and more wounded flooded the hospitals and private homes such as Mrs. Osborne's.

As Sean gained some strength, he also tried to help, giving water and encouragement, even washing bandages. He felt guilty taking up a bed, but even two or three hours on his feet exhausted him, and, white and strained, he would be forced to lie back down.

Panic in the city intensified when news came that Mrs. Jefferson Davis had left. Sean wanted Ryan to go, but she wouldn't leave without him, and he was still too weak to travel.

Justis and Jimmy visited at the end of March and were delighted to see Ryan and how well Sean was doing. They were there just a brief time before hurrying back to their lines, promising to return for the Mallorys if the city was abandoned.

In what little time there was to talk, Sean told Ryan about his journey to Virginia, leaving out many of the dangers. His voice saddened as he described the almost total destruction in Georgia and the armies of hungry and homeless they encountered on the way. They had switched uniforms repeatedly at first, then divided into small groups and posed as peddlers. It had been a long perilous journey, and not all had made it, Braden among them. Sean asked several times about Ben, noting the reserve that immediately invaded Ryan's eyes and her unusual reluctance to talk. Something was wrong, very wrong, but Ryan would say only that she planned to return to Fort Scott, no matter how much Sean probed.

On Sunday, April 2, President Davis and the cabinet were summoned during church services, and rumors ran rampant: the cabinet was meeting; President Davis had left the city; Petersburg had fallen; the Yankees were fast approaching.

Fear swept the city, and thousands clogged the streets. Carrying only small bundles, they fled along the northern bank of the James, competing with retreating soldiers for the small broken roadway.

In the late evening, Justis and Jimmy appeared with Sean's horse. Sean decided he was strong enough to leave; he knew he would otherwise be taken prisoner, and he worried about Ryan's safety among the first wave of jubilant Yankee invaders.

It was a scene from hell, Ryan thought. Fires and explosions were everywhere; mobs were pillaging stores, and whiskey ran in the streets. It was miles upon miles of fire and black smoke, a ceaseless babel of human voices—crying, pleading, grieving.

Several times Justis and Jimmy had to resort to firearms to keep their horses from being taken. Ryan had dressed as a boy, the easiest way to both ride and avoid the scavengers of both sides. She had been through sickness and Indian raids, but nothing compared to this. She knew she would never forget it.

They followed Lee's tired, defeated, hungry troops for miles, turning frequently to see the red glare spreading over the capital of the Confederacy, a bloody red halo that cried defeat for a cause that had been doomed from the beginning.

Seven days later, camping at the end of a wood, they heard the news. General Lee had surrendered at Appomattox. The war was over.

The journey to Texas was equally devastating. Ryan had never seen such hunger, such hopelessness. Endless lines of battered humanity mindlessly put one foot in front of the other: Southern soldiers, tattered and often shoeless, trying to get back home; Westerners leaving the East; prisoners returning starved from the North. It was a constant churning of humanity trying to find a way back to homes that no longer existed and families scattered to the winds.

Their money ran out quickly, for they often found those worse off than themselves and by common agreement shared what they could spare. They still had horses and guns, and a limited amount of ammunition. They had clothes on their backs. It was more than many.

Their financial condition improved substantially when they were attacked by scavengers, who found more than they expected. Justis and Jimmy had gone to hunt, leaving what the outlaws thought would be easy pickings. They didn't expect the young boy to be able to shoot so accurately nor the rail-thin man to be so fast with a knife. When Justis and Jimmy returned, they discovered three dead bodies and a pouch full of gold and valuables.

When they reached Baton Rouge, they found fresh Union troops, who, to their amazement, were being sent to Fort Scott as replacements for the Federal officers who had assumed control after the surrender. Dressed in his tattered gray trousers and filthy shirt, Sean met the commander and asked if Ryan and Justis might accompany them. He explained that Ryan had family there and was engaged to a Union officer. After meeting Ryan, the man quickly agreed.

Satisfied that Ryan was safe and that Justis would provide further protection, Sean and Jimmy headed south. He wanted to stop and see Braden's family and the families of some of the others who had died. He owed them that much. He would meet Ryan at Fort Scott. He gave her most of what was left of the purse they had taken from the renegades and spurred his horse south. There were far too many Yankees here for his taste.

Andrews was at his desk when the dispatch rider came in. He knew instantly it was more than the usual packet. The rider asked to see the commanding officer—an unusual request under any circumstances.

The trooper came into his office, his face tired and worn...and something more. Andrews took the mail pouch and army packet. Something kept him from asking questions; he instinctively knew the answers. He read the contents quickly and nodded to the rider, who abruptly turned and left, other destinations ahead of him. There was an escort waiting.

Andrews sunk in his chair. It was only an acknowledgment of what he had known for many months, but the reality of it hurt more than he thought possible. The South had lost, had surrendered in Virginia, was surrendering throughout the Confederacy. His orders—more of a message—urged him to seek the best surrender terms possible. He was on his own.

Andrews weighed the alternatives. There were not many, he admitted. He was sitting in the middle of the plains with six hundred troops and three hundred prisoners. He could easily envision the slaughter of both by Indians if antagonism between the two continued. If his men had to give up their arms, they were doomed.

He called in his principal officers: Captain Woodward, his second in command; Lieutenant Frazier, whose responsibility had been the prisoners; Captain Seldon; and four other lieutenants.

He quickly relayed the essence of his orders. Lee had surrendered. Grant had given generous terms—the men were to keep their horses and sidearms. Rifles were contraband. All independent commands could make their own terms. Fort Scott was considered independent.

"Any suggestions?" Andrews queried.

There was a silence. They had all known it was coming. The realization of defeat, however, was a different thing.

Andrews broke the uneasy quiet. "I don't think we have any choice but to negotiate with Colonel Morgan. I'll tell you frankly,

I don't know what he will do. I do know I won't surrender the fort under less than honorable terms."

Frazier broke in. "Sir, I may be alone in this, but I think Morgan will be reasonable."

"I hope to God you're right," Andrews replied. He sat down wearily. "Tell your men what's happening. That Lee's surrendered and we're negotiating. I want them ready to accept what might come. I won't give their lives away. Make them aware of that."

His officers started to leave. Andrews stopped Frazier, then waited until the others were gone.

"Lieutenant, bring Morgan to me."

As the door closed, Matt Andrews leaned back in his chair, wondering about Morgan. The man's reputation had been hard, his demeanor rebellious, his attitude hostile. Even the strange relationship between Morgan and Beth didn't impress him. Even the hardest man had some soft spot. He didn't have a lot of optimism about the coming confrontation.

Frazier stopped in his office briefly, preparing himself. He said nothing yet to his sergeant about the impending surrender. Finally, he gathered his wits and told the old sergeant to open the door.

Frazier went straight to Morgan's cell and waited while the sergeant opened it. "Colonel, would you please come with me."

Ben stared at him with surprise, then stood and almost leisurely sauntered to the door. He started out of the cell and suddenly realized there were no outstretched handcuffs. He looked at Frazier, one eyebrow arched in question.

Frazier just smiled ruefully and shrugged.

Morgan followed him, optimism growing within him. Could it possibly be over?

When they arrived at Major Andrews's office, Frazier ushered him inside then stepped back out, closing the door behind him. Morgan found himself looking at Andrews, who was playing with an official-looking paper.

Andrews finally spoke. "Please sit down, Colonel."

Morgan sat, his face inscrutable.

Andrews silently handed him the message and studied the man as he read it.

Ben's face did not change, nor did his eyes. He handed it back. "What do you intend to do, Major?" he asked quietly.

"Surrender to you . . . if I can get the right terms for my men."

"And what might those be?"

"The same as Grant's terms and a bit more. My men keep their horses, their sidearms . . . and their rifles. In this country, a rifle means life or death. As," he added wryly, "you have found out."

Ben's face didn't change as he heard the offer. Without hesitation, he nodded to Andrews. "Done."

Andrews's face was a study in astonishment. He started to rise, then settled back down. "I want it in writing."

Ben took some paper and a pen from Andrews's desk and quickly scribbled some words. He handed it to Andrews.

Morgan almost laughed at Andrews's expression. "You didn't expect it to be this easy?"

Andrews gave him just a trace of a smile. "To tell you the truth, I didn't know what to expect. You have a difficult reputation, and you've been anything but cooperative."

Ben's expression was intent. "It wasn't the best of circumstances," he replied slowly. "But I've never taken pleasure in another's defeat—nor in their pain."

Andrews nodded. "I'll vacate my quarters today."

"No," Ben said sharply. "I prefer the bachelor quarters. You've been very good to Ryan and Beth. I'm not going to toss you out. You and your wife stay here as long as you're at Fort Scott." With his heart in his eyes, he asked the question that had been hammering at him since he came in. "Have you heard anything about them—Ryan or Sean?"

Andrews could only shake his head.

"I would like to see Beth later," Ben said. "Right now, I've men out there who have been waiting years for this. I owe them first." His eyes met Andrews's. "I want this to be an easy transition. I'll see to the release and talk to them at the same time you talk to yours. Let's avoid any hostility we can. We'll work out the details later."

Morgan started to leave again, stopping only when he heard the soft Southern drawl. "Colonel?"

Morgan turned around.

"I would consider it an honor if you'd have dinner with us tonight."

Ben smiled, a slow hauntingly sad smile. He wished Ryan was here.

"That's kind of you," he said softly. "I know how hard this must have been. I accept. And I thank you."

He met Frazier outside. The lieutenant was resting on a porch step, his back against a railing. He rose lazily, pushing his nonregulation hat to the back of his head.

"I take it you and the major came to an understanding?"

Ben studied the man in front of him. He had admired the evenhanded way the Reb had managed an assignment he obviously didn't like. He had been reasonable and fair, more than fair, really, even at the time of Ben's attack on the guard.

"Yes," he said slowly. "Would you like to check with Andrews inside? I'll need your help."

"I don't think I need to do that," Frazier drawled. They both turned when they heard the door open, and Andrews appeared. His face looked years older, and his eyes were blank as he glanced at his lieutenant.

"You were right, Frazier," he said slowly, nodding at Ben. He looked around the fort sadly, recognizing the tenseness in the air.

"Frazier," he continued finally, "go with Colonel Morgan and release the prisoners. I'll talk to our men." He turned and left without another word.

Ben Morgan turned to Frazier. "What did he mean when he said you were right?"

Frazier shrugged. "I just ventured the opinion you would be reasonable."

"No one else thought so?"

Frazier turned to him. "You haven't exactly been the easiest man here. They didn't know what to think. They hadn't seen you like I did. I watched you with your men. I saw you put pride back into them. It wasn't exactly helpful to me, but I respected it. You're a good officer, and good officers don't usually demand a pound of flesh."

They were silent the rest of the way. The cell area was quiet when Ben entered, the men tense and watchful. Some had watched their colonel and the Reb lieutenant walk across the parade area, and they had sensed a distinct change in roles. They had also been very aware of the strained emotions among the Reb guards.

Ben didn't waste words. "The war is over. Major Andrews has surrendered the fort to me. Lee surrendered to Grant two weeks ago in Virginia. You're free."

He watched as the Rebs unlocked the doors, studied the men as they sought to understand but couldn't seem to grasp the meaning. There were no shouts of jubilation until Lieutenant Hart pulled out his harmonica and started playing "The Battle Hymn of the Republic." They all stood there, the eyes of many wet with unshed tears. As the last strains slowly disappeared into the air, Ben grinned. "It's true. It's really true."

The last words finally made an impact. They looked at each other and came into the hall, grabbing each other, hugging indiscriminately, pounding on backs.

Ben left them alone but turned to Frazier. "Let the men in the other barracks out into the yard. I want to talk to them."

He gave them the same short speech. A ragged cheer interrupted him, and he allowed himself a wide grin. "Go ahead, you deserve it."

"What now, Colonel?" yelled one. "What do we do now?"

Morgan looked across the field, where groups of Rebs were gathered. "They're being told now. Give them an hour or so to get adjusted. I'll have two of the barracks cleaned up for you. They'll just have to double up for the next few days."

He hesitated. "We're going to have to live together for a little while. We may even have to fight together. They have honorably surrendered, and they have been a valiant foe. I don't want any trouble from our side. I won't tolerate any from theirs. Is that understood?"

Morgan watched carefully as the men nodded slowly.

"All right, Frazier and the sergeant major will return any belongings they've been keeping safe for us." This was said with a rueful smile. "And you can go as damn close to the fence as you want. You can even tear the darn thing down if you want. But I'm asking you to stay in this area until Captain Forster informs you differently. Agreed?"

There was a chorus of approval, all of them too stunned from the rapid turn of events to protest.

"What about home, Colonel?"

"We'll get you there as soon as possible. I'll be sending a request for relief immediately. As soon as it gets here, we'll start processing you out of here." He turned and left.

There was one last errand he wanted to complete.

Ben strode over to the infirmary, briefly knocked on the closed door and opened it.

Wyeth was standing, packing instruments in his black medical bag. He looked up as Ben entered.

"I've been expecting you, Colonel."

"Have you now?" Ben said softly. He looked at the bag. "Planning to leave so quickly?"

The answer was curt. "Yes."

"I'm asking some to stay," Ben said, his eyes studying the Louisiana doctor.

"I wouldn't think that would include me," Wyeth replied, a bitter tone in his voice.

"May I sit down?" Ben asked, his face emotionless.

"I think you can probably do any darn thing you want on this post right now," This time the bitterness was explosive. Wyeth turned angry eyes on Ben. "Why bother to ask?"

"Because I've been a fool, and I've come to ask you to stay...at least until we hear about Ryan. And," he added with a small smile, "we don't have a doctor."

It was Wyeth's turn to stare. There was surprise in his dark gray eyes, and he dropped suddenly into a chair. "Why the abrupt change?" he asked suspiciously.

Ben sat down across the desk from Wyeth, his eyes veiled.

"I made a mistake fifteen years ago and lost the best friend I ever had. I swore I would never let my temper lose me something that valuable again. And yet I've done exactly that. Repeatedly. I would like to blame it on the prison over there, but I can't. It's something inside me that just seems to boil over. And I'm the loser." He stopped. "That's an apology, Doctor. You have been good to my men, and you've tried to be decent to me. I appreciate it."

Wyeth listened in amazement. There was a painful honesty in the Yankee officer and a charm he hadn't expected.

Ben stood up and held out his hand. "I wouldn't blame you if you refused it," he said.

But Wyeth didn't, and the handshake was unexpectedly firm.

Ben made his way over to Andrews's empty office and sat down. He wanted to be alone. He knew he should be elated. The war was over, he and his men free. But freedom meant nothing at the moment, and he was only filled with a vast loneliness. Ryan was gone. Sean was wounded, perhaps dead. Both were lost in the boiling caldron that was the South. He would never forget his last words to her; perhaps they had forever lost her to him. But he would look for her. He would find her. As soon as he could, he would resign his commission and search for Ryan and Sean Mallory if it took the rest of his life.

He buried his head in his arms in total grief.

Chapter Twenty-six

Apprehension battled with hope as Ryan rode into Fort Scott with reinforcements. She was almost sick with uncertainty, still totally baffled from her last meeting with Ben. She had to make him understand why she had left him to go to Sean.

Ryan looked frantically for the tallest officer, her eyes inevitably traveling quickly to Major Andrews's old office.

She saw him, Fortune at his heels, on the porch, and her heart surged with the old familiar jolt. How tired and worn he looked, how strained. But how completely wonderful. Her hands tightened on the reins as she became a mass of pulsing, undefinable feelings. Except for love. That she knew, and it was stronger than ever as she watched the sure figure turn their way and saw the beloved sad face change as he identified her.

Ryan had been prepared for anything: anger, studied indifference, even the contempt of that last day. Everything, except the fierce joy that suddenly blazed in his face. And then he was coming toward her, not walking but running, dignity and reserve gone. He reached her horse and looked up, his eyes searching, wondering, fearing, hoping. So much was in them, Ryan thought, so much that he had been afraid to show before.

She thought she would die. No one could experience the intense happiness, the bubbling exhilaration, the absolute euphoria she felt, without dying. Unthinking, she kicked her feet out of the stirrups and propelled herself out of the saddle and into Ben's arms, which wrapped protectively, possessively around her. And then the miracle. Regardless of all the watchers, the troopers standing in complete astonishment, Ben's lips touched hers with a force and energy that swept her away into some incredibly sweet world that was theirs alone. He was tender and fierce, giving and taking, exulting and fearful. His lips told her a thousand things, asked so many questions, and hers gave him every answer he needed.

He whirled around, Ryan still cradled in his arms and against his chest, and, completely oblivious to his officers standing dumbfounded, to the new reinforcements watching with wide grins, he strode with strong confident steps to his office.

Once there, he lowered her to the floor. He wanted to see her face—her wonderful, beautiful, giving face.

He studied every lovely curve, each beautiful feature and the love shining so brightly in her eyes.

He said nothing, just held out his arms again and clasped them around her as she floated into them. They stood there for a long time, exulting in the nearness of each other. "Ryan," he finally whispered. "My beautiful Ryan."

Ryan, her hands wandering gently around his back, rested her head against his broad hard chest, her eyes filling with silent tears. There was too much happiness to bear; the joy could express itself no other way. She said a silent thanks to God and pressed herself even more tightly into his gentle embrace. He was now her life. They were irreparably entwined. She felt the old currents charging and singing between them and knew again the familiar understanding that made words unnecessary.

Ben finally stepped back and lifted her chin so that her eyes met his. A sudden shadow crossed his face as he saw them glimmering with tears. His lips touched them, kissing away the wetness.

"I love you, little Reb," he said softly, gently. "I love you so very, very much."

Ryan stood, unable to answer, her emotions swelling to a crescendo. She finally forced herself to nod and stood on tiptoes to kiss his lips with an almost ethereal sweetness.

Ben could no longer contain his elation. He put his hands around her small waist and swung her around, rejoicing in her quick, musical laughter.

"I never would have expected," Ryan said teasingly, "you had such an exuberant nature."

"Ah, there's a lot of things you never expected." He laughed back. "Are you sure you want to find out?"

"Very, very sure," she answered, delighting in his openness and the happy laughter on his face. "You really should do that more often, you know."

"What?"

"Laugh," she said, again with the teasing, loving music in her voice. "It becomes you."

"It will be easy with you," he answered. Then, so abruptly she almost didn't catch the words, he added, "Will you marry me?"

Ryan stood absolutely still as the words sunk in. The corners of her mouth wriggled. Only Ben could make a proposal in such a brusque way.

"How soon?" she answered, her eyes fairly dancing with delight.

He looked at her, his usually stern, stoic features creasing with amusement. "I didn't know what an impatient young lady you were."

"Want to change your mind?" She could ask it now; she knew the answer.

"Oh, no. I won't let you off now. I have you now, and I won't ever let you go." He added with fierce emphasis, "Never."

She rested against him again, feeling the confident strength in his body and reveling in it. "I don't ever want to go."

"You haven't really answered me," he said. "Will you marry me?"

"Yes, a thousand times, yes." She reached up and kissed him again, unable to get enough. She wanted to touch every part of him, to assure herself the doubts were truly gone. She wanted to take away every hurt he ever had and to make sure he would never be hurt again.

"When?" she asked.

"Whenever you wish...as soon as possible," he said quietly. His face darkened for a moment, searching for a way to ask the question, afraid of destroying the happiness between them. But he had to know. "Sean?"

Her smile answered him. "He's fine.... He should be here soon." Some of the joy left her face. "He had to visit some families. So many of them are dead, Ben. So many. Braden, Scottie, Sandy. Nearly half of them." Her voice faltered and he held her tight, his chin resting on her silky bronze hair.

"I'm sorry," he whispered, "but I'm glad, so glad about Sean." And then hesitantly, not wanting to meet her eyes, he explained, "I didn't know about Sean...that day you left. I didn't know." His voice broke, and Ryan knew the agony he had been going through. "I thought...I was afraid you were leaving with Seldon. I saw you in the window." He couldn't go on.

She suddenly understood everything. It answered all the questions that had been tormenting her.

Ryan forced him to look at her. "There has never been anyone but you, Ben. There never will be," she said softly. "Can you believe that?"

His dark blue eyes were stormy with warring emotions. He wasn't certain that all distrust, all suspicion of good fortune was gone. But he would try. God, how he would try. His eyes cleared and his mouth relaxed. "I love you," he told her again, wanting to repeat the words over and over again, wanting to drive all the doubts away.

She felt the hesitancy and flinched. Then she brightened. She would teach him. How lovely it would be to see those smoldering embers quenched. And she *would* do it.

"Beth . . ." Ryan suddenly asked, "she's all right?"

"She's fine." Ben smiled. "She's still too quiet, but she's getting better. She keeps asking about you."

"Where is she?"

"She's with Matt and Anna in town. There's a school there. Matt has a job at the bank."

Ryan stared at him. So much had changed in three months. Blue uniforms replacing gray, Matt gone, Beth gone. Wyeth? It was a question she was afraid to ask.

She didn't have to. Ben saw it. "Seldon's still here," he said softly. "I asked him to stay until we could get a replacement . . . until we knew something about you."

Nothing could have told her more of the changes in him. Maybe she wouldn't have much of a job, after all. Her smile illuminated the room. "I love you, Ben Morgan."

He grinned at her, pleased with himself, pleased at her surprise and obvious approval. "I do learn some things . . . occasionally," he said smugly.

She had never loved him quite as much. That imp of a little boy looked out of his beautiful blue eyes, which were now glinting mischievously with self-satisfaction.

"Hmm," she said, throwing her arms around him and squeezing as if she could never get enough.

They made plans then. They talked about marriage and adopting Beth. The Andrewses had enough to worry about now—they knew hard times were coming.

And then there was Sean. Ben kept avoiding the subject until they had exhausted everything else.

"Sean won't be very happy about this," Ben finally said hesitantly.

Ryan smiled. "I don't know about that." She leaned back against his arms and looked at him with tenderness.

"Sean loves you. He loves you in that rare way men sometimes do. His battle wasn't so much with you. It was with that special relationship you once had, that I think you still do despite everything. I think you feel the same."

Ben stared at her. "How did you become so wise?"

"I love both of you, remember? I watched you together. I'll never forget our rescue by that young lieutenant, nor the way the two of you laughed together at his reactions. There was a genuine bond there, one not easily broken, no matter what. It was also," she added with delight, "the first time I discovered you could actually laugh."

Ben buried his head in her hair, smelling the sweet scent of it. "It had," he admitted, "been a long time. I plan to improve."

He leaned down and kissed her again; this time the gentleness turned to desire, and he pressed against her, feeling his manhood reacting to her closeness. She returned his passion measure for measure. Her body felt on fire, and her fingers dug into his back. She treasured the feel of his lips as they traveled from her nose to her eyes to her hair, then back to her open, inviting mouth.

He suddenly realized they could be interrupted at any time. With the new troops, there were a thousand matters needing attention. He gently pulled back, kissed her lightly and rested his large hands on her shoulders.

"I don't know if I can wait," he groaned, "but I want it to be right for you."

Ryan's face reflected the same doubts about waiting, but she said nothing, unable to put into words the soaring feelings that made wave after wave inside her.

He took a ring from his finger and placed the heavy crested heirloom in her hands, closing her fingers around it.

"Until I can do better," he said, "I want you to have something of mine, to remind you every minute how much I love you."

She started to say something, but his lips stopped her. After he kissed her thoroughly, he released her. "I'm moving to the bachelor officers' quarters. You stay here until we're married."

Ryan started to protest, then saw his eyes. They were pleading, and she understood how much he wanted everything perfect for her, wanted her to have a proper wedding. It was his gift to her.

"All right," she whispered, "but I won't wait long."

* * *

Sean was tired, dusty and aching when he and Jimmy reached Scottdale. It had been a long, often sorrowful trip, and both were relieved it was over. Sean was anxious now to see his sister, to assure himself that all was well with her. He still didn't trust Ben's capacity to love or to make Ryan happy, though he knew he would see to her physical welfare.

It was with this disquieting thought that he and Jimmy approached the stable. They had precious few coins remaining between them, not much more than what would be required to stable and feed two very tired hungry deserving horses.

The stable was where Sean remembered it, a few buildings down from the hotel and sheriff's office. He guided his horse gently; it had more than obediently carried him through three years of war and its aftermath.

The stable keeper was currying one of the horses inside. He looked at the ragged Rebs; they were only two more of the many Texans heading home, nearly all of them penniless.

His look was unsympathetic. "No credit," he said curtly. "It will be fifty cents each for the horses. In advance."

Sean nodded briefly. He had grown used to the new hardness in the business keepers. He really couldn't blame them. There were so many like himself, all trying to reach home. The money had disappeared. Almost all of it had gone into Confederate paper, none of it worth even the shoddy material on which it was printed. He knew the stable owner had to pay cash to feed the horses, and charity went only so far.

He dismounted carefully. He still had twinges of pain in his chest and stiffness in his arm. He put the reins in the man's hand. "Take good care of them," he said softly. "He's carried me from Richmond."

The stableman reappraised the man. "You were there ... at the surrender."

"Not far away," Sean replied, his face reflecting the sadness he felt each time he remembered the mass despair when they'd heard of Lee's surrender and his farewell message.

The man's look of mixed caution and greed changed quickly to interest. "You're the first to come from Virginia."

"It's a long way ... a very long way," Sean said quietly.

"Where do you plan to stay tonight?" the man asked.

"I don't know. We can't afford the hotel...."

"You can stay here," the man said. "My name's Brown, Dan Brown. You and your partner can bed down in one of the stalls.

Business is not exactly good right now.'' The last words were bitter.

Sean's face relaxed. "We would appreciate that. Thank you."

The man started to take the two horses as Sean asked, "Fort Scott? What's happening out there?"

"Them Yankees," Brown said contemptuously, "they've taken over. Some of the Southern troops have stayed." He spit on the ground. "Damn traitors."

"What about the Indians?"

"Well, some have been rounded up, but there's still renegade bands around. Still ain't safe to travel alone toward the fort. It's okay going north. But south . . . I wouldn't recommend it."

"Okay if I leave my gear here?"

Brown shook his head. "Only if you don't want it," he said frankly. "Anything loose is liable to be gone. It ain't like it used to be."

Sean took his guitar from the saddle and slung it on his back. It was really the only thing of any value left. There was one dirty change of clothes in the saddlebags and one clean shirt. He took the shirt and inquired about the bathhouse. "Same place?"

Brown nodded.

Sean started in that direction; Jimmy turned to him. "You take a bath. I'm going to see if we can't win some money."

Sean grinned. Jimmy's luck with the cards had become legendary. He had an unfailing instinct for winning. It was, Jimmy admitted modestly, an unexpected talent. He had won his shoes from the trooper who first taught him poker and had rarely lost since. Sean thought it was Jimmy's ingenuous face and manner; no one took him seriously until it was too late.

At the bathhouse, Sean luxuriated in the hot bath. It was his first in more than six months—well worth the ten cents it cost. A young boy poured hot water into one of the wooden bathtubs in the room, and nothing spoiled the effect, not even the lack of privacy. Afterward he pulled on his clean shirt, reluctantly struggling back into the dirt-caked trousers.

Feeling halfway human again, he strode over to the sheriff's office. The arrival at Scottdale, the bath, the near climax of his journey all brought back his natural resiliency.

Sheriff Tanner was behind his desk. He looked up as Sean knocked briefly, then entered.

"What can I do for you?" he said, immediately absorbing the worn Confederate clothing, the stiff arm, the careful brown eyes.

"I want to go to Fort Scott. What's the situation between there and here?"

"Bad," Tanner said shortly. "I wouldn't advise going alone. The Indians are only too aware of what's happening in Texas, the confusion going on. Why do you want to go?"

Sean's Irish temper began to simmer at the question. He forced himself to relax. "I think my sister's there."

"A pretty girl? Hair sort of like yours?"

"That's her," Sean said quickly. "Do you know if she's still there?"

Tanner nodded. "She's fine. Came in a week ago with a regular detachment for supplies and medicine. Seems she was planning a wedding."

Sean stiffened visibly.

"You didn't know?" the sheriff questioned.

"No," Sean replied. "No, I didn't."

"There should be soldiers coming through in the next day or so," Tanner continued. "They come into town pretty regularly."

"Much obliged," Sean mumbled as he turned and left the office. He couldn't stop the waves of confusion that assaulted him as he went over the news in his mind.

Two days later, Ty led a patrol into Scottdale. The young Yank lieutenant had retained his antipathy toward Southerners and wasn't pleased to find the two Rebs waiting to accompany them back to the fort. He started to refuse, then remembered that Sean was to be Colonel Morgan's brother-in-law. He liked Ryan, even if she was Texan, and he had admired her spirit the night of the escape.

"All right," he consented. "We leave town in one hour."

Sean felt both expectant and hesitant as he neared the gates of Fort Scott, his emotions still very much in conflict as far as Morgan was concerned. He didn't like coming back as a defeated foe; it was too much as if the tables were turned. But he needed to see Ryan, to make sure for himself that this was the right thing for her, that she was absolutely positive in her decision to marry Ben Morgan. He still wasn't all that confident he wanted Morgan for a brother-in-law.

The gates opened, and he had no more time to think. As his horse crossed the parade field, his eyes easily found his nemesis.

Ty brought his horse to a stop in front of Morgan and saluted.

Ben saluted absently, his eyes never leaving Sean's face.

Sean stayed on his horse, knowing the height gave him brief advantage. "Ben," he said noncommittally. "I see you stayed put for once."

An unfamiliar wide grin spread over Ben's face. "Not by choice. Damn, I'm glad to see you." His face creased with worry. "How are you? Ryan said the wounds were bad."

It was Sean's turn to smile, a slow easy smile. The warmth of Ben's greeting, the old smile, disarmed him. It was almost as if the past fifteen years had disappeared. Almost, but not quite. "I decided it wasn't quite right for me to go all the way through the war without a scratch.... I couldn't let you have all the wounds...and glory."

Just then, he saw Ryan. She was coming out of the infirmary, her hair back in a braid and her dress wilted from heat. She looked up toward him and started running. He quickly dismounted and caught her up, giving her a quick hug, then setting her away from him as he scoured her face. The reserve he had noticed in Richmond was gone. There was only laughter and joy now.

He leaned down, kissing her forehead. "I obviously don't have to ask how you are, Kitten. You look like you've just finished the world's largest saucer of milk."

Ryan beamed. "You're just in time. Ben and I are getting married." She hesitated then, knowing Ben was watching Sean's face closely, that he desperately wanted Sean's acceptance and approval. "You will give me away, won't you?"

The silence was long. Sean knew what she wanted, and he wasn't quite sure if he could wholeheartedly give it to her.

She finally broke the quiet. "I love him, Sean. I love him more than life itself." It was said quietly, but the intensity behind the three words left no doubt in Sean's mind that she would marry Ben regardless of what he thought.

He looked up at Ben, noting the wariness in the other man's face. There was also hope, a hope that seemed to leave Ben oddly defenseless.

Sean looked back at Ryan. "I know," he said softly.

Realizing that the two men needed a moment to talk things over, Ryan looked down at her wilted dusty dress. "I have to change clothes," she stated, and was gone before either Ben or Sean could reply, both of them staring after her. Sean couldn't stifle his laughter at Ryan's turnabout. He heard Ben join him and, much as they had eight months earlier, they found pieces of the old friendship in shared amusement.

Ben's smile all too quickly disappeared. "You've not answered Ryan's question."

Sean grew serious. "It doesn't matter what I think. You don't need my approval. You never did."

"It means a lot to Ryan," Ben said slowly. He was silent a moment. "It means a lot to me." The last comment had been difficult for Ben to say, and Sean knew it.

Sean was suddenly tired. "There's been a lot between us, Ben. I would be lying if I said it was all gone, all forgotten. But Ryan's obviously happy, happier than I thought possible, and I thank you for it."

Ben stood there quietly. It was more than he had expected, less than he wanted. He stretched out his arm, and two hands met . . . and tightened in understanding.

"I hope," Ben said, "you will stay with me. I'm in the bachelors' quarters. Ryan's staying in the commander's home."

Sean nodded. "I expect I know where it is. Can someone take care of my horse?"

Ben nodded and watched as Sean took his near empty saddlebags and walked to the officers' quarters.

Sean made himself at home. It was typical of most bachelors' quarters, consisting of two rooms, one in front, with a few chairs, a table, a desk and bookcase, and a second room in back, with two narrow beds. He threw his saddlebags on one of the beds and returned to the front room, his eyes roaming over the bookcase. There were five tattered volumes on one shelf, several bottles and glasses on another. He helped himself to a glass of Ben's whiskey and sprawled in one of the chairs.

He sipped it slowly, having had none of its quality for more months than he wanted to remember. He had been delighted to see Ryan, to see her unreserved happiness, but he wanted time to think. He had been startled at the change in Ben, at the open happy man he had just encountered. Even the reserve he knew so well as a young man, the reserve that had been there even before Melody, was gone. Ryan had evidently wrought a miracle. Sean had enjoyed very little sleep in the past few nights, and lulled by the whiskey, he dozed off.

Sean woke as Ben noisily entered his quarters, his boots pounding a drumbeat on the floor.

He opened his eyes, feeling a little fuzzy from the unaccustomed afternoon nap and alcohol. He watched as Ben poured himself a drink and offered one to him.

Straightening up, Sean refused. It was time to clear his thoughts, not cloud them further. He watched Ben prowl around the room restlessly, the old power and confidence apparent in every step. He felt a fleeting twinge of envy. Ben now had everything while he, Sean, didn't know where his next meal was coming from. He dismissed the thought immediately.

"I'm resigning my commission," Ben said abruptly. "I'm tired of fighting and all that goes with it. And I don't want to drag my wife and children from one dismal army post to another."

Sean nodded, understanding. He, too, had had more than enough of fighting. "Are you going back to Boston?" he asked, dreading the answer. It would take Ryan thousands of miles away.

Ben smiled slowly, reading Sean's thoughts. "I told you months ago I would never go back to Boston. I meant it. We want to buy some land here in Texas, start a ranch. Ryan loves it here." A bleakness appeared on his face as he remembered the past months. "I like any place where there's open spaces and sky. We need your help in finding some land, and we want you to join us as a partner."

Sean just stared at him. "I think I'll take that drink, after all," he finally said. Ben handed him the glass he had already poured and watched as Sean took a large gulp.

"We've asked young Avery to come join us and Beth—you haven't met her yet.... I think she's in hiding."

Sean smiled faintly. "That's quite a family."

Ben frowned, then permitted a wry smile. "I know, but it's what Ryan wants ... and I want."

Ben *had* changed, Sean thought.

Ben continued. "I need your help. You grew up on a ranch. You know about land and cattle and, God knows, I've never known a better horseman."

Sean stared at his drink. The offer was the last thing he had expected. He had already discussed starting a ranch with Jimmy and Justis and some of the others who had ridden with them. They had planned to round up range cattle, which roamed free throughout Texas, drive them up to Kansas for sale, then buy some land with the proceeds. It would take several years, but it would all be theirs, bought by the fruits of their own labor.

"You wouldn't be welcomed here," Sean said flatly. "It's going to take years before Yanks will be accepted in Texas."

"That's why I need you," Ben said bluntly. "I'm not offering charity. I need you. I need your knowledge."

Sean shook his head slowly. "No, I have other plans."

"Damn it, Sean," Ben said. "We would make a good team...a damned good team."

"We haven't been that for a long time," Sean replied quietly. "And I have to do things my own way. I remember something else you once told me, that you didn't want to be a part of a business someone else built. I feel the same way. I won't take a handout from you."

"Then I'll ask one from you. Will you at least help us find some land? For Ryan, if not for me? You know Texas. I don't."

Sean smiled, his eyes sparkling with the old devilment. "I'll call it my wedding present," he said. "Now what about dinner? I'm starving."

Chapter Twenty-seven

The wedding took place in the parlor of the commander's home. It was crowded, and the minister, summoned from Scottdale, eyed the congregation with bemusement.

Blue uniforms mixed with tattered gray ones in the audience, while the groom, whom the minister knew to be the temporary fort commander, was dressed in civilian clothes. Ben had not wished to widen the sea of division and distrust. Sean had also swallowed his pride and borrowed a pair of finely tailored trousers and coat from Ben.

Others had not been so accommodating for the event. Dr. Seldon, Justis and Jimmy all stubbornly wore their gray trousers, having little else in their possession and adamantly refusing to borrow clothes from those they still viewed as enemies.

Ty wore his uniform as though he were waving a red flag in front of a bull. Others, such as Forster, merely thought it the proper dress.

In any event, the temporary coexistence heartened the minister, who felt there might be some hope for civilization, after all.

With exquisite joy Ryan looked around the church, thinking everyone she loved was there today. Sean was wonderfully grave and dignified as he led her down the aisle and put her hand in Ben's. Avery had arrived several days earlier. Beth, quiet little Beth, even emitted a slight giggle as she led the procession, dropping an occasional petal they had stolen from Major Andrews's rather neglected garden.

As the ceremony proceeded, Ben scarcely heard the words. Ryan was breathtaking in a white gown, her beautiful golden hair laced with flowers and her eyes glowing with a thousand twinkling amber lights. He thought his heart would shatter with the wonder of it. She had chosen him; all that beauty and courage and love was his. His hand shook for a moment as he felt a tremble of fear—he didn't deserve such an enormous gift. It couldn't last...nothing this glorious could last.

But then her hand tightened on his, and he felt the strength and love as it closed reassuringly around his fingers. Even now, he thought with amazement, she sensed the core of his feelings.

"...for richer, for poorer, in sickness and in health...until death do us part...."

He heard her repeat the words in a strong confident voice, and he thought of the first time he heard it.... *"You should be honored. He doesn't give his attentions lightly...."* It had been the beginning. The beginning of so much.

He heard his own mumbled vows through a haze of images: that silly hat after Sean's misadventures in Center; her defiant kiss the night of his escape; the stricken look when she went to find Sean; the uncertainty when she returned. *Dear God, don't let me hurt her again.*

His voice broke, then found its strength, and he finished loud and clear. Her eyes applauded him, and her lips twitched with gentle amusement.

When it was over and he leaned down to kiss her, she whispered, "I was afraid you were going to bolt."

"I might have," he answered teasingly, "but I knew you were too fast for me." And then his lips met hers and clung there with such fervent possession that she felt dizzy with desire.

He finally let go and was immediately aware of all the amused stares. "This is," he whispered, "going to be the shortest wedding party in history."

And it was. For Ben and Ryan, at least. They accepted the congratulations of their guests, amiably led the first dance to the music of a hastily assembled group of musicians, and, to no one's surprise, disappeared. As laughter followed them, Ben picked Ryan up in both arms, and with his usual hurried pace, carried her to one of the unoccupied married officers' quarters, where they would spend this one night in privacy. He had arranged it earlier, and both had already left clothes and champagne there.

Once inside, he swung her down while keeping a hand on her shoulder, as if afraid to let go.

"I'm afraid you'll disappear...like a will-o'-the-wisp."

"Never, Ben, I love you so much. I love everything about you." She held up her arms to him, and he needed no more words. He took her in his arms, his mouth reaching down to hers in an infinitely tender touch. His lips then moved to her eyes, her cheeks and finally nibbled on her ears in a way that started a conflagration in Ryan.

"Hmm," she murmured, her own hands busy as they fondled, teased, stroked his neck, creating similar blazes in him. She could sense their heat and feel the trembling under her caresses. Could she ever, ever have enough of him?

He led her into the bedroom, his hands tight and possessive, as if still disbelieving of her presence. She felt his hands at the back of the dress, felt button after button open, felt the burning touch of his flesh against hers, and her body tensed with the feelings his fingers aroused. And then the dress was falling, and his sure steady hands discarded the chemise and other underthings.

She heard the intake of his breath as he looked at her. There was no fear in her, only an entrancing trace of shyness as her eyes searched for his approval. Her body unconsciously stretched toward him with undeniable yearning.

"You are so incredibly beautiful," he said softly. I knew... but..."

She stopped the words with a kiss, and now it was her turn. As his fingers had freed her, now she freed him from the seemingly endless layers of clothes. He stood absolutely still, reveling in the ritual as she slowly unclothed him, her hands taking every opportunity to touch him. With timorous but instinctive movements, her fingertips played with the dark fur on his chest as the shirt parted, and he couldn't contain the shudders her touch sent rippling through him.

She slowly reached his trousers, and he seemed suspended as she searched for buttons, finally releasing the swelling manhood that held so many beckoning enticing mysteries. She touched it with wonder, exploring its masculine beauty as he went taut with sensation.

Ben could stand it no longer. Tenderness fought with burning desire as he quickly pulled off his boots and stripped off his pants. He held his hand out to her, and, once more inexplicably shy, she accepted it and was pulled gently into the bed.

His hands roved lovingly over her, playing every nerve, every sense as a musician might coax a finely crafted violin. He wanted tonight to be as exquisite, as joyful as he could possibly make it, and he would sacrifice his own growing need to that end. His lips nuzzled the firm tips of her breasts until they grew hard with passion and she cried out in pleasure and torment. His tongue moved again, making fiery trails up and down her body until it was a quivering mass of sensation.

Bursting with a sweet agony, Ryan pulled Ben to her, no longer able to stand even the slightest distance between them. "Oh, I want you, Ben," she said, her voice trembling. "Teach me."

He needed no more encouragement. His mouth joined hers, and its urgency was contagious. Unable to withstand the millions of burning pinpoints he had created in her, her body instinctively arched toward his, and she knew his wonderful warmth as expectant flesh ignited flesh....

Ryan felt the probing throbbing touch of him as he entered slowly, ever so carefully, and his tenseness told her how much the effort cost him. There was a surge nf pain, and her breath caught, but it didn't matter. Not now. Not as she was being consumed with crashing waves of ecstasy that grew greater with his every movement. Her body caught his rhythm, and together they whirled and spun as if waltzing in a storm-swept heaven. When she thought there could be no greater wonder, his movements quickened until the storm became a hurricane inside her, and they climbed together to a pinnacle of rapture, cresting in an explosion that sent shock waves through both of them. Ryan's hands clutched his back, feeling the straining muscles as her lips tasted the wet saltiness of his skin. She savored his fragrant aroma of tobacco and bay and musk, and she knew a fierce all-consuming possessive savagery as she pressed him even closer to her. She arched toward him again, marveling at the slow sensuous movements that brought her to the edge of an abyss before sending her soaring to paradise.

After, they lay there silently, hands locked together, her head on his chest. There were no words. Nothing could possibly describe what had happened. It was enough to be there together, to hold each other, to know there would be so many more days and nights to share and explore and love.

"Love," he finally whispered. "My beautiful love. My magical little enchantress." It was the first endearment he had ever used with her, and Ryan's heart surged with warm pleasure.

With a compulsive deviltry, Ryan turned her head and started nibbling his chest, letting the tiny black hairs tickle her face. She felt the beginning rumbling of his laughter, and she experienced a bliss so great it hurt. How wonderful his laughter sounded. How completely enchanting his slow smile. And now he was hers. All hers. Forever.

She felt herself go warm inside again and pulled him to her.

Epilogue

The next few months were so incredibly happy for Ryan that Ben's withdrawal, when it came, was particularly painful.

The trouble came in Ryan's sixth month of pregnancy. She had had difficulty from the beginning, but she had successfully hidden it from Ben. She didn't want to frighten him with the constant sickness and bouts of pain that she knew were unusual. She knew only too well how loss, or even the threat of loss, affected him.

But when she found herself bleeding, she finally went to the doctor in town, who didn't disguise his concern. He ordered her to bed, a direction that she couldn't, or wouldn't, obey. It would mean telling Ben, and it wasn't in her to stay still, to let others wait on her. She tried, however, to curtail her activities as much as possible without alarming anyone. She didn't want to lose this child.

When the doctor showed up at the ranch on an unannounced visit, everything exploded.

He had scolded her for not staying in bed and then said he was going to talk to Ben. She had begged Doc Adams for silence, but to no avail. "He has a right to know," the doctor said, "especially if you don't follow orders."

Ryan had to withstand Ben's subsequent inquiry. "Why," he demanded, his face changing from worry to impotent anger, "didn't you tell me?"

It had been a long time since she had seen his fury directed at her, and she winced. In a small voice, she replied, "I didn't want you to worry."

"Worry? Worry? My God. You're risking your life going around like nothing's wrong, and you don't want me to worry?"

He stared at her almost as if he hated her at the moment.

She held out her hand. "Ben . . ."

His eyes were great storm clouds, his mouth compressed into the tight line she had seen before. It had always warned her. It was doing it now.

"I'm fine, Ben. Dr. Adams is a worrier. That's all. I really have been careful. I haven't done any riding..." Her voice faded as she saw the implacable look on his face. It wavered for a moment, then returned.

"You will not," he said, "get out of bed again."

The harshness of his voice and stark order angered her. "I will if I wish," she said, and then would have given her soul to have withheld the words. His eyes burned into her, then he turned and left.

Ryan kept expecting Ben to return to the loving man she had come to know; he had changed so much in the past year. But he didn't. He moved out of her bedroom, and except for short cold visits, mainly, she believed, to see that she obeyed his orders, he stayed away. He would disappear for days at a time, growing colder each time he returned. When she would try to touch him, to hold his hand, he would jerk away as if burned and make an excuse to leave. But even those times grew scarcer, and Ryan started to believe that the only thing that mattered to him was the child. Not her.

A month went by, and the final blow came. Ben came by Ryan's room after several days' absence. He smelled of whiskey and cheap perfume, and his face was uncharacteristically stubbled. It was obvious he had not shaved in days.

Ryan, whose temper could match Sean's, exploded with hurt and rage. She threw a book at him, and he caught it neatly and with an emotionless face and returned it to her bedside. For a moment Ryan thought she saw pain and confusion in his eyes, but then it was gone, and his eyes were once more hooded and fathomless. He merely nodded and left. Ryan cried herself to sleep, and Ben drank himself into oblivion as he had done nearly every night for a month.

Ryan was going to die. Ben was thoroughly convinced of it...just as he was convinced it was all his fault. It was his seed that was killing her. It was his bad star that was ruling her life. Nothing of value to him had ever lasted, and now the most important thing in his life was being taken. In his total misery, he had come to one possible hope. If he could let her go, perhaps the Fates would allow Ryan to live. Ryan with her laughing eyes and heart so filled with love. Ryan. His heart broke every time he whispered her name, every time her face appeared in his mind.

He stood on a hill overlooking the river. It had been his thinking place since he first came here. It had been a place of hope and thankfulness. Now it must give him the strength to let Ryan go, to let her live, to let their child live. He had tried, oh how he had tried to make her hate him, to make his departure easier. But he would look at those confusion-filled eyes as they first filled with hope when he entered the room and then silent tears as he left, and he died inside, piece by piece. Last night, he had visited a saloon, hoping for relief, but there was none. A woman hung around him through the evening, but all he felt was disgust—total absolute disgust—and he finally, rudely told her to go away.

He was glad Sean had been gone this month on a cattle drive. He couldn't explain this feeling of doom he carried within him, this knowledge that those he loved were endangered by him.

How could he live without her now? How could he forget the touch of her? How could he erase those merry eyes from his heart?

Ben sank to the ground he loved, which he would soon leave. But Ryan would live. She and the baby would live.

His disappearances lasted longer. Even Avery, with whom he had forged a close bond, was ignored. Beth's overtures were met with an almost indifferent pat on the head. And that was when he was there. Which was seldom. More and more of the ranch business was left in the hands of Justis who had joined him as foreman.

Ryan knew she had to take care of herself because of the baby. And she knew exactly what had happened. She blamed herself for much of it. She had not told Ben about the doctor's fears, nor had she obeyed his orders to stay quiet. She knew Ben's deep distrust of life, and yet she had added to it by not confiding in him. She had feared this reaction and had made it worse by her silence.

What hurt more than anything, however, had been that smell of perfume the one evening. And his abandonment of their bed and room. She so missed the warmth of his body next to hers, the comfort of his touch.

One night she woke up and felt him standing at her door, but she was afraid to move or open her eyes. She could smell the rich scent of tobacco, and she longed to reach out to him. But he would have to come back on his own.

And then Sean returned for a visit. He found a house almost in mourning. He talked to Ryan, who would say little until he pressed her and she finally confided all her fears, including the cheap perfume. In a rage Sean went searching for Ben, who had left the house at sunrise.

Instinctively he knew where Ben had gone, and soon found him leaning against a tree, looking morosely down at the river flowing swiftly between the cottonwoods.

Ben didn't look up or pay attention to the intrusion. He simply ignored it and continued to brood alone.

"I was right about you, Ben," Sean said softly. "I was right about you ever since an ill wind brought you into my camp. You hurt everything you touch."

Ben whirled around, his hands in tight fists. "It's none of your business." His eyes were cold and threatening.

"It is my business. Ryan is my sister, and right now I wish to hell I had killed you when she first brought you in."

"Get away from me, Sean."

"Not before I do something I should have done long ago." Sean's fist whipped out and caught Ben on the chin. Ben went whirling against a tree, found his balance and went after Sean like an enraged bull, his own uncertainty and fear for Ryan crystallizing into violence.

His blow went to Sean's stomach, and the Texan went down. He rolled over twice and warily got to his feet. Both men eyed each other carefully, waiting for an opening. Ben was the first to move, his right hand meeting Sean's chin and the left going once more to the stomach.

Sean went down again, but his hand grabbed Ben's and the two rolled over in the dirt, pummeling each other without mercy.

Nothing mattered now but their own personal rage. Ben's was against fate—his almost hopeless belief that Ryan's salvation lay only in his abandonment of her. Sean was only a convenient target. But Sean didn't know that. He only saw the damage being done Ryan, and he hated Ben for it.

It went on, blow traded for blow, no quarter asked and none given. The violence slowed only as exhaustion drained the two, but still they continued. Their clothing was torn and bloody, their faces bruised and swollen. But still they went on. All the anger and frustration of fifteen years spent itself.

The sun was setting when it came to an end. Ben swung, missed and fell. Sean sank to the ground. Neither had the strength to move. They lay there together, a fiery sky framing their prostrate bodies. Neither moved for a long, long time.

Sean was the first to speak. "I knew you would hurt her...damn you. How can you see another woman...especially now? God damn you," he added with helpless rage.

At first the words didn't register with Ben. Then slowly they penetrated, and he lifted his head to look at Sean. "Another woman?"

Anger was strong in Sean's voice. "Perfume.... Ryan smelled perfume. Damn. Don't you have any idea what you're doing?"

There was genuine puzzlement in Ben's voice. "There's no one. How could there be?" His voice broke. "There could never be anyone but Ryan."

Now it was Sean's turn to be confused. He lifted himself slowly, painfully up onto one elbow and studied Ben's face. There was no questioning the truth in it.

"But your absences...the way you've been avoiding her...your drinking...and the perfume...."

Ben's face was tortured. "Oh God, is that what she thought?" His voice broke again. "I went to town one night...there was a woman who tried...but I couldn't."

Completely dumbfounded, Sean could only stare at Ben and at the moisture that now clouded his eyes.

"Not another woman...never another woman," Ben repeated, wondering how anyone could ever think that.

"Then what?" Sean's voice was harsh.

Ben was silent for a long time before the words came seeping out in a dirge of anguish. "You were right—I hurt everything. I have to leave her. It's the only way...." He paused, then continued in a hopeless monotone. "I'm so afraid...so very afraid—afraid to touch her...afraid that I've killed her with the baby. Maybe if I go, she and the baby will be all right. No one..."

Sean knew Ben well enough to finish the sentence for him. *No one has ever loved me before.* All of a sudden he understood. Ben's fear made him believe he was at fault, that if he left, everything would be all right for Ryan. He simply had no idea what it would do to Ryan, what it had done. For, as he had almost said, "no one has ever loved me before." He still couldn't quite understand it or deal with it.

Sean was suddenly filled with pity. For Ben, who had such a hard time believing in love. For Ryan, who had never quite conquered Ben's lingering doubts. "Ben. Ryan's not going to die. Women have babies all the time. The doctor just wants her to be careful."

Ben buried his head in his hands. His face was ravaged when he looked up. "My mother died in childbirth. Melody—"

"Melody died by her own hand," Sean said rudely. "She went to a butcher. It had nothing to do with the normal course of child-bearing. When are you going to let her go, damn you!"

"But . . ."

"You're a fool, Ben. I have never seen anyone loved like Ryan loves you. Accept it. Treasure it. Don't let Melody destroy it the way she destroyed so much of your life. Don't let her destroy Ryan, because that's what you're doing. You're letting her win. My God, you're lucky. You and Ryan have something rare, special. Even if it's only a year or two or five, you have more than most people have in a lifetime."

A groan rose from Ben. And then tears. They flowed from his eyes and mixed with blood and sweat and dirt and made rivulets down his cheek. Sean had never seen anything as anguished, and his own hardened heart cried with his friend. His hand reached over and touched Ben's shoulder in comfort and reassurance.

They stayed like that as the wind turned cool, and the raw angry sky melted into soft muted colors and finally into star-sprinkled velvet.

It was very late when they finally found the strength to mount their horses and slowly, silently, painfully plodded through the night. But there was something else riding with them—an almost visible cord that had been repeatedly tried and tested and stretched and, now, tonight, strengthened to the consistency of tempered steel.

When they reached Ben's ranch house, only one light shone in a window. Sean waited while Ben dismounted and turned toward him, and the two men shook hands silently. Ben went up the steps and inside.

He walked down the hall to Ryan's room. As he looked inside he cursed himself for making it that—Ryan's room. He knew she was awake, even though her eyes were closed. He lighted the oil lamp and sat on the bed, his hand touching her smooth cheek.

Her eyes opened slowly, as if afraid, and he winced at the pain in them.

"Did you really think there could be another woman?" he asked in a broken voice.

"If you were angry enough. If. . ." Her voice was very small.

"I wasn't angry, love. I was terrified. I was terrified of losing you. I couldn't stand looking at you and knowing you might disappear." He picked up her hand and kissed its fingertips, one by one, then clutched it almost desperately.

"It seems I am always hurting you, always causing pain. I'm sorry, Ryan. God, I'm sorry."

She drew him down to her, urging his head to rest on her breasts. Her hands investigated the cuts and bruises and feather-light fingers soothed them.

"It doesn't matter," she said. "Nothing matters now that you're back. I've missed you so much."

A shudder ran through his body as he realized how much he had nearly lost. His arms went around her, holding her with an extraordinary gentleness. He felt the baby move within her and felt a surge of tenderness so great his heart seemed stilled.

She snuggled against his fully clothed body, rejoicing in his presence and warmth.

Ryan moved slightly and she heard the quick withdrawn breath of pain. With worry, she moved from him and turned, searching his face.

"What happened?"

"I ran into a bear," Ben answered evenly.

"And the bear...did he fare as poorly as you?"

"Almost," came the slightly smug answer.

"And am I going to have to contend with this bear tomorrow?"

"I don't think so, love. I think he's decided he no longer needs to protect this particular den."

She released a small sigh she had been holding. "You need to do something about those cuts."

"Tomorrow," he said. "Tomorrow will be soon enough. Now I just want to hold you."

Ryan snuggled carefully back into his body, fitting her own into his hard curves. It was all the answer he needed.

"I love you, Ryan," he whispered. "All my days...all our days. I love you."

And for the first time, he knew total peace. He had Ryan, and no one, ever, could ask for more.

* * * * *

Harlequin Historicals

COMING NEXT MONTH

A GENTLE PASSION—Cassie Edwards

When orphaned Faye Poincare was forced to make the rough journey to her brother's mission in Arkansas, she met the challenges of the trail without flinching—until she locked horns with the arrogant army scout Joe Harrison. And both discovered that the raging tempest between them had become...*A Gentle Passion.*

WILD HORIZONS—Jeanne Stephens

Innocent Megan Riley fled town to escape her mother's tarnished legacy. With a crotchety old cowboy as her only friend, she joined a wagon train bound for Oregon. But the young woman's trials were only beginning as the fires of passion flared between her and the aloof wagon master Jed Dossman. From Kansas westward they surmounted danger and hardship, and learned to face the one power that would sustain them in their quest for a new life....

AVAILABLE NOW:

BETWEEN THE
THUNDER
Patricia Potter

PROMISES
Pamela Wallace

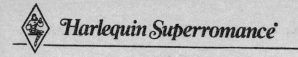
Harlequin Superromance

CALLOWAY CORNERS

Created by four outstanding Superromance authors, bonded by lifelong friendship and a love of their home state: Sandra Canfield, Tracy Hughes, Katherine Burton and Penny Richards.

CALLOWAY CORNERS

Home of four sisters as different as the seasons, as elusive as the elements; an undiscovered part of Louisiana where time stands still and passion lasts forever.

CALLOWAY CORNERS

Birthplace of the unforgettable Calloway women: *Mariah*, free as the wind, and untamed until she meets the preacher who claims her, body and soul; *Jo*, the fiery, feisty defender of lost causes who loses her heart to a rock and roll man; *Tess*, gentle as a placid lake but tormented by her longing for the town's bad boy and *Eden*, the earth mother who's been so busy giving love she doesn't know how much she needs it until she's awakened by a drifter's kiss . . .

CALLOWAY CORNERS

Coming from Superromance, in 1989:
Mariah, by Sandra Canfield, a January release
Jo, by Tracy Hughes, a February release
Tess, by Katherine Burton, a March release
Eden, by Penny Richards, an April release

Harlequin Temptation dares to be different!

Once in a while, we Temptation editors spot a romance that's truly innovative. To make sure *you* don't miss any one of these outstanding selections, we'll mark them for you.

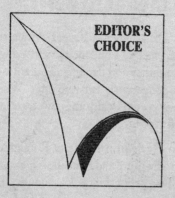

EDITOR'S CHOICE

When the "Editors' Choice" fold-back appears on a Temptation cover, you'll know we've found that extra-special page-turner!

THE

Temptation

EDITORS

Harlequin Regency Romance™

Romance the way it was *always* meant to be!

The time is 1811, when a Regent Prince rules the empire. The place is London, the glittering capital where rakish dukes and dazzling debutantes scheme and flirt in a dangerously exciting game. Where marriage is the passport to wealth and power, yet every girl hopes secretly for love....

Welcome to Harlequin Regency Romance where reading is an adventure and romance is *not* just a thing of the past! Two delightful books a month, beginning May '89.

Available wherever Harlequin Books are sold.